Second Chance Christmas

LORI WILDE

Second Chance Christmas

A TWILIGHT, TEXAS NOVEL

AVONBOOKS

An Imprint of HarperCollinsPublishers

Excerpt from *The Christmas Backup Plan* copyright © 2020 by Laurie Vanzura.

SECOND CHANCE CHRISTMAS. Copyright © 2021 by Laurie Vanzura. All rights reserved. Printed in the United States of America. No part of this book may be used or reproduced in any manner whatsoever without written permission except in the case of brief quotations embodied in critical articles and reviews. For information, address HarperCollins Publishers, 195 Broadway, New York, NY 10007.

First Avon Books mass market printing: November 2021
First Avon Books hardcover printing: October 2021

Print Edition ISBN: 978-0-06-295322-3
Digital Edition ISBN: 978-0-06-295324-7

Avon, Avon & logo, and Avon Books & logo are registered trademarks of HarperCollins Publishers in the United States of America and other countries. HarperCollins is a registered trademark of HarperCollins Publishers in the United States of America and other countries.

FIRST EDITION

21 22 23 24 25 LSC 10 9 8 7 6 5 4 3 2 1

To Bryan Duncan who gave me a key to freedom.

Second Chance Christmas

CHAPTER 1

THE GIRL

What on earth was she going to do?

Three days before Christmas and she had no money, no food, and no place to stay. Every measly thing she owned was tucked inside the battered backpack weighing heavily on her thin shoulders.

Shivering in her threadbare jean jacket, not nearly warm enough for the winter storm rolling through North Central Texas, the teen tightened her grip on the tiny bundle in her arms.

Some dude she barely knew had said she could couch surf with him for a couple of days, but he'd been adamant.

No brats allowed.

Panic rose in her throat, swelling and bubbling like the sourdough starter Grammy fed on her kitchen counter.

No, not anymore. Grammy and her sourdough were gone forever, and she was all on her own.

A gust of wind blowing off Lake Twilight shook the tinsel garlands that were strung from quaint lamppost lanterns. Gaily colored lights flickered through the thickening darkness like fickle beacons. On-off. On-off.

Her teeth chattered, braces clicking together. Her bare knee, poking from the hole in her shredded jeans, turned as numb as her nose.

For the past three hours, she'd ringed the entire town square, entering boutiques and restaurants to get in out of the cold. Leaving when shop owners shot her dirty looks.

In one restaurant, with hunger gnawing her stomach, she'd pretended she needed to use the restroom. They didn't want to let her in—no public restrooms—but the hostess saw the baby and nodded.

She hadn't gone into the restroom. Instead, she'd slipped into the dining area, targeting an unbused table and filching leftovers.

It wasn't stealing, she'd told herself. The food was getting thrown out.

A ten-dollar bill on the next table beckoned. Her heart leaped. *That is stealing.*

She inched over, reached for the ten, and had it in her fingers when one of the servers caught her.

"Put that back!"

She dropped the money. "I wasn't—"

"You were."

"I—"

"Get out. Now!"

Ducking her head, she moved toward the door. As she passed, the server whispered, "You're disgusting," with a curled lip. The woman's gaze landed on the baby tucked up underneath her jacket, and the curl became a full-on snarl. "For shame! What kind of mother are you?"

That was a knife through her heart. She was a horrible mother. She knew it. The baby would be much better off without her.

"Get out," the server said, pointing a furious finger at the door. "Before I call the cops."

She'd slunk away, slipping into the shop next door, but they were closing up, and she'd had to move on. Now, the only place open on the square was Fruit of the Vine, the storefront for a local winery. It would be almost seven years before she was old enough to legally go inside.

Fighting back tears, she hitched the baby to her shoulder. He'd been really quiet today, as if he understood the trouble that they were in.

"Good boy," she cooed to him, pulling the little knitted cap down securely over his ears. "You're such a good boy, and Mommy loves you so much."

Earlier, the town square had been packed with shoppers, but now the streets were nearly empty. The vendors on the courthouse lawn had battened down their kiosks, and the Santa Land display was shutting early because of the weather. From the outdoor speakers mounted on the courthouse, Christmas music played. "It's the Most Wonderful Time of the Year."

She bit her bottom lip, so dry and cracked from the cold wind that it hurt. The hot tears she'd been battling spilled over the rim of her lower lids and trickled down her face.

Hopeless.

Everything was hopeless.

She fisted her hands against the baby's back. If only she didn't have him to worry about. Closing her eyes, she groaned. That server was right. She was a horrible, horrible mother. She sucked in a deep breath of frigid air and opened her eyes.

A white church spire topped with a cross rose up behind the buildings on the square. Grammy used to take her to church every Sunday. Her grandmother liked to sit in the front row, to be "closer to God."

"Sorry, Grammy," she whispered, her heart plunging into her throat. "Right now I'm as far away from God as I can get."

She'd tried praying—oh yes, she had—but God must have turned his back on her, because she'd had no answers, and her problems kept stacking up like cordwood.

Maybe the church spire is an answer.

She'd seen a program on TV that said churches were considered safe havens. A place to anonymously leave your baby if you couldn't take care of it. The only catch was that there had to be someone around to find the baby or it would be considered child endangerment. Or so the program had said. That is, if she was remembering correctly.

Trembling now, at her wits' end, she walked toward the white steeple sticking up out of the darkness, with no real plan. The wind slashed her face, and she ducked her head to shield the baby, cradling him to her chest. She could feel his little heart beating against hers.

If only things were different.

But they weren't, were they?

She walked a block, turned right, then left, another block and there it was, the First Presbyterian Church of Twilight.

The church looked old, like it had been built back in the cowboy days, but it had a fresh coat of paint and was decked in holiday decorations, including an elaborate nativity scene on the front lawn, complete with live animals milling around in a wooden corral.

Her gaze fell on the straw bed where the Baby Jesus lay nestled, surrounded by life-sized plastic figures of Mary, Joseph, the three Wise Men, and five shepherds. The bed looked really warm, and it was located underneath a shelter out of the wind.

Should she? Could she?

Her heart was pounding a million beats a second, and her face was so cold she could scarcely breathe. But how could she leave the baby when there was no one around to find him? Despair knocked against her chest. A hollow, numb feeling that bewildered and frightened her.

She chewed a ragged fingernail, gnawing off the chipped polish—Cotton Candy Daydreams. Last year, Grammy had put the polish in her Christmas stocking. This year there would be no stocking, no presents, no loving grandmother, nothing.

Fresh tears welled in her eyes, stinging her cheeks.

"I'm not leaving you for good," she mumbled, trying to convince herself it was true. "Just until I can find a safe place for us to stay. This is the best thing for right now."

The sound of voices sent her shrinking into the shadows, hiding in the thick shrubbery surrounding the church. She crouched, grateful that the baby was sleeping. He was such a good boy. He deserved a good mother. A mom who knew how to love him the right way. He deserved a good dad and a happy home too. All things she couldn't give him.

Salty tears filled her mouth as her heart broke.

Okay, okay. She would do this, but only if the people looked nice and kind. Otherwise, she'd wait until someone else came along.

The voices grew louder. From around the opposite side of the church, closest to where the animals were penned, two people appeared.

The guy was really tall and looked to be the age of her dad when she'd last heard from him. Kinda old. Thirtyish. The woman was younger and not much taller than she was. Five-four maybe. She wore black motorcycle boots, thick black leggings, a short red plaid skirt, and a cute white ski jacket. Dope outfit. She had wicked fashion sense.

"You should have worn gloves," the man said to her. "Your hands are turning blue."

"I loaned my gloves to one of my elderly customers. Midge keeps losing hers. When I picked her up for her doctor's appointment, her hands were like ice. What was I supposed to do?"

"You're too generous." He shook his head, but he smiled at the woman as if he was proud of her.

She wished someone would look at her with the same sweet kindness.

"It's okay." The woman tucked her hands into her jacket pockets. "It'll be fine."

The man stopped underneath the security lamp that cast a soft glow over the nativity scene, took off his own gloves, and tucked them under his armpit. "Give me one of your hands."

"What?" The woman drew back. "Why?"

"C'mon, Tink." The man grinned. "Stop being so suspicious. I swear, if Jesus himself turned up on Christmas Day, you'd insist on interrogating him."

"Well, yes, I'd have lots of questions." Narrowing her eyes but laughing, the woman slowly took a hand from her pocket and held it out to him.

The tall man took her hand and rubbed it vigorously between his. Then he repeated the process with her other hand.

Aww, that was so sweet. She wished she had a nice boyfriend who would warm her hands for her. Feeling jealous, she pressed her back against the side of the building, watching the couple tease and banter as they went about turning off the inflatable Christmas decorations.

They were so nice to each other. Smiling and joking. No yelling or hitting. She could tell they liked each other. She liked them too.

Safe haven.

The words popped into her head again. People were here now. The church was officially a safe haven.

The baby whimpered, a soft little mewl.

If she was going to do this, now was the time while the couple was still here, and their attention was on the opposite side of the church lawn from where she crouched. But first, she needed to write a note explaining that she'd be back for him as soon as she could.

Quietly, she twisted around, grateful for the relentless wind because it muffled her sounds. She fished a Sharpie from her backpack. Then she realized she didn't have any paper.

How could she leave a note with no paper? She dug in the backpack, desperate for something to write on, and her hand hit the diaper.

His last diaper.

The one she'd been saving for when he did number two.

In the darkness, she wrote a heartfelt note on the diaper, tucked it inside the blanket with him, and as the couple's backs were turned, she crept to the manger and replaced the plastic Baby Jesus with her son.

Chapter 2

The Manger

"Shh, did you hear that?" Jana Gerard touched her companion's wrist and canted her head, listening for the sound to repeat.

Lean, tall, dark-headed, a former college-basketball star, and her part-time boss, Joel MacGregor looked down at her hand and smiled softly.

Joel ran the Brazos Queen, a paddle-wheel boat for the tourist trade that offered daily and nightly tours during the summer and holiday dinner-and-dancing cruises on the weekends in November and December.

Jana, who ran her own handywoman business, Jana-of-All-Trades, worked for him seasonally as the Brazos Queen's entertainment coordinator, mostly because it was pure fun. Although, the extra money never hurt. Jana liked to have a strong financial cushion. Multiple streams of income were important when you were self-employed.

Feeling awkward and wishing she hadn't touched Joel, Jana tucked her hands into her pockets. They got along like a house on fire, but she was his employee, and she didn't want to be overly familiar, no matter how much they enjoyed each other's company. Boundaries were important. She was certain that Joel's girlfriend, Ursula, would agree.

"Hear what?" he asked. "Christmas music?"

"No, no. *Listen*."

Joel tilted his head, mirroring Jana, and paused for a moment. "I got nothing beyond the music and the wind rattling the leaves. What did you hear?"

"I dunno. I thought I heard a soft bleat, like a lost kitten or an infant's whimper." She felt silly saying it. Who would bring a newborn outside into this blustery December weather?

Then again, who knew?

This was Twilight, Texas, and she'd learned a long time ago not to ask too many questions of the quirky, lakeside community if she didn't want fanciful or far-fetched answers. Jana was from Austin, the Capital of Weird, but even that hadn't prepared her for the whimsical shenanigans that went on in this tourist town that she'd adopted seven years ago when she'd been running from . . .

Well, she wouldn't think about *that*. The past was well behind her, and she was *not* a ruminator.

"I'm sure it was the sheep." Joel gestured to the ewes in the little wooden corral beside the nativity scene.

Jana rolled her eyes. "Who on the town council cooked up the idea of using live animals in the nativity scene? Taking care of them is a pain."

"There's no telling. One of the usual suspects, I imagine." Joel shrugged and polished up his grin. The man did have a prince of a smile that he whipped out often to charm and stun.

Before Thanksgiving, the chamber of commerce had come begging for local business owners to help ride herd on the animals and tourists alike. Joel had tried to tap-dance out of the obligation, but his gregarious twin brother Noah, and Noah's wife Kelsey, who ran the Rockabye Boatel, an adjunct to Joel's riverboat cruise business, had told the chamber of commerce they could count on all the MacGregors to volunteer.

The nightly roster rotated, and Joel had signed up for Wednesday evenings throughout the holiday season, and he'd twisted Jana's arm to join him.

Truth?

He'd begged his butt off and promised to cook Jana a vegan version of his famous mulligan stew if she'd agree to help. Always on the lookout for great vegan meals, she'd been persuaded.

Tonight, in this inclement weather, the tourists had skedaddled, leaving them with nothing more to do than round up farm animals. The pen had a divider between the sheep and the donkey because Antonio Banderass was known to nip.

Joel hooked his finger through the miniature donkey's halter.

Antonio hee-hawed at them, his sides billowing with the bray as if asking why it had taken them so long to show up. Joel pulled a molasses treat from his pocket.

Seeing the treat, the donkey hushed right up.

"Storm's comin' in faster than the forecasters said. Let's get these critters into Pastor Luther's barn ASAP and then hustle back to stake down anything that could get carried off by the wind. You want Banderass or the sheep?"

"There's three sheep and one donkey. I prefer the easy option."

"The sheep it is." Joel laughed and took down the crook that was hooked on the side of the corral and handed it to her.

Joel had the best laugh in the world. Low, seductive. Women flocked to him because of that laugh and his rich baritone voice.

Honestly, he could have been a TV announcer, his voice was that hot. Not that she noticed all that much. He was just a nice guy she worked for sometimes.

Uh-huh.

"Remind me again why we volunteered for this?" Jana grumbled, opening the gate to the sheep's side of the pen and guiding them out with the crook.

"Peer pressure."

"Oh yeah." She chuckled. "From your twin brother."

"Look at the bright side." Joel winked. He didn't mean it provocatively. She knew that. The winking was a dashing trick to win people over. "No one could locate a camel. If you think Antonio is a handful, you've never wrangled one."

"And you've wrangled a camel?"

"Yep."

"When?" she asked, turning her back to the north wind and flipping up the collar on her jacket.

"I worked at the Fort Worth Zoo, cleaning cages the summer between my junior and senior years in high school. Camels spit. A lot."

"I didn't know that about you."

"Hey. I can be an enigma too."

She rolled her eyes.

"Okay, you're right. I'm lousy at secret-keeping. I don't have your flair for subterfuge."

He wasn't wrong.

If Jana had a spirit animal, it would be an iceberg. She kept most of herself hidden far below the surface. She knew her secrecy bugged some people, but life was safer when you kept your mouth shut and the spotlight focused on others. Although, keeping her secrets wasn't easy in a town of good-hearted busybodies. They all wanted to get to know her better.

To which her suspicious side asked *why?*

A gust blew her hair in her face, and for a second, she wished she still had her dreadlocks. That hairstyle wouldn't move in a hurricane. Since she'd been working on self-improvement, and healing from her tumultuous childhood, she'd toned down the flashy appearance she'd worn like a freak flag when she'd first rolled into Twilight at age nineteen.

Over the course of the past seven years, she'd ditched the dreads, most of her numerous piercings, and the heavy goth attire, and she'd let her hair go back to its original color—a honeyed brown that was prettier than she'd remembered. The only thing left that said she'd led a full and varied life by age twenty-six were the twenty-six tattoos inked onto her body. One for every year of her life.

Each tat told a story.

Her past was laid out there on her skin. She didn't hide her history; she just inked it instead of talking about it.

The lead sheep bolted and broke for the street.

"Whoa! Get back here, Freda!" Jana flew after the runaway.

"That's not Freda," Joel yelled as he tugged on Banderass's rope. "That's Chelsea. Hang on. Let me get Banderass to the barn, and I'll come help."

The donkey dug in his heels and brayed loud enough to wake the dead.

Jana winced. Freda? Chelsea? Who cared what her name was?

The lead sheep frolicked like she was in a commercial for Little Bo Peep's Yarn, kicking up her heels and bleating. The other two ewes wouldn't let her have all the fun and trotted after her. As one unit, the ovine trio barreled across the street, heading for the Twilight Library.

"Get back here, you rascals!" Jana charged after them, waving the crook.

"Remember, they're the easy ones." Joel laughed. He really did have a spectacular laugh. Deep and commanding. It made her want to throw back her head and join him.

That impulse scared her. She was starting to like him too much. *Simmer down, he's got a girlfriend. He's just a friendly guy. Don't read anything more into it.*

Jana raised a middle finger at him over the top of her head.

"Love you too!" he shouted above the blustering, braying, and bleating.

Love you too.

Jana didn't take his declaration personally. He was one of those people who threw the word *love* around willy-nilly. He was teasing. It was a figure of speech. He didn't mean he *loved her* loved her.

Pfft. She knew that. The only reason her pulse was pounding in her ears was she'd jogged across the street in her vegan-leather motorcycle boots to retrieve the errant sheep.

Naughty creatures.

"Get back here, you three," she scolded.

The sheep collected on the front stoop of the library and peered at her with *nah-nah, nah-nah* looks in their eyes.

"Do not poop on the porch! My handywoman business has a contract with the city to do yardwork for the library. I do not want to clean your poop."

Freda, Chelsea, and whatever the other one's name was had no regard for her sob story. They swished their tails, bleated, and pooped in unison.

"You're pushing your luck, ladies." Jana kicked sheep dung off the porch and into the grass. "Good thing I'm a vegan, or you'd end up in a big pot of mutton stew for that stunt."

With deft movements—she'd spent some time on a farm with one of her foster families—Jana rounded up the sheep and guided them toward the big red barn next to Pastor Luther's house, their hooves clomping against the asphalt.

Christmas music from the town square drifted out into the windblown night, currently "Away in a Manger."

Jana cocked an eye toward the sky, grinned, and muttered, "A little on the nose, don't you think?"

Joel was still tugging on Antonio Banderass's halter, the donkey digging his hind legs into the dirt and braying nonstop, as a flurry swept up leaves and spun debris eddies across the yard and into the darkness beyond.

"Stubborn jackass," Joel muttered.

A fat drop of rain hit the top of Jana's head, and she rushed the sheep ahead of her. "C'mon, girls. Let's do this."

Pastor Tom Luther came out of his house, ski cap perched on his head, body bent against the gale, and hurried over to open the barn door. He waved them inside.

"Big storm's on the way," Pastor Luther said, stating the obvious.

He was an amiable, round-faced man in his late sixties. He wore reading glasses on a chain around his neck, a puffy down coat, rubber wading boots, and baggy cargo shorts that hit him just below the knees.

"Please hurry," he urged.

It was hard to see in the darkness, the area lit only by a lone flood lamp overhead, and the icy blue Christmas twinkle lights dangling from the eaves.

Jana narrowed her eyes and moved the crook from side to side, keeping the sheep in tidy order. With Pastor Luther's help, she got the ewes into the barn and turned to see Joel luring the donkey inside with yet another treat.

After they'd fed the critters and locked them into their stalls for the night, Joel sagged against the barn door and mopped his arm over his forehead, only half exaggerating. "Whew, what an ordeal!"

"Do you need help with anything else?" Pastor Luther cast a longing glance toward his house and rubbed his palms together.

Joel gave an amiable shake of his head. "We've got this. All that's left is to secure the nativity scene."

"Well, holler if you change your mind." The minister hurried across his yard to the back steps of his Victorian home, leaving Joel and Jana alone again.

Joel flashed a smile, and his gaze lingered on her lips for a disturbingly long second. Or maybe she was just imagining it.

Unnerved, she ducked her head. "Get a move on, MacGregor. I'm jonesing for that mulligan stew. My mouth has been ready for it all day."

"Um, about the stew . . . I forgot to plug in the Crock-Pot and didn't notice until I was headed over here, so I stuck it in the freezer for later. My bad."

"Rain check, then. And I'm being literal." Three raindrops in quick succession hit her face. *Splat, splat, splat.*

They closed up the barn and trotted back to the church in the quickening rainfall. The crowds who'd earlier strolled the streets on and around the town square had vaporized.

Not a soul in sight.

The sky was midnight black, and the wind bone-chilling. Since she wasn't getting mulligan stew, Jana yearned instead for a steaming bubble bath, streaming hard-rock music, and hot chamomile tea. She was a sucker for her creature comforts.

Joel staked down the Christmas blow molds, while Jana pulled up the wooden cutouts and stacked them underneath the awning at the side of the church that afforded a windbreak. When she'd finished, she returned to the manger for one last check . . .

And she heard it again.

The soft mewling whimper.

A baby.

You're hearing things, she told herself and put a hand to her belly to quell her fear. *It's that time of year again.*

Perhaps, but the sound reminded her she hadn't yet secured the Baby Jesus swaddled in the nest of straw. She would just fetch the doll, run him over to Pastor Luther's house, and then they were out of here.

She squatted beside the makeshift crib.

Felt Joel come up behind her.

Reaching for the corner of the blue fleece blanket that had blown over the face of the plastic Jesus, Jana pulled back the covers.

And that's when the bundle let out a long, demanding wail.

"HOLY THROAT CHAKRA!" Jana shouted, stumbled backward, and fell on her butt. "It's a *real* baby."

Dumbstruck, Joel stared. First at Jana sitting on her backside at his feet and then at the straw crib where a tiny human wriggled, red-faced and squalling louder than the storm.

"It's a real baby," he echoed, stunned.

Before he could put a hand down to help Jana up, she bounced to her feet. Squinting hard in the darkness, she circled the child as if it was a time bomb that might explode at any moment and it was her job to defuse it.

What Joel knew of babies from his niece and nephew, the explosive scenario wasn't that far-fetched. Babies were forever spewing bodily fluids.

"How did it get here?" She blinked and shook her head and blinked again.

"I dunno." Joel scratched his head.

"Is this some kind of prank? Are we on that show *What Would You Do*?" She glanced around as if John Quiñones was lurking inside the church with a camera crew for a Twilight, Texas, version of the programming that delighted in setting up unsuspecting people in faked moral dilemmas.

Joel glanced around too and settled his hands on his hips. It was a legitimate question. He cupped his palms around his mouth and called, "Hello! Whoever left the kid, come on out. This isn't funny."

"Do you think someone could have actually abandoned him?" Her voice scraped hard against the word *abandoned*.

"Seriously." Joel glared into the darkness. "Come get your baby. The joke has gone on too long."

"Where's its mother?" Jana wrung her hands. "Who would do this? Why did she leave her baby?"

"The answers don't matter right now." Joel scooped the infant into his arms. "We gotta get this little guy in from the cold and sort the rest out later."

Stark lightning flashed, and the sky grumbled.

He cradled the baby against him. "Jana?"

"Huh?"

"Shake a leg."

Jana looked dazed.

"C'mon, Tink," he said teasingly yet worried about her. "Snap out of it."

He'd started calling her Tinker Bell a few weeks ago when

Jana had confessed, during a children's birthday party she was helping him host on the Brazos Queen, that Tinker Bell, the feisty pixie fairy, was her favorite Disney character.

No surprise there, since she was pretty darn feisty herself. But Tinker Bell had sounded a bit too delicate for Jana, and he'd shortened it to Tink. She hadn't complained, so he'd kept using the nickname. He liked it.

Assuming Jana would follow, Joel sprinted toward his pickup truck, the baby held tight against him as the raindrops morphed into a full-blown downpour. Soaked to the skin, Joel pried the driver's-side door open and hopped inside, the kid crying at the top of his lungs.

Jana got in on the passenger side, her wet hair plastered to her face. They both needed dry clothing, but first they had a more pressing problem.

"Oh my gosh, we're drenched!" Jana shivered. "Thank heavens you tucked him under your coat, or he'd be soaked too."

In his arms, the tiny wailing infant turned his head to the sound of Jana's melodious feminine voice.

"Hey, kid," she said. "What's your dealio?"

The baby quieted, blinked, and let out a loud hiccup.

"Wow," Joel said. "Jana has charms to soothe the savage beast. I mean, I knew that all along, but hey, *evidence.*"

"Breast."

"What?" Joel startled, and dang if his gaze didn't fall to her chest so well-endowed by Mother Nature. *Knock it off, MacGregor. Stop ogling her. Not cool.*

"The quote," she explained. "It's 'soothe the savage breast.'"

He wrinkled his forehead. "No kidding?"

"Google it."

"I believe you, but why *savage breast* when *beast* works so much better?"

"I dunno." Jana lifted her shoulders. "It's an old saying. Maybe that's how they talked in the seventeenth century or whatever."

"*Breast* equals *beast*? Huh. Who knew?"

The newborn stuck his tiny fist into his mouth and started chewing. Outside, hard rain drummed against the roof of the pickup truck. On the buildings, Christmas lights blurred like Monet's paintings viewed too close up.

"And speaking of breasts," Jana said, "the kid looks hungry, and he needs dry clothes before he catches cold."

Joel peered down at the infant.

The baby, sucking on his hand, cast wide, frightened eyes at Joel. Someone had abandoned this helpless little one in a Christmas manger. His chest tightened, and his ears rang as reality sank in.

Overwhelming emotions flooded his body, and one singular thought filled his mind. An insistent thought that knocked the air from his lungs and the innocence from his eyes. A thought so resolute it became an insistent imperative.

Protect this child at all costs.

CHAPTER 3

THE CHILD

Watching Joel with the baby melted Jana's heart.

Joel was a large guy, built more for a basketball court than the confines of a pickup truck, and the padded plaid mackinaw coat he wore accentuated the breadth of his shoulders. He'd raked his wet dark hair, just long enough to curl around the tops of his ears, back off his forehead, leaving finger furrows like plowed rows. His big palm almost covered the baby's entire back.

Poor defenseless little kid.

Overcome with unsettling emotions she had no name for, Jana glanced away and saw that the truck windows had steamed up from the warmth of their breath against the cold, damp glass.

The baby's cry was high and strangled.

"Hang on, kiddo. Let me get the engine going and the heater on." Joel shifted the baby from his shoulder to his lap, started the truck, turned on the heat full blast, and angled the vents toward the infant.

Jana shivered, thankful for the welcome warmth, and rubbed her upper arms as her fanny heated. How considerate of Joel to turn on the seat warmer for her. The radio came on along with the engine, spilling out Christmas music from a local radio station, an extra jivey version of "Jingle Bells."

Joel cleared his throat.

She looked over and met his gaze.

They stared at each other wide-eyed and dumbstruck as the full implications of what was happening sank in.

"Wow," he said, shifting his gaze from her to the baby.

"Oh, Joel! Look how tiny he is. He can't be more than a week old." Jana placed both palms over her heart.

"Who could abandon something this small and helpless in the cold and just hope someone found him?" He clenched his jaw, and the muscles along his chin twitched. "This is serious stuff."

"Someone pretty desperate, I guess," she said, ignoring the slap of guilt that hit her. This was not her burden or her pain. She didn't have to carry it, but she ached to reach over and stroke the baby's cheek with her knuckle.

Why?

She was not a kid person. Kids were too needy, and Jana was too independent for needy. A jittery feeling bounced on her stomach like a trampoline.

Ah, Anxiety, my old friend. I remember you.

"Tink? You okay?"

"Yes," she croaked. "Just trying to wrap my head around this."

Joel moved the child to his shoulder again to calm him. His hand cradled the infant's spine, while his long fingers cupped the back of the little one's head. The heartstring-tugging contrast of tiny baby and big, masculine man unfurled something inside her, and she was back in the mushy bog of her chest.

Nope. Not going there. Not again.

Quickly, as if she was deadheading roses, she pruned those silly romantic thoughts. Sure, Joel was hot. He was handsome, buff, and personable, but he was her boss, and he had a girl-friend.

What if he wasn't her boss?

But he was. And even if he wasn't and didn't have a girlfriend, they were incompatible. Too different to ever be a good match. Here's what she knew of him.

Joel was traditional. Reliable. A protector type. He was an upstanding citizen who mowed his lawn to a two-and-a-half-inch height—yes, he measured; she'd seen him. He painted the white-picket fence around his house yearly, and he had his pets duly spayed or neutered and annually vaccinated.

He was pretty straitlaced, despite being something of a goofy, fun-loving cutup. He vowed an unwavering allegiance to Lone Star beer, never mind the lovely microbreweries that had cropped up in the area. He insisted on turkey and dressing for both Thanksgiving and Christmas. He drove a Chevy, wore flannel shirts and cowboy boots. It went without saying his favorite pie was apple, his favorite ice cream was vanilla, and baseball was his favorite sport, even though he'd played basketball in college and his twin, Noah, had played in the NBA.

He valued community, family, and the American way. He loved holidays and celebrations and family reunions of any kind. He flew both the US and Texas flags on his paddleboat, for crying out loud. Yes, the tourists ate up the corny patriotism with a long-handled spoon, but Jana knew far too much about human nature to be sucked in by the idealized fantasy of an America that had never really existed.

While his stalwart traits might appeal to the majority of women in Twilight, Joel was a bit too upstanding for Jana's tastes. For better or worse, she was attracted to bad boys, and she'd found a few when she'd first moved to Twilight. Those relationships had burned out as soon as the sex got routine. As she'd gotten older, she'd learned to avoid those lightning-hot, lust-filled flings that ended like the crash of a sugar rush.

And now?

Shh, but it had been eight months since she'd been with anyone. She felt like a clean slate, and she wasn't in any rush to write on the slate again.

Jana was edgy, adventuresome, and thrived on variety. Anything that made the general public clutch their pearls tended to put a spring in her step. She could be rebellious, argumentative, colorful, and creative. She loved to have a good cause to fight for and, man, did the town council hate to see her at public hearings, which tickled her no end.

She gave people the space to be themselves and tried not to judge. She knew firsthand what it was like to be the focus of gossip, innuendo, and speculation, and she didn't want to do that to anyone else. And yes, okay, she even courted the rumors sometimes, just to keep people off balance.

Coffee—strong and black—was her beverage of choice, and it was her favorite ice-cream flavor too. She ran on caffeine. She adored Thai food and Indian curry, two cuisines hard to come by in Twilight. She played the high plains flute on her back patio every morning as part of her sunrise ritual. She kept in shape by jumping on a rebounder, and just for fun she visited a psychic once a year, even though she didn't believe a word of it. She did yoga, used essential oils in place of cologne, and believed in green causes even if she couldn't always live up to her ideals.

Face it. In the personality department, she and Joel were total opposites. She wasn't going to be sucked in by the fact he looked adorable with a baby and her body was reacting in ways she had not seen coming.

"Any idea what we should do about him?" Joel asked.

She raised one shoulder to her ear, alarmed by her tender feelings. "Take the baby to the police station, I guess."

"We can't drive around with him without an infant car seat."

"Good point. I hadn't even thought about that. What I know about babies would fit into a teaspoon."

"All I know about kids is from taking care of my niece and nephew."

"That makes you the expert. I've seen you with Ian and Grace. You're a natural. Could we call your sister and ask her to bring us a car seat?"

Joel rubbed his chin. "It's eight o'clock on a stormy winter night. I hate to ask Flynn to come out in this mess. She dislikes driving in bad weather."

"I'm sure Jesse would drive her."

"Then, they'd have to bring the kids."

"What if Flynn sent Jesse?"

"Jesse is heading this year's toy-drive distribution efforts. He and his team are slammed prepping for the Christmas Eve deliveries."

"Noah?"

"My twin and his wife are having an early Christmas in Dallas with her dad and stepmom this year."

"Oh yeah, I forgot about that." Jana crinkled her nose.

The baby whimpered again, fussier this time.

"He'll only get louder," Joel said. "We gotta feed him."

Icy rain slapped against the windowpane. No time to waste. They had to act. Jana and Joel stared at each other and said, at the exact same time, "Pastor Luther."

TEN MINUTES LATER, they were sitting in Pastor Tom Luther's kitchen. The preacher was at the stove making hot chocolate from scratch to warm them on the cold winter night. The house smelled like Christmas: pine and peppermint.

It was a welcoming home.

Hands gnarled with rheumatoid arthritis, Pastor Luther's wife, Irene, perched in her wheelchair next to the kitchen table where Joel and Jana sat, gazing at the baby with wide, concerned eyes.

"A baby in the manger?" Irene shook her head. "It's a Christmas miracle."

Joel shot Jana a *what the hell?* expression. Miracle? What was she talking about?

Irene must have seen the look pass between them, because she waved a knobby fist. "I don't mean it's a miracle his mother abandoned him. I meant it's a miracle you were there. Can you imagine if you hadn't been?"

Simultaneously, everyone shuddered. Seen from that point of view, finding the baby was most definitely a Christmas miracle.

"It's God's plan," Irene said.

Joel wasn't sure about that. He wasn't terribly religious, but neither did he rule anything out. Miracles *did* happen.

"I bet Joel and Jana were the reason the mom left the baby in the manger," Pastor Luther said. "I prefer to believe most people act with positive intent."

The baby let out a wail as if he knew they were talking about him. Although, who knew? The baby might not be a boy. Joel had just assumed because of the blue blanket and his blue onesie.

"We need formula," Jana said. "And diapers."

"There's a spare diaper tucked in the blanket with him," Joel said. "I noticed it earlier. I'm sure he needs changing. Any volunteers?"

Silence fell.

"I'm making cocoa." Pastor Luther stirred the pot on the stove.

Irene lifted her contracted hands. No need to say more.

Jana had her palms up and was shaking her head just as vigorously as Pastor Luther stirred the cocoa.

"Fine." Joel sighed. "I'll do it."

"Cowboy up." Pastor Luther chuckled.

The infant's wails grew louder.

"You can use the guest bedroom to change his diaper," Irene offered. "Down the hall, first door on the left."

Joel shot Jana a desperate look. "You wanna come along?"

"All right," she said. "I'll go with you for moral support, but you're doing the changing. I can smell him from here."

"There's clean washcloths in the guest bathroom," Irene said.

"The cocoa will be ready when you get back." Pastor Luther turned the heat down under the pan. "In the meantime, I'll call Shep and ask him to bring over Henry's old infant car seat so we can transport him safely."

Pastor Luther's daughter Naomi and her husband Mark

"Shep" Shepherd lived next door. Jana was good friends with Naomi. The pastor said something else, but Joel didn't hear him. The infant was putting up a pretty good fuss, wailing nonstop. At least they knew his lungs were in good shape.

"Transport him where?" Jana asked, her voice coming out in a strange squeak.

"The hospital. He needs to be checked out by a doctor. No telling how long he was out there in the cold."

Right. Joel hadn't even thought of that.

"We're going to need some formula too," Jana said.

"I'll make a call." Pastor Luther's brow furrowed. "Although, you're the one I would normally contact for an evening supply run."

A big part of Jana's income came from taxi and delivery services since there were no major rideshare or delivery companies in Twilight. Through her handywoman business, Jana-of-All-Trades, she also did yard work, housecleaning, in-home elder day care, and dog walking. Her schedule was varied, and she worked fifty hours a week or more. Joel had no idea how she juggled it all.

With the baby in his arms, Joel stood up from the table and headed down the hall. Once they were in the guest bedroom, Jana shut the door.

"Since we don't have baby wipes, I'll get a washcloth and dampen it with warm water while you . . ." She flicked a glance at Joel as he laid the crying baby in the middle of the full-sized bed. ". . . do the deed."

"You're acting like the kid is radioactive." Joel laughed. "It's just poop."

"Which is why you get to change him." She grinned and shuffled to the bathroom.

Joel turned his attention to the little guy on the bed. The baby was peering up at him, his wide dark blue eyes tear-stained and unfocused. He had to be missing his mother. Joel got a strange pang in his heart. He'd lost his mother when he was four, and it had deeply impacted him. His mother passing away at such a young age was probably the reason he had this abiding urge to protect the infant at all costs.

The baby made loud suckling noises, chewing on his tiny hand.

"Diaper first, kiddo," Joel said. "Then food. Mainly because we've got a diaper. I hope Pastor Luther has put out the call for formula. That fist isn't going to satisfy for long."

Leaning over the mattress, Joel unwrapped the blanket, revealing the diaper tucked against the baby's side. There was writing in marker on it, and some of the ink had smeared.

"Jana," he called.

She poked her head from the bathroom. "Just letting the water run to heat up for the washcloth."

"C'mere."

"What is it?"

He held up the diaper. "I found a note."

Instantly, she was at his side. "His mother wrote a note? What's it say?"

"Haven't read it yet." Joel handed her the diaper. "Read it out loud."

Jana sucked in an audible breath, and she held the diaper up to the light. "It's hard to read. The lines are all over the place. It's as if she wrote it in the dark."

"Which is why I gave it to you."

Squinting, she cleared her throat and read. "*Please look after my baby. You are such a sweet couple and the perfect people to take care of him. I saw you two together and just knew you'd keep him safe. I will come back for him by New Year's Day if I can find a safe place to stay. His name is Gabriel because he is such a little angel and . . .*" Jana paused. "The rest of it is smeared beyond deciphering."

"So his mom *didn't* abandon him," Joel mused.

"Well, technically she did, but she's promising to come back."

Joel scratched his chin. "I don't know if we can bank on that. She did say *if* she could find a place to stay."

"I agree her reliability is questionable." Jana nibbled her bottom lip. "She dots her *i*'s with little hearts. I think she must be really young and fooling herself about returning for him."

"Denial." Joel shook his head and looked down at the baby. "It can be a powerful defense mechanism."

"It sounds like she was watching us. That's kinda creepy."

"And she mistook us for a couple."

"I hate to imagine what drove her to this." Jana looked sad, her mouth dipping down at the corners.

Joel felt pretty sad too. "Should we go ahead and use the diaper?"

"From the smell? Yeah. He's got to be miserable. I'll go get the cloth." She disappeared into the bathroom again and returned with a damp, warm washrag.

Joel changed the diaper while Jana hovered.

"Too bad we can't just keep him until his mom comes back," she said.

"*If* she comes back."

"I suppose we don't have a choice. If we take him to the hospital like Pastor Luther suggested, by law the staff have to notify law enforcement."

"He has to get checked out by a doctor."

"I know." She sighed.

That weary sigh stirred weird feelings inside of Joel. He had a wild urge to make all her dreams come true, even though he didn't know what those dreams were. "I thought you weren't big on babies."

Jana put a hand to her mouth. "I don't have anything against babies, I just don't have any experience with them. I was just thinking . . ."

"What?" Joel prodded.

"I just know what it's like in the foster-care system, and if there's any chance to help this little guy avoid that . . ." She bit her thumbnail. "I mean, most people who serve as foster parents do it for the right reasons, but it's still a revolving door, and sometimes folks are in it just for the money. If we can keep him out of the system and give his mom a chance to make things right . . ."

Was it his imagination, or did the sudden fire in Jana's eyes suggest that her mind was running on the same track as his?

"Tink?"

"I know we should turn the baby over to Child Protective Services right away but—"

"What are you saying?" Joel raised his eyebrows and jostled the fussy Gabriel in his arms.

"I dunno."

"You're hedging. I can see it in your eyes."

"I just had a wild thought. It's nothing. Forget it."

"Maybe. Maybe not. Let's hear it. I'm open to suggestions. That fist isn't going to satisfy this kid for long. I swear he's eyeing my earlobe as an appetizer."

"I hate to turn him over to CPS right away. We don't know what's going on with his mother. Maybe we can find her. Or help her out by keeping Gabriel until New Year's Day."

Their eyes met over the baby, and he felt a mawkish tugging of his heartstrings. Keeping the child, even for a night, seemed absurd. They should let the professionals handle the situation.

"We're ill-equipped," Joel said.

A knock sounded on the door.

"Y'all doing okay?" Pastor Luther called.

"Just dandy," Joel called back, but his gaze was trained on Jana. She looked as if she was on the verge of begging. Wow. He'd never seen her like this.

"We might be ill-equipped, but we have friends and a busy-body, meddlesome community who'd love to help, and Christmas *is* about love, hope, and charity. We could consider it **our** good deed for the season," Jana said.

She surprised him completely, but maybe he shouldn't have been so bowled over. He knew very little of her past except that she'd grown up in a string of foster homes. She just didn't share that kind of stuff with people. He didn't even know *how* she'd ended up in the system.

But her concern for Gabriel was easy to read. She jammed her hands in the pockets of her jacket and lowered her head.

"It's a generous thought, Jana, but taking on a newborn is a big responsibility, even if we had lots of help and convinced our family and friends to get on board."

"Please," she said. "It breaks my heart to think of putting him into the system before we've given his mom time to correct her choice."

Yeah, that right there? How could he turn down those big puppy-dog eyes of hers? Or ignore the needs of the little one wriggling against his shoulder?

"Tink, it'll be a lot of work, and both of our Christmas schedules are jam-packed already."

"True."

"I've got the Christmas Bards thing tomorrow night," he said, referring to the all-male review who put on a *Magic Mike*–type show every year for charitable donations to amyotrophic lateral sclerosis, the disease that had killed his mom on Christmas Eve twenty-six years ago. "And aren't you tending bar at the Horny Toad Tavern tomorrow night as well?"

"I am." She looked disappointed. "We *could* make it work if we tried. I bet Flynn would be happy to babysit tomorrow night."

Joel was shaking his head. Jana pushed herself harder than anyone he knew, but that wasn't the problem. She worked so hard she tended to neglect her own care. "You overload yourself every year."

"It's only for ten days, Joel. How bad could it be?"

"That's ten days *if* his mom returns."

"If she doesn't, we can take him to CPS then, right? At least we'll give her a chance to reclaim him."

Joel's mouth formed the word *no*, but his heart was already saying *yes*.

"Once the baby is clocked into the system, his mom will have a hellacious legal battle trying to get him back. I'd hate for a moment of weakness to escalate into a whole child-custody thing. What I can gather from that note, she seems very young and scared and all alone, and I think she loves her baby very much." Jana pressed her palms together in front of her heart and got a faraway look in her eyes as if she was reliving something from her past.

"I'm not convinced it's the right thing for him," Joel murmured, wondering what that look was all about. "Or us."

"But it's Christmastime, Joel, and what if the mom is a local girl? What if she's someone we know?"

"What if Gabriel's mom's *not* from Twilight? What if she's from another town around here? What if she was just a tourist and she's long gone by now?"

"Baby-dumping tourism?" Jana laughed, no humor in the sound.

"You're right. That was dumb of me. If she's gone for good, she's gone for good. Under the circumstances, it won't make much of a difference if we turn the baby in tonight or tomorrow."

"Or on New Year's Day."

Ah hell, what could he say to that? He was a goner. No way was he letting Gabriel and Jana down.

"All right." Joel nodded, knowing full well this wasn't the brightest thing he'd ever done. Jana's desire to keep the baby was problematic in several ways, but damn if Joel wasn't on board with keeping him.

Why? This was a delicate matter that deserved the utmost thought and care, and he wasn't an impulsive guy. A child's future was at stake. Why wasn't he insisting they immediately turn the infant over to CPS?

Why?

For one thing, Jana had rallied a solid argument. It was almost

Christmas. How could they let the little guy be whisked into the system tonight when they could easily wait a few days while they gave him a good first Christmas?

For another thing, he hadn't ever seen Jana looking so earnestly vulnerable, and it touched something inside him. Usually, she pulled out her tough, gruff exterior to deflect when tender emotions entered the picture.

Not that he knew her all *that* well. Sure, she'd lived in Twilight for seven years and had worked for him seasonally the past two of those seven, and they did run in the same social circles. At parties and family gatherings, he gravitated to her because she had a pretty wicked sense of humor whenever she let it out, and he enjoyed her wry take on their kooky community.

But . . .

At heart, she was an enigma. She had walls. Tall walls. Even though the walls had slowly shortened over time, she still trusted very few people.

Joel had the ridiculous urge to smash her defenses to rubble, prove to her she could trust *him*, and the baby was his wrecking ball. Tears welled in her eyes over the child, and he'd never seen her cry. He felt as if she was so close to an emotional breakthrough, and well, damn, he wanted to be there to see it.

"If you can convince Pastor Luther to get on board with the scheme, I'm right there with you, Tink," he said. "All the way."

CHAPTER 4

THE CALL TREE

Pastor Luther not only hopped right on board Jana's plan, he activated the Twilight call tree, and within thirty minutes, his kitchen was packed with well-wishers.

His daughter Naomi had shown up first, rushing over from right next door, with a car seat and diapers, while her husband, Shep, stayed home to watch their kids.

Three years ago, Naomi had adopted her late brother's son, Hunter, and then she and Shep had a son of their own named Henry. Naomi was also seven months pregnant with a daughter they planned on calling Heather.

The minute Naomi spied Gabriel, she'd pounced, taking the infant away from Joel and cooing over him.

On Naomi's heels, the neighbor from across the street, Terri Longoria, showed up with baby formula. Her surgeon husband was chief of staff at Twilight General Hospital. Terri was in her late forties, owned Hot Legs Gym, and had a sixteen-year-old son named Gerald. Gerald worked part-time for Joel, cleaning the paddle-wheel for an hour in the afternoons three days a week.

"I popped right down to H-E-B as soon as I heard," Terri

said, sweeping into the kitchen, the grocer's brown shopping bag in her arms. "The roads are really slippery, FYI, but thank heavens the temp's not supposed to drop below thirty-two degrees. Although the windchill makes it feel like it's in the teens."

A few minutes after Terri shook the rain from her coat, Joel's cousin, Paige MacGregor Colton—who was married to country-music star Cash Colton—showed up with baby clothes, receiving blankets, and more diapers. Cash and Paige had a two-year-old daughter named Zinnia, and they were expecting a son in April. Paige was petite, bubbly, and down-to-earth despite her husband's fame and fortune. Jana didn't know Paige well, but she liked her a lot.

After much oohing and aahing over the baby, Paige persuaded Naomi to let her hold Gabriel.

Jana felt a strange possessiveness toward the baby, and she had absolutely no reason for the feeling. She hadn't even held him yet.

Ahh, maybe that was it. She'd found the baby, and everyone else had gotten to hold him but her. Even Irene took a turn, and it was all Jana could do not to fuss. Irene's hands were pretty gnarled. What if the baby slipped from her arms?

Still, that was weird because Jana wasn't particularly enamored of children. The house was overly warm with the extra people, and she wanted to shrug off her coat but keeping it on felt safer somehow. Cushioning. Against what, she couldn't say, but in response to the sweat collecting at her neck, she burrowed deeper into the coat.

Joel leaned down and whispered, "Are you cold?"

His breath was heated against her ear, and it feathered the fine hairs along her hairline. He smelled of the peppermint candy cane he'd used to stir the hot cocoa Pastor Luther had doled out to his guests.

Unnerved, she suppressed a thrilling shudder and shook her head. What was wrong with her? Sure, he was a hottie, but he had a girlfriend, and he was her boss.

Stop getting turned on, Gerard.

A circumspect expression crossed Joel's face, and he stepped away from her.

She blew out her breath, both disappointed and relieved. Why was her body reacting like this? It never had done this before around Joel.

It's the baby.

Finding the abandoned newborn must be triggering these unexpected feelings inside her. Feelings she hadn't known she possessed: the need to nurture, the desire for . . .

What?

Something more in her life?

She cast a sidelong glance at Joel, trying to gauge his mood. Even in his rumpled mackinaw from a day working on the Brazos Queen, his chocolate brown hair mussed, and a beard stubble ringing his jaw, he was drop-dead gorgeous.

He met her gaze, and the air seemed to crackle between them.

Where was this electricity coming from? She had no business thinking sexy thoughts about her boss. Looking at him, she realized for the first time how much they matched. Joel in a red plaid coat. Jana in a red plaid skirt. She wore thick black cotton leggings. He was in black denim jeans. Both of them had on boots, although his were cowboy and hers were motorcycle with lots of shiny buckles. They looked like a paired set.

No wonder the baby's mom had thought them a couple.

Irene passed the baby to Terri, who cooed at him. Jana pulled her arms from her pockets and crossed them over her chest. She wanted to snatch up Gabriel and clutch him close to her.

In her mind, a memory triggered.

A vivid snapshot of another baby, another Christmas. Overwhelmed by the imagery, she closed her eyes and put a hand to her belly, air slipping from her lungs in a long shallow leak.

She adored the people of Twilight—most of them, anyway. They were some of the nicest folks she'd ever met, but right now, Jana kinda hated their comradery, and she wished she and

Joel had taken the baby to her house, car seat or not, instead of coming over to the Luthers'.

Why had they come over here? Oh yeah, diapers, formula, a car seat. They had all those things now. Could they go?

She sought Joel's gaze, hoping to telegraph that message with her eyes, but he was over by the stove near Pastor Luther, getting a refill on his cocoa and having a conversation she couldn't hear.

"Jana?" Naomi asked. "Are you okay?"

"Fine." Jana forced a smile. "Fine, fine, fine."

Great. Why had she repeated the word? That made her sound anything but fine. She again wished she still had her dreadlocks. Wished she hadn't let most of her piercings close up. Wished she'd kept her goth clothes.

Calm down. Chill. Your anxiety is showing.

She concentrated on her breathing, deepening and slowing it. And smiling. Smiles made people feel better. *Fake it till you make it, right?*

"It's got to be unsettling," Naomi said. "Finding a baby in a manger."

Jana just kept smiling.

Naomi glanced around at the people gathered in her parents' kitchen. "What are we going to do about him?"

We? Naomi was co-opting the baby?

Jealousy curled a hard knot in the pit of her stomach. Geez, what was going on with her? She didn't like these runaway feelings. Not one bit. Jana caught Joel's eye, seeing if she could get a read on him.

"Jana and I plan to keep him until his mother returns," Joel said, meeting Jana's gaze and smiling at her.

Her heart lifted. He was still on her side.

"Both of you?" Terri asked. "Together?"

Jana notched up her chin. "Sure. Why not?"

Terri's eyes widened. "I . . . you—"

"Yes." Jana dropped the smile and drilled the gym owner with a steady stare. She'd been told her stares could freeze molten lava. The skill came in handy when she needed to quell nosy questions.

"I remember when you first came to Twilight." Terri's smile widened, and her eyes softened with kindness.

Instantly, Jana felt like an ass for getting defensive. She'd been reading things into Terri's words that the woman clearly hadn't intended.

"You were this feisty little kitten, all claws and teeth." Terri chuckled.

Yeah, well, that sounded lovely.

"Your car had broken down just outside of town on Highway 51. Your tires as bald as Mr. Clean's head."

Which was how Jana had ended up living in Twilight. Nineteen. On the run from her past, penniless, and hopeless with nowhere else to go.

Terri added gestures to her story, the jingle bells on her sweater jangling as she waved her hands. "When Steve and I pulled up behind you, you locked all your doors and told us you had someone coming to help you. We could tell right away you were lying, and we said we wouldn't leave you until your ride came. We all sat there for an hour before you admitted you needed help."

Okay, okay, she'd been distrustful and suspicious and . . . scared. Guilty as charged. But that was seven years ago. Move on, people.

"Oh, you are so right, Terri," Irene added. "I remember when Naomi brought Jana to her first Sunday service at our church. One of our more . . . er . . ." Irene paused as she searched for the right word. ". . . conservative members—"

"Mrs. Lewis?" Paige guessed, making kissy faces at Gabriel.

"How did you know?" Irene asked.

"I had a brush with Mrs. Lewis when I first came here," Paige said. "Thankfully, she is not indicative of the general citizenry of Twilight."

"Mrs. Lewis was taken aback by Jana's colorful appearance," Irene went on with her story. "And she dared to confront Jana about her tats. Without missing a beat, Jana asked Mrs. Lewis for her cell phone, took a selfie, handed the phone back, and said, 'Now you have a picture to remind yourself just how much better you are than me.'" Irene giggled and met Jana's gaze. "Tom and I secretly got a kick out of you putting Mrs. Lewis in her place."

"You did that?" Joel laughed. "That's priceless, Tink."

Jana's cheeks heated. "I'm not proud of it. I was a teenager and not smart enough to know when to pick my battles."

"I loved it," Pastor Luther said. "Trust me, Mrs. Lewis had it coming."

"She's mellowed," Irene said.

Pastor Luther looked startled. "Mrs. Lewis?"

"Oh no, she's still a challenge." Irene laughed. "I meant Jana. She tried hard to keep us at bay, but Twilight slipped underneath her defenses, and now look at her! Here she is, rescuing an abandoned baby."

"I was there too," Joel said. "I helped save him."

"Oh *pfftt*," Naomi said. "Everyone knows you're a hero. Jana is the one who's grown by leaps and bounds."

Okay, enough about her past. People got it. She'd been a pugilistic little snot, prepared to fight her way out of any situation, but she'd grown up since then. She and Joel had the baby gear. Time to get out of here.

"It is surprising you'd want to keep the baby," Paige said, lifting Gabriel to her shoulder and patting his little back.

Jana watched, still feeling that possessive jealousy. "Oh?"

"When I asked if babysitting was part of your handywoman services and you said you didn't 'do' kids, I got the feeling you didn't like children. What's changed?" Paige seemed honestly curious.

It wasn't that she didn't like children. In fact, it was the opposite. She cared about kids so much she had to keep them at arm's length in order to keep her heart safe.

She stared at Gabriel, and Paige's question circled her head.

What's changed? Why did she want to go out on a limb for this baby?

C'mon, you know why. She might be fooling everyone else, but she shouldn't lie to herself.

"How did you end up in Twilight?" Terri asked, canting her head. "You've never told us. What on earth happened?"

Jana squirmed. Seriously? Terri was bringing that up now?

"I got in my car and started driving north until I ran out of gas." She chuckled so she wouldn't seem like a smart-ass.

Joel moved to put an arm over her shoulder. The weight of it felt both comforting and disquieting. "You guys lighten up on Jana. She might look tough on the outside, but inside she's a marshmallow."

"I can fight my own battles, Joel," she said, stepping away from him.

He dropped his arm to his side, looking chastised. "I didn't mean to violate your boundaries."

Great, now she felt as if she'd overreacted. It was just that his touch had set off a wave of body tingles she didn't want to think about.

"My goodness, we were ganging up on you, weren't we?" Irene looked upset. "I'm so sorry. Putting you on the spot is the last thing we intended. We're here to help, Jana."

Yeah, Jana had never been good with accepting help, but this wasn't about her. The little baby needed them. *That's* what mattered.

"I didn't feel ganged-up on," Jana denied.

"Because we *do* love you." Irene placed both her knobby fists over her heart and met Jana's gaze. Gave her a tender smile.

Love.

Many of the townsfolk—including Joel—dispensed that word so easily. It was a habit Jana hadn't picked up. If she ever said the *L*-word, she meant it. It wasn't a figure of speech to her. Love was too precious to throw around lightly.

Precisely at nine P.M., an hour after they'd found the baby, a solid knock sounded against the Luthers' back door. Three no-nonsense fist raps in quick succession. *Whap-whap-whap.*

"Who's that?" Paige asked, passing the baby over to Terri, who'd been standing beside her making *gimme* hands.

Jana felt another jealous-green pang. *Holy Heart Chakra, what was happening to her?*

"Come on in," Pastor Luther called out.

The back door swung open, and in walked Sheriff Hondo Crouch.

"You called Hondo?" Joel asked Tom Luther, irritated that the pastor had betrayed them.

Now they'd have to turn Gabriel over to CPS tonight. This was going to crush Jana, who'd clearly developed some kind of instant attachment to Gabriel. Not that he could blame her. He was head over heels for the newborn too.

Joel peered over at Jana to see how she was taking this. She stood still as a statue with her hands fisted at her sides. She looked so self-contained, needing no one.

An odd sadness squeezed his heart.

She was so beautiful bundled in that white ski jacket that complemented her honey brown hair, her dark blue eyes pinned on him. She possessed a gymnast's body, petite yet muscular, compact and powerful. Admiring her jazzed him up in ways that weren't smart. He shifted his gaze off her curves and back to her inscrutable eyes.

What was she thinking? He'd never really gotten a good read on her. Just when she'd start to open up, she'd catch herself and pull back.

For sure, she wasn't as guarded as she'd been when she'd first come to work for him, when every word had seemed measured. But she rarely shared anything personal about herself. Even just now, she hadn't been able to answer Terri's question about why she'd left Austin.

It didn't take a rocket scientist to figure out she'd faced some pretty big challenges in her young life and those experiences had put her constantly on guard. It must be exhausting monitoring everything you said and did around other people.

"I texted him, actually," Pastor Luther said, with an apologetic half smile.

"So you were never on board with us keeping Gabriel?" Jana said. "Why did you call everyone and ask them to bring baby supplies?"

"Because . . ." said Sheriff Hondo, stalking into the kitchen, the sound of his cowboy boots striking the hardwood floors and echoing off the tall ceiling. He was in uniform, the gold name badge pinned to his pocket. "Tom wants this situation on the up-and-up."

"Huh?" Joel scratched his head.

A second knock sounded at the back door, and Naomi moved to open it.

Terri's husband, Dr. Steven Longoria, entered. The physician was tall and lanky, but not as tall as Joel's six foot five, and he had a serious case of male-pattern baldness. His straight, over-sized nose and round, wire-framed glasses gave him an owlish appearance.

This was feeling like an ambush. Tom Luther had brought in the sheriff and the hospital chief of staff. This is exactly what he and Jana had wanted to avoid—turning the baby over to the authorities.

Terri held up Gabriel for her husband to see. "Isn't he the most adorable thing *ever*?"

"Somebody left that precious bundle in the manger?" Dr. Longoria shook his head. "People confound me sometimes."

Me too, Joel thought and glowered at Tom Luther.

"What's going on?" Jana asked, planting her clenched fists on her hips, narrowing her eyes, and notching up her determined chin. "Have you come to take the baby away?"

"Not yet," Hondo said mildly. "We came to hear the story and make a decision."

"A decision?" Joel gulped, surprised by how invested he felt.

"On what to do about the baby." Hondo swept off his cowboy hat, settled it on the counter and took a seat at the bar. "Tell me what happened."

Jana folded her arms over her chest and stared at the sheriff. "How much do you know?"

Hondo waved his cell phone. "Tom said you found a baby in the nativity scene, but that there are extenuating circumstances. Let's hear it."

Jana met Joel's eyes. "Do you want to tell him?"

"You found the baby. It's your story."

Jana sucked in a breath and told Hondo and Dr. Longoria what had happened and about finding the note written on the diaper.

"His mom *is* coming back," she said. "So really, technically, we'd just be babysitting."

Hondo scowled. "*If* his mom is telling the truth."

"I do need to check him out," Dr. Longoria said. "Whether you keep him until his mother returns or we turn him over to CPS, he needs to be seen by a doctor."

"May I see the note?" Hondo asked.

Jana winced. "His mom wrote it on his diaper."

"I'll unwrap him," said Terri, who was still holding Gabriel.

His muscles spring-loaded with tension, Joel moved to stand by Jana. He could smell her scent, like pumpkin spice and pine cones. He wanted to put his arm around her again, but she hadn't reacted well when he'd done it before, and he didn't want to make her uncomfortable, so he jammed his hands into his jacket pockets instead.

Everyone watched with bated breath as Terri uncovered Gabriel. Holding him gingerly, she turned him over for Hondo to read the note written on the diaper.

Joel should be relieved at the prospect of washing his hands of the baby. He already had so much on his plate this holiday season, and he figured he would have been relieved if it hadn't been for the expression on Jana's face. For whatever reason, that look of pure longing in her eyes said she wanted to care for this baby.

But what staggered Joel to his core was his own compelling urge to move heaven and earth to give Jana what she wanted. And that, friends and neighbors, turned him inside out.

When had he started feeling like this?

She raised her hand to press the heel of her palm against her forehead, which gave him a good view of the angel with the sweet face of a newborn baby tattooed on the inside of her wrist. He'd seen the tat before but hadn't thought much about it. Now, looking at it set his curiosity whirling.

Hondo nodded, and Terri bundled up Gabriel again.

"Well?" Joel prodded, puzzled by the hard knot forming in the center of his chest.

"It seems as if his mother did select you to care for him, and her intent is to return for him," Hondo said. "So unless she doesn't show up on New Year's Day, I'm inclined to view this as a babysitting situation."

Air burst from Jana's lungs in an audible whoosh, and the sudden joy on her face took Joel completely by surprise. Why did this mean so much to her?

Hondo held up an index finger. "As long as Dr. Steve says the baby is healthy."

Terri handed the baby to her husband, and the look of longing on Jana's face as she watched the transfer filled Joel with a sense of wonder and . . .

Dread.

She was already attached to the kid. He didn't know how that had happened. Jana was not someone who gave her heart freely. Dang, but was he feeling jealous of that baby?

"But . . ." Hondo held up a second finger. ". . . before you two undertake this responsibility, I suggest you take some time to think about this. It's not a decision to enter into lightly."

"All right." Joel nodded.

They did need time. The events had unfolded at a blinding blur, and they'd had no opportunity to think it through.

"How long will it take you to examine the baby?" Hondo asked Dr. Longoria.

"Terri and I will take him to my office, feed him some formula, check him out thoroughly, and run some basic blood work. It shouldn't take us more than an hour."

"Great." Hondo picked up his Stetson and held it in his hand as he got to his feet. "In the meantime, I'll do some digging and see if I can get a lead on his mother."

Joel saw Jana cross the fingers of both hands behind her back. Was she wishing that Hondo would find the mom?

Or would not?

"You two go get some coffee or a bite to eat at Moe's," Hondo suggested, referring to the all-night diner four blocks from the square. "Steve can call you to come pick up the baby. Or if you decide that taking on a newborn at Christmas isn't for you, then just let me know, and I'll handle the rest."

"I *want* to take care of him," Jana said. "I already know that."

"But . . ." Joel added, nodding. ". . . we're not going to make a snap decision. This is important."

"There's a lot to consider," Hondo said, "and I want you to factor that into your decision. Who will watch the baby when you both have to work? Who will be the primary caretaker? Where will you stay? How is this going to affect your relationship with each other? What happens if the baby gets sick? How will you handle it when his mom shows up? How will you feel if she doesn't?"

Wow, those were all solid questions Joel hadn't had time to consider in the mad rush of getting the baby to safety. He was glad Pastor Luther had called Hondo. This wasn't something to be undertaken lightly, and it was smart to get the chief law-enforcement officer in Hood County on their side.

"I have answers for all those questions," Jana reassured him.

"That's fine, but since Joel is on this adventure with you, you need to discuss your answers with him." Hondo headed toward the back door.

"All right." Jana nodded solemnly.

On his way out, Hondo stopped and rested his palm on the doorframe, leveled them both a serious stare. "I'll go along with you and call this *babysitting* until New Year's Day because it's the holidays, and I know there are so many good-hearted people in Twilight to help look after this baby, but if his mom doesn't show up as planned, no more messing around—I *am* getting CPS involved."

CHAPTER 5

THE DECISION

"I miss Gabriel already," Jana murmured as she and Joel settled in across from each other in the booth seating at Moe's. "Is that crazy?"

The diner smelled of bacon and strong coffee. The Christmas tree at the back of the room stood so tall it scraped the ceiling and that was without a topper. Holiday music seeped from the speakers, "Run, Run, Rudolph."

"Not crazy at all," Joel said. "Being around babies stirs up feel-good hormones. At least according to my sister, Flynn. Oxytocin or something."

Ahh, okay. That explained a lot. Now she didn't feel so weird about all these strange new emotions churning around inside her.

After Dr. Longoria and Terri had left with Gabriel, Jana insisted they load up the donated baby supplies in the back of Joel's truck. She'd decided she was keeping the baby through the holidays whether Joel was on board or not. There was no way in heaven she could walk away from the tiny, helpless baby. Sure, it'd be nice to have Joel's help, but she didn't *need* it. Jana had been on her own since she was fifteen.

She *would* figure it out.

Joel's gaze met hers across the table, and the smile moved all the way to his eyes and sent her heart beating faster.

Wildly unnerved, Jana studied the menu, even though she knew it by heart. There were only three vegan options on the menu, all put there at her suggestion—veggie burger patty melt, baked potato with roasted broccoli and cashew cheese, and a Hawaiian salad.

"I'm getting the veggie burger," she announced. "Normally, I don't eat this late at night, but I'm starving."

"Denver omelet for me," he said stretching out his legs in front of him, taking up more than his fair share of room underneath the table.

At his height, that must be a chronic issue for him. How to be comfortable living in a world built for people a foot shorter? Good thing she didn't take up much space. Accommodating him, Jana angled her knees sideways.

"Yoo-hoo!" A woman at another booth waved madly at them. It was Belinda Murphey, Joel's across-the-street neighbor. She was there with her husband and two of her five kids. "Joel! Jana!"

Belinda was a sweetheart, but she had a matchmaking streak a mile wide—she'd once owned a matchmaking service on the town square before online dating put her out of business—and she hadn't lost her meddlesome nature. She was constantly trying to hook Jana up with someone.

Of all the people to run into.

Full-figured, round-cheeked, flame-haired Belinda was wearing a god-awful, brightly colored Christmas sweater. She hopped up from her seat and barreled over.

Jana didn't want to chat. She and Joel had important things to discuss, but she hated to be rude. Especially since Belinda had been so kind to her when she'd first arrived in Twilight. While Terri Longoria had given her a job working at Hot Legs Gym, Belinda had been the one to supply lodging, letting her stay in her garage apartment for half the usual rent. That was before the Murpheys moved to the house across the street from Joel.

"Hello, hello, hello!" Belinda went in for a hug.

Jana half stood for the awkward embrace, and then it was Joel's turn to get squeezed. He winked at Jana over the top of Belinda's head.

"We just dropped by for a bite to eat after Kevin's Christmas piano recital." Belinda straightened and flapped a hand in the direction of her family. "Otherwise we wouldn't be out so late, but I'm thrilled to run into you!"

"How'd Kevin do?" Jana asked.

"He was fabulous!" Belinda lowered her voice and got a Proud Mom look on her face. "Shh. I think he was the best in the recital. But I want to hear about *you*." She held up her cell phone she'd been clutching the entire time. "I just got a text from Irene that you guys found a baby in the nativity manger!"

"Oh."

Bubbly Belinda oozed enthusiasm, and sometimes her glee could be a little much. Like now. The redhead plunked down in the booth next to Jana and said, "Tell me all about it."

Truly, there were no secrets in this town. Her fault though, for not asking everyone who'd shown up at the Luthers to keep a lid on the secret. At least for tonight while she and Joel oriented to the idea of keeping a newborn for ten days.

But this was Twilight, where the trade-off for a loving, tight-knit community was loss of privacy. What else did she expect?

Especially with a baby involved.

As Jana quickly filled Belinda in, several other diner customers came over to hear the story. They stopped her frequently to ask for details.

Crap. Coming to Moe's had been a bad idea.

"Oh my goodness. Oh, the poor little thing." Belinda plastered a palm over her heart.

"I'm so glad it was you two who found him," said a woman named Carol, who hired Jana every year to clean out her gutters.

"And I'm thrilled that Sheriff Hondo isn't going to make you turn him over to CPS right away," added a third woman named

Gretchen, who was a receptionist at the dental office Jana used. "That was so kind to give the baby's mother a chance to return for him."

"That's only because she left a note asking us to watch the baby until New Year's Day," Joel said. "Without that, we wouldn't get to keep him."

"I'll help any way I can. I don't have any baby things left. Donated those after my last one turned ten." Belinda chuckled. "But I'll babysit if you need me. Just say the word."

"Me too," Carol said.

"Me three," Gretchen added.

A couple of other people who'd been eavesdropping from neighboring tables volunteered for babysitting duty as well.

"Thank you, all. That's really very sweet." Jana smiled at her and tried not to flinch when Belinda pinched her cheek.

The group then started speculating about who the baby's mother could be. They all assumed she had to be young, but no one knew of any teens in Twilight who could have recently given birth or would leave a baby in the manger.

"This is delightful!" Belinda applauded. "What a Christmas miracle! You and Joel together with a baby! It's the stuff of legends!"

"We're not together, Belinda," Joel said. "In fact, we don't know for sure that we're even going to do this. We're here to discuss the situation and make a final decision while Dr. Longoria examines the baby."

Joel might not be sure, but Jana was.

"But of course you'll do it! You two are an *adorable* pair. Taking care of a baby will deepen your relationship. Mark my word." Belinda smiled sappily.

"Don't go playing matchmaker," Joel warned. "I'm Jana's boss, and we're just friends. There's nothing romantic going on here."

Not to mention that Joel had a girlfriend. Belinda's statement got under Jana's skin. Would taking care of the baby with Joel change their relationship? Could it cause trouble with their work? Or cause problems between Joel and Ursula?

She didn't want that. Now that she had so many offers of baby-sitting help, maybe she should just tell Joel she'd take Gabriel on her own. After all, she was the one who wanted to do this. He was just along for the ride.

"Bee," Belinda's husband, Harvey, called from across the room, "leave those folks alone to order their food."

Belinda heaved a sigh and rolled her eyes. "That man doesn't have a romantic bone in his body, but I love him to pieces. See you later, and call me for babysitting duty. I mean it."

They waved goodbye to Belinda, and the other people drifted off back to their tables.

"Whew." Joel chuckled and met Jana's eye. "That was a lot."

Before Jana could respond, their waitress appeared. She was new to Twilight and had just started working at Moe's.

"Hi!" she greeted them with a big smile and a bounce in her step. "I'm Mandi, and I'll be your server today."

"Hi, Mandi," Joel said. "Sorry for creating a stir."

"Oh no, I loved the story. It's so romantic. Twilight is the sweetest town I've ever lived in. I'm so glad I moved here." Mandi took a small spiral notepad and pen from her pocket.

"That's how I felt seven years ago when I ended up in Twilight," Jana said. "It's a magical place . . . if a bit strange at first."

"It's exactly my cup of tea," Mandi said. "And nice couples like you are what make the town so special. I can see why that baby's mom asked you two to care for him while she's away."

"You've made a mistake." Jana shook her head vigorously. "We're not a couple. We're just friends."

"Ooh, sorry. I misunderstood." Mandi's cheeks reddened.

"He's really just my boss, and I only work for him part-time seasonally, anyway," Jana said, knowing she was overexplaining, but not wanting anyone to get the wrong idea.

"And we run in the same social circles," Joel added.

Jana met Joel's eyes. "Maybe *friends* is the wrong word. More like *friendly acquaintances?*"

"*Associates.*" Joel's sharp gaze never left her face.

"*Colleagues.*" Jana nodded, observing a darker layer of brown near the pupils of his eyes. She'd never noticed that before.

"*Teammates.*"

"*Contemporaries.*"

"That's putting a fine point on it," Mandi said.

"We're both too busy for a deeper friendship," Joel said. "We both run our own businesses, and honestly, we struggled to find the time to monitor the nativity scene for the chamber of commerce."

"And yet, here you are, planning to take on an abandoned baby at the holidays." Mandi laughed softly.

"Well," Jana said, wondering why Joel hadn't mentioned Ursula, "this is an emergency situation."

"Sure. Right. Go ahead. Stick to that story. But from where I stand, the only people you two are fooling are yourselves." Then she took their orders, picked up their menus, and walked away laughing.

JOEL DIDN'T COMMENT on the server's analysis. It was best to allow that conversation to die a quick death.

Instead, he rested his palms flat on the table, looked Jana in the eye, and said, "It's time we talked about the questions Hondo raised."

"Okay."

He couldn't get a read on her. Her face was noncommittal with just the hint of a smile. He returned her smile with an equally bland one of his own. Two could play the sphinx game.

"I gotta ask straight up, Tink, do you think keeping Gabriel is really the right choice? A newborn is a lot of work."

"It's just until New Year's Day. Ten days. A person can do

anything for ten days. And we've had a lot of offers of help. We wouldn't be doing this alone."

"That has a downside too. Nosy people getting all up in our business."

"How is that any different than any other day in Twilight?"

"Busybodies on steroids? It's a baby abandoned in a nativity-scene manger at Christmas. The entire town will be invested. You just saw it at work."

"This isn't about inconveniencing us. This is about what's best for Gabriel."

Joel canted his head, studied her. "When did you start caring so much about kids?"

"I've never *not* cared about kids."

"At the Thanksgiving party on the paddle-wheel, when Paige asked you to hold Zinnia while she went to clean kid puke off her sweater, you said, and I quote, 'Eew, no thank you.'"

Jana crinkled her nose. "Okay, that was rude of me. I need to apologize to Paige the next time I see her."

"What'll you do if Gabriel throws up?"

"Give him to you." Jana laughed.

"I'm being serious." Joel drummed his fingers against the table.

"I'd handle it, obviously."

"Why does this mean so much to you?"

Jana bit her bottom lip and glanced away, but before she closed off to him, he caught a swift glimpse of stark yearning. An expression he'd never seen in her eyes before, and her intense longing touched his soul.

Was she aching for a baby of her own? That surprised him. As far as he knew, she'd never dated anyone for more than a few weeks.

"It's Christmas, Joel. We gotta give his mom a chance to come back. Even Sheriff Hondo agrees."

"But we don't have to be the ones to look after him."

"His mom chose us. She said so in the note."

"Realistically? We were in the right place at the right time. *That's* how she picked us."

"I know." Jana sounded deflated.

He wasn't trying to be discouraging. He just wanted her to understand what she was getting into. He'd babysat for his niece and nephew enough times to know that instant parenthood wasn't the piece of cake she seemed to think it was.

"Let's move on down Hondo's list of questions." Joel pulled a piece of paper from his jacket pocket.

"You wrote down his questions?"

"Just jotted a few notes."

"When did you do that?"

"When you were hovering over Gabriel telling him goodbye."

"You work fast, MacGregor."

"I didn't want to forget anything."

"I didn't bother because my answer is yes."

"All right, then . . ." Joel consulted his notes. "Which one of us will be the primary caretaker?"

"Me." Her tone was unequivocal.

"Where will we stay? My place or yours?"

She blinked at him. "Why is that even a question?"

He tapped the piece of paper. "It's Hondo's question, not mine."

"I'll stay at my house, and you'll stay at your house. What? Did he think we were going to move in together?"

"The question seems to suggest yes."

"Why did he think that?" She seemed genuinely confused.

"Gabriel's mom picked us both to take care of him. I suppose the moving-in-together thing was a logical conclusion on Hondo's part. Otherwise, I'm seven miles away from you if something should come up with Gabriel in the middle of the night."

Mandi arrived with their food, placed it in front of them, giggled, and waltzed away.

"What was that about?" Jana mumbled, turning to stare at the departing server.

"I think Mandi believes we're madly in love with each other and deluding ourselves about it."

"Please." Jana waved a hand and rolled her eyes. "This town and its goofy romantic legends are pure nonsense."

Hmm. Now he was intrigued. He understood that Jana wasn't interested in romance, but the idea that a stranger would assume they were a couple wasn't *that* far-fetched. He had a lot to offer. He owned his own business and his own house. He was smart enough and fairly good-looking. He had all his teeth and a full head of hair, plus he was tall.

Why did she dismiss a relationship with him out of hand? Was there something about his personality that rubbed her the wrong way?

Ouch.

He watched her cut her veggie burger in half with a determined, self-confident slice, and darn if he didn't feel a bit miffed. Because he certainly thought she was hot and quite beautiful in a quirky, unconventional way. He liked her dry sense of humor and her ability to focus on the tasks at hand and get them done well. She was the best employee he'd ever had. He trusted her. She was clearheaded and logical and street smart. All valuable, admirable qualities. Honestly, he'd love to get to know her better.

"Which brings us to Hondo's next question . . ." Joel consulted his notes again. "He asked how taking care of the baby together is going to affect our relationship."

"It's not going to affect it at all." Frowning, Jana shook her head.

"No?"

"Why would it?"

"We'll be around each other all the time. For ten days."

"So?" Jana shrugged and chewed her veggie burger.

Face it, MacGregor, you might think she's awesome sauce, but she doesn't feel the same way about you.

Which was why maybe coparenting an abandoned baby with her—even temporarily—might not be the best idea in the world.

"Next quest—"

"Joel, there's really only one question."

"What's that?"

"Are you up for this challenge or not? I'm in. If you don't want to do it, please don't say yes."

"I want to do it."

The moment he said it, Joel knew it was true, and this was about much more than just helping out a friend. It was about much more than taking care of a vulnerable baby. It was about the miracle of Christmas. It was about making a difference.

And it was about getting closer to Jana.

She'd worked for him for two years, and he barely knew anything personal about her. That last thought led him to one more question. One for which he didn't have a quick answer.

Why did he want to get closer?

"You sure?" She lifted her eyebrows at him.

"Positive. Gabriel needs the best start in life he can get."

"Thank you," she whispered, and then she reached out and put her hand over his.

A strong bolt of static electricity snapped their skin, and they both jumped back, staring at each other wide-eyed.

Jolted, and oddly breathless, Joel fumbled for his smile and tacked it up quickly. "Well." He laughed. "That was shocking."

Jana's cell phone buzzed with an incoming text.

She picked up her phone from the table and peered at the screen. "It's Dr. Longoria. Gabriel is in tip-top shape. We can go pick him up whenever we want."

CHAPTER 6

THE GIRLFRIEND

By the time they pulled up in front of Jana's house with Gabriel, it was after eleven. Earlier, she'd left her Jeep Grand Cherokee parked under the carport and walked over to the church, not expecting the storm to hit until after midnight as promised by the weather service. So much for accurate predictions.

She lived in a small stone bungalow, built in the 1920s, that she rented on a side street off the town square. On the opposite side of the road from her cottage stood the old Twilight jail that had been transformed into a museum filled with the scandalous history of Hood County rogues. It was a popular tourist attraction rife with ghostly rumors.

Her friends thought she was nuts, but Jana got a kick out of living near the historic building, and the rent was cheaper because of the heavy foot traffic.

Tonight, at this hour, in the misty drizzle, no one was around.

Jana had ridden in the back seat with Gabriel who was sleeping in the car seat Naomi had given them to use. She sat close to him, unable to stop staring at the vulnerable little bundle.

Joel parked at the curb, retrieved an umbrella from the floorboard, hopped out, and opened the back door. He took great care to cover her and the baby with the umbrella, leaving himself exposed.

He was such a good guy. Why wasn't he married already? Why was Ursula dragging her feet? Someone should have snatched him up years ago. What was wrong with the women of Twilight?

Although, to be fair, a few years back he'd had a fiancée. Jana didn't know the details of the breakup. Just that it had ended badly. Was that the problem? Had he, like she, adopted a once bitten, twice shy outlook? What was his future with Ursula?

Unlike her holiday-loving neighbors, Jana had no Christmas lights decorating her house, no tree in her window to welcome her home. Who had time for that when you lived alone? What was the point?

Besides, she spent much of her days decorating and celebrating for other people. Who wanted to work when they were off the clock?

Joel took the baby while she fumbled for her house key. It felt weird letting him into her home. The place was her sanctuary. She didn't socialize here, it was too small for that, so she rarely had anyone over, and it was Joel's first time inside.

It's okay to let down your guard. Joel's safe.

Yes, she knew that, but old habits died hard, and she couldn't deny the tension running along the back of her shoulders. It had been an eventful day.

In the darkness, and her nervousness, it took her a minute to get the key in the lock, and the door swung open. Seconds later they were over the threshold dripping water onto the tile in the chilly foyer.

Jana dropped her house key on the entry table, spied an envelope on the floor, and bent to pick it up. Someone had slipped it in through the doggy door that had been there when she rented the house and she'd never bothered closing it up.

"Who's it from?" he asked.

"Dunno. Just has my name on it." She tucked the envelope in her back pocket and led the way into the small living area.

"Probably just a Christmas card from one of my ladies." She had a regular group of senior citizens she drove to their doctor or hair-salon appointments.

"*Brr!*" Joel shivered. "It's chilly in here."

The rental was within her modest budget, but the house had no central heat or air, so it would take a while before the room warmed enough to allow them to take off their coats. To save money and for safety's sake, Jana switched off the gas heaters when she wasn't home.

If she'd known she'd be bringing back a baby in wet, thirty-degree weather, she would have left the heaters burning on low. But once the little eight-hundred-square-foot house heated, the thick plaster walls, stone exterior, and metal roof kept it toasty.

"I'm on it." Jana hurried to turn on the gas heater installed in the house in the 1950s, and then she started a fire in the fireplace. In the winter, she kept the grate stocked with wood and kindling to use as an adjunct to the gas heaters.

The baby stirred, fretful in his carrier. Dr. Longoria and Terri had fed him, but that had been over an hour and a half ago. How often did newborns eat?

Joel looked unnerved, his eyes wide and his face wan in the dim lighting from the foyer.

Join the club, MacGregor. Me too.

Reaching over, she switched on the floor lamp, bathing the room in a soft yellow glow from the energy-efficient bulb, giving her a much better view of Joel. His cheeks and the tip of his nose were ruddy from the cold. Raindrops caught in the dark brown strands of his hair. He stood in a wide-legged stance before the fireplace, even though the wood hadn't fully caught yet, the baby carrier looped around his arm.

MacGorgeous took her breath away, and that's all there was to it.

Terrified of the thought and eager for a distraction, Jana fished the Christmas card from her back pocket and opened it up.

"Oh wow, it's from Jenny Cantrell. A thank-you for dog-sitting when her family got called out of town for an emergency. I wouldn't let her pay me because I considered it a favor for a friend in need, but she's gifted me with a hundred-dollar gift card to a big-box store. This will help take care of Gabriel's needs and maybe buy him a Christmas present or two."

"That's some perfect timing."

Jana stuffed the card back into her pocket. "In my woo-woo past, I would have considered it a sign that the universe was looking out for me."

"You don't have to be woo-woo to appreciate good fortune when it drops into your life, Jana Gerard."

"Why did you say my full name like that?"

He grinned. "I like it when you give me a peek into your past. You rarely do."

"If you understood the boring reality of my past, you wouldn't be so intrigued."

"Tink, when it comes to you, I'm *always* intrigued."

What was with that tone and the look in his eyes? He sure was complimentary tonight. What had gotten into him? Was it the baby or something else? Worst of all, she liked it. She shouldn't encourage him.

Why not?

He had a girlfriend.

And if he didn't?

But he did.

She zipped up the smile itching to break across her face, picked up the fireplace poker, and prodded the wood.

"You don't have a Christmas tree up," he said.

"Who has time?" She shrugged, kept stoking the flames. Christmas was no big deal to her even if she did sometimes pretend to love the town's over-the-top holiday celebrations. Truth? The holidays brought back sad memories that she was better off forgetting.

"Maybe you should make time now." He settled the baby in

his carrier onto the rug between the fireplace and the gas heater. "For this little guy's sake."

"He has no clue what's going on."

"Kids can pick up on the mood around them. If you're in a holiday spirit, he'll feel it."

"You're an expert on babies now?"

"I know more about them than you do."

Touché. "Why are you such a Christmas nut?" she asked. "Didn't your mom die on Christmas Eve?"

Joel nodded and pressed his lips together, forming a tight seam.

"I figure that would turn you off of Christmas forever," she said, thinking of her own holiday losses.

"No." Joel's voice was solid as concrete. "Christmas was my mom's favorite time of year. I celebrate to honor her memory."

"I guess that makes sense." She bobbed her head. She couldn't help admiring his loyalty to his family. She wished she had that kind of holiday spirit, but she was just too skeptical. The difference between them was stark. Would he be so optimistic about Christmas if he'd grown up in foster care? Somehow, she doubted it.

From his carrier, Gabriel whimpered.

Joel stuffed his hands into his pockets. "I'll go unload the baby supplies. Sounds like we need a diaper change and another bottle."

"Thanks." She smiled and reached for Gabriel as Joel headed out the door.

The second Joel left, a wash of silly loneliness swept over Jana. It was the same loneliness that had dogged her for her entire life. The loneliness of an abandoned child.

"Don't worry, Gabriel," she whispered, holding him in her arms and falling instantly in love. She pressed her nose to his head, inhaled the sweet baby scent. "I'm here. I've got you. Joel will be right back. You are not alone, little one. Not by a long shot. Just wait until you meet the rest of the MacGregor clan. Trust me. I've been around this bunch for seven years now. Soon enough, you'll be begging for some me time."

Joel rang the doorbell, and Jana hopped up to let him in. His arms were filled with the generous donations. She relieved him of a couple of the bags, and he came into the house, stamping his boots on the welcome mat.

Gabriel's whimper turned into a full-blown squall the way it had at the Luthers'.

Joel tossed Jana a box of diapers. "You change him. I'll put the formula on to heat. We'll double-team this."

"Aye, aye, captain." Laughing, she spread a blanket out on the rug in front of the brightly flickering fire and unwrapped Gabriel. From her place on the floor, she could see Joel in the kitchen heating the formula in the microwave. "But next time, you get diaper duty again, and I get to make the bottle."

"Deal."

"You know," she said, taking off the wet diaper while Gabriel flailed his sweet little arms and legs, "if I had my own kid, I'd use cloth diapers and wipes. It's so much better for the environment."

"A noble aspiration. That's what Flynn said with Grace."

"But Flynn used baby wipes with her kids."

"You're making my point. It's good to have goals, but watching my sister and Jesse with their kids, I've seen heartfelt principles fall by the wayside."

"I care about the environment and the future of our little ones."

"And I've seen you set unrealistic aspirations and then beat yourself up whenever you can't meet those lofty goals."

"You're acting like I don't usually meet my goals."

"You almost always meet your goals, but the few times you don't, you run yourself through the wringer for not living up to them."

Jana let out a sigh. Guilty as charged. "This kid stuff is complex."

"No joke."

The microwave dinged. Joel took out the glass bottle of formula and capped it with the nipple. Jana watched him test the temperature against the inside of his arm.

"Lukewarm. Perfect," he said.

"Where'd you learn to do that?"

"Like most things, from Flynn. She's my shero."

"I admire the close relationship you have with your family," Jana said, feeling wistful. "You're lucky."

"I know," he said, strolling into the living area with the bottle. "I try never to forget that."

While Joel fed Gabriel, Jana fashioned a bassinet from her largest dresser drawer the way she'd seen in an old movie. Once they had the baby snugged in his makeshift crib, they sat down on the couch together in front of the fire. It was a nice moment after a hectic night.

"We need a crib for him," Jana said.

"We're only going to have him for ten days." Joel shook his head. "And if we're going to take turns caring for him at our separate houses, a portable playpen is in order. I think Flynn's still got Ian's Pack 'n Play. I'll swing by her place tomorrow and see if she'll let me borrow it."

"Good idea."

"Although, I think it makes more sense for us to stay under the same roof as long as we have Gabriel. It'll just be easier on all of us."

Jana winced. "I don't like living with other people."

"I'm not 'other people,' Jana." His tone held a low, sultry quality, as warm and comforting as the flames in the fireplace.

Goose bumps popped up on her arms. *Whoa, okay.*

"I like my own space," she said simply, not wanting to get into the reasons she didn't believe in roommates. Living with people complicated things.

"Does this have anything to do with the way you grew up?"

It did, but she didn't like talking about that. So she didn't.

Joel brought up a palm to cover his yawn. "Sorry, I was up at five this morning."

"You should go home. Get some sleep. We've got a lot to do over the next two days."

"Yes, and we need to get you a Christmas tree, ASAP. Put it on the list." Joel mimed taking notes.

"Forget the tree." Amused, she shook her head at his persistence. The man did love his Christmas. "There's too much chaos for tree-trimming."

"Not even a little tree?" He measured off an inch with his thumb and forefinger. "It *is* Gabriel's first Christmas."

"He's not going to know anything about it."

"But *you'll* know." Joel winked conspiratorially.

Instant heat shot to her groin. A heat so searing it scared the pants off her. What on earth was that about? Startled, Jana blinked and stomped on her baser instincts. *"Joel."*

"Jana," he said using her same exasperated tone.

"Go home."

"I'm not leaving you to take care of Gabriel all by yourself."

"Don't be silly. Both of us shouldn't lose sleep. Keeping him was my idea. I'll make the sacrifice. I don't need you. I've got this."

"You know something, Gerard?" he asked, his voice dropping lower, and his smile growing lazier. He only called her by her last name when he was about to disagree with her.

"What's that, MacGregor?"

"You're too independent for your own damn good." He stayed welded to the couch as if he had no intention of ever leaving, and that threw a knot of panic into her throat.

"Bye." She stood and went to the door and held it open to a blast of cold, damp air. "Scoot. I'll see you tomorrow . . . Oops, I guess it's today now."

The cell phone in her pocket dinged. Good grief. It was after midnight. Who was texting her this late?

She pulled out her phone. *Uh-oh.*

"What is it?" Joel asked, getting to his feet.

"I've got a fare."

He steepled his fingers, stretched out his legs, and grinned like he had a monopoly on smiles. "So you need me to babysit?"

She wanted to tell him no, that she could handle this just fine on her own, but that would mean bundling Gabriel up and taking him with her, which didn't seem the wisest move just so she could prove a point.

"I shouldn't be long," she said, pulling her coat off the hook where she'd hung it when they'd come in. "Ladies' Night Out at the Horny Toad Tavern. Someone needs a ride home."

"Who?"

"Raylene and her posse," she said, referring to a colorful septuagenarian who'd been a Dallas Cowboys Cheerleader in the 1960s and '70s. Raylene also worked as a desk clerk for Noah and Kelsey at the Rockabye.

"Tell them you can't come."

"Excuse me?"

"Tell Raylene to find another way home."

She shot him the evil eye. "I'm currently the only ride service in town."

"How about Raylene calls her husband or daughter, Shannon?"

"It's *my* job."

"I don't like you going out this late at night in bad weather." Joel scowled.

"I make a third of my income off ridesharing, MacGregor, and surprise! I've done this for the last four years, and nothing untoward has happened to me yet."

"First time for everything."

"And you wonder why I don't like living with other people." She picked up her purse from the bench seat in the foyer and hitched it up on her shoulder. "Make yourself at home." She thought about telling him he could crash in her bed, but that felt way too intimate, so she said, "Nap on the couch. There's blankets in the hall closet. I'll be back in two shakes of a lamb's tail."

Joel stood up. "Tell you what. I'll go get the ladies."

Jana gritted her teeth and growled at him. "Back off, Mac-Gregor, and let me take care of my own business."

He held up both palms. "Okay. I'll hang here with Gabriel until you get back."

"Thank you." He was a great guy, and Ursula was a lucky woman. Jana hoped his girlfriend knew that.

She headed out the door, the scent of the baby still clinging to her skin. Unexpected tears pushed at the backs of her eyelids, but she blinked them away, got into her Jeep, and started the engine.

What the hell? She was feeling maudlin over leaving the infant? Why?

She backed out of the driveway, and as she pulled into the street, she glanced back at her house and saw Joel standing in the window, the curtains parted, Gabriel tucked against his side as Joel lifted the baby's tiny hand to wave goodbye.

The Horny Toad Tavern was still crowded at twelve twenty when Jana parked on the street, engine idling, and texted Raylene that she was waiting outside.

Music blared from the establishment. Inside her Jeep, she could feel the throbbing vibrations of "Merry Christmas Baby," the Bruce Springsteen version. A poster on the side of the building advertised the upcoming Christmas Bards show poetry-strip-jam.

Joel and Noah had started the Christmas Bards to raise money for ALS research, and the event had become so popular they'd been able to raise prices to include other charitable organizations as well.

It was the largest fundraiser in Twilight, and every year the tickets always sold out within an hour of going on sale. Noah had retired from the group after he'd gotten married, but Joel still participated. Jana wondered how Ursula felt about that.

Vapers and smokers were hanging out on the sidewalk, huddling in groups for warmth, laughing and talking loudly in order to be heard over the music. The bouncer at the door, a burly guy named Brick, who Jana had dated for half a second, spied her and rushed over.

Great. What did *he* want?

Suppressing a sigh, Jana lowered her window. "Yes?"

"Hey." Brick's gaze traveled to her breasts.

"Hey, yourself. My eyes are up here."

He grinned and didn't look the least bit embarrassed for ogling. "You here for the old ladies?"

"I'm not sure they'd appreciate being called that, but yes, I'm here for Raylene and her friends."

"K." Brick kept standing there, his hands jammed in his pockets.

"Is there something you want?"

"Just wondering if you're solo on Christmas Eve. I thought—"

"We're over, Brick. It was a one-time thing. Accept it. Move on."

"I'm not asking for your hand in marriage." Brick snorted. "I've just been thinking about you and—" He pulled mistletoe from his pocket, dangled it over his head, and leaned in through her window, lips puckered.

Jana drew back. "Kiss me and die, Jughead."

"Well, *someone's* not in the Christmas spirit." Looking disappointed, he withdrew.

The door to the bar banged opened. Jana put up her window, waved Brick away, and turned to see who'd come out of the Horny Toad.

It wasn't Raylene and her crew.

Rather, it was Joel's girlfriend Ursula, and she was with another man.

Jana's eyes bugged.

They were looking friendly. So friendly, that they staggered across the sidewalk arm in arm. The man pressed Ursula against the side of the building and ran his hands up and down her body. Joel's girlfriend threw her arms around the guy's neck, and they got lost in an R-rated kiss.

Watching the couple paw each other, anger exploded inside Jana. *Holy Sacral Chakra!*

Ursula was cheating on Joel!

CHAPTER 7

THE MOVE

While Jana was giving senior citizens a ride home from the bar, Joel made an executive decision. He was taking her and Gabriel to his place.

End of story.

Considering the unpredictable nature of Jana's business, never knowing when she'd be tapped to give someone a ride, she couldn't reasonably expect to take care of Gabriel on her own. Even with Joel as a backup caretaker.

They had to do this together, and that either meant him moving into her place or moving her into his. Considering she didn't have a guest bedroom and her couch was apartment-sized, there was nowhere for him to sleep. His place won by default. Plus, there were his dogs to look after.

Jana would kick up a fuss, but he was whisking her and the baby off to his house tonight, and he didn't care if she liked it or not.

Determined, he left Gabriel sleeping in the dresser drawer and, in one overloaded trip, carried the baby supplies back to his truck and started the engine to idle with the heater on, then raced back inside.

He checked the time. Twelve thirty.

Jana should be back soon. Raylene and her friends didn't live far from the Horny Toad Tavern. He extinguished the fireplace embers with baking soda that he found in the kitchen, turned the gas heater down as low as it would go, and covered Gabriel with an extra blanket while they waited for her return.

He needed to gather up her things for an extended stay at his house. He wanted to be packed and ready to go as soon as she pulled into the driveway.

That meant entering Jana's bedroom. He paused at the invasion of her privacy. He could wait until she got home, but that would add time and a prolonged discussion. There was a baby to consider, and Gabriel trumped everything.

Joel wouldn't be nosy. He'd efficiently grab some clothing and get out. Trying to convince himself this was the right way to handle things, he went to her bedroom, opened the door, and flicked on the overhead light.

The bedroom was tidy and well organized, and the room smelled of her provocative essential-oils scent. She slept in a small full-sized bed, and her possessions were minimal. A lamp. A dresser. A sound system.

In her closet, he found a gym bag and threw in enough clothes for a few days, pulling from hangers outfits he knew she wore regularly. He tossed in sneakers and a pair of ballet flats, her makeup bag that was lying on the bathroom counter, a thick button-down sweater that his sister Flynn called a cardigan, and . . .

Underwear.

She'd need a change of underwear.

He went to the dresser. There was a stack of pajamas and sleep shirts on top, from where she'd emptied the contents of a drawer to make a bed for the newborn. He grabbed a pair of pajamas and stuffed it all into the bag.

Now for the underwear drawer. He paused again with his hand on the knob. This really was a privacy violation.

Time's a-wasting, MacGregor. Move it. You can apologize later.

In the top drawer, Joel found an array of sexy lingerie in a variety of colors and textures.

His idiotic pulse thumped. Never in a million years would he have imagined that his tough-as-nails employee liked dainty, silky, lacy underthings. All this time when they'd been working on the Brazos Queen, she'd been dressing this way underneath the vegan leather and denim she favored.

He wished he was ignorant of this find. From now on, whenever they were together, he'd wonder what she had on beneath her clothes. This wasn't a good development. Especially when he saw the label. Pandora's Box. No kidding.

Suck it up.

Joel erred on the side of plenty and stuffed five silky panties, in different colors, into the bag. He added a black bra and several pairs of thick winter socks. She could always do laundry at his house or come back home for more clothes later.

On the way to the door, he spied her jewelry box on the nightstand and tossed that in too. Just as he finished, her Jeep pulled into the driveway.

He didn't wait for her to walk in.

Putting Gabriel in the baby carrier, he picked him up in one arm and shouldered her gym bag in the other. Retrieving her house key from where she'd left it on the foyer table when they'd come in, he then stepped out into the cold and locked the house up tight.

Jana was halfway up the sidewalk when he turned to face her, feeling breathless and weirdly excited, his pulse strumming fast and hard.

"Hey," he murmured.

She stopped, her face cast in shadows from the streetlamp. "What's up?"

He braced himself for the fuss he knew she'd give him. "We're moving to my house. I packed your things." He raised his shoulder with the gym bag. "And I took care of the fire and locked your front door. Let's go."

Expressionless, she stared at him.

"I don't want any arguments, Jana. The two of us living together until New Year's Day is what's best for Gabriel."

"It's a done deal?"

He clenched his jaw and narrowed his eyes. "Done deal."

"All right."

"Wh-what?" He had not expected that.

"You're right. I can't take care of him alone."

Wow. Hmm. Okay. "Do you want to ride with me and Gabriel or take your Jeep?"

"I never go anywhere I don't have an exit plan," she said. "I'll follow you."

"Let's roll."

EVEN UNDER THREAT of torture, Jana wouldn't admit how grateful she was to Joel for taking charge.

With the baby, she felt out of her league. Everything Joel had said and done was on point. He'd taken care of business, and she would spend the night at his place because it was the sensible thing to do and the best for Gabriel.

Those reasons, plus she felt terrible about Ursula.

How was she going to break the bad news that she'd seen his girlfriend kissing another man? Her stomach roiled. Poor Joel.

As she followed his taillights, her chest squeezed as if someone had strapped a thick, wide band around her and was slowly twisting it tighter and tighter until she was only breathing from the top part of her lungs in short shallow pants.

Deep breath.

By the time they got to his house on the opposite side of the lake from the town square, it was one thirty. Joel's three golden retrievers greeted them at the door with wagging tails and sniffing snouts.

"Oh!" Jana sank to the floor to greet the dogs. She loved

animals, and if she didn't work such oddball hours, she'd have a cat. "What are their names?"

"Muffin, Puffin, and Filbert."

"I want to hear the story of their names—"

A howl from Gabriel set the dogs barking, and for a minute it was chaos.

"How about I take the baby," she said, "and you take care of the dogs?"

"Deal."

Laughing good-naturedly, Joel fed the dogs and let them into the backyard while Jana changed the baby and warmed up a bottle. By two thirty, Gabriel had eaten and was out like a light in the drawer from the dresser in Joel's guest bedroom.

Jana lay in the twin bed listening to the sound of Gabriel's soft breathing and thinking about Joel sleeping across the hall. She was exhausted to the bone, but the events of the day kept circling her head.

Mentally, she walked through the evening wondering how, in six short hours, she'd become a temporary surrogate mom for a baby abandoned over the Christmas holidays. Thinking about that stirred memories of another abandoned baby. Another mournful Christmas. Except this time, she wasn't alone.

Joel was on her side.

She smiled into the darkness.

Joel was right there with her all the way. He was a solid, dependable guy. Someone she could trust. She thought about how he'd swooped in and taken charge right when she needed him most. Packing her clothes. Insisting she and the baby come stay at his place.

This alpha-male image was appealing if somewhat uncomfortable for her. She'd never seen him so commanding, and it stirred butterflies in her belly.

Big time.

What if, a voice whispered in the back of her head, *what if she and Joel . . .*

Good grief!

He didn't even know that Ursula was running around on him. And even if he and Ursula did break up, he'd need time to grieve the loss of the relationship, and she certainly didn't want to be the rebound woman.

Why not?

Huh? She rubbed her eyes. Why *not* be the rebound woman? She simply wasn't wired for romantic commitment. She knew that about herself. Rebound woman was precisely the way to go if she wanted a sweet fling with Joel.

Yeah? Devil's advocate here. Wouldn't a fling ruin your working relationship? Wouldn't it make things awkward?

And if she initiated a hookup with him, wouldn't she be taking advantage of his vulnerability? That was icky.

Heavenly stars, why was she thinking this way? When had she become obsessed with Joel? Because—news flash—she *was* suddenly obsessed.

She kept remembering the pressure of his arm at her elbow as he'd escorted her into the house over the rain-slick ground. How his familiar masculine scent had tangled up in her nose. How the sound of his deep voice sent shivers up her spine.

How she wanted him to kiss her.

Her mind toyed with the concept, tracking it back. She'd always thought he was good-looking, but so what? Just because he was hot didn't mean she should jump his bones. Except now, she couldn't stop thinking about it.

It's the baby, she told herself.

She'd been feeling all these feels over the course of the past few hours, right? Ever since the baby came on the scene. After seeing Joel with Gabriel, her brain flooded with estrogen and oxytocin and dulled her objectivity.

Then watching his girlfriend kiss another man outside the Horny Toad Tavern had added empathy to her pile of emotions, and that empathy had her longing to comfort him.

That was her story, and she was glued to it. These feelings

were temporary and hormone-induced. Situational. They would go away. Nothing to flip out about.

Reassured, she fell asleep.

Two hours later, she awoke, disoriented, and it took her a second to remember where she was. She got up to check on Gabriel and found the baby wasn't in the drawer.

Had someone kidnapped him?

Instant panic gripped her, but then, embarrassed, she realized Joel must have taken him. Had she slept through Gabriel's crying?

She tiptoed down the hallway and peeked into the living room.

Joel sat rocking the newborn, and her heart did a cartwheel at the sight. *Aww.* They looked so cozy.

He hadn't seen her standing in the doorway. His head was lowered, and his adoring gaze fixed on the baby in his arms. Multicolored twinkle lights from the nearby Christmas tree cast the man and baby in a soft halo glow.

Jana's breath stilled, and she almost forgot to breathe. Why had she come in here? She should have stayed in bed, trusting him to care for the baby. Now those sweet flutterings in her stomach were back harder than ever and completely undeniable.

He's a big dude feeding a tiny baby. Big deal. Turn off the mush.

Yes, it was greeting-card precious, which was exactly why she should dismiss the feelings. That sappy stuff had no basis in reality. Case in point, cute as the scene might be on the surface, the ugly truth underneath marred everything. Gabriel's mother had abandoned him at Christmas. Nothing greeting-card happy about that.

"How's he doing?" she murmured, moving into the room.

"Shh." Joel raised his head, an easy grin on his face. "He's asleep. Like you're supposed to be."

"I couldn't sleep."

"Why not?"

"I'm freaking out."

"About Gabriel?"

And because I saw your girlfriend kissing another guy, and I don't know how to break the news to you. "Yes."

"Yeah, me too. This is a big responsibility." Joel sniffed the top of the baby's head, and his smile widened. "He smells so darn good."

"Right? And his tiny fingers and toes are so adorable."

"Did you see the little stork-bite birthmark he has on the back of his neck? It looks like a misshapen heart. Some woman is going to adore kissing that spot someday." Joel chuckled.

"I'm worried." Anxiety cinched her chest.

His smile faded, and he gave her his full attention. "About what?"

God, why had she said that? She'd killed the sweet mood. She pressed a palm to her nape and sank down on the couch opposite his rocking chair. "Me staying at your house. I know it makes sense logistically, but . . ."

"But?"

Suddenly realizing she was braless in her pajamas, Jana picked up a cushion to hold over her breasts. "You know this town. You saw how people acted at Moe's. Me staying at your place will add fuel to the fire of this town's crazy romanticism."

"Oh?" His eyebrows dipped inward.

"You know, they'll try to turn this situation into a Hallmark movie. Baby found in a manger by two friends. Sparks fly, yada, yada . . ."

"And they fall madly in love?" His voice deepened, and his gaze locked on her.

"Yeah. That." She gestured. "Silly, huh?"

"Preposterous," he agreed. His tone was light, but the look in his eyes seemed serious.

"I mean, a person doesn't suddenly wake up one day and change the way they think about someone overnight, do they? That's fiction. Right?"

"No." A serious expression came into his eyes. "That doesn't happen. At least, not too often."

"People are already building a legend around this kid. We should nip that in the bud."

"Snip, snip."

"Right?" She was saying *right* too often. Why was she seeking his validation?

"This situation is the stuff of long-lasting Twilight mythology. We can't egg that on."

"No indeed."

"So . . ." He looked amused, the rocking chair creaking as he moved slowly back and forth. "Any idea how to corral the rumors?"

"Mmm." Jana rubbed her palms over the top of her thighs. "There's something I need to tell you."

"I'm listening." He stopped rocking and cocked his head to study her.

Her stomach sank. "Joel, you should brace yourself."

"For what?"

"It's about Ursula."

"What about her?"

Just say it. Rip off the Band-Aid.

"I saw Ursula kissing some random dude outside of the Horny Toad when I went to pick up Raylene and her crew." She cringed, watching his face for his reaction.

Joel blinked. "Um . . . okay."

She shook her head, befuddled. "You're not upset?"

He shrugged. "Why should I be?

"Ursula is groping a guy in public for anyone to see!"

"I get that."

"Her behavior will add fuel to this fire." She drew an imaginary circle encompassing her, Joel, and Gabriel. "People will think I came between you two."

"Jana?" he murmured, his voice whisper-soft.

Pleasurable tingles ignited the nerve endings along her scalp. "Yes?"

"Ursula and I broke up two months ago."

Oh my. That's nice.

Jana gulped. "Really?"

"Really. We're over, done, kaput."

He doesn't have a girlfriend.

"And you're okay?"

"Perfectly fine."

"How did I not know about this? Why didn't you tell me?" she asked.

"There was no need to make a big announcement. Ursula and I were never serious," he said. "The relationship had run its course, and the breakup was mutual."

She snorted. "*That* sounds like a press release."

"It's the truth. I don't know why you find it far-fetched."

"It feels disingenuous."

"It's not. Ursula and I were casual. You of all people should understand casual."

Huh? Was that a jab? "Excuse me?"

"In the seven years you've been in Twilight, you've never been serious about anyone," Joel said. "At least, not to my knowledge."

"Is that a judgment?"

"No. Statement of fact."

"Yeah, well . . ." Feeling defensive, she rubbed a knuckle along the bridge of her itchy nose. "I like my freedom."

"You're entitled to your choices, which is why I don't think people will make anything romantic of you staying at my house. Everyone knows you're a commitmentphobe. Although granted there'll be hot goss speculating a hookup, no one will mistake us for happily ever after."

"I am not a commitmentphobe!" she protested, startling herself with her raised voice. "I just committed to ten days of tending a baby with you."

"You're upset. Hang on. Let me put Gabriel down, and we'll

talk this through." Joel got up from the rocking chair, left the empty bottle sitting on the side table, and moved toward his bedroom.

"Where are you going?" she asked, hopping to her feet.

"I just said I was putting the baby down."

"In your bedroom?"

"Sure. Why not? My turn to watch him for a while. You get some sleep."

She gritted her teeth, feeling possessive of the baby again. "I'll take him."

"No need."

She tapped her foot, held out her arms, repeated, "I'll take him."

"No, Tink. We're in this together."

"Are we fighting over the baby?"

"No."

"Then, let me have him."

"Are you going to deny me the chance to cuddle this sweet-smelling bundle?"

She felt her bottom lip quiver. "I want to cuddle with him too."

"My bed is king-sized." He paused. "Just saying."

Narrowing her eyes, she gaped at him. "What does that mean?"

"It means, in my bed, we can both cuddle him. We'll put Gabriel in the middle between us."

Now, that was a thought.

Jana caught her breath. She liked the idea far too much. What was wrong with her? "What about your dogs?"

"Hey, they've got dog beds."

"Are you asking me to sleep with you, Joel MacGregor?" She was joking, but her voice came out sultrier than she intended.

He doesn't have a girlfriend.

Alarmed, she pressed three fingertips against her mouth. "That was a stupid thing to say. Ignore me."

"I intended on just sleeping. Unless . . . Do you have a different idea?" He wriggled his eyebrows comically.

"There is no *unless*. Stop with that."

"I've rattled you. Never mind. It was a silly suggestion."

"No. Not at all. Sure, we can sleep in your bed," she said blithely as if it was no big deal. "Just as long as Gabriel is between us."

"Of course he'll be between us."

"Okay." Truth was she didn't want to be alone. She *wanted* to sleep in Joel's bed. It wasn't smart, it wasn't sane, but there it was. She didn't want to be by herself, and he made her feel safe.

That was saying a lot.

He held her gaze with a sharp-edged expression. Was he waiting for her to back down? Had this been a test? What in the world was going on between them tonight? And what was he thinking? Better question, what was *she* thinking?

Jana tossed her head. Despite her fears, she refused to cut and run.

"Tink, are you okay?"

"I'm fine."

"You sure?"

"Are we going to stand here bickering for the rest of the night, or are we going to get some sleep before this one"—she nodded at the baby—"wakes up for another feeding?"

"The bed it is." Joel turned for his bedroom.

Heart pounding, Jana followed.

He doesn't have a girlfriend.

CHAPTER 8

THE PILLOW TALK

Sliding beneath the covers in Joel's bed felt inflammatory and dangerous. What was she doing here?

Better yet, *why*?

She liked to think she was pretty good at controlling and camouflaging her impulses, but suddenly, her emotions threatened to overtake her. How had this happened? It was too damn cutesy for words. A rom-com waiting to happen.

And Jana was a sucker for it.

That was the problem. Lying on her side, facing Joel, Jana couldn't resist searching his features in the dim illumination coming from the night-light. Shadows cloaked his face, adding to the illicit air of mystery.

It was as if he had transformed in some fundamental way and she'd never again be able to see him as nothing more than a boss or a friend. No matter how hard she might try. She'd gotten a peek into a new world. Joel as a father and as a potential romantic partner—er . . . that is, for a woman who wanted those things, which she did not.

But a heart-splitting, bone-deep yearning shook her soul.

Alarmed, she flopped onto her back and stared up at the ceiling. She brought her knees together and folded her arms over her chest as if lying in a narrow coffin. Quickly, she went through the techniques she'd cultivated over the years to temper unwanted emotions.

First, she didn't deny what she was feeling. Jana had learned that denying her feelings kept her asleep to herself and her true motives. Denial of feelings wasn't the answer. Awareness was the key.

Understand and accept your feelings, then neutralize them.

Fine. She practiced this often. Had used this method each time she'd changed foster homes to reorient herself in her body. Closing her eyes, she focused on the sensations churning inside her.

She explored the odd heaviness settling at the bottom of her stomach like silt and the languid slowing of her heart rate as if her blood was too thick for her veins. She noticed the fine muscles at the corners of her eyes jerk oh-so-slightly and observed how her nostrils flared as if desperate to inhale more of Joel's scent from the bed linens. She listened to the sound of her scratchy breathing as she filled her lungs and heard how different it was from Joel's smooth, long breaths.

As she cataloged all her physical experiences, the dampness of her upper lip, the soreness of her hamstrings, the coolness of her fingertips, Jana felt her body relax and the tension ebb.

Yes, she was feeling so many things inside her tissues—fear, worry, sadness, loss, gain, joy, and tenderness that overwhelmed her. But as soon as she brought attention to an emotion, it shifted.

Ahh, there it is.

The thing she'd been shooting for. You couldn't trust feelings. They always changed. Emotions were nothing to bank on.

Comforted, Jana exhaled low and long. She'd had a few sexy feelings about Joel. Big deal. Nothing to freak out over. The feelings would pass. They always did.

Whew!

But in the meantime? What would she do about the intense, hot throbbing lodged between her legs?

Nothing.

Absolutely nothing.

All she needed, whenever she felt tempted to take her relationship with Joel beyond friendship, was to stay as far away from him as she could get. Except, for the next ten days with a baby to care for, that would be darn near impossible.

"Jana?" he called.

Should she answer or pretend she was asleep? She closed her eyes in the darkness again, breathing in the masculine scent of him that smelled better than the vegan cinnamon rolls from the Twilight Bakery.

"Guess you're asleep," he murmured.

"I'm awake," she replied, unable to resist, feeling like a stranger in a strange but wonderful land. A land that felt too good to be true.

Thank heavens there was a baby between them, because if Gabriel wasn't here . . . *Well, Dora the Explorer, if Gabriel wasn't here, you wouldn't be either.*

She pulled the covers up to her chin, waited.

He cleared his throat, and then his wonderfully rich voice spun a hypnotic web around her in the darkness. "You smell so good."

That's what he wanted to tell her?

"Essential oils," she said. "I went through a kick when I was younger thinking oils could actually heal you. While I soon discovered there was no scientific basis that essential oils can cure anything, they smell nice, and there's always the placebo effect. That can be huge in the healing process."

"You've done a lot of work to overcome your bumpy childhood."

"Amen to that. I made a lot of mistakes and bought into some silly ideas during my search. If my past has taught me anything, it's that I can't expect other people to be there for me. If they are, that's great and I appreciate it, but I can't expect it, so I learned to take care of myself."

"And what a beautiful job you've done! You've formed your-self into an admirable human being, Jana Gerard."

"I wouldn't go that far. I've got a long way to go to live up to my dream self, but hey, it gives me something to shoot for."

"What do you see as your main area of growth?"

"How I've already grown, or ways in which I need to grow?" The conversation was not one she would have had with him under normal circumstances. She tended to squirm when talk got too personal, but here, in the dark, in his bed, the words just rolled right out of her.

"Either. Both. Whatever you want to tell me."

"What if I say I don't want to talk about it?"

"That's fine too."

Silence settled over the room, the sound of his slow, deep, calm breathing soothing her. "As a young child, I was a feral little thing. I had more detention time than any kid in the history of my elementary school."

"You gave your teachers a run for their money." He chuckled.

"They were really pretty decent to me. They knew I didn't have parents and made allowances, but they didn't let me get away with bad behavior. Which, while I didn't appreciate it at the time, was actually a great gift. It taught me to consider the consequences of my actions."

"I'm glad you had that."

"Later," she said, "when I was in high school, one of my friends' mom was a yoga instructor, and she taught me about mindfulness and using my breath to control my emotions. Yoga was so helpful. Yes, her community came with some wacky be-liefs that I've since discarded, like the healing power of essential oils, but they gave me some tips and techniques that helped me self-soothe. I'm eternally grateful for those gifts. Yoga helped me survive some pretty dark days."

"Do you want to talk about those dark days?"

"No."

"Okay," he said easily, just like that.

Jana exhaled slowly, relieved, but a part of her wanted to keep talking—just not about herself.

"Tell me about your dogs," she said.

"Muffin is my oldest. She'll be ten in April."

"You got her while you were still in college?"

"No, I didn't get her as a pup. She belonged to my ex-fiancée, and when we broke up, she asked if I wanted Muffin."

"She abandoned her dog?"

"Her changing lifestyle wasn't conducive to pets."

Jana wanted to ask more about his ex-fiancée, but that felt too personal in this intimate situation. Besides, asking more questions about his personal life left her open to being asked similar questions from him.

Instead, she said, "So you didn't name Muffin?"

"No, but I know how she got her name. Not long after my ex brought her home, and before she'd settled on a name, the puppy tore into a box of banana nut minimuffins, ate them all, and ended up at the vet with tummy problems."

"And Puffin? Who named her?"

"Me."

She heard the grin in Joel's voice, felt him shift in the bed beside her. "Oh?"

"When we were little my mother loved to recite the puffin poem."

"What poem is that?"

Laughing, Joel recited the lovely kids' poem about a puffin bird who stopped eating fishes in favor of becoming their friends and took up eating pancakes with them instead.

"That is a delightful poem." Jana joined in with this laughter.

"Plus," he said, "Puffin rhymed with Muffin. It fit."

"Does Puffin like pancakes?"

"Adores them the way Muffin loves muffins."

"And Filbert? How does he fit in with the two girls?"

"Ever heard of the children's social-simulation video game *Animal Crossing*?"

"No."

"Filbert is a character in the *Animal Crossing* village. He's a lazy squirrel whose main focus in life is eating and relaxing."

"Ahh, and I'm guessing your Filbert exhibits the same qualities?"

"That, and Filbert the dog doesn't chase after squirrels like Muffin and Puffin. My niece, Grace, named him. She's a huge *Animal Crossing* fan. She says Filbert and I have a lot in common." His affection for his niece was unmistakable.

"Oh?" Jana giggled, surprising herself. She wasn't a giggler, but the thought of Grace pegging her uncle was too delightful to resist. "Filbert the dog or Filbert the squirrel?"

"The squirrel, I think. Grace says Filbert and I are both laid-back, our eyes are wide open, and we're always smiling."

"Your eyes *are* wide, and so are Filbert the dog's," Jana mused.

"Filbert the squirrel's too."

"And when I first moved here, I remember thinking I didn't really trust you because you smiled too much."

"Smiling too much is bad?"

"To nineteen-year-old Jana, it was."

"And now?"

"I've grown accustomed to your smile."

"Aww."

Jana gave a friendly snort. "Seven years old, and Grace already has you pegged. That girl has mad insight."

"Yep."

"The squirrel game sounds charming."

"Get Grace to show it to you sometime."

"I'll do that."

The conversation petered out. Then she felt his fingertips very lightly brush across her forehead in the dark and linger. For one hopeful moment, she thought he might lean over and boldly kiss her.

But then he moved his hand away.

Leaving her feeling as if she'd barely avoided tumbling into a bottomless pit and was already regretting not taking a headfirst dive.

Tucked on the other side of his bed, with the dim yellow glow seeping from the night-light, the sight of Jana's silhouette underneath his covers stirred Joel's fantasies. He kept thinking about her colorful, silky underthings.

He hadn't expected this level of desire for her. The hot tick of his pulse as it pounded loud and hard through his arteries and veins. The dry, hungry flavor that filled his mouth. The craving inflamed by her fragrance.

C'mon, if he was being honest, he'd had these kinds of enflamed feelings for her before, but he'd stuffed them down. Either because he'd been in a relationship with Ursula or because Jana worked for him occasionally or because he didn't want to risk damaging their friendship. But cards on the table? He'd wanted more than friendship from her for quite some time.

He'd just been too laid-back to go for it.

Like Filbert the lazy squirrel, he'd allowed his desire for ease and comfort prevent him from taking calculated risks.

Until now, thoughts of having Jana in his bed were theoretical, but here she was in the flesh, no longer just a figment of his fevered imaginings, so beautiful and real she stole his breath away.

"Good night, Jana."

She didn't answer. Had she fallen asleep already? They'd had a full, exciting evening, and the baby would wake up again soon. He needed to get some sleep himself.

But that was easier said than accomplished when he could feel the heat of her body radiating across the sheets.

His hand ached to cross that invisible barrier again. To finger her chin, her jaw, her lips. He curled his hands into fists to keep them on his side of the bed, trapping himself in his moral imperative.

He shouldn't have touched her a while ago. It had only stoked the fire burning inside him. She didn't know how he felt. He couldn't tell her now. Not under these circumstances.

Feelings he'd locked down and buried for months battled against his instincts, but his resolve held strong. He cared about her too much to put her on the spot. He'd waited this long. He would wait for the right time. The right place. He would wait until she was ready to receive what he had to give.

His undying devotion.

Joel might be a bit lazy, a bit too laid-back for his own good, but he was loyal to a fault. Once he gave his fidelity to someone, it was a done deal. He didn't flip-flop or vacillate. When he was all in, he was in one hundred percent.

Which was why he'd wait.

"Good night, Joel," she finally whispered back, her voice tight as a vise.

Or maybe the tension he thought he heard was all a projection of his own taut emotions.

Was she as wound up as he was? God, it pleased him to think so. She sounded so vulnerable and sweet, not at all like Jana usually sounded. Why did that charge him up?

"I never really expected you'd crawl into my bed," he said.

"I never expected I'd do it."

"It's just for Gabriel."

"Right. Just for Gabriel."

"Easy having the two of us together." He cleared his throat.

"Yes."

He had so much he wanted to say to her, so much that couldn't be spoken. If he could wave a magic wand and grant himself any wish in the world, it would be to fast-forward his relationship with Jana until she was ready to hear what he had to say.

But he didn't have a magic wand, did he?

And she wasn't ready. While he might have been having serious thoughts about her for months, she was just now sticking her toe into the water. The baby had drawn her into his bed, but having her here was far trickier than he'd believed.

It would have been much safer if he'd let her take Gabriel back to the guest room. He'd gotten himself into this fix. A pickle of his own making.

"What are you thinking?" he whispered.

"Worrying about his mother," Jana confessed. "If she's as young as I think she is, she's out there alone in the cold."

She was so kind and caring. Here he'd been thinking about his own sexual desires, while she'd been worrying about someone else.

Feeling ashamed, he turned on his side, putting his back to her and icing down his spicy thoughts.

"She'll be fine," he mumbled.

"You can't know that."

"I choose to believe it."

"Why?"

"Because I can't worry about every single person, Jana. To spare myself, I have to compartmentalize. The baby is my main concern. Keeping him safe is my goal. Anything else I have to leave up to a higher power. Try to get some sleep."

"I wish I could turn my worries off like that," she confessed. "But I can't."

"What helps?"

"Music sometimes."

"Really?"

"If I get caught up in a song, it can help circumvent my worrywart tendencies."

"No kidding. Okay, then, I've got this." He reached for his cell phone on the table, switched it on, and picked a Christmas music album. As "Away in a Manger" played, Joel added his baritone to the music and sang a soft and low lullaby as Jana drifted off to sleep.

CHAPTER 9

THE PUSHBACK

"Wait, wait. Slow down. You need *what*?"

Joel stood in his sister's large country kitchen at nine A.M. on Thursday, the day before Christmas Eve.

Sleeping with Jana in his bed had proved damn near impossible, and he'd only managed a couple hours of shut-eye before the baby woke him again at seven thirty.

Jana had been zonked.

Smiling the entire time, he'd fed and diapered the infant and put the little guy back into bed beside Jana. On his way out the door, he suppressed an overwhelming impulse to lean in and kiss her cheek as she slept. Last night had been magnificent in an unexpected way.

That unexpected urge sent him jamming into his clothes, feeding Muffin, Puffin, and Filbert and letting them out to frolic in the fenced yard, before zooming over to see Flynn and ask to borrow her Pack 'n Play.

But he wanted more than a portable playpen from his sister. He needed reassurance that he and Jana had done the right thing taking Gabriel in for the holidays.

Flynn was a grade-school teacher on winter break. At this

moment she was looking at him as if he'd lost his ever-loving mind.

He reached for one of the freshly baked kismet cookies cooling on the sideboard, but she was quicker than he.

She leaned over and smacked his hand. "Those are for the kismet-cookie bake-off contest."

"They won't miss one little cookie," Joel protested, but he had the good sense to stick his hands in his pockets away from temptation and Flynn's halfway serious swats.

"That's how it starts. You take just one cookie, then Jesse takes just one cookie, then Grace and Ian each take one cookie. Boom! We're already down half a dozen cookies."

"Wait a minute, Teach, that doesn't parse. That's only four cookies, not half a dozen," he said.

Flynn's eyes narrowed. "As if you and Jesse would stop at just one."

The kismet cookies were part of the town's whimsical allure that brought tourists flocking to Twilight during the holidays. The myth was encouraged and hyped through recipe cards and free cookies passed out at local businesses during the month of December. Local legend had it that if you slept with a kismet cookie underneath your pillow on Christmas Eve, you would dream of your one true love.

Many people in Twilight, including Joel's three siblings, fed the lore with claims they'd followed the kismet-cookie fable to the letter and dreamed of the people who'd later become their spouses.

Despite peer pressure, Joel had never slept with cookies underneath his pillow, although more than one former girlfriend had tried to persuade him to take the plunge whenever Christmas Eve rolled around. But sleeping with cookies was just too damn silly and messy to boot. Besides, what if he did sleep with a cookie under his pillow and then he didn't dream about the woman he was with?

No thanks.

He didn't court complications. Call him laid-back or lazy, but he enjoyed nice and easy.

Right now, Flynn's two children sat at the kitchen table eating steel-cut oatmeal with banana slices and maple syrup. Grace was seven and quite precocious, and five-year-old Ian was all boy and dinosaur-crazy. Joel's cheek was still sticky from the hello kisses they'd given him, and he wasn't in any rush to wash off the gunk.

Ian sat in a booster seat with a small green plastic brontosaurus hanging by the neck on the edge of his cereal bowl, while Grace drizzled more syrup on her oatmeal. Dang, but he loved those kids with all his heart.

His sister's curly dark hair was pulled up into a messy bun, and she wore black yoga pants and a Santa apron over an intentionally ugly Christmas sweater in anticipation of brunch at the Cheeks', who were close family friends. The Cheeks had also invited him to their annual pre–Christmas Eve festivities, but with the Brazos Queen in the float parade tomorrow morning, he had work to do.

Flynn had been the one to raise him, his twin Noah, and their other sister, Carrie, after their mom died and their dad turned to alcohol to cope. Flynn had carried the brunt of that burden. It had been a rough few years before Dad had his moment of clarity, attended an AA meeting, and got sober. He'd just received his twelve-year chip, and Joel was proud as hell of his father. Getting clean and staying that way wasn't easy. Dad had since remarried, and he and his bride had moved to another town, but they'd be in Twilight for Christmas.

At thirty-nine, Flynn looked a decade younger and kept herself in tip-top shape through a dedicated exercise routine. Joel admired his sister deeply, but sometimes Flynn could be pretty bossy, as if it was still her job to keep him and Noah in line, even though they'd just celebrated their thirtieth birthday.

"Where's Jesse?" he asked.

"He left for the fire station at four this morning. You know how early they have to start on the logistics of the toy distribution."

"Oh yeah." Joel had volunteered on the toy-drive committee for several years running. He knew.

"Back to the Pack 'n Play," Flynn said, bending over to load the dishwasher. "Why do you need it?"

Joel was honestly surprised the news hadn't yet reached her through the Twilight grapevine. As quickly as he could, he told her the story of what had transpired the previous evening. Leaving out the part about Jana sleeping in his bed.

"Wait, wait." She made a football referee time-out sign with her hands. "Someone abandoned a *newborn* in Twilight?"

"Yes."

"In the *manger*?"

"Yep."

"In a *winter* storm?"

Technically true, but discovering Gabriel had been far less dramatic than Flynn was making it sound. "Uh-huh."

"At *Christmas*?"

"That's the holiday."

"But that's crazy. It's like something from a movie."

"Maybe that's where the baby's mom got the idea. We're assuming she's really young."

"Who on earth could do such a thing?" Flynn clicked her tongue and shot a melancholy glance at her kids. "Even a young mom?"

"Someone pretty desperate, I guess."

"Pastor Luther and Hondo are in on this?"

"Yeah, Dr. Longoria too."

"I can't believe they're condoning this. That baby needs to be turned over to CPS straightaway." Looking alarmed, Flynn tucked an errant curl behind her ear.

"In the note the baby's mother left, she did say she'd return

for him on New Year's Day. We wanted to give her a chance. If
we turn the baby over to CPS right now, it'll turn into a big legal
issue for her to get him back."

"And you believe a woman who writes a *please look after my
baby* note on a diaper with a marker? Who does that?"

"Someone in a rush who didn't have any paper?"

Flynn tapped her foot and twisted her mouth around. She
did not look appeased. "So your first instinct is to scoop up this
newborn and take him home with you, just like that?"

"It was raining. In a manger. In the winter. Below freezing.
At Christmas."

"Smart-ass." She sank her hands on her hips and studied him
as if he was a total mystery to her.

"I learned from the best." He winked.

"Stow the soft soap. What on earth compelled *you* to take
this on?"

"Again, manger, winter, Christmas, rainstorm . . ."

"It's not a puppy, Joel."

"Hence the reason I need to borrow your playpen. If it was a
puppy, I'd be borrowing a training crate."

"This has Jana written all over it," Flynn muttered. "I love
her to pieces, Joel, but she's got you in over your head. Why did
you let her talk you into this?"

"I don't *let* Jana do anything. She's her own person, just as
I am." He paused and gave his sister a pointed look. "Just like
you."

Flynn moved her arms from her hips to cross them over her
chest. "Is there something going on between you two that I need
to know about?"

Hmm, how would his sister react if he told her they'd slept in
the same bed last night? "We rescued a baby together. That was
pretty significant."

"And now you're playing house with her? What's next, Joel?
Patty-cakes?"

Joel stroked his chin with his thumb and index finger, trying to slip away from the trapped feeling Flynn's disapproval built inside him. "What are patty-cakes, anyway?"

"Don't act dumb. You know what I mean."

"I should text Christine," he said, referring to Christine Noble, Flynn's friend who ran the Twilight Bakery, "and find out just what in the hell a patty-cake is."

"*Aahmmm!* Mom, Uncle Joel said a dirty word." Grace pointed an accusing finger at him.

"I thought you liked me, kiddo." He winked at her.

"It's not you that I don't like," Grace said with a queenly slant to her dark blond head. "It's your potty mouth. Watch out or Mom'll wash your mouth out with green soap."

"Green soap?" Joel lifted his eyebrows at Flynn. "What the frick?"

"Irish Spring. Jesse loves the smell."

"Go get it, Mommy," Grace said. "Uncle Joel said *frick*, and he looks like he's about to cuss again."

Joel laughed. "She gets that bossiness from you."

"Excuse me?" Flynn glowered.

"Oops, sorry, she gets her *assertiveness* from you," Joel amended.

"That's better. Now, back to your baby."

"It's not *my* baby."

"Sounds like it is to me. At least until New Year's."

"Unca Jo'l got a baby?" Ian asked around a mouthful of oatmeal.

"Please don't talk with your mouth full, son, and yes, Uncle Joel has gotten himself a baby."

"I have a new cousin!" Grace squealed and clapped her hands.

"No, no. I'm babysitting," Joel explained, drilling Flynn with a glare.

"That's one way of putting it." Flynn chuffed.

"It's the only way we're putting it." He put steel in his voice, and his tone sent Flynn's eyebrows dipping.

"Yay!" Grace enthused. "I love babies. Can we play with him?"

"No, sweetheart, you can't play with Uncle Joel's baby. He's too little."

"Why do you sound mad?" Joel studied his sister. "If borrowing the playpen is such a problem, I'll just ask one of your friends from the First Love Cookie Club to lend me one of theirs."

"You'll do nothing of the sort."

He knew that would light a fire under her. The idea that her brother would turn to someone else for help didn't sit well with his big sister. Although she was loath to admit it, Flynn needed to be needed, and therein lay her kryptonite.

"C'mon." Flynn took off her apron and dropped it on the table. "The baby things are in the attic." She turned her attention to her kids. "Put your dishes in the sink when you're done, and go get dressed. We're going to story time at Ye Olde Book Nook today."

"Yay!" Grace did a little jig in her seat.

"But first we have to go help Daddy sort toys for the toy drive."

"Mom?"

"Yes, sweetie?" Flynn paused and kissed the top of her daughter's head as she led Joel through the kitchen toward the back stairs.

"Why do we have to give toys to poor kids? Why can't Santa do it?"

"Ask your daddy the next time you see him," Flynn told her daughter. To Joel, she said, "This one gives me a run for my money."

"Grace reminds me of Mom," he murmured as they climbed the stairs to the second floor. "She's got that same triumphant tilt to her head when she's asking button-pushing questions. Like she already knows she's going to win the argument."

"How do you even remember Mom? You were only four when she passed away."

"Come to think of it," he mumbled, "you're the one I remember. Flynn, I don't know how you did it. Stepping in to take care of all of us when the unthinkable happened."

Flynn flicked her hand. "I did what I had to do."

"With an enormous amount of love and care."

"Lordy," she said as she pulled down the attic door, "you're being sweet. What's gotten into you?"

"I just want to thank you for all you did for us. It wasn't easy. I get it now. You even gave up Jesse for us."

"It took Jesse and me a long time to find our way back together, but look at us now. He's the love of my life." Flynn's entire face softened at the mention of her husband. "I wish the same thing for you."

"Without the stint in prison for a crime I didn't commit," he said. When his brother-in-law was eighteen, Jesse had gone to prison for blowing up the Brazos River bridge, but the real perpetrator had been a rival for Flynn's affection who'd framed Jesse so he could date Flynn.

"Of course not *that*."

They climbed the stairs and squared off in the finished-out attic, staring across the open hole between them.

"I'm worried about you keeping this baby with Jana," Flynn said.

Hairs rose on his nape, and Joel felt a hot tightness in the pit of his stomach. "What are you talking about?"

"I fear sharing this baby will stir up your feelings for her."

"Jana and I are just friends. Why does this town have a problem with that?" Joel shoved his fingers through his hair. "It's a sickness, you know. The way this town tries to romanticize everything."

"Romanticism is the town's appeal. That's why tourists come to Twilight." She sounded logical, but downstairs on her sideboard she had four dozen kismet cookies that said otherwise. "For the legend and lore. People need to believe in something magical and the power of true love."

"It's not like that with me and Jana. We enjoy each other's company, and we work well together. That's all it is."

"Uh-huh." Flynn stared at him.

Joel thought about the restless night with Jana in his bed and watched a broken cobweb drift down from the rafters and attach to his sister's hair. He didn't tell her about it. If she was so smart, let her figure it out.

"I've seen the way you look at Jana, bro, when you think no one is watching. Whether you'll admit it, you have feelings for her that go far deeper than friendship."

"I don't know what you think you saw," Joel said. "Whatever *it* I have for Jana is platonic. I respect her, admire her, and like being around her, but that's as far as it goes."

"You sure?" Flynn's eyes struck flint.

"Positive."

"Good." She let out a long-held sigh and poked around some boxes.

"Why did you say it that way? What if I *did* have romantic feelings for Jana? Would that bother you?"

Flynn made a face. "I love Jana . . ."

"But?"

"It's like she's always got one foot out the door. As if she's come to a party and never taken off her coat. I mean she has every right to be that way. It's her choice to live her life any way she pleases. But, little brother, you deserve someone who can commit to you one hundred percent, and I doubt Jana's ability to fully trust anyone. And how can you have a successful, intimate relationship without trust?"

Joel moistened his lips. Flynn had a point. Jana did have trouble opening up. But she had opened up to him a little bit last night. "You, dear sister, worry too much about things that you can't control."

"I know." Flynn sighed. "I'm working on it."

"A good step in that direction would be to keep your nose out of my business."

"Touché." Flynn paused. "But you *don't* have romantic feelings for Jana, right?"

"Right," Joel echoed, but a sense of wrongness curled up tight underneath his rib cage.

His feelings for Jana were changing, growing more complicated and complex. When he and Ursula had parted company, she'd told him that she believed he had unresolved feelings for his employee. He had blown off the comment, but now here it was coming from his sister as well.

Flynn pushed aside a dresser mirror to get to the playpen stacked against the wall. "You'll need more than the Pack 'n Play if you're keeping the kid for ten days." Flynn said. "Take the car seat and stroller too."

"Naomi already gave us a car seat, but we'll take the stroller." Joel looked at the baby things Flynn was unearthing and felt his chest tighten again. Okay, this was officially overwhelming.

It's just until New Year's, he reminded himself. *No biggie.*

"Why'd you keep all this baby stuff?" he asked.

Flynn shrugged and leaned back and looked as if his question had caught her off guard. "I suppose in the back of my mind I'd always wanted a third baby, but I'm staring down the barrel of forty and thinking maybe that's not the best idea in the world."

"Why not? You're healthy and strong."

"Kids are a lot of responsibility, Joel. If you do it right, raising human beings is the hardest thing you'll ever do in your life."

"Well, you and Jesse are doing a bang-up job with Grace and Ian."

"Mommy," Grace called from the bottom of the attic stairs, "Ian spilled his milk, and it's dripping on the floor."

"I'll be right down, sweetie. Don't come up the stairs. They're rickety, and there are lots of cobwebs up here." Flynn finally brushed away the loose spiderweb caught in her hair, and Joel felt a twinge of guilt for not telling her about it.

"What do I clean the mess up with?" Grace asked. "Ian's tracking milk footprints all around the kitchen."

"I'll be right down." She turned to Joel and lowered her voice.

"I mean it about being careful with Jana. Remember, cuddling babies stimulates oxytocin, the bonding hormone."

"Be honest with me. What do you *really* have against Jana?"

"I have nothing against Jana . . ." Flynn bit down on her thumbnail. "She's just not the one for you."

Joel got irritated then. "Why?"

Flynn crinkled her nose and ran her hand through her hair again, as if making sure no cobwebs lingered. "She's a little weird, Joel."

"Meaning?" He scowled at her, protective instincts snatching at his chest. Flynn was being unfair.

"Because of her upbringing, I believe she doesn't know how to fully love. She keeps people at arm's length. I mean, what does anyone really know about her? She's had seven years to embrace our community, and still she holds herself apart."

Flynn made good sense, but Joel wouldn't tell her that. His goal was simple. Help Jana take care of Gabriel until the baby's mother returned. His real motives, however, might be more convoluted, and he couldn't explain them to Flynn because he didn't fully understand them himself.

"Here's the dealio, sis," Joel said, stealing one of Jana's favorite words. "Jana is my friend, and I would appreciate it if you didn't disrespect her."

"I'm not disrespecting her."

"You're running her down behind her back."

"No, I'm not. I think Jana is amazing. She's just not the woman for you."

"And you know what's right for everyone?"

Flynn's shoulders dropped, and she slowly shook her head. "Fine. I'm staying out of it, but don't come crying to me when you get your heart broken."

"I won't."

"Good. C'mon, I'll help you drag the baby things to your truck and get you on your way."

Despite her warning against Jana, his sister really was a good sport and helpful to boot. He could overlook a little bossiness.

"Mommy," Grace interrupted, back at the foot of the stairs, "Ian's finger-painting on the wall with milk."

"Lord, give me patience," Flynn muttered and rolled her eyes. To her daughter standing at the bottom of the stairs she said, "Tell him to please stop."

"I already did."

"You sure you want to take in a newborn?" Flynn chuckled. "If you're aching for kids, I've got a couple you could borrow."

"They're all yours. Have fun."

"You too."

They grinned at each other and Flynn helped him load the things into his vehicle.

"One last word of warning though, and I'm being serious about this, and then I'll shut up. Don't fall in love with the baby. The next thing you know, you'll be applying to be a foster parent, and after that it's just a hop, skip, and a jump to the manger baby calling you Daddy." Flynn gave him a goodbye hug.

As Joel got in his truck and backed out of the drive, he couldn't help thinking, *What's so wrong with that?*

CHAPTER 10

THE BUMP

The baby wouldn't stop crying.

Muffin, Puffin, and Filbert were so alarmed, they'd run cowering under Joel's bed an hour ago and hadn't come out since.

Jana had tried everything she knew to do, but the kid was still squalling his head off. She'd fed him, changed him, and rocked him. She'd sung nonsense songs to him, swaddled him, done Reiki on him—yes, it was a throwback to her Austin roots, and while she didn't really believe in the woo-woo stuff anymore, she *was* desperate.

But no matter what she tried, he still wailed as if his tiny little heart was broken. Which in turn broke her heart.

He missed his mommy, and that's all there was to it.

As she held him close to her chest and paced the hardwood floor in front of the fireplace, the past came blasting through her mind like a supersonic train, scary fast and overpowering. It wasn't a memory per se, but it was more than just a feeling. It was a persistent aching deep inside her bones.

An entombed loneliness she'd ignored for her entire life.

That night, on Christmas Eve twenty-three years ago, the uniformed police officer had gotten down on his hands and knees to coax her out from under the pool table in a noisy honky-tonk with a candy bar he'd plucked from the pocket of his coat. He'd picked her up in his big, brawny arms and cooed to her that everything would be all right.

The muscle on the left side of Jana's mouth twitched.

The taste of that candy bar was forever etched on her tongue. Three Musketeers. She'd hated that candy ever since. Actually, she hated any candy that resembled it—Milky Ways, Mars Bars, and yes, Snickers too.

It was the nougat. She hated the spongy quality and the way it stuck to her teeth, just like that ugly memory. Jana shuddered.

Gabriel howled louder.

"What's wrong, little guy? What's your dealio?" Yep, she heard the despair in her voice. "Please stop crying."

His face scrunched, and fat tears rolled down his cherubic cheeks. Something else had to be wrong.

She took him to Joel's bedroom to investigate. It smelled so masculine in here: orange peel, pine, sandalwood, and musk. Her nose twitched as she remembered the night spent in his bed.

Focus.

"I'm in over my head, kid," she whispered. "Doing the best that I can."

As Gabriel sobbed uncontrollably, she steeled herself against the hopelessness tangling up inside her and took off his clothes, looking to see if something was poking him. A quick search told her everything was okay on that front.

She redressed him and lifted him to her shoulder again, gently jostling him as she circled the rug. Why had she thought keeping the baby for ten days was a good idea?

There's an easy out. All you have to do is notify CPS.

She could wash her hands of the whole situation. Go back to her life. The baby wasn't her responsibility. No one would blame her. She'd have to turn him over eventually if his mom didn't return. Why not now?

Why?

What if his mom *did* return?

"I've got this," she told him. "We've got this. Your diaper was dry, so let's try the formula again. Unless you have a tummy ache. Do you have a tummy ache?"

A tummy ache might explain everything. What should she do about that? Jana settled him back onto the bed and curled up beside him, her booted feet hanging off the end of the bed. She rubbed his tummy and hummed "Hush, Little Baby."

It didn't help.

He cried harder, his little face scrunched and red, tears soaking his cheeks.

"Ah baby, ah sweetheart. I am so sorry you're suffering." *Geez, if he didn't stop crying soon, she would call 911.* She couldn't let him go on like this.

A few minutes later, the sound of Joel's truck crunching the driveway gravel jettisoned her from the bed.

"The cavalry is here! We're not alone anymore. Joel will know what to do. He's a good guy. We can trust him."

Jana met Joel in the mudroom as he came through the back door, juggling the Pack 'n Play, a stroller, and a brown paper bag.

"Thank God you're here!"

"What's going on?" He looked startled and set down the supplies. The three golden retrievers swarmed him.

"Gabriel won't stop crying. I don't know what to do. I've tried *everything*."

Looking concerned, Joel nodded. He leaned back to open the door and let the dogs flow outside, then closed it and reached for the baby.

Beyond grateful to have him back, Jana deposited Gabriel into his big powerful arms and felt relief grab hold of her. At last! She wasn't alone anymore.

"Hey, little dude," Joel said. "What's up?"

Jana's hopes that Joel's presence would magically calm Gabriel shattered as the baby's cries grew louder still.

Panic-stricken, she ticked off the things she'd tried on her fingers. "I fed him, changed his diaper, checked him for irritants, sang to him, rocked him, paced the floor . . ."

With a calm, lazy smile that settled her nerves, Joel lifted the baby to his shoulder and patted his back with a firm, gentle pat.

Gabriel let out a belch rivaling that of a full-grown man and instantly stopped crying.

Jana's eyes met Joel's, and they burst out laughing. "He just needed to burp."

"Gas bubble." Joel gave her a humble smile.

"How did you know to do that?"

"Ian was a gassy baby."

"My stars." Jana sagged against the counter. "I was within inches of rushing him to the ER."

"Never fear, Joel's here," he teased.

"I am thrilled you came back." Her voice came out gruff and ragged.

"It's my house. Where else would I be?" He kept patting Gabriel's back, but more softly now. The baby's eyelids drooped. Nonstop crying was exhausting.

Jana grinned, so relieved to have Joel here it was all she could do not to throw her arms around him, baby and all, and squeeze tight. "He's falling asleep."

"I'm going to put him in the middle of my bed while we set up the playpen." Joel headed for his bedroom.

Jana picked up the folded playpen he'd rested against the wall and followed him. "Did everything go okay with Flynn?"

Yes, okay, her anxiety was getting the better of her.

"Fine." His back was to her, and she couldn't see his face, but his voice sounded weird, as if everything hadn't been fine. It was a subtle change, but she caught the elevated inflection.

Good grief, Jana, stop being so suspicious. This is Joel. Relax.

"You sure?" She could have bitten off her tongue. She sounded way too needy.

He straightened. "Why wouldn't it?"

"Sometimes I get the feeling your sister doesn't like me."

"She likes you."

"I think it's the tats that put her off," Jana mused.

"It's not the ink."

"Aha! So she *is* put off by me."

"Not put off, no." He shook his head too vigorously. "Flynn's just overly protective of me and Noah. She hasn't learned how to butt out of our business. She just wants to see me happy. I'm the only sibling left who hasn't settled down."

"And she thinks I'm going to corrupt you with my Austin weirdness?"

"She thinks you keep too many secrets."

"Honestly?" Jana smacked her forehead with her palm. "She doesn't like me because I don't broadcast my life history for the town to gossip about and dissect endlessly?"

"She thinks you shut people out."

"Just because I have good boundaries, unlike most people in this town, doesn't mean I'm closed off."

"Don't worry about it. Flynn doesn't run my life as much as she might think she does." Chuckling, he settled the baby in the middle of the king-sized bed to sleep.

Outside the window, the goldens barked, the lighthearted, energetic barks of dogs at play. Gabriel didn't stir.

But Jana *did* worry about it.

Was she too secretive? Should she open up more? Had the strong boundaries she'd developed shut people out? Was she too coldhearted?

The thoughts sent a shiver straight through her heart. Flynn might be right, but Jana had learned the hard way the more information you gave people, the more things they had to use against you.

Once the Pack 'n Play was up, Joel moved Gabriel into the makeshift crib all without waking him.

"You're pretty smooth at that. The daddy thing."

"It's not hard. I like kids." He pressed his palms to his back and gazed down at the sleeping infant, an endearing smile on his face.

"How come you don't have any kids of your own?"

"I want to do things the right way."

"You mean the traditional way?"

"Let me rephrase. I want to do it the right way for *me*."

"Meaning?"

"The traditional way." He laughed. "Go ahead. Call me old-fashioned. I'm not ashamed. I want to fall madly in love. I want to get married before I have kids. I want a big church wedding, and I want time with my bride before we plunge into having a family."

"It sounds nice." Her words came out wistful.

He shrugged, a casual gesture that was anything but dismissive. "I believe kids do best with two parents who love each other."

"So do I," she said, wondering why her heart was thumping so hard. "But not everyone gets to have that."

"I know. I only had it for four years. Then Mom passed."

"What happened between you and Tory?" she asked, referring to the woman he'd been engaged to when she'd first moved to Twilight. "What went wrong?"

"You really want to know?"

"Yeah."

"Then, you have to tell me something personal in return."

Her curiosity warred with her need to keep herself safe. "Okay," she said. "But I reserve the right not to answer questions I think are too intimate."

"Okay." He bobbed his head. "Tory and I had great chemistry, and we'd had this on-again off-again thing since high school. She was my first girlfriend. Then we went off to college and broke up. Then we got back together. Then I asked her to marry me. She said yes, and it was the happiest time of my life . . ."

"Until?" Jana prodded.

"She told me she didn't want any kids. It was a deal-breaker."

"Where's Tory now?"

"She moved to Dallas. Married a banker. Has a fancy house in Highland Park. Globe-trots. She got what she wanted, and I'm happy for her." He sounded so sincere.

"That sounds very mature."

"I didn't always have that point of view," he chuckled. "But I came to understand that you have to be true to yourself. If we had gotten married, one of us would have had to sacrifice who we were. Either me by agreeing not to have children or her having a child she didn't want. It was sad, but that's how life goes sometimes."

Jana had the strongest urge to give him a big hug.

He studied her for a long moment. "Your turn."

She moistened her lips, hoped he didn't ask anything too intrusive. "What do you want to know?"

"How many foster homes did you live in when you were growing up?"

She shook her head. She didn't want to talk about this. *This is why Flynn doesn't like you. You're too closemouthed.*

"Half dozen," she mumbled.

"I don't know anything about the foster-care system. Is that typical?"

"Search me. I'm not a caseworker." She hoped that would shut him down. She hated to rehash the past. It served no purpose except to stir up miserable memories.

"Did anything happen to you in any of those homes?"

"Do you mean was I abused?"

He nodded.

She blew out her breath. "Not physically. Look, I wasn't an easy kid. Sometimes I just wasn't a good fit for the families."

"How old were you when you went into foster care?"

"Three."

"How did that come about?"

She shook her head. "I don't want to talk about it."

He nodded, honoring her wishes. "A couple of Christmases back, didn't you return to Austin to take care of your mom when she had surgery? Was that—"

"I lied. I didn't want people asking questions." Oh crap, she could *not* get into all that. It was just too much.

Joel sank his top teeth into his bottom lip as if holding back more questions and drilled her with his gaze.

Jana squirmed, tensed, begged him with her eyes. *Please don't ask.*

His soft smile returned, and in that moment, she knew he would drop the interrogation. He was easygoing in that way. Swift gratitude washed over her.

"C'mon," he said. "You need a break. Let's take one while Gabriel is sacked out. I've got a surprise for you."

The air left Jana's lungs as relief warmed her heart, but then he reached out to take her hand and *bam*!

Back draft.

Joel had taken her hand before. This was nothing new. Once, when they were in a dance competition for charity and had held hands awaiting the results—they'd lost. Another time when they'd gone hiking with Noah and Kelsey, and Jana had fallen into a shallow ravine, Joel had been there to help her out, taking her hand and pulling her up beside him. Over the course of the past two years, they'd shaken hands and high-fived numerous times.

Touching him should not be a big deal.

But none of *those* incidents had lit her up like a Christmas tree. Well, except for last night at the diner, but that had been static electricity.

But now?

Today?

His touch was pop, crackle, snap without the static electricity. Sending red-hot spikes of sensation skipping along her nerve endings.

What was happening? Where were these new and exciting feelings coming from? She darted a quick glance up at his face.

He smiled down at her.

Fear had her wanting to let go of his hand, but her palm seemed fused to his, and she let him lead her back to the mudroom. She hadn't noticed it when he'd come in, she'd been so distraught over Gabriel, but there on the counter was a rectangular white window box from the Twilight Bakery underneath the brown paper bag.

She dropped his hand and rushed to the box. "Oh, my gosh are these—"

"Vegan cinnamon rolls."

"You truly are my hero, Joel MacGregor!" Jana exclaimed, plastering both hands over her heart. "I love . . ."

Dear heavens, she'd been about to say *I love you.*

Holy Crown Chakra! She was turning into a Twilightite. Loving things, and giving voice to it willy-nilly. She meant she loved him as a friend for bringing her a special treat, but suddenly the word was fraught with meaning, and she quickly amended by saying, ". . . love these cinnamon rolls!"

"I know." Joel's gleeful grin did strange things to her.

"Thank you."

"I enjoy putting a smile on your face. You don't smile nearly often enough, Jana." His tone sounded serious, and he looked a bit sad.

"Bring me these cinnamon rolls, and I'll smile every time." She injected glibness into her voice and patted her tummy.

"I'll put in a standing order with Christine." He eyed her up and down. "What else makes you smile, Tink?"

Rattled by the question and the inquisitive expression in his eyes—he had the look of a man who wanted to know too much—Jana grabbed the box and scampered to the kitchen.

That's when it dawned on her that she was still in her pajamas and she was braless and jiggling around all over the place. She'd been too absorbed with Gabriel to think about getting dressed. Naomi had once told her that, after Henry was born, she didn't put on real clothes for six weeks.

At the time Jana had thought that was bizarre. Now, she completely got it. Newborns took all your attention.

"I'll put on a fresh pot of coffee," Joel said, moving to the coffee maker on the counter.

"Does that mean you think I'm going to share my cinnamon buns with you?" she teased, strategically holding the bakery box against her chest to camouflage her breasts.

"A man can only hope." His eyes twinkled.

Ack! Why had she said *buns*? The word had connotations she hadn't intended.

Or had she?

Jana tilted her head and studied him. The way his hair fell sexily over his forehead gave him a jaunty, rakish look that left her breathing shallow.

"You take your coffee black?" He dumped the old, grounds-filled filter from the coffeemaker and put in a fresh one.

"I do." She was trying to figure out a way to slip past him without having to explain she needed to put on a bra. She didn't want to call attention to her free-swinging girls.

He ground coffee beans, and the rich aroma enlivened the kitchen, weirdly deepening the intimacy. She felt trapped in one of those coffee commercials where drinking caffeinated beverages bordered on orgasmic.

Jolted, she turned toward the cabinet, intent on getting plates for the cinnamon rolls, at the very same moment Joel moved toward the coffee mugs dangling from hooks underneath the cabinet where the plates were kept.

They crashed into each other. Smack dab. Her unharnessed breasts bumping hard into his muscular abs.

Holy Gut Chakra!

They both sprang back. The alarm on Joel's face as shocking as the overwhelming sensations swamping her body.

"Sorry, sorry," he mumbled.

She ducked her head, her breasts tingling crazily. "No, no, all me."

Then confused and flustered, they simultaneously surged forward again, each headed for their goal. Her for plates, him for cups.

And damn if they didn't bump into each other a second time. As if acting of their own accord, her breasts smashed flat against him.

This time, they jumped to opposite sides of the kitchen, Joel landing near the coffee maker, Jana by the microwave.

"I-I . . ." she stammered.

"S'kay, s'kay."

"It's—"

"You."

"Me."

His eyes locked hers down. "We."

"No."

"I get it."

"I gotta . . ."

She was panting so hard she couldn't catch her breath or rip her gaze from his. All she could hear was the sound of her own heartbeat galloping in her ears. All she could feel was heat blasting liquid fire from her belly to her groin. All she could smell was cinnamon and Joel's masculine fragrance mingling into some mad sensory experience that turned her brain to mush.

"Put on a bra?" he finished her sentence.

Nodding, she hiccuped and fled the room.

CHAPTER 11

THE BANNER

A few minutes later, Jana returned to the kitchen as reinforced as a jousting knight in a suit of armor. She'd put on a bra, buttoned her cardigan up to the top button, and had her arms folded tightly across her chest.

But it was too late.

Joel knew what her bare breasts felt like beneath the thin layer of her cotton pajamas, and the knowledge knocked him out. He couldn't stop thinking about it, but he didn't want her to feel uncomfortable or embarrassed. He forced himself to keep his eyes on her face, offered her a reassuring smile, and waved at the dining nook.

"Coffee's ready. I heated up the cinnamon rolls."

"Thank you." She looked as if she might say something else but didn't.

He dropped his gaze to her lips, which were so damned kissable it was all he could do to *not* kiss her, and that rattled him so hard the back of his teeth hurt.

In a world where she was his part-time employee and casual friend, the sexual thoughts blasting through his body were definitely coloring outside the lines. He didn't know what to do with the feelings. They sat on his chest like oil on water. Something he should skim off, but he didn't want to.

The morning sun filtering through the blinds glinted off the amber highlights in her shoulder-length, honey brown hair. Amber? *Sheesh, MacGregor, you're an artist now?* Where had he fished out that vocabulary word?

Amber Waves of Grain.

The name of the microbrewery beer that she preferred popped into his head, and dang if her hair wasn't the same color as that drink.

Face facts. He was intoxicated: drunk on her soft hair, her deep blue eyes, her enigmatic half smile, her resilience and badassery.

Except right now she looked hesitant and vulnerable which, damn him, turned Joel on in a whole new way. She was usually so tough. Spying a chink in her defenses stirred his protective urges, and he wanted to scoop her into his arms and tell her everything would be all right.

This was getting really real, and honestly, he didn't know what to do about his changing feelings.

She dazzled him. Looking just as hot in the faded jeans and wool sweater as when she'd worn a red cocktail dress and spike heels to Noah and Kelsey's wedding last year. It blew his mind how a down-to-earth country boy found himself in proximity to a woman as intriguingly sexy as Jana.

Cheeks flushing, eyes widening, her exotic, essential-oils scent thickened the weighted air between them. And those lips! Why had he never noticed before their pillowy perfection? Pink, soft, and stunningly kissable.

But, but, but . . . here was the problem. Well, four problems actually.

1. *The baby.*
2. *She was the best employee he'd ever had.*

3. *He wanted more than hot sex, and she was far right of skittish.*
4. *They were friends, and he didn't want to blow it.*

Joel couldn't imagine his life without Jana in it in some capacity which, now that he was aware of his growing feelings and no longer tamping them down, explained why he'd never considered kissing her before.

Not seriously.

Not until now.

That weighted air between them became a solid thing. Denser than butter. The expression in her eyes said she felt it too and was just as uncomfortable with this as he was.

"Um . . . are you okay?" he asked.

"I'm fine." She frowned. "Why wouldn't I be?"

Aching to pry, he opened his mouth but then shut it again. He shouldn't be worrying about her emotions. Her feelings belonged to her, and if she didn't want to share them, that was her right.

Okay. Message received. Got it. She did not want to talk about the bump, but his chest was *still* tingling from where her breasts had crashed into him.

They sat down across from each other at the breakfast table, in a small, intimate, cozy little nook.

"Let's talk about work," he said to keep his mind off those lips. Sublimating his desires, he bit into the cinnamon roll.

"Work?" She had a dollop of icing on her upper lip.

Dammit. He wanted to lean across the table and kiss it off. Instead, he motioned to her that she had something on her face.

"Oh, sorry. I turn piggy over these cinnamon rolls." She dabbed away the enticing icing. "What were you saying about work?"

Joel dropped his gaze to his plate. "You promised you'd help me finish decorating for the float parade, remember?"

"Oh yes, right. BG."

"BG?"

"Before Gabriel. It's like everything BG flew right out of my brain. Sure, sure, I'll still help, but we gotta take him with us."

"We could find a babysitter. We had offers all over the place last night at Moe's."

"We'll already have to leave him with a babysitter tonight, when I'm tending bar at the Horny Toad and you do your thang with the Bards. I don't want to shunt him off all day, especially since we had such a rough morning over the burp."

He got that. "Sure. We'll bring him along."

"Next, we just have to find a sitter for tonight."

"I don't think that's going to be a problem, but I'll put out some feelers."

"Me too," she said, pulling her cell phone from her pocket to send a few texts.

He polished off his cinnamon roll and dusted crumbs from his fingers onto the plate. "I'll walk the dogs while you get Gabriel ready. Unless you want to swap roles. I didn't mean to suggest you get baby duty just because you have a uterus."

Jana's head shot up from leaning over the phone screen. "What?"

Why had he said *uterus*? Joel cringed inwardly. "Um . . . er . . . I didn't mean to offend."

One corner of her mouth quirked up. "It's fun watching you squirm, MacGregor. I'm not offended. I'm amused at your discomfort."

"Whew."

"You thought I'd be offended because you mentioned a part of my anatomy?"

Yes. No. He had no idea what he thought. Not wanting to permanently wedge his cowboy boot in his mouth, Joel just shrugged and prayed he looked nonchalant.

"Tell you what. I'll take care of the baby, and you can walk the dogs. Just because they're your dogs, not because you have a penis."

Penis.

Her tongue wrapped glibly around the word, and her wicked smile was downright gleeful.

His body part in question jumped to attention, straining against the zipper of his jeans. It had been many moons since he'd gotten a boner with so little provocation.

Ah hell, Flynn was right about his living situation. If he didn't get a handle on himself, this wasn't going to end well.

Reality was a kicker. Getting through the next nine days with his heart intact would be one helluva hard grind.

An hour later, Joel and Jana walked up the gangplank of the Brazos Queen together, Joel carrying Gabriel in his carrier.

For a second, as he did every time he climbed aboard, Joel paused to lob a prayer of gratitude skyward.

He was living his dream life, and he knew he was a lucky guy. Growing up on the river, he and his twin had talked of owning their own water-related business, and four years ago their childhood fantasies had come true when they'd bought twin paddle-wheel boats and formed a partnership together: River Dreams Inc.

It had taken them a year to renovate the paddle-wheels, transforming Noah's boat into the bed-and-breakfast permanently moored on Christmas Island, and turning Joel's boat into the pleasure cruiser. Then they'd grown the business, adding seasonal scuba-diving packages, featuring lodging, cruising, and scuba lessons taught by their handyman, Sean Armstrong, an ex–Navy SEAL. They also sold diving equipment and River Dreams–branded merchandise online and through Jesse's motorcycle retail shop in town.

"What is it?" Jana stopped and looked over her shoulder at him.

"Just appreciating what I've got," he said, tracing her face with his eyes.

"Oh."

"In this moment . . ." He held her gaze. ". . . things are pretty freaking fantastic. I want to enjoy every second of it."

"Wow, MacGregor. Better watch out. I'm rubbing off on you."

"I think you are." He smiled. "You are the one who taught me about mindfulness. Remember the time when we got horn-swoggled into participating in the dunking booths at Wine Walk Weekend?"

Her cheeks flushed prettily. That weekend, they'd been seated on precarious perches in side-by-side dunking booths to raise money for charity.

"You couldn't stop complaining," she said.

"You were so Zen, sitting there cross-legged, and barely re-acting whenever you got dunked."

"While you squawked your head off every time."

"Hardly anyone was dunking you, and they were lobbing at me like crazy."

"Who knew so many tipsy people would get off on dunking *you*?" She laughed, and it was a beautiful sound in the still of the morning.

"I think the peacefulness you projected sent off *don't mess with me* vibes," he speculated.

"Your bitching was driving me bananas. I had to teach you mindfulness for my own sanity." She chuckled. "Or I was going to get out of that booth so I could dunk you myself."

"The mindfulness worked too, mostly. I still couldn't get into water shooting up my nose, but other than that part, I was able to temper my response."

"Glad I could help." She spanned the distance between them, went up on tiptoes, and patted his cheek.

The gesture wasn't the least bit sexual, but the message that shot through his nerve endings was *hawt, hawt, hawt.*

He felt sweat bead around his collar, despite the cool breeze ruffling the water. So much for mindfulness: his errant thoughts blew around like dandelion seeds, the majority of them sexually charged and lusty.

"Let's get inside," he urged, putting a hand to her elbow.

Big mistake.

The muscles of her arm bunched underneath his touch, and she sucked in an audible breath. But worse, his body hardened just as it had at the breakfast table.

Quickly, he let go of her and leaned forward to open the door, praying she did not look down at his zipper.

They stepped into the ballroom of the main deck where Joel and Noah had pulled out boxes of decorations on Tuesday. If someone had told him the wild twists and turns his life would take within two days of then, he wouldn't have believed them.

Jana took the baby carrier from him and eased the blanket aside for a peek at the infant. "He's still asleep. Let's get to work while the getting is good."

She sat the carrier in an out-of-the-way spot near the windows and moved back to where Joel was opening up a box of decorations.

"Hey, y'all," a female voice called from the door. "Where's this miracle baby I've been hearing so much about?"

They turned to see Tasha Williams-Armstrong, a spunky thirtysomething Black woman, holding a tray of canapés. Tasha was a trained chef, married to Sean.

Jana waved at the baby carrier.

Tash beelined it to the fridge, stowed the food for tomorrow's float parade, and rushed over to Gabriel.

Jana followed her.

Joel's gaze followed Jana.

She moved with such grace and ease. Her lithe sway captivated him. Even in motorcycle boots, she walked as if she had clouds on her feet. Watching her stirred a funny sensation in his gut.

Did Jana have any clue how gorgeous she was? He thought maybe not. She seemed to do everything in her power to downplay her natural beauty in favor of flamboyant style that cried *Look at this persona I created to hide the real me.* A guy could spend his entire life with a woman like that and still be mystified by her.

Most everyone in town knew Jana. She showed up for all the main events, whether working or volunteering. She had lots of casual friends, but no one she let get truly close. Pastor Luther's daughter Naomi probably came the closest.

No one truly knew who she was deep down inside. She was a "riddle wrapped in a mystery inside an enigma." The Winston Churchill quote ran through his mind. It fit Jana to a *Z*. The letter *T* was too tame for a maverick like her.

"Can I hold him?" Tasha asked, gazing down at the baby.

"He eats every couple of hours, so I try to let him sleep between feedings." Jana widened her stance, holding her ground, cementing those boundaries she held so well. If it had been Joel, he'd have let Tasha hold the baby.

"Oh, gotcha," Tasha whispered and crouched beside the carrier. "Ooh, I wanna pinch those sweet little cheeks."

Looking as serious as any bodyguard, Jana folded her arms and loomed over Tasha. Joel could almost see Jana smacking Tasha's hand away if she dared touch the baby without permission, and he smothered a laugh.

"Man," Tasha said, tucking her fingers into her back pockets as she straightened. "I hope I can toe the line like you whenever Sean and I have kids."

"No skill." Jana shook her head. "Just self-preservation."

The baby moved in his sleep.

"He's awake!" Tasha said. "Can I hold him now?"

"It would help to have Tasha watch him while we hang the banner," Joel said. "Otherwise we'll have to wait until tomorrow morning for outside decorating when Gerald Longoria is here to assist."

"Yes! Yes!" Tasha clapped her hands. "Go hang the banner. I'll chill with Gabriel."

Jana's phone buzzed, and she pulled it from her hip pocket, silently read the text on the screen, and then looked over at Joel.

His pulse blipped. God, he enjoyed looking into those dark blue eyes so full of mystery and possibilities.

"It's Kelsey. She and Noah would love to watch Gabriel tonight while we work." Jana was a few feet away, but he got a whiff of her fragrance.

"That's great." He adored the way she smelled, and he inhaled deeply, savoring.

She looked a bit unnerved, trod across the room, grabbed a box marked OUTDOOR DECORATIONS, and headed outside.

He followed, his gaze lingering on her backside as she climbed the stairs. What a beautiful butt!

Once they were on the upper deck, Jana stopped, box still in her arms, and stared down at the dock.

He looked to see what had captured her attention.

There, several yards away, stood a thin young woman standing off by herself, wearing a blue jean jacket that seemed far too flimsy for the winter cold. She was staring up at the Brazos Queen, but when Joel met her gaze, she ducked her head and shuttled away, joining a group of carolers strolling the marina.

"Do you know her?" Joel asked.

"No." Jana shook her head. "She just reminded me of someone I once knew."

"Your past self?" he asked.

She looked startled, clutched the box tighter. "How did you know?"

"A hunch. You got a sad, faraway expression on your face."

"Do you think she could be . . ." Jana shook her head. "Nah."

"Could be what?"

"Gabriel's mother."

"Checking up on us?"

Jana nodded. "I'd like to believe that."

"Odds are it's not her."

"I know. It's just that she looked so—"

"Much like a broody teenager?"

"She seemed more tragic than the average broody teen."

"You got that from a fleeting glance?"

"You're right. I'm being fanciful."

"Totally understandable. You want Gabriel's mother to come back. I do too."

Jana bit down on her bottom lip and stared off in the direction where the teenager and the carolers had disappeared.

"You okay?"

"Fine. I'm totally fine." She looked as if she might say something, but then she shook her head.

"I get the feeling there's something more going on with you."

"There's not."

"You sure?"

"I'm dandy," she said, but she drew her shoulders up and her head down in a protective slump. "Let's get to work."

It had been a long time since he'd seen that defensive body language in her. When she'd first come to town seven years ago, it had been her go-to stance. But as time rolled by and she'd grown more comfortable in Twilight, he'd watched her gradually grow stronger, more self-confident, and bolder. He liked who she'd become.

What caused her to regress? Was it the teenager on the dock who'd reminded her of herself? Did it have something to do with her feelings for the baby? Or was it because they'd shared a bed last night? Or was it the chest bump in his kitchen?

Truth?

He was rattled too. Then again, maybe he was imagining things. All he knew was that something had shifted between them, and their normal, comfortable comradery was not so comfortable anymore.

She leaned over to grab one side of the eight-foot-long banner that was supposed to say *Merry Christmas, Twilight*, giving him a straight-shot view down the front of her sweater.

She waited for him to pick up the other half.

His eyes bugged. Joel stopped in his tracks, gaze fixed on Jana's cleavage. His pulse jumped right off a cliff. *Last night, this gorgeous creature was in my bed.*

"Joel?"

"Huh?"

"You gonna stand there all day with your mouth hanging open?"

He shut his jaw, picked up the other end of the banner, and followed her outside to drape it from the railing of the upper deck.

"Before we anchor the banner securely, let's make sure it's even," she said and hit the stairs for the lower deck so they could stand back and examine their handiwork.

He followed her, hunching his shoulders against the cold air blowing off the water. Jana cleared the stairs ahead of him, turned, and stared owl-eyed at the message on the unfurled banner above them.

She gasped. "What's this?"

He stared up.

The banner read WILL YOU MARRY ME?

Seeing the words spelled out in red letters across the boat yanked the breath from his lungs, and he startled, moving forward on the ball of his foot.

Whoa, what is this? For one insane second, he wondered . . . Was Jana asking him to marry her? Was this some wild, covert setup? He peeked over, his heart in his throat.

The confusion in her eyes matched his own.

Dumbass. No, of course not.

She lifted terrified eyebrows, and they asked the question on his mind, *Are you asking me to marry you?*

He shook his head. Hard. Held up both palms. "No, no."

"Whew." She wiped her arm across her forehead.

"You thought I—"

"No."

"But you said—"

"*No.*"

"This banner is from when Sean borrowed the paddle-wheel so he could ask Tasha to marry him."

"I figured that out."

"It took me a minute too. You're not going to believe this, but for half a second, I thought *you* were asking *me* to marry you." He chuckled nervously.

"Good Lord, Joel, are you serious? Why would I do that?"

"Not for real, as a joke."

"That's hilarious. I wish I *had* thought of it. This was pure accident."

"I know, right?" Joel peered at her. "Wait, why is that hilarious?"

"Hilarious that, even as a joke, you thought that I'd ask you to marry me."

"Because you wouldn't." His stomach was in his boots, and he had no idea why or why he was stirring this particular pot. "Ever."

"That's right."

"Because being married to me would be such a horrible thing?" *Just shut the hell up, MacGregor. You're making things worse and worse.*

"It's not you. It's me."

"That's what people say when it *is* you."

"*Joel.*" Her voice carried a coaxing tone. "Why are we even having this conversation?" She flipped her hair back off her shoulders with a blasé flick. "It's silly."

"Because for some weird reason, you thought I was asking you to marry me."

"I didn't think that." She paused. "Not really. I thought it was a poor joke. Can we stop talking about it?"

"Okay, but I am curious about one thing."

"Yes?"

"Why, in all the seven years you've been in Twilight, you've never had a serious boyfriend. At least none that I've heard of."

"Stupid banner," she mumbled.

"You're like a slippery catfish," he said.

"If you're trying to flatter me, you're failing miserably. I don't fancy being called *slippery* or a *catfish*."

"Every time someone tries to pin you down, you manage to slip off the hook."

"What hook?"

"You don't talk about your past."

"Why should I? Ancient history. No one cares."

"I care."

"I don't. The past is over. No point wallowing in it."

Why couldn't he just let it go? "So there's no alternate universe where you could imagine you and me hooking up?"

"Hooking up is one thing . . ." She jerked a thumb over her shoulder at the banner. "Marriage is a whole other thing entirely."

"Because you're not the marrying kind?"

"Ding, ding." She made a motion as if she was ringing an invisible bell.

"We gotta get back inside to the baby," he said. "Tasha's got things to do—"

"Yes."

They stared at each other again, then simultaneously shifted their gazes back to the banner, their movements so smooth it felt choreographed.

Without another word passing between them, in synchronized tandem, each grabbed one side of the banner—Jana had to jump to reach—and they yanked it right down.

CHAPTER 12

THE KISS

After that awkward moment on the deck, Jana vowed to ignore her deepening feelings for Joel. Yes, she was seeing him in a whole new light, picturing him as a dad, and it was a very lovely portrait. He'd make a splendid father someday.

But it was more than that. One look at that banner, and she had really thought for one wild moment that Joel had been asking her to marry him.

Idiot.

What was wrong with her? Did she secretly want Joel to propose?

No, no, of course not. She wasn't wife material. She knew it. Accepted it. Didn't really get bothered by it . . . except . . .

There was this longing. Ever since finding Gabriel, she'd had a yearning burning deep inside her. A yearning she didn't know how to satisfy. A yearning she didn't fully understand, but it was all tied up in Joel MacGregor.

He doesn't have a girlfriend.

Joel put the wrong banner away and went back to digging through the boxes, on the hunt for the right one. Tasha left with a wave.

Gabriel whimpered, and Jana rushed to attend to him, happy for an excuse to shift her attention away from Joel. She fed the baby, cooed to him, rocked him in her arms, sang goofy Christmas songs. She might not have much experience taking care of newborns, but she was a quick study.

Gabriel seemed to like her singing this time. His little eyes didn't focus well, but at the sound of her voice, he'd turned his head toward her.

Aww! She kissed the top of his fuzzy little head and fell deeply, madly in love with him.

"You're gonna break my heart, little guy," she whispered. "I know that, but it's all worth it."

Then she looked up and caught Joel watching her, a hungry expression in his eyes filled with his own brand of yearning.

He studied her lips.

She studied his.

No, no, no. She wouldn't acknowledge these feelings he stirred inside her. Nope. Not gonna do it. The baby clouded everything. This was nothing to count on.

Her nose twitched as Joel's scent embedded into her brain. From this moment forward, she would forever equate the scent of pine and peppermint with lust. Because that was the horrible, terrible, rapturous truth.

She was *hot* for Joel, and damn if she just hadn't gone and slapped a label on it.

LEAVING GABRIEL WITH Kelsey and Noah was much harder than Jana expected. She'd been taking care of the baby for just twenty-four hours, but already he felt like an appendage.

She was getting too attached.

The second Jana and Gabriel set foot in the lobby of the Rockabye Boatel, Kelsey pounced. "Oh my gosh! Cute, cute, cute! Let me have at that baby."

Jana slipped the diaper bag off her left shoulder and let it drop onto the floor beside the reception desk. She'd brought way more supplies than the baby would need for a short stay, but she liked being prepared.

There was a roaring fire in the fireplace and a Christmas tree in every corner, each decorated in a different color. They were all real trees, and they filled the place with the scent of the holidays.

"Can I hold him?"

"Sure, but remember, he's a newborn." Jana unlatched Gabriel from the carrier.

"I'll be gentle, I promise." Kelsey kept her arms outstretched.

"Hold your hand behind his neck to support his head," Jana instructed, anxiously shifting her weight from foot to foot as she demonstrated how Kelsey should hold the baby. Joel was the one who'd shown her how to hold him. "He's like a little rag doll."

Just then Noah strolled into the room. He and Joel were identical twins, and it gave Jana a start to see the good-natured grin that matched his brother's. For a crazy second her wild heart thumped *Joel*.

"Omigosh, he feels light as a feather." Kelsey lifted the baby to her shoulder, holding him exactly as Jana had told her.

"He is really tiny."

"I can't imagine his mom leaving him at Christmas. It breaks my heart." Kelsey kissed his little cheek.

"Mine too." Jana rubbed her palms against her hips, wondering why they felt so sweaty.

"At least he's too young to know any better," Noah said. "But we're going to help you and Joel give him one heck of a holiday, aren't we, Firefly?"

Noah had given Kelsey the nickname Firefly when they'd met at grief camp the summer that they turned eleven. She'd heard Noah had gifted Kelsey with a jar of fireflies so she wouldn't feel lost and lonely in the dark in a strange place. Jana hadn't ever been nosy enough to ask if the story was true.

Kelsey and Noah exchanged loving glances so sweet it felt like an invasion of privacy to watch them.

"We should get ourselves one of these." Kelsey swayed with Gabriel in her arms.

Noah matched his wife's wide grin. "We really should."

Kelsey audibly caught her breath, and her eyes rounded. "You mean it?"

Grinning, Noah said, "It's time."

"Can we get started right away?" Kelsey giggled.

"I'm not sure now is the right time since we promised Jana that we'd keep an eye on Gabriel." Noah wrapped his arm around his wife's waist. "But tomorrow *is* Christmas Eve, and you might just get to open your present early."

Laughing, Kelsey rolled her eyes at her husband. "I didn't mean *right now* right now." To Jana she said, "What time will your shift be over?"

"Eleven," Jana said. "But Joel will be finished with his set first, so he'll be coming by to pick him up."

"You know what? That's kind of late. What if"—Kelsey turned to her husband again—"we just keep Gabriel through the night?"

Noah nodded. "Sure, sure. Great idea. Let us get in a little practice before we take the plunge. It'll give you and Joel a little breather. What do you say?"

She longed to say no. To snatch the baby back and run off with him. Geesh, why was she feeling so possessive of the kid?

Honestly, it took everything she had inside her not to cancel her shift at the Horny Toad Tavern. She only worked there once in a blue moon whenever she needed extra money. Or someone else wanted time off. That's what had happened tonight. Her friend Camilla was out of town for Christmas, and she'd promised to fill in. If she bailed, she'd put Camilla in the hot seat.

But, my stars, it was tempting to call in.

Especially since Joel was performing with the Christmas Bards at the Horny Toad. After what had happened in his kitchen and on the boat that morning, the last thing she wanted was to see him stripped bare and shaking his Magic Mike in front of other women.

She *was* jealous, but there was no way she would ever let him know that. She would keep her head down, fill drink orders, and try not to sneak peeks at him onstage. Then she could go home. *Home.*

No, not home. Back to Joel's house where they planned to spend what remained of the evening wrapping gifts for tomorrow's Christmas Eve celebrations.

"Jana?" Kelsey asked, breaking through her thoughts. "Can we keep Gabriel for you overnight?"

She'd packed enough formula, diapers, and clothing to last until morning. Damn her preparedness. Now she had no good excuse to refuse.

"Please?" Kelsey added.

"Sure." Jana tried for a laid-back smile but didn't quite pull it off. "If you're sure you're up for it."

"It'll be nice," Noah said.

"Nice," Jana echoed, but she was missing Gabriel already.

THE PARKING LOT at the Horny Toad Tavern was overflowing, so she parked on the street and walked past the long line of women snaking around the block as they waited to get in to see the show. The air buzzed with excited female voices.

Jana felt grouchy. Soon these randy women would be inside ogling the dancers.

Ogling Joel.

Disgruntled, Jana scowled and pushed her way through the crowd.

"Hey!" one woman hollered. "No cutting in line."

"I'm not cutting. I'm tending bar," Jana growled. She would have gone in through the back entrance, but a delivery truck was pulled up to the dock unloading beer kegs and blocking her way.

"Oh! Proceed, then. We'll need plenty of liquor to cool us down after the Bards heat us up." The woman laughed and fanned herself.

At the door, she discovered Brick was the bouncer on duty. He seemed quite pleased with his job of corralling a bevy of ladies. He was chatting up a couple of them, but his grin widened the minute he saw Jana.

Ugh.

"Hey, doll." He winked at her like some 1930s troglodyte and put up a hammy arm to block her way. "You working tonight?"

"I am." She forced a smile.

"Whatcha doin' after?" He leaned in closer.

She could smell the scent of his overpowering cologne. "Did you take a bath in the Paco Rabanne?"

"You remembered my signature scent." He leered. "I've been on your mind."

"You have not."

"C'mon," he said. "It's okay to admit it. You're still hot for me."

"Please remove your arm from the door so I can get by."

"If you were with me, you wouldn't have to just get by. I'd take care of you like the princess you are."

"Hey," said one of the women he'd just been talking with, "you said the same line to me."

"Sorry," Brick said, looking the opposite of apologetic. "You're nice and all, but my heart belongs to Jana."

"It does not." Jana turned to the woman. "You can have him. Be my guest. Brick, please step aside."

Brick moved his arm, but he aimed it right for her ass as she pushed past. He had a history of butt-grabbing.

"Touch me and draw back a bloody stump," Jana warned.

The two women closest to the open door gasped. Several people farther down the line giggled.

Brick threw back his head and let out a loud hoot. "God, I love your spunk. If you think a sassy mouth is a turnoff, think again. If you were my lady, I'd make good use of that mouth by—"

"But she's not your lady, is she?" Joel's voice punched a hole in the night.

Jana jerked her head up to see that Joel had stepped from inside the bar to the open doorway. He had his hand clamped around Brick's raised wrist and his face shoved just inches from the bouncer's nose.

"No," Brick squeaked.

Outside, the women were swooning at the sight of Joel, who was wearing a tuxedo that Jana knew was Velcroed on just so he could rip it off when he danced to "Pony."

And damn if her mouth didn't water. Sisters on the street weren't the only ones swooning.

"An apology is in order." Joel tightened his grip, the muscles in his fist contracting.

"I—I'm sorry for messing with your woman," Brick stammered.

"Don't apologize to me." Joel's face darkened. "To her."

"Oh." Brick dropped his gaze, shuffled his feet, and mumbled, "Sorry, Jana."

"From now on you'll keep your hands and your scummy comments to yourself, right?" Joel said smooth as steel.

"Y-yes." Brick pulled back on his wrist.

Joel held steadfast. "I'm serious. You give her one ounce of grief, and you'll be answering to me. Got it?"

Jana's heart was slamming like a rock-band drummer, and her knees were barely holding her up.

Brick nodded, still tugging against Joel's grip.

Joel released him suddenly.

Brick stumbled backward, crashing into the women who'd crowded around to watch what was happening. Amid the commotion and tittering, Joel ushered Jana through the empty bar. The sound and light crew worked on the stage as employees cleaned tables and swept the floor, preparing for the crush that was about to descend when the show began.

"You didn't have to do that," Jana said. "I can take care of myself."

"Brick was out of line."

"Some might say you were too." She tilted her chin up at him. "Charging uninvited into something that's none of your business."

"Did I violate your boundaries, Tink?"

Truth? She'd loved watching him take Brick to task, but she didn't *want* to love it because then she'd come to depend on Joel having her back, and well . . . she just didn't do dependency. People always let you down eventually. Better to never lower your guard than risk opening your heart and getting blindsided by love.

Love?

What the hell, Jana?

"Thank you," she said. "For intervening. I didn't need your help, but it was kind of you to care."

"Anytime." He lowered his head and his voice. "Just say the word and I'll be there. But in the future, I'll wait for you to ask before I insert myself into your business."

"I'd appreciate that."

His gaze swept over her body. "You look fantastic, by the way."

Huh? She was wearing holey jeans and an oversized sweater. Okay, she'd slapped on a little makeup, but there was nothing glam about her outfit.

"Jana." The main bartender waved at her from behind the bar. "Could you mull the cranberries? Cranberry Sauce Margarita Martinis are on special tonight. We're gonna be slammed."

"I saw the line," Jana called to her. "Be right there."

"We cool?" Joel asked.

"We cool. Go get ready to do your thang, tall man." She patted his chest.

Oops. Bad idea.

Instant sparks volleyed through her palm, hit her bloodstream like scattershot, pelting her with heated waves of erotic tension.

"Pony boy!" called one of Joel's fellow dancers from the doorway of the dressing room just off the bar. "Saddle up, it's time to ride. Group huddle before the games begin."

Joel waved off his friend, his gaze locked on Jana. "I'll see you back home when this is over. I can pick up Gabriel. I'll be out of here before you."

"Kelsey and Noah asked to keep him for the night."

"Really?" Joel looked surprised.

"Apparently they're ready to become parents and want a trial run."

"And you're good with that."

"I wouldn't say *good*, but I did agree."

"Wow." He whistled.

"Feeling intimidated your twin is thinking of procreating?" she asked.

"No."

"Why are the tops of your ears turning red?"

"They're not." Joel cupped his hands over his ears.

"You're embarrassed." Jana laughed.

"Maybe," he said, wriggling his eyebrows suggestively. "But not for the reason you think."

"What reason?" She eyed him suspiciously. Joel, when the mood struck him, could be a prankster. What did he have up his sleeve?

"We're going to have my house all to ourselves."

Oh crap. They would.

Panic seized Jana then. Closed her throat right up.

"Hey, MacGregor. Chop, chop. We're waiting!" Joel's fellow bard, a guy named Magnus, called again.

Joel swept a heated gaze over Jana's body, and his grin gobbled her up. "Can't wait to get you alone."

"Why?" she asked, scared stiff by the hope and fire rolling through her veins.

"So we can have time to talk undisturbed."

"Talk about what?"

"This upcoming week. Coordinate our schedules, plan the

prep work . . ." He paused, his eyes lit up from the Christmas twinkle lights overhead, and he lowered his voice and added, "Our relationship."

Jana gulped, her pulse thundering so loudly in her ears she couldn't think, much less form a cohesive response.

"MacGregor!" Magnus barked.

Brick was letting women enter, and they surged into the room, bringing the electric buzz with them.

"I gotta go," Joel said. "We'll talk later."

"Shoo." Jana waved him away as if the idea didn't strike terror in her heart. "I'm off to mull cranberries."

Joel grinned and then did the darndest thing. He leaned down and softly kissed the top of her head as if she was as cute and helpless as Gabriel.

Chapter 13

The Grind

Joel waited with the six other dancers in the storage room that doubled as the Christmas Bards' dressing room, his mind exploding with a billion unwanted thoughts. He should be focused on the dance moves ahead of him, not obsessing over Jana. There was time for that later. Now, he had a job to do. A charity to fund.

A striptease to perform.

Why the hell had he kissed her on top of her head as if she were one of his dogs? She must be feeling weird about that. He sure was.

If he was going to kiss her—which he shouldn't have, not in a noisy bar with everyone watching—he should have kissed her on those sassy, sweet lips.

Hells bells, MacGregor, you sound like that creepy bouncer.

His damn brains had left his skull and slunk straight down to his penis. Being in proximity to Jana, and yet having to keep his desires to himself for fear of chasing her away, was pure torture. He was a complete failure as a trustworthy friend.

The Bards were lined up at the door, Joel bringing up the rear.

As the tallest, he would enter last and take center stage, flanked on each side by three other men dressed in breakaway tuxedos just as he was, all biting a single red rose between their teeth.

From the bar came the sound of the warm-up music and the loud chants of "Bring on the Bards!" accompanied by feet-stomping, hand-clapping fervor.

Stage fright took hold of him, squeezing his stomach flat. He'd been here before and knew it would pass as soon as he was in front of the audience.

But tell that to his bladder.

He cast a glance at the adjoining bathroom. The first dancer was preparing to leave the room, clenching the thornless rose between his teeth, slanting his top hat at a rakish angle, straightening his tie. Each solo number lasted ninety seconds before the next dancer joined the stage for his spin. Joel had exactly nine minutes to take care of business.

Quickly, he darted into the restroom.

And that's when he discovered the stitching on his black sequined G-string was hanging by a thread.

Spptt!

Jana was pouring mulled cranberries into the martini glasses lined up in front of her as the music swelled. "Santa Claus Wants Some Lovin'" played as she struggled to ignore her Lamborghini pulse that had taken off at top speed the second Joel kissed her, and hadn't slowed since. The top of her head still burned from the pressure of his lips. How was that even possible?

Obsessing. She was obsessed with him.

Spptt.

The place was rocking. Women catcalling and clapping, standing on tabletops and shouting, "Bring on the Bards!"

The DJ turned up the volume on the song, an indication that the first dancer was about to burst onto the stage.

Jana could feel the sexual tension building.

Spptt.

Finally, it dawned on her someone was trying to get her attention. She set down the pitcher filled with pulverized red berries, turned toward the sound, and saw . . .

Joel.

Peeking at her from the door of the dressing room, looking panicky and motioning to her with a frantic finger.

Hmm. What was up? She dried her hands on her apron.

"Bring your purse," he hissed.

Umm, okay. She reached under the counter for her handbag, motioned to the other bartender that she'd be right back, and headed over to Joel. The crowd and music were vibrating so loudly the noise could shake loose fillings.

She went to the door. "What is it—"

But she didn't get to finish the question. Joel grabbed her by the wrist and yanked her inside the dressing room.

She stood blinking and, okay, gaping at the seven tuxedo-clad, muscular men, the air filled with the collective scent of their Christmassy colognes.

"You got a needle and thread in your purse?" Joel asked.

"Lucky for you, big guy, that I like to be prepared." She waved her oversized handbag in his face.

"Great. Perfect. Come with me." Still holding on to her hand, he dragged her toward the bathroom.

"What about us?" Magnus, the first dancer, asked as he peeked out. "The crowd is going insane. I don't think we can put them off much longer."

Joel stopped and looked at Jana. "How fast can you sew?"

"Depends on what I'm sewing."

"A couple of basting stitches."

"Bring on the Bards! Bring on the Bards!"

"A minute or two?" Jana hazarded a guess.

"That should be plenty of time. Hit it, Magnus." Joel waved at the first dancer.

Magnus burst through the door and onto the stage as Joel yanked Jana into the bathroom and shut the door behind them.

"What's going on?" she asked.

"My G-string broke."

"Why don't you just change?"

"No time and no spare G-string."

"Seriously? You didn't bring an extra?"

"Color me stupid."

"Not stupid, just . . ."

"What?" he prompted.

"Too much of an optimist."

"Is there such a thing?"

Yes, absolutely, and he was it.

"We have exactly nine minutes to get 'er done before I have to be out there."

"So no pressure, right?" Jana pried open her purse and went right to the sewing kit. She wasn't one of those women who just tossed things into their handbag randomly. She was a *place for everything and everything in its place* kind of gal.

"Thank you, thank you, thank you. You're an angel."

"Not quite." As she pulled out the needle and thread, Joel leaned over and switched the lock on the bathroom door.

Sealing them inside.

Alone.

Together.

And he was ripping off his Velcro trousers.

Yikes!

Ducking her head, she closed the toilet lid and sat down. Concentrating on threading the needle as fast as she could, she heard the clock inside her head ticking off the seconds.

"Santa Claus Wants Some Lovin'" shook the walls. The bathroom seemed impossibly small.

Joel held the ends of the glittery black G-string clutched in his hands. He was practically naked in front of her, except for the

tuxedo top and the unraveling banana hammock barely camouflaging his junk.

She struggled not to notice.

"Hurry," he urged.

"I'm trying. It's hard to hit the hole."

"Title of your sex tape?" he teased.

"Title of *your* sex tape." Despite her anxiety, Jana laughed
and looked up at him.

He was staring down at her with heat in his eyes.

Way too hot to handle.

Quickly, she dropped her gaze to the garment in need of
sewing. *Holy Root Chakra!* She was going to have to rest her
hand on his bare thigh to get the job done.

He shifted, presenting her with his left hip where the G-string
was coming undone. He could be an artist's human-form model.
No joke.

Gulping, Jana leaned forward. Great. She must look wildly
attractive sitting on a toilet. *Never mind that. Sew.*

Joel's sexy bare skin was right in front of her. His masculine
fingers holding the skimpy material, waiting for her to stitch.

Tick tock.

She took a deep breath. Rested the side of her palm on his hip
bone.

He inhaled sharply.

She exhaled.

He squirmed. "That tickles."

"What?"

"Your breath against my skin."

"Oh," she said. "I'll hold my breath."

"Don't pass out."

She wasn't making any promises. Not when his sequin-sheathed
penis was in touching distance of her pinky. Good grief. How had
she ended up here?

"Tink?"

"Uh-huh?"

"You okay?" His tone was light, jokey, but she took it seriously. Absolutely not. She was *not* okay.

The music changed. "Sassy Sexy Wiggle." A door slammed. The second dancer had gone out onstage.

"Hurry," Joel urged again.

Her hands were sweaty and yet at the same time felt frozen. The beautiful gluteus medius muscle in front of her—she hadn't gone to college, but she'd had a bit of anatomy in her yoga teacher-training classes—twitched. Yeah, he was nervous too.

Just do it.

She plunged the needle into one end of the fabric, made a quick anchoring stitch, and zipped over to poke the opposite side.

Her naughty gaze had a mind of its own and drifted to the left. Was it her imagination, or was he getting a . . .

Jana jerked her gaze back where it belonged. On the sewing.

"Sorry," he whispered.

She didn't ask what he was sorry about, but she inched her hand as far away from his crotch as she could get while still being able to sew. She pulled the ends of the material together with the knotted thread.

"Sassy Sexy Wiggle" turned into "You Can Leave Your Hat On." Another door slam. The third dancer gone.

"Got it?" he asked.

"I need to add a few more stitches," she said, wishing she could just run away. "This sewing kit has been in my purse for ages. I don't know how reliable the thread is at this point."

"Great, great, great." His hand that was still holding on to the G-string was so tense his veins at his wrist bulged.

Oh yeah, he was nervous too.

"You can let go," she said, her voice coming out way too high, as if a bee had stung her while she was singing.

He moved his hand. She didn't look around to see what he did with it. She lasered in on her task, weaving the threaded needle in and out, in and out.

A fourth song change. Another door slam.

Why did it feel as if she was moving in slow motion? Sweat popped out on her brow and rolled down the bridge of her nose.

One last stitch. A knot tied. Where were those sewing scissors?

"You done?"

"I just have to clip the thread." The sewing kit was in her lap, but she couldn't find the scissors. They'd been in the kit, but now she couldn't find them!

A fifth song change.

A knock on the bathroom door. "Joel? You gonna make it?"

"Be right there!" Joel called out to his fellow bard.

"Do you see the scissors?" Jana asked, pushing her hair out of her way so she could get a good look at the bathroom floor. The scissors must have slipped off her lap.

"No, but hurry, please."

Tick tock.

The scissors had vanished.

"Screw it," Jana said, leaned in, and pressed her lips against his newly sewn G-string and the bare skin beneath.

"What are you doing?" He rested his hand on her head.

With the smell of his hot, masculine body in her nose, she bit the thread, severing the cotton strand with her teeth. It felt wild having her mouth on him in such a compromising spot. Every nerve ending in her body was burning and jumping.

She glanced up, the needle and thread dangling triumphantly over her bottom lip.

"Dang, woman," he said. "You're one helluva badass."

She jumped up. Stowed the needle. Found the scissors. She'd been sitting on them, and in her overheated emotional state hadn't even realized it. She could kiss him right now.

Just roll forward on the balls of her feet, go up on her tiptoes, and . . . if he didn't lower his head, she'd end up kissing his chin. Not a smart plan. Not with the tock clicking. Tock clicking? She was losing her ever-loving mind.

Ack! So out of control. She hated losing control.

"I'll leave you to it." She spun on her heels, desperate to get out of that bathroom.

"Jana, wait."

Schooling her features to hide her panic, she threw him a quick glance over her shoulder. Joel stood there looking deadly earnest in that faux tuxedo.

"Yes?"

"Thank you," he said. "You saved my life."

And just destroyed her own.

She snorted. Being tough, righting the world. Waved him off and zoomed straight back to the bar.

The customers were lined up for drinks. The other bartender shot her a scowl.

Apologizing, Jana put her mixology skills to work. Wonderful distraction. Especially when the DJ cued "Pony" and out came Joel.

He was slinking across the stage in his long-legged stride. The audience let out a heated, collective moan.

Don't watch, don't watch.

She watched.

He oozed up to the mic and started reciting to the rap poetry that the Bards had written. Sexually explicit lyrics.

Jana was no prude, but she felt her cheeks flame hot.

He bumped. He grinded. He rapped.

Just minutes ago she'd been up close and personal with that hot male body, her teeth actually pressed against his skin. Her blood was lava, rolling through her veins like liquid fire.

The cheers and catcalls were deafening, drowning out the music. Jana darted a sidelong glance at the stage and . . .

Holy Eyeball Chakra!

Joel ripped off his top, revealing washboard abs so taut you could seriously do laundry on them. Soaping and slipping, rubbing and scrubbing.

Her mouth watered. Her skin felt flayed. And below the waist? Twinges. Urges. Needs. She tingled and ached and burned. Fully charged and ready to rock.

Joel executed more sexy striptease moves that had the crowd going completely insane. Jealousy was a missile, exploding inside her. She wanted to snatch every single one of those overheated females bald-headed for lusting after her man.

Her man?

Oh, what fresh torture was this? Her own mind was turning on her. Thinking things that she should not be thinking. Lusty, hungry things.

Joel had missed his calling. Seriously. He could outdance Channing Tatum. Then he did a spectacular twirl, jumped back, and shook his booty for all he was worth.

Her heart pounded in her throat. *Boom-chicka-boom-chicka-boom.*

He leaped back around to face the audience again, yanked off those shiny Velcroed trousers, wiggled and jiggled. The black sequined G-string catching the spotlight and drawing every eye in the place to Joel's impressive package.

There was much gasping, some of it from her.

One more fine maneuver. One more loose hip swivel and . . .

Her hurried stitches didn't hold.

The G-string fell right off his magnificent body and hit the floor, showing Joel in all his resplendent glory.

The entire room gasped.

In that moment, Jana saw *exactly* what she'd been missing.

Chapter 14

The Escape

Joel stared down at the text on his cell phone.

> Since Gabriel is with Noah and Kelsey, I'm spending the night @ my house.

Simple. To the point. Jana was on the run.
Dammit.
Dressed in jeans and a burnt orange University of Texas sweatshirt, Joel stared down at his cell phone feeling lonelier than a hound dog howling up the wrong tree. So much for the romantic fantasies he'd been building in his head after Jana had sewn up his G-string in the bathroom. He'd thought maybe she was starting to trust him.

Stupid wardrobe malfunction.

"Hey." Magnus clamped a hand on Joel's shoulder in the dressing room. "After that performance, we gotta change your song from 'Pony' to 'Horse.'"

"Or," said one of the other Bards, a guy who went by the nickname Duke, who delighted in imitating John Wayne, "'Save a Horse, Ride a Cowboy.'"

Magnus hummed the tune, did a little bump and grind. "Yeah. That'd work."

"That way we could get *his* action." Duke snorted a laugh.

Magnus made clip-clopping noises and pranced around the room like he was riding a stick pony.

Joel expected the ribbing, but it didn't make it any less humiliating. Especially with the text message on his phone. Jana had gotten a good look at him buck naked, and she was running.

Just when things had started to get good between them.

Don't accept this. Go after her.

He thumbed his phone, and texted U planning on coming back? Joel waited.

No immediate response.

He wanted to march into the bar and ask what was going on, but the place was still packed with adoring women. He didn't want to run *that* gauntlet. Shuddering at the thought, he took his jacket off the coatrack, jammed his arms into the sleeves. Besides, he had a much better idea.

"Where you going?" Magnus asked. "We're supposed to sign autographs."

"I've got something else to do."

Duke opened the door and peeked out. "No one's leaving, Pilgrim. There's a string of women waiting at the bar, eyes trained on this door, and after your performance, Horse, I'm guessing most of them are staying for you."

"You guys handle it," Joel said. "I'm slipping out the back way. Cover for me."

"Yee-haw," Duke said. "I'm not too proud to take your leavings, pardner."

"What do we tell them?" Magnus asked.

"'Save a Horse, Ride a Cowboy.'" Duke laughed. "My new motto."

New text from Jana. Not tonight.

Ok, he texted back and added the sunglasses-wearing emoji as if that could make him cool.

Yeah, because it *wasn't* okay. Not at all. Whenever things got tricky, Jana ran. He wasn't going to let her get away with it.

Not this time.

Settling a baseball cap on his head and turning up his collar as if he could actually hide in a crowd with his six-foot-five height, Joel stuck his phone in his pocket and left the building.

RELIEVED TO DISCOVER that Joel had slipped out the back and wouldn't be hanging around signing autographs—or cleavage, the way Duke was doing right now—Jana felt her shoulders relax for the first time since she'd come into the bar.

She needed space.

And not just because Joel's G-string had popped off during his number, although that was a factor. She had to get control of her runaway lust before seeing him again. Starting tomorrow, they still had eight more days together taking care of Gabriel.

After that, they would go their semiseparate ways. But here was the question: Could she keep her hands to herself for the next eight days?

Um, why do you even want to? Seriously, did you not see his—Jana slapped her palm to her forehead. She had to stop this. *Excuse me. Knock, knock. Why?*

Nope. She wasn't entertaining this conversation with her baser self. Not doing it. She had one goal tonight. Home. Hot bath. Herbal tea. Her own bed.

Alone.

Lonely.

Lonely was her middle name. Her oldest friend.

Ack. No. Shut up.

Determined, she shoved aside her inner monologue and gave her full attention to the customers. *Shush it, monkey mind.*

Her shift ended at eleven, and by the time she left the bar, she was starving and added *hot meal* to her checklist.

She turned down her street, her spirits soaring at the sight of

her house but then swiftly careening to her feet when she spied
Joel's pickup truck parked at the curb.

Keep driving!

Don't you dare!

Bully!

Coward!

Monkey mind was off the chain, scampering madly from
perch to perch. But she was in charge. Not her fears. Not her
insecurities. And certainly not her lust. This was her house. She
lived here. She was going inside.

She pulled into the driveway and got out of the Jeep. Why
was her pulse going nuts? What was happening to her? She was
usually so good at tempering her expectations. But there was
chemistry between them and, if she was being honest, there
always had been. Back burner, Low on simmer. Something she
could ignore.

Apparently, not anymore.

Somehow the dial had gotten turned on High, and that soft
simmer had turned into a rolling boil.

The sound of her boots striking the sidewalk rang out into the
night. She could hear her own breathing. Too shallow. Too fast.
Hyperventilation was a real possibility.

In the light from the streetlamp and the glow from her neighbors' Christmas lights, she could see him sitting on the top step
of her porch, his long legs extended out over the other two steps,
his heels planted on the sidewalk. On his head, he wore a Santa
cap with a jingle bell attached to the end and cocked at a dapper
angle.

A covered stoneware Dutch oven rested across his muscular
thighs. Thighs she had been oh-so-near not so long ago.

"Nice hat," she said.

"Thanks." He tossed his head as if he were an arrogant sham-
poo spokesperson deeply proud of his hair. The bell at the end of
his cap jumped and jangled.

She suppressed a smile. No sense encouraging him. She was sending him straight home because she wanted to do the exact opposite—invite him in and beg him to stay. "What are you doing here?"

He tapped the lid of the pot. "I nuked the mulligan stew that I froze the other day. It's cold now, but we can reheat."

"We?"

"As in you and me."

"Why are you here, Joel?"

"To find out why you ran away."

"I needed to come home and check on things."

"Pinocchio."

"Fine. I thought you'd get the hint that I wanted to be alone."

"No."

"What do you mean *no*?"

"You might *think* you want to be alone," he said. "But you really don't."

"Oh, so now you know what I want."

"Right now?" His gaze flickered to her lips. "Yeah, I think I do."

"Because you know me so well?"

"No," he said. "Despite being acquainted with you for seven years, including two of those years working with you, I barely know you at all, Jana. But *nobody* wants to be alone on Christmas Eve."

"It's not Christmas Eve."

"Check the time. I believe it's close to midnight. Soon it'll be officially Christmas Eve."

"It's not *Christmas Eve* Christmas Eve."

"You're running away. Scared of your feelings."

Well, duh.

"You couldn't handle staying at my place without Gabriel as a buffer."

"And yet, knowing that, you show up here anyway."

"That's because I want to help. Withdrawing isn't the answer."

She arched an eyebrow and laced her voice with sarcasm. "What is the answer?"

His gaze snapped onto hers like a bear trap, and she wished like hell she hadn't asked the question. "Connection."

She wanted to rush past him, flee into her house, and slam and lock the door behind her. Shutting him out. Shutting out her feelings.

"Good night, Joel." She injected iron into her voice, but the iron was rusty.

"Seriously? You're not going to invite me in? Aren't you the least bit curious how the vegan mulligan stew turned out?"

She was starving. She hadn't eaten since the cinnamon rolls that morning, and Joel looked so endearingly sweet. Besides— and here was the tricky part—she wanted him to come inside. More than anything.

"Okay, then, you're right. You said no. I'll respect that and go. I don't want to be pushy or talk you into something that makes you uncomfortable." He slapped a palm on the porch railing as if about to lever himself up.

"Wait. Where are you going?"

"You asked me to leave, and I'm leaving."

"Um . . . I might have been too hasty."

"Oh?" He looked so hopeful it was comical.

"I *am* starving." *Oh, you weak, weak woman.* "C'mon in."

He laughed like a kid who'd just been told he was going to Disneyland. "Um, could you help me up? My butt's gone to sleep."

Remembering exactly how fine his butt was, Jana shivered. "I'll take the stew. You can boost yourself up."

He curled the pot against his body. "I don't trust you not to take the stew and lock me out in the cold."

"It did cross my mind," she admitted as if she was a badass, but in reality, she was a total marshmallow who couldn't stick by her guns.

"I know." He grinned.

She put out a hand.

He took it.

Snap. Sizzle.

She pulled him to his feet. Tried to drop her hand.

He held on.

She glowered.

He grinned and finally let go.

Seconds later, they were in her foyer, kicking past packages and holiday-card envelopes on the floor that friends and neighbors had slipped through the doggy door. She really should get a new door since she didn't own a dog. If she ever did get a pet, it'd be a cat. She much preferred cats and their cool aloofness over dogs and their goofy friendliness.

Hey, that's you and Joel. Cats and dogs.

"Wow," Joel said, glancing around the floor and sending that irritating hat to jingling again. "That's a lot of Christmas presents and cards."

"I know a lot of people."

"And you think you don't belong here?" He clicked his tongue.

"I never said that." She took off her coat and hung it on the coatrack, stepping over the packages.

"No, but your behavior does."

"What are you talking about?" She was truly perplexed. She'd lived in Twilight longer than she'd ever lived in any one place.

"I get the impression you don't feel like you belong anywhere."

"I really don't know what you mean. I'm in the big middle of this community. I go to almost every flipping event this town holds, and they hold a lot of them. I volunteer. My work takes me into the public. I'm not some recluse."

"And yet, you never really connect with anyone. You're hiding in plain sight."

"All right," she said, tossing her keys on the foyer table. "I need your definition of *connection*."

"Letting your guard down. Letting people in. Letting yourself be vulnerable. Sharing a secret or two. Trusting people to have your best interest at heart."

"Yeah, okay. Maybe you're right. If being *connected* means blabbing about all your past mistakes and sorrows to everyone you meet, then I'm not connected."

"Not to everyone you meet," he said. "Just to the people you'd like to get close to. The people who want to get close to you."

"I'm close to tons of people." She waved at the packages and cards. "Proof!"

"Yes, but do any of them know the *real* you?"

No. Not fully. She was too scarred by the past to ever really let down her guard with anyone, but she *was* getting better about sharing. At least the small things. No one in this town knew her ugly secrets, and she liked it that way. She wouldn't allow Joel to goad her into spilling her guts about things that were none of his business.

"Here," she said, reaching for the pot. "Hang up your coat. I'll go turn up the heat and warm the stew."

He passed her the pot and that Disneyland grin again.

Now, that's what turned up the heat. Suddenly, she was hot and sweaty beneath his sultry gaze.

Gulping, she hurried to the kitchen, put the pot on the gas stove to simmer, and went into the living area to dial up the heater. Joel was retrieving packages from the hallway and stacking them in the corner of the room.

"This is where you'd put them if you had a tree," he said.

"Yes, MacSanta."

"Ooh!" He picked up one of the boxes that came from the Twilight Bakery. "Looks like we've got dessert."

"Who sent it?"

He peeked at the label. "Sesty."

Jana had worked for Sesty, a professional party planner, a few years back before Sesty married former NASCAR-driver Josh Langtree, had children, and went part-time. Jana's work experience with Sesty was what had spurred her to start Jana-of-All-Trades.

"What do you suppose Sesty sent?"

"It's your package." He thrust the box at her. "You open it."

"Fine." She took the box into the kitchen, grabbed a pair of shears, and cut through the wrapping. "Vegan kismet cookies! Yum. Sesty is so sweet, but I didn't get her anything. What's she going to think?"

"I'm sure Sesty gave you cookies because she wanted to give you cookies, not because she expected a gift in return," Joel said in an attempt to soothe her.

"I meant to get her something, but we found Gabriel, and everything flew right out of my head. Oh crap, I've even got presents I need to wrap for tomorrow. Oh gosh, I'm not going to get a wink of sleep."

"Everything will work out. Don't worry so much. I'll help you wrap them."

She threw him a dirty look. "Don't tell me how to be."

He held up his palms. "Poor word choice. I don't mean to minimize your feelings. I've just noticed you have a tendency to borrow trouble."

She narrowed her gaze at him. "What's that supposed to mean?"

"When you go looking for problems, you'll find them, whether there are any real problems or not."

"Said by someone with a head-in-the-sand approach to life." She moved to the cabinet and took down two soup bowls.

"Excuse me?"

"If I maximize problems, you minimize them. I know it's partly a product of growing up in a town like Twilight, but sometimes your optimism flies in the face of reality."

"Can you give me an example?" He seemed truly nonplussed that his relentless confidence could ever be problematic.

"How about tonight?"

"What about it?"

"You assumed I could sew."

"You had a sewing kit."

"That doesn't mean I'm a seamstress. You assumed I could sew, and because of your optimism in me, you ended up bare-ass naked in front of a hundred screaming fans."

"I'm not seeing that as a disadvantage. Embarrassing sure, but the audience got their money's worth. Magnus texted me that donations skyrocketed after my oops, so the ALS Association owes a debt of gratitude to your lack of sewing skills."

"See? That's really annoying. Taking those lemons and making lemonade. Only problem? Newsflash: not everyone likes lemonade."

He chuckled.

Jana was just being contrary at this point. She knew it, and so did he. She took the lid off the pot, turned down the heat, and started ladling out stew.

"You could have been a spy."

"What?"

"You would have made a fabulous CIA operative."

"With these tats?"

"Ink aside, you've got all the attributes. You're inquisitive, action-oriented, and closemouthed."

"I don't know whether to feel flattered or insulted."

"Neither. You are who you are. I hoped you'd feel seen."

"By you?"

"I'm the only one here."

"What do you want from me, Joel?" She sighed.

"You know," he drawled, "when I was in college, I took a course in Greek mythology, and we read a fable that reminds me of you—"

"*You* took Greek mythology?"

"I did."

She canted her head, ran the tip of her tongue along her bottom lip. "You don't seem the Greek-mythology type."

He shrugged and tossed the tail of the Santa hat over his shoulder. Jingle all the way. "I thought it'd be an easy A."

"Was it?"

"No."

"What did you learn from that experience?"

"Don't make assumptions?" he said.

"I dunno." She shrugged. "It's your lesson. I wasn't giving you a moral imperative. Only you can decide what you got out of it."

"Still seems you were angling for a theme."

"That's for you to figure out. So about this fable that reminds you of me . . ." She settled the bowls onto the saucers. She handed one of them to him, and took her bowl to the table.

He joined her. "It's the story of newlyweds Orpheus and Eurydice."

"Um." She blew across a spoonful of stew to cool it. "Which one am I? Orpheus or Eurydice?"

"Listen to the story, and you'll figure it out." His eyes darkened.

Her nipples got hard. *Oh shit.*

"Orpheus and Eurydice were truly, madly, deeply in love, but soon after their wedding, Eurydice was bitten by a poisonous snake and died."

"What kind of snake?"

"I don't know. It doesn't matter. She's dead."

"How sad."

"Devastated by his grief, Orpheus descends to the underworld to bring her back."

"Little far-fetched," Jana said, "but go on."

"It's a myth. Roll with it."

Gingerly, she took a bite of stew, got a tangy taste of rosemary, thyme, tomato sauce, and stewed veggies. "OMG, so good! And you added lima beans! My fave."

"I know. I'm glad you like it."

"Anyway, back to your story." She waved her spoon. "Orpheus goes looking for his dead wife and . . ."

"He goes through many trials and challenges to rescue her. From his pure heart, he finally convinces Hades, the king of the underworld, to let his beloved go. But there's a catch."

"Isn't there always?" She was getting interested in the story now.

"Hades tells Orpheus he can have her, but he must lead Eurydice to the land of the living without looking back at her."

"Yikes. Is she a zombie? I bet she's a zombie."

Joel laughed so hard he banged his leg into the table. "Orpheus did exactly the same thing you're doing. He started obsessing."

"Ah, so I'm Orpheus."

"The doubtful thoughts circle his brain. Orpheus wonders if Eurydice is even behind him. Has Hades tricked him?"

"Yeah, by sending him off with a zombie wife." Jana took another bite of stew and gave a low moan of pleasure.

"You slay me, Tink." Joel held his belly as his body shook with laughter.

"Well, don't die, because I'm not going to the underworld to fetch you. Let's be clear on that."

"Orpheus and Eurydice are almost back to the land of the living. Orpheus can see the light. It's just right there. All he has to do is keep facing forward."

A chill chased through Jana, and she sat down her spoon. "Orpheus is gonna blow it, isn't he?"

"He's plagued with doubt. Overrun by uncertainty. His feelings are running away with him. He can't stop wondering if she is there."

Jana covered her mouth with both palms.

"Orpheus can't stand it a second longer. He *must* look back. He turns, and there's his beautiful—"

"Zombie wife!"

"No! She's not a zombie. She smiles, extends her hand to him, tells him she loves him. He reaches for her—"

"And she eats his brains?"

Joel gasped, unable to stop laughing. "No . . . no . . . he's already rotted his brains with obsessive worrying."

"So what happens?"

"Eurydice vanishes right before his eyes, forever consigned to the underworld because he could not control his suspicious fears."

"Well," Jana said, "that story truly sucks."

"Yes." Joel's laughter ebbed and his gaze latched on to hers. "Orpheus battled the monster of grim prospects, and Tink, my love, it's the exact same thing I've watched you battle."

"What battle is that?"

"Nursing your fears in an attempt to stay safe versus letting go of those fears so you can find your heart's desire."

CHAPTER 15

THE MIRROR

Tink, my love.

The look in Joel's eyes set off bottle rockets and Roman candles and cherry bombs spinning and sparking inside Jana. Her nerve endings came alive, jiggling and wiggling, tingling and twitching.

Not knowing how to handle it, she pretended she needed to use the bathroom and darted from the kitchen with that mumbled excuse.

She shut and locked the bathroom door and sank against it with her hands clasped behind her back, listening to her heart pound out a crazy little drumbeat.

He'd nailed her with that story about distrustful Orpheus. *Hard.* So hard that her knees were shaking.

The last words he'd spoken before she'd zoomed from the room were at the core of her inner conflict. Because of the turbulent life she'd led before coming to Twilight, she had a hard time trusting. But she was never going to find the safety she cherished unless she took a risk. And that meant she could be betrayed, which sent her on the spiral again.

She had to trust someone. Trust someone fully. Show her true self, warts and all.

And this someone was sitting in her kitchen eating the vegan stew he'd made just for her. Joel had been completely vulnerable in front of her tonight. He put himself out there again and again. He was interested in her. Of that she had no doubt, and she was interested in him too.

But, but, but . . .

She let out her breath through pursed lips, raised her head, and caught sight of herself in the oval mirror mounted over the sink. Her breath stilled in her lungs. Who was this woman in the reflection?

What the hell was happening to her?

She was turning into someone she didn't recognize. If she kept going down this path, playing house with Joel and the baby, where was she going to end up? Who did she want to be? The woman who kept everyone at arm's length to keep her heart safe, or the woman who let people in and risked everything for love?

In equal parts terrified and mesmerized, she stared down her effigy. If she chose the latter option, what would she have to sacrifice for love? The answer came to her in bright neon letters. The thing she treasured most.

Freedom.

But to quote an old song, freedom was just another word for nothing left to lose. Freedom had been her comfort for so many years because it was all she had. Now she had the possibility of so much more.

Enough excuses. She'd been running from her past long enough. The only way to get over it was to face it, and who better to face it with than Joel?

She moved to the mirror, stared herself down, and whispered, "Aren't you tired of running?"

Yes. Yes, she was.

Then, do something about it. Go out there and tell Joel you need his help to get over your fears. Tell him the truth. Tell him everything.

Her stomach roiled, and she pressed her palm flat against her belly. No, she couldn't handle that. Too much. Too soon.

You've been friends with him for two years.

Yes, but it was two years that she'd thought he had a girl-friend. The idea that they could become a couple was a startlingly new one.

This is it. The time was now. If she wanted to explore these fresh feelings churning inside her before he found another girl-friend, she had to make a move.

Yipes!

What if she had read him all wrong? What if she was imagining feelings on his side that weren't there? She'd done *that* before, and it hadn't been fun.

Tink, my love.

C'mon. If he wasn't interested, would he have said *that*? Would he have kissed her in the bar?

He kissed the top of your head, numbskull. Not exactly romantic.

She put her hand to her head where his lips had touched. This was the beginning. They could take their relationship to a whole new plane. He'd left the ball in her court. Now all she had to do was hit it back.

One step.

That's all it took.

One step in his direction, and she might find the happiness she'd never dared dream could be hers.

All she had to do was face her fears.

Yeah, as easy-peasy as Orpheus not looking back.

BY THE TIME Jana came back into the room, Joel had put the leftover stew in the fridge, cleaned off the table, and washed the dishes.

He turned from the sink and saw her standing there, her

gaze fixed on him, looking more beautiful than he'd ever seen her look. She wasn't wearing anything special, just jeans and a sweater, but the way the light hit her hair, the softness in her eyes, took his breath away.

"Hey," he whispered.

"Hey," she replied.

"Did you say you had packages to wrap tonight?"

"I did." She let out a soft sigh.

He cocked an eyebrow. "Want some help?"

"I've got it."

"It'll take half the time if you let me pitch in." He knew she would say no. While Jana loved helping others, she was pretty proud, and it wasn't easy to convince her that sometimes she needed help too.

She paused and then slowly nodded.

"Really?" He was surprised. Delightfully so.

"Sure, if you want to spend the next hour wrapping my gifts, who am I to deny you the thrill?"

"Wow, I was sure you'd say no."

"I decided maybe you were right. Maybe it was time I started trusting people to have my back."

"Hot dog!" He did a humorous jig around her kitchen that got her laughing.

"Simmer down, MacGregor. It's too late at night for shenanigans." She shook her head with a smile. "I'll go get the gifts from my bedroom if you'll fetch the wrapping paper, scissors, and tape from the hall closet."

He saluted her. "On it! I'll bring the kismet cookies."

"There's a bottle of red wine someone gifted me on the counter next to the fridge, if you want to open that too."

Wine and cookies with Jana. Hells to the yeah. He was on that like butter on toast. With his heart thumping faster than it should, he assembled everything in the living room and leaped up to help her when she came from the bedroom with arms stacked with presents.

They sat cross-legged on the floor, wine and cookies on the nearby coffee table, the gifts and wrapping supplies a divider between them. For several minutes they sipped wine and munched cookies and wrapped presents.

It was nice. Really nice. They had an easy comradery.

They chatted about the upcoming float parade and little Gabriel. Jana confessed she'd texted Kelsey several times throughout the evening checking on him.

"I think I was driving her crazy," Jana admitted. "She finally told me at ten o'clock that they were going to bed, and she'd see us tomorrow. Although, to be honest, I was kind of rattled after your costume fell off, and I needed something to ground me."

"No kidding?" Joel studied her lips. Damn she had beautiful lips. "*I* rattled *you*?"

"Don't pretend you don't know the effect you have on women."

"I don't care about *women*," he said. "I care about *you*."

"You rocked me to my core, dude."

"Why didn't you say so?"

"I just did."

He wanted to kiss her so badly he could already taste her lips, but he couldn't get a read on her. What did she want?

"Hand me the tape." She held out her hand.

He put the roll of Scotch tape in her palm, and she closed her fingers around the dispenser. He didn't let go.

She tugged.

He held on and pinned her with his gaze. "Jana?"

"Uh-huh?" She darted out the tip of her tongue and moistened her lips.

Kiss her, kiss her, kiss her.

"I enjoy being with you like this."

She sucked in her breath and said in a murmur so low he could barely hear her, "I enjoy being with you too."

"Having the baby around has opened my eyes."

"To what?" she whispered.

"Possibilities."

"Possibilities?"

"You and me . . ."

"What?"

He gulped, treading lightly. She got spooked easily. "Dating. After this is over, I mean."

"Mmm," she said, noncommittally. "We'll see."

Well, what did he expect? One intimate moment in a dressing-room bathroom did not a romance make.

She dropped her gaze, taped up the present she'd been wrapping, and reached for another gift from the pile.

"I'm spooking you."

"No, no." She raised her head and met his stare again, unflinching now. "I'm just . . . I need time."

"Take all the time you need," he said. "I'm not going anywhere."

He watched a flicker of emotion move across her eyes, but he wasn't sure what he saw. Trepidation? Hope? Wariness? Longing? A mix of all? Or was he just projecting his feelings onto her?

His arms ached to hold her closer, feel her heart beating against his chest. He was out of his mind with the need to kiss her. His imagination going insane with what it might be like to have her in his bed.

Except they were at her house.

They'd be in her bed.

Would the sheets smell like her, essential and earthy? He inhaled deeply, breathing in the air between them. Holding her scent in his nose. Considering himself a damn lucky man.

Her gaze was hooked on his lips. He wasn't imagining that. And yet, she was holding her body away from him, not leaning in.

She wasn't ready.

He dropped his gaze. Reached for another present to wrap. Racked his brain for a safe topic of conversation. Took a swallow of wine.

She mirrored him. Sipping from her glass, peering at him over the rim.

"What was the best Christmas Eve you ever had?" Joel asked.

A happy smile stretched her face. "That's easy. Two years ago, when I first came to work for you on the Brazos Queen, and we threw that huge party on the paddle-wheel. What a blast! I didn't want the evening to end."

"That was the year Kelsey and Noah reconnected?"

"Yes, but they weren't at that party."

"They were partying all on their own." Joel chuckled. "I'm touched that I was part of your best Christmas Eve."

"This one is shaping up to be even better than that one," she murmured, sending his pulse into overdrive.

He could hardly get his breath. "Why's that?"

"Gabriel."

"Oh," he said, disappointed.

"And . . ." She lowered her lashes and gave him a shy sidelong glance. It wasn't like her to play coy. "Because of what's developing between us."

"Yeah," he said. "I agree."

She put the tip of her tongue to her upper lip and widened her grin. "What was *your* best Christmas?"

Joel shook his head, hope knocking against his rib cage. "I've had so many good ones. It's hard to say. Each Christmas is special in its own way. Although there were one or two that truly sucked buckets."

"The year your mother died."

"Yes, it was the worst. No one wanted to open the packages Mom had under the tree for us." He had to pause and get his emotions under control. "We wanted to keep them forever, knowing it was the last thing she ever bought for us."

Jana reached over and took his hand. Her touch was tender and comforting. "I'm sorry that happened to you."

"Hey," he said, "everyone has loss and pain. We got through it. Although my dad did take a header into alcohol, and it was several years before he righted the ship and got sober. If it hadn't been for Flynn, the family would have wrecked on rocky shoals, but she kept us together."

"Your sister is amazing."

"She's the second-strongest woman I know," he said, his gaze searching her face.

"Who's the first?" Jana asked.

"You."

She looked blown away. "Me?"

"You face life head-on. You don't shy away from trouble. You're kind and compassionate with people. Look at all the gifts you've gotten. Look at all you're giving." He flapped his hands at the packages scattered around them. "Coming from the background you did, it's stunning how generous and caring you are."

An embarrassed expression crossed her face, and she ducked her head again.

"The only place I can see where you trip yourself up is that you keep your walls so high you can't fully receive the love you so richly deserve."

She peeked up at him. "I know I have trust issues. I'm working on that. Please be patient with me."

He squeezed her hand. "I'm not going anywhere."

Her smile was thin and wavery, but it was there.

"How about you?" he dared and braced himself to be rebuffed. "What was your worst Christmas ever?"

She blinked, and a pained expression crossed her face.

She's not going to share. Disappointment hit him. He'd thought they were making progress.

"Are you really prepared to hear it?" she whispered, surprising him again.

"Absolutely." He'd sit here with her until dawn if necessary.

Inhaling deeply, Jana drew her knees to her chest and rested her head on them, allowing her hair to fall across her face, hiding her expression from him. "It was the Christmas Eve my mother left me in a honky-tonk underneath a pool table when I was three years old. At closing time, the bartender found me clutching a bald, armless Barbie someone had given me to play with."

"Oh, Tink, no." His heart broke right in two. He moved toward her, intending on wrapping his arms around her and holding her close, but she held up a restraining hand.

"Please," she said. "Don't touch me."

She covered her head with her hands and sobbed. He'd never seen her cry, and her grief scared him to the marrow of his bones. "She left me. They searched the bar. They waited for an hour before calling the cops in hopes she'd return. She never returned. My very own mother didn't want me."

"That's why taking care of Gabriel means so much to you," he murmured, kneeling beside her, hovering his hand above her body, wanting so badly to comfort her, and yet knowing she couldn't handle it, and respecting that enough not to do what every instinct inside him urged him to do. Hug her.

"Yes," she whispered. "Yes."

"I'm so sorry." It was all he could think to say.

"My mom never returned, but I never gave up hope. That's why I can't give up hope on Gabriel's mom. She said she'd come back. I cling to that. It's probably stupid. She's probably long gone, but I can't help wanting it to be true for that little guy."

Rage was a strange emotion to feel for a woman he'd never met. But anyone who would leave a three-year-old in a bar deserved the brunt of his anger. Especially when that three-year-old had grown up to become this fierce, independent young woman who so desperately deserved to be loved.

"I understand. I'm with you all the way." He brushed his fingers against her wrist, and she didn't draw back. Good sign. It heartened him.

"Thank you." She turned her head to look up at him, offered a small smile.

"That must've been so hard for you," he said. "I can't imagine how difficult that was."

Tears glimmered in Jana's eyes, and the sight of those tears almost stopped Joel's heart.

Giving her his full attention, he leaned over to place a hand on her knee and waited for her to continue. The only value he had in this moment was to serve as her sounding board and leave his opinions to himself.

"She left town with some cowboy she'd met in the honky-tonk." Jana's voice turned small, and she drew herself inward, shoulders slumping forward in a C shape.

From her body language, Joel could see that she'd gone back to that night. She was three years old again. Alone and afraid.

"The authorities tracked her down months later in Phoenix, Arizona. She was dancing in a strip club, and they charged her with child abandonment. She signed over her parental rights, and I never saw her again as a child."

Part of him wanted to make excuses for the woman so that Jana would feel that her mother loved her on some level, but he couldn't minimize what she'd gone through. Feeling inadequate, he cleared his throat and waited for her to continue.

"Of course, I was too young to remember any of this. I only found out later from the foster mom who wanted to adopt me."

Protective instincts muscled against Joel's chest. He ached to go back in time, find Jana underneath that pool table, and save her himself.

"What about your dad?"

"No one has any idea who he was."

"Grandparents? Aunts? Uncles?"

She shook her head. "My mom was estranged from her family, and none of them could or would step up to the plate."

It was so damn sad. No wonder finding Gabriel had triggered all these old feelings inside her. Together, they would make sure that baby was taken care of. One way or another.

"How come the foster mother who wanted to adopt you didn't?" he asked.

"Mama Marjean," Jana said softly and got a faraway look in her eyes. "I loved her so much. She used to brush my hair and sing to me. She'd take me to the mall and let me ride on the carousel, and then we'd go for ice cream."

Joel got a lump in his throat as he imagined a little Jana finding happiness with her foster family, but she'd lost that too.

"Marjean got cancer and died after I'd been with her and her husband for four years. Chuck couldn't take care of me on his own, and I ended up with a new foster family. But by then, after so much loss, I was hell on wheels. I acted out. I bit the other kids. I threw temper tantrums. I trusted no one."

Those words might've brought a chill to someone who didn't understand Jana. Whether she realized it or not, Joel *did* understand her, and he knew behind everything she'd said and done was a deep fear of being hurt again.

"Because of my bad behavior, no one ever wanted to adopt me." She paused, hitched in her breath. "No one has ever *really* wanted me since Marjean."

"I want you," Joel said.

She jerked her head up, and he saw so much fear on her face, he realized too late it had been exactly the wrong thing to say.

CHAPTER 16

THE SHARE

She'd shared way too much, and her loose lips panicked her. Jana played her cards close to her vest, but this time she'd let him see her hand, and it felt like free-falling. "You don't want me."

His jaw tightened. "I do."

"You can't want me."

"Why not?"

"You wouldn't if you really knew me."

"Why not?" he repeated.

"I'm messed up."

"That's not true. Everyone has a past and has done things they regret."

"You've had an easy life, despite losing your mom. Not to be rude, but you have no idea what you're talking about." She hardened her jaw.

"You're right that I have a close, loving family, but that doesn't mean I can't understand where you're coming from."

"That's exactly what it means."

"Jana, why are you pushing me away?"

She bit her bottom lip, didn't want to speak, but finally shoved the words past her teeth. "I'm ashamed."

"You have nothing to be ashamed about."

"Trust me on this. You're far too good for me, Joel."

"Ha!" He barked out a laugh.

"I'm a horrible person. That's why I keep people at arm's length. It's not about keeping my heart safe. It's about protecting other people from *me*."

"You are *not* a horrible person."

Anxiety tightened her neck muscles, and she heard the flint in her voice. "You have *no* idea what I'm capable of."

"I don't care what mistakes you've made in your life. You are one of the best people I've ever known."

It was her turn to say "Ha!"

"Okay, the rubber has met the road, Gerard. Tell me, just how horrible are you? Because I don't see it. What have you done that's so unforgivable? Murdered someone?" He sounded irritated.

She raised her head and gave him a piercing stare. He understood *nothing*, and she wasn't in the mood to give him a lesson on the hard side of life.

"I ran away from my last foster home," she said. "It was bad in the house. There was verbal abuse, and when my foster father tried to come into my bedroom one night, I knew I had to get out of there."

"Oh, Jana, *no*."

He thought that was bad? What happened in that foster home was nothing compared to what had happened to her on the streets. But she wasn't going into those details. It was too much for one night. Maybe too much to ever tell him the full truth of her past.

"So what did you do that was so awful?"

"I fell in with a rough crowd." She kept her gaze downward. "On the streets I got involved with other kids headed in the wrong direction. We shoplifted, did drugs, and had risky sex."

"None of those things make you a horrible person. You were

a kid. You'd never had a stable environment, and your one good role model died. You had no tools with which to make smart decisions."

Her nose itched. "I did bad things."

"Okay, that wasn't great, but maybe the things you did were bad." He made air quotes around *bad*. "Not *you*."

"I was looking for love in all the wrong places and ended up with—" Something else she wasn't ready to tell him for fear he'd think less of her. At least, not all of it.

"With?" he prodded.

"I got into a relationship with an older guy. He bought me things, and he had a nice house. At first it was great, and then I found out he was into a lot of shady stuff—gambling, drug-running—although, I was a kid and didn't fully understand what all he did to make money. He turned physically abusive three months into the relationship. I'd try to leave. He'd love-bomb me. I'd stay because I had nowhere else to go, and honestly . . ." She hitched in a breath. "I was scared he might kill me."

A darkness came into Joel's eyes, and he clenched his fist. They'd both stopped wrapping packages. There was a green bow stuck to one knee of his jeans. She stared at the bow to keep from meeting his gaze.

"Jana, that's horrific." He gritted his teeth. "I wish I could have been there to help you."

She lifted her shoulder. She'd survived. She didn't think about it much. That was one of the reasons she didn't like blabbing about her history. She preferred to let the past stay buried and keep her face turned to the future.

And right now, the future was staring at her intently.

"That's what brought me to Twilight," she said. "I was on the run from him."

"I hate that the bastard was after you but am so happy you ended up in my hometown." His chin hardened, and a lock of his dark wavy hair fell across his forehead.

Oh gosh, he was so handsome.

"I'm happy too," she said. "Twilight saved my life in more ways than one."

"We're a kooky place, but once you're one of us, you're one of us for life."

What a sweet thing to say. It wasn't just talk. She felt it too: accepted, welcomed, respected.

"I'm so glad you got out," he said. "I've always admired you, Jana, but finding out all that you've overcome . . ." He shook his head, awe in his eyes. "You're the bravest woman I've ever known."

His words warmed her, and the panic that had gripped her earlier vanished completely. He wasn't disgusted or turned off by where she'd come from. He didn't judge her.

"I . . . you . . . still want to date me after all that?" she asked tentatively.

"More than ever." His tone was so earnest and sincere, it took her breath away.

"Really?" She could hardly breathe.

"Really."

Smiling, she dropped her gaze again, overwhelmed by the positive emotions her sharing had generated. Hope was a scary thing. Previously, she'd gotten her hopes up, only to have them dashed.

But this was different.

This was Joel.

The most steadfast man she'd ever known, and right now, she was feeling all kinds of complicated feelings for her boss. Nice feelings. Sexy feelings. Wondrous feelings.

She didn't know what to do with them.

Maybe *this* was the real reason she didn't talk about her past. The raking of the muck left you raw and vulnerable.

Jana didn't do vulnerable.

Except now, looking into Joel's eyes, she had a reason to change her ways. He wanted to be with her.

And she wanted to be with him too.

*   *   *

Looking into Jana's rapt blue eyes, Joel felt two opposing emotions, both so strong they bounced off him like a missed foul shot.

Desire and doubt.

He wanted her. Oh hell, yeah. His body ached for her in a way it hadn't ached in a very long time—if ever.

That was world-rocking right there.

Ah, then came doubt, kicking into his mind like pointy-toed cowboy boots.

Joel picked up another gift, this one a fluffy pair of grippy Christmas socks, and reached for the candy-cane wrapping paper lying on the floor between them. He suspected there was so much more she hadn't told him. There had to be for her to believe she was a horrible person. He wouldn't push. She'd already shared so much with him tonight, and he was honored she felt safe enough to open up as much as she had.

But, but, but . . .

Would she ever be able to trust him with all her secrets? Or was she so closed off there would always be parts of her she could never let him see?

He took the scissors and snipped off the proper amount of paper with a long precision cut. He remembered what Flynn had said about Jana. *She doesn't know how to fully love.*

That was the thing, wasn't it? The one time Jana had been loved, by her foster mother Marjean, she'd lost that too. She'd never had a pattern for love, didn't understand the template.

Maybe that was a good thing? A template gave people a mold to pour themselves into, shaping them before they had a chance to form themselves. Maybe Jana had invented her own way of loving. A way that didn't fit the image Flynn had in her head but was just as legitimate as any other kind of love.

On the other hand, Joel need to be clear-eyed about this because he was falling fast.

Did he want to get into a relationship with a woman who

could never completely give him her heart? He was a patient man. He could wait a long time. If he were honest with himself, he'd admit he'd been waiting on her for years.

Waiting for her to wake up to her own awesomeness.

She was on the verge. He could feel it.

Her head was down, her fingers creasing the ends of the paper as she folded it over the box she was wrapping. A dinosaur for Ian.

Joel sprawled beside the coffee table, studying the reddish strands of her hair glistening in the light. His heart just went *boom*!

"You okay?" he asked.

"Of course." She shrugged but didn't look at him and reached for a roll of silver ribbon.

"You sure?"

"Why wouldn't I be?"

"Wishing you could retract everything you told me?" he asked.

"Yes, kinda." She gave a nervous laugh.

"*Awk*-ward," he quipped in a sing-song voice. "How can we fix this?"

"What do you mean? There's nothing to fix."

"You're uncomfortable because you revealed so much, and now it's weird between us."

"Yeah? So what? I've been uncomfortable before. It won't kill me. Unless . . ." She eyed him. "*You* feel uncomfortable."

Did he? "I don't feel uncomfortable."

"Then, why are we talking about it?"

"Because you won't look me in the eyes."

Snorting, Jana raised her head and drilled him with a prolonged stare. "Happy now?"

"I know what's wrong. We need to even the score."

"What score?"

"I could tell you something about me that you don't know, and that way we've both revealed secrets."

"Ooh," she said, a soft smile appearing at her lips. "That sounds interesting. Whatcha got?"

Relieved that he'd shifted her mood, Joel went all in. "Is there anything you've ever wanted to know about me but were reluctant to ask?"

"Let's see." She tapped her chin, getting into the game. "How old were you when you lost your virginity?"

"Who says I'm not a virgin?" Joel batted his eyelashes comically.

"Oh, you." Jana grabbed a couch pillow and threw it at him.

Enlivened, Joel caught the pillow and tucked it behind his back. "It was senior year. I was seventeen and had been hankering after Lyndsey Pruitt since freshman year."

"Where'd you do the deed?"

"High school, behind the bleachers after our team won the basketball game."

"How was it?"

"Fumbling first attempts." Joel chuckled. "I didn't last long, and Lyndsey was disappointed. We dated a bit, but her parents moved shortly afterward, and that was the end of my first burning romance."

"Did you ever look her up on social media?"

"Nope."

"Why not?"

"I prefer to look to the future, not the past." He shrugged. "Or maybe I wasn't carrying much of a torch to begin with."

She dropped her smile and glanced away, reaching for the last present to wrap, a ballerina music box.

Oh dang, he'd rattled her.

Quick, say something to smooth things over.

"Anything else you want to know about me? Now's your chance." He held his arms wide.

"How did you get that scar?" She pointed to his chin.

He reached up to finger the edges of the small, faded scar

along his jawline. Honestly, he rarely thought about the scar anymore, even when he shaved. It was part of the landscape of his face.

"This? I got into a fight."

"Deets, MacGregor. I need deets."

"It's embarrassing."

"Remember this was your idea to even things up between us. Spill it."

"Back when we were kids, there was this bully who kept picking on Carrie. One day we found her crying, and Noah and I decided to put a stop to it."

"Carrie? She's no shrinking violet. I'm surprised she didn't handle the situation herself. Besides, you guys are several years younger than she is."

"The bully was teasing her about her weight. Back then, she was chubby and sensitive about it."

"Aww, poor Carrie."

"The next day, the three of us were walking home from school together, and the bully popped up from the riverbank and blocked our way. There was name-calling, and things got wild, and I got punched. My knees buckled, and I fell face-first onto a rock, and this was the result." He touched his scar again.

"That was pretty cool of you and Noah to protect your sister."

Joel cringed. Although he could just drop it and let Jana assume that he was a hero, she'd been so honest with him he felt obligated to tell her the full story. "Well . . . it didn't quite go down like that."

"How did it go down?" Amusement tinged her voice.

"We didn't exactly protect Carrie."

"No? What did you do?"

"She was whaling on the bully so hard that Noah and I felt sorry for him and went to his defense."

Jana burst out laughing. "That's priceless! I love Carrie even more than before."

Sheepishly, Joel laughed too.

"Wait, so if you were protecting the bully, who punched you? Was it Carrie?"

Joel shrugged. He was happy his story had lifted Jana's mood. "She didn't mean to punch me. She swung, the bully ducked, and she clocked me instead."

"So what happened to the bully?"

"Turns out he had a crush on Carrie, and that's why he was teasing her. Since I believe in second chances . . ." He gave Jana a pointed look. He wanted her to know that she too deserved a second chance for youthful mistakes. "Noah and I went out of our way to befriend him, and now he works for me."

"Sean?" Jana asked with disbelief in her voice. "Sean Armstrong was Carrie's bully?"

"We learned Sean had a rough upbringing, and he didn't know what to do with his feelings. Joining the Navy helped him channel that."

"I'll say. Sean is the coolest cucumber around." Jana chuckled. "Wow, I'm impressed how you and Noah turned a potential enemy into a great friend. Kudos."

"We even convinced Carrie to go on a date with Sean. It didn't work out—she was in love with Mark Leland—but she and Sean ended up as good friends."

"Hey, thank you for sharing that story. You brightened the evening." She finished wrapping the music box and added a label, writing *Grace* on it in black Sharpie. She'd bought gifts for his niece and nephew, and he loved her for her generosity.

"You're welcome." Joel peered into her eyes.

Jana held his gaze.

Then without even knowing for certain why he did it other than he'd been aching to do it since they'd found the baby, Joel leaned over and kissed her.

CHAPTER 17

THE SAFE WORD

The second Joel's lips touched hers, Jana's entire body lit up, on fire for him. For two years she'd buried her desires and denied her feelings.

She wanted Joel.

Why, oh why, had they waited so long to do this? Kissing Joel was, in a word, *glorious*, and yet it felt wrong, but in all the right ways.

Oh! This was why she'd kept her distance emotionally.

He tasted like Christmas. Minty and bracing, sweet and yet with a spicy tanginess underneath.

When he broke the kiss and pulled back, it was as if the sun had suddenly gone dark and she was left alone in an empty world.

"Jana?" His voice was ragged.

Slowly, she opened her eyes and stared into his. Those murky pools of intense dark chocolate searched her face.

"You okay?"

Silently, she nodded.

"You sure?"

"Are *you* okay?" She injected a dollop of sauciness into her voice, just to protect herself. She'd been alone too long, and it was hard to express the tender emotions threatening to overwhelm her.

"That was some kiss," he said. "I don't know if I'm okay or not, which is why I asked after you." In that moment, for all his height and broad shoulders, he looked flummoxed and nervous.

Her breath came to her on a hiccup, and when she answered, it almost sounded like a burp. "Fine."

Joel took her hand in his. "You're trembling. You're not fine."

"You took me by surprise. You got to me. I'm all shook up." She paused and glared at him with a smile. "And don't you dare start singing an Elvis song."

"I'm shook up too, Tink. More than I can say."

"*Sooo . . .*"

"So," he echoed.

They stared at each other. Here it was. Their moment of truth. Walk away and forget that kiss or . . .

They were both breathing hard and in the same jagged tympany. Neither one of them said a word. They just took hold of each other and started kissing again.

All righty, then, here we go.

They kissed and kissed and kissed, until she feared her lips would chap. His hands were on her, and her hands were on him—feeling, touching, exploring. He took her breath away. Ran off all common sense.

"Should we?" he whispered against her lips.

"Yes!" She gasped, ignoring all logic for why this was not a bright idea.

"You sure?" Joel asked, hope in his voice.

"Sometimes, MacGregor, you talk too much."

"I do, don't I?" He grinned at her as if after years of mining a tapped-out mine, he'd finally found gold.

She grinned back.

Something fresh and exciting took root in her small living room, surrounded by a stack of presents, and unearthed an embarrassing, long-forgotten sex dream she once had about Joel.

Holy All Seven Chakras, she thought, *this was finally happening!*

Something precious blossomed in that Christmas-scented room packed with gifts and abundant joy. Odd how the holiday epitomized the very fabric of their relationship, based on mutual respect and admiration.

"Let's do this, MacGregor," she said, whipping off her sweater and revealing the purple plaid shirt she wore underneath.

"Damn, I love how strong and direct you are." Joel cupped his palm against her jaw and kissed her again.

This kiss was slow and measured as he took his time, but his other hand, that sly thing, eased open the buttons on her shirt.

One button.

Two buttons.

Three buttons.

They were all undone.

The heat from the fireplace kissed her skin along with his hot damp mouth. His hands were equally hot and wildly curious, trailing over her body and slipping around her back to search for the clasp of her bra.

She let out a hungry whimper, urging him on.

Joel didn't need any more encouragement than that.

She leaned forward, giving him better access to the stubborn bra clasp, and gave a sigh of triumph when he got it undone and freed her breasts. She whipped off the bra and tossed it over her shoulder, where it landed—*plop*—on the floor.

Joel laughed and hugged her closer.

Jana looped one arm around his neck and tugged his head down, and they got back to hot, furious kisses.

While she kept his mouth busy with her tongue, his hands palmed and stroked her breasts. They didn't bother with prolonged foreplay, and she didn't want that, anyway. Leisure foreplay was too tender, too dangerous. This was about hot, hungry sex. She had no room in her mind for any other interpretation. She wanted to feel something primal, something physical and real. Beyond that . . . well . . . she couldn't let herself hope for things she had no business hoping for.

Joel ducked his head, and his amazing mouth was at her nipple, and he was doing the most stunning thing to her. She felt the effects through every cell inside her. The pleasure was so intense she feared she just might faint, although never in her life had Jana fainted.

While he was busy stirring up her nerve endings, she wasn't sitting idly by. Passivity was not her jam. She clawed at the button of her jeans, but her urgent fingers couldn't seem to undo it, and she fumbled clumsily as if she'd forgotten how to undress herself.

She managed the button, but then the zipper—that damn zipper—caught and hung on the material of her panties. Oh no, she was not getting stuck in these jeans!

"Stupid, stupid zipper!"

Chuckling, Joel eased her onto her back so that she was staring up at him as he hovered over her. "Allow me, Tink."

Her breath was so short and fast she felt the fainting sensation again, but how could you faint when you were lying down?

Patiently, he jiggled the zipper until it gave way like buttered magic beneath his masterful fingers. "Slow and methodical, that's how you do it, babe."

"If you were a superhero, they'd call you Captain Painstaking."

"I'm taking that as a compliment."

"Considering that you got my zipper unstuck, it is one." She wriggled out of her jeans while he attended to his own denim, yanking them off, along with his boxer briefs, in a move so quick, it belied his avowed leisurely methodology.

For which Jana, as she slithered out of her panties and kicked them aside with the tip of her toe, was eternally grateful.

And then she took hold of him and pulled him down, in an efficient way, on the rug in front of the fireplace, flaming with warmth. Without missing a beat, she took him in her hands and stroked his rock-hard shaft.

"Holy *sssssss*," he hissed. "You go right for the jugular."

"Clearly, you flunked biology if you think this is where your jugular vein is located." She laughed.

"Tink," he said in a helpless tone, and she knew she had him right where she wanted him. "You are *amazing*."

She pressed her mouth to his ear and whispered, "You ain't seen nothing yet, tall guy."

He made a noise, half groan, half chuckle, and she felt like her own kind of superhero as his body grew even harder between her hands.

"You keep that up, and we will never get to the good part," he warned.

Although he was pantless, he still had a shirt on and looked hilariously handsome. Business on the top, party on the bottom. His body was poised over her in plank position looking ready and willing for a long, strenuous set of push-ups.

Hungrily, she slid her palms underneath his shirt and up the sides of his waist. His honed muscles were a joy to caress. It had been far too long since she'd had a man hover over her like this, body locked and loaded, gaze welded to her face.

It was heady. No way she could deny that.

Just for fun, she strummed his nipples with her thumb, and they turned to stone pebble as a heated moan escaped his lips.

They were kissing again in time to the soft murmur of Christmas music coming from the boom box on the mantel. Joel had turned on the music when they'd sat down to wrap presents.

It was a jazzy, sexy tune, "Santa Baby."

Time stretched out and elongated as they submersed into each other. She got him out of that damn shirt. They gasped and sighed, whispered and moaned. They explored each other's bodies like pioneers forging a new country, searching for exciting, new experiences with each other.

Jana savored every second and saw in Joel's face that he was struggling to hold out, to make this last for as long as possible. She tingled from her head to her toes: everywhere he touched felt as if he'd branded her with his own special heat. She wanted this. Wanted him. And that's as far as her thoughts went.

Lust, desire, desperate and unyielding yearning.

"Please," he begged. "I can't last any longer. Please, Jana. Gotta have you now, babe."

"Hang on," she said. "We need a condom."

"Hurry," he croaked.

"BRB." She hopped up and ran naked through the house, horny and panting.

Her goal was to burst into that bathroom, snatch a condom from the drawer, and race back before her ardor cooled and common sense stopped her from taking this to its logical conclusion.

When she returned, she found Joel holding up a condom and grinning. "I had one in my wallet in my pants."

She looked up at him, so stalwart and strong, as noble as a pine tree. Reliable. Dependable. Always there for her. She'd never had that. Ever.

It scared her.

Her feelings got all jumbled up. Forget simple lust. This was so much more. It wasn't just about the desperate need for sex with a hot guy. Joel stirred something greater inside her. Something that rocked her to the center of her soul.

But at the same time, he utterly fascinated her on a level so profound she couldn't sort it out.

Joel must've seen her confusion and feared she might put an end to everything, canceling out all that had gone before. Without a word, he bent and scooped her up as if she weighed no more than Gabriel.

Laughing joyously, Jana surrendered. Gave up her fear. Gave in. Allowed this man, this big, tall, wonderful man, to make love to her.

Not that it was all that difficult.

Her body was charged up like a new battery.

He stretched her out on the rug in front of the fireplace, the flickering flames casting his hands and face in intriguing shadows, and her heart skipped several beats.

Oh boy, oh wow, this is happening now.

"Jana. Lord . . . you are so beautiful." That last word came out clotted and the sound told her he was full of *feels*.

So was she.

Yikes!

The depth of emotion in his voice should have terrified her, would have terrified her, if it had been anyone else but Joel. He was her friend and her boss. Was she really willing to screw up their relationship for one night of hot, glorious sex?

Apparently so.

Desperately, Jana reached up, wrapped her arms around Joel's neck, and pulled him down beside her, then quick as a wink, she flipped him onto his back and straddled him.

"Aha!" she cried. "Turnabout, fair play."

"Look at you." The firelight shone in his admiring eyes. He liked her as much as she liked him, and that stirred her stronger than ever.

If he hadn't settled his hands at her waist, she might have bolted. Did he know that? Or was he just hanging on tight?

She leaned over him, and her breasts dangled not far from his inquisitive mouth. Yes, she was tempting him, eager to feel his hot tongue.

He raised his head and tried to capture one dangling nipple, but with a wicked grin, she drew back, just out of reach.

"Ooh, Jana in charge."

"Tink, when it comes to me, you're *always* in charge."

"Not true. You're my boss."

"In name only. No one is ever the boss of *you*."

She knew he meant it as a compliment, but it bothered her a teeny bit. He was right. She had trouble letting other people be in charge, had problems relinquishing control. In the past, too many times people in positions of authority had turned out not to be all that responsible or trustworthy.

Did she have control issues? Probably. Was it an issue that needed addressing? Maybe. Who knew? Now wasn't the time to think about all that.

What if, just this one time, you let go and let him take charge?

Yikes! Super scary. If she was going to let go and risk, she'd need a safe word.

"Wait."

"What?" A lock of hair fell over his forehead.

She rocked back, resting her bare butt on his thighs. "Motorcycle boots."

"Huh?" His eyes were glazed, and she realized she hadn't prefaced her thoughts with context.

"Motorcycle boots. It's my safe word."

"Umm, hang on." He moved her aside and sat up. "We need to unpack this."

Jana groaned and rolled her eyes. "Should've kept my mouth shut."

"I'm not the guy who's going to blow past your concerns just to get my needs met."

"Why not? Just go with the flow."

"I want to hear about this safe word."

Jana blew out her breath through pursed lips. "You're making a thing."

"Okay, fine. I'm making a thing. I need to know why you feel the need for a safe word. Do you feel unsafe with me?"

"I grew up in an unsafe world. Comes with the territory." She said it as quickly as she could, hoping he would get the hint to get back to kissing her nipples.

"We're not going to do anything that needs a safe word." His tone filled with humor. "At least not tonight, but if having a safe word makes you feel more comfortable, okay."

"Great! Let's get to it."

"However . . ."

She held her breath. "What?"

"*Motorcycle boots*, while fitting, is a phrase, not a word. In a moment of passion, *motorcycle boots* might be too unwieldy."

"Good point."

"We need one word, and preferably a one-syllable word."

"Suggestions?"

"How about a simple *no*?"

"Won't that harsh the vibe?"

"*Stop*?"

"You have the lyrical prose of a pooper-scooper, MacGregor."

"Hey, what can I say? I'm a literal guy. How about *boots*?"

"Good enough." She laughed, pushed him down on the rug again, and leaned forward so he could capture her breast lightly between his teeth once more. She splayed her palms over his chest, her fingers eager to feel the hot strength of him.

While his miracle mouth worked her nipple, his hand moved slowly between her thighs. With determined but delicate movements, his fingers tickled her tender skin.

Multitasking. She liked that.

Jana shivered as pleasure slid down her spine. All her focus went to the spot where his calloused fingertips stroked. Wherever he touched, she instantly went wet, aching and ready for him.

"Joel," she gasped. "More pressure."

"Your wish is my command, Tink." He increased the pressure, giving her exactly what she had asked for, caressing her in all the right places and in all the right ways.

Then it got really good.

At some point, she rolled the condom on him and, fully in charge, she orchestrated a spectacular pole dance, with his hard shaft as the pole.

His breath came out in a hot, tortured hiss between his clenched teeth, and he croaked, "Ride 'em, cowgirl."

There was much more kissing, stroking, licking, teasing, and various other forms of sex play.

Joel groaned and sighed and grunted. Oh, who was she kidding? Jana was groaning, sighing, and grunting right along with him.

At some point, Jana couldn't really say for sure when, they changed position, and now Joel was on top, looking down at her with admiring eyes.

It was too much, really. The smack of his affection slamming squarely into her heart.

Joel was planting blistering kisses over her throat. Kisses that bloomed and spread, sending goose bumps to every nook and cranny of her body.

If she shivered one more time, she was going to fly into pieces, like a poorly welded spaceship blasting through the atmosphere.

"You like?" His growl was low and sexy.

"Yes," she urged, "yes, yes, yes. Likey, likey, likey."

"Hmmm," he teased. "You're just a tad too eager. Maybe I should slow down and make you wait for it."

"No, please, no," she begged.

He stopped moving inside her.

"Don't . . ." She gasped. "Stop."

"Don't?" His eyes turned wicked in the weak but colorful lighting. "Or stop?"

"Go!"

"You're the go-getter. Come and get me."

And then that rascal pulled right out, moved to sink back on his heels, and laughed despite her cries of "No, no, no."

He just kept grinning.

"You, sir," she said, "are no superhero. You are quite villainous."

"You think?"

She sat up so that she could swat his shoulder. "You're pushing your luck, buddy. I could toss you out on your ear."

"I'm not scared."

"Calling my bluff, MacGregor?"

"You got it." Oh, he was definitely smirking, and she swatted him again just for good measure.

He loomed over her, that wicked, wicked smile firmly in place, looking like a wolf going in for the kill.

She'd never thought of Joel in this context. The rugged alpha male, but he surely was. She'd just been too afraid to admit it. Knowing somewhere deep down inside that if she saw Joel in all his facets, both his gentle side and his rough masculinity, she'd lose herself. And that was Jana's greatest fear: losing herself, losing control, trusting someone else to take the reins for once.

Right now, Joel was fully in charge. He leaned down, ready to slide into her again, but she stiff-armed him, planting one palm on the center of his chest.

"Boo."

He waited. Paused. Hovering.

Her mind was blank. Why was she stopping him when she wanted this more than she wanted oxygen?

"Change your mind, Tink?"

"*You* don't have a safe word," she babbled. "You can't use my safe word. You have to come up with your own."

From the gleam in his eye, she knew he could tell a stalling tactic when he saw one. "Oh yeah?"

"What's your safe word?"

"Jana."

"That's a lousy safe word," she said with a determined shake of her head. "You can't use a name. Just think of it. We're rocking along, doing the wild thing, and you call out 'Jana,' and I'll stop right when you want me to go."

"I wasn't suggesting that my safe word be *Jana*. I was calling your name to get your attention."

She blinked. "You were?"

"Could we please stop talking now?" he asked. "I just want to be with you, be inside you."

"Pick a safe word, and it's on."

He looked into her eyes and said, "Gabriel."

CHAPTER 18

THE HOT SEX

Dude, why did you mention the baby? You're harshing the vibe.
Joel heard his twin brother's voice in his head.

But Jana pushed him onto his back and crawled right up his body.

Oh yeah, babe, you do whatever you need to do. Boss me around, turn me upside down—just be with me.

She was straddling him again. Enveloping him in her warmth. Riding up and sliding back down, a rhythmic stroke that was driving him straight out of his ever-loving mind.

He stared into her wide-open eyes, and their gazes fused. He couldn't look away if he tried, but he didn't try.

Joel was locked in this moment with her, making memories, because he didn't know whether or not this moment was going to send her running away from him. It was a risk they'd taken without really discussing it, falling from friends to sex partners.

Bam. Bam.

To be honest, this had been simmering for two years. The only thing that had held Joel back from pursuing more was Jana's skittishness, so he'd engaged in mutually casual relationships like what he'd shared with Ursula. At some point a man had to make a move.

If their friendship crashed and burned because of this, well, that would be damn sad, but it was a risk worth taking. He just hoped she saw it that way.

Skittish she might be, but Jana wasn't a coward. Not by any definition of the word. Other than his sisters, she was the strongest woman he'd ever known, and he lived in a town filled with strong women.

They'd made their choices. Jana was a big girl, and she knew exactly what she was getting into. Their eyes were wide open, and they were staring into each other as if they were tethered by a titanium cord.

In her face, he saw that she felt the same way he did. It would take something monumental to sever that bond.

Neither one of them said another word, and they just let their bodies do the talking. Their pace was as timeless as the rhythm of the ocean, leisurely sliding in and out, ebbing and flowing. Slow and languid, entrancing each other.

Joel watched her surf him with happy eyes. *Hang ten, Tink, hang ten.*

She leaned over so that she could kiss him while she rode his body.

Their breath mingled.

Her pupils widened, growing large enough to block out the pretty color. He felt her tense, squeezing him tighter.

For one freak of a second, he thought the impending orgasm just might kill him, so strong was the electrified feeling buzzing through his nerve endings.

"I wish I could sketch a picture of you . . . the way you look right now . . . so I'd have it for reference when I'm an old lady in a rocking chair, dreaming of this night," she murmured.

Her words were sleepy, hypnotic as she whispered against his ear. She kissed his cheek, his jaw, and then the hot pulse jumping at his throat.

"I want to lick every inch of you. I want to rim every hollow, explore every angle, delve into your spaces."

Her words sent a shiver through him. He wanted that too!

She kept talking and moving and licking and stroking until Joel didn't know which way was up. He did his best to give as good as he got, but he feared he fell short of her finesse. But what he lacked in flair he made up for with enthusiasm.

They talked dirty and clung to each other like life rafts in the ocean. It was raw and real and beautiful.

Soon, their bodies were bathed in sweat, and they were long past the point of no return. She seized his hips and urged him faster, a soft, desperate moan rolling from her throat.

He was right there with her, knees shaking, pulse pounding, breath halting, earth quaking . . .

"Make me come, Joel." She threw back her head, and he could see the paleness of her graceful neck in the flickering firelight.

Joel went wild then, in a frenzy, flipping her over onto all fours. He could speed things up this way. She was fully on board with the position, and if he hadn't been so dazzled by lust and need, he might have fully realized she'd goaded him into the change.

He would've wondered if she had urged him into it, because she couldn't bear the bonding of such intense eye contact.

As it was, his brain blew past all caution.

Too late now. This was happening the way that it was happening. Joel couldn't hold on any longer, and apparently neither could Jana.

They arched together, and he spilled into her. He could feel the power of their simultaneous orgasms passing through them in a powerful shudder.

She called his name.

He called hers and held on to her tightly until both of them were completely spent.

His mind was gone. Just loose and blank and drifting, but he took her with him as he tumbled to the floor, kept her right up underneath his arm, and held her tenderly.

Her breath was warm against his skin, the earthiness of her scent tangled up in his nose, the sound of her soft sighs driving him crazy.

This was better than any fantasy. Better than any hidden dream he'd dared imagine. This was Twilight magic, pure and simple. It was a very good Christmas indeed. A second chance Christmas for both of them. Maybe even the best Christmas ever.

"Wow." Jana exhaled. "Wow."

"The same forward as it is backward."

"Huh?"

"Wow. It's a palindrome. A word that's spelled the same forward as backward."

"How," she asked breathlessly, "can you talk after what we just did?"

"You energize me, Tinker Bell."

She lay resting her head against his shoulder, one side of her cheek turned against his chest, inhaling his magnificent after-sex scent.

He had his arm around her, holding her close, and they clung to each other, as if by close contact they could make the moment last.

Because it *was* a very special moment, the changing of their relationship. Jana wasn't sure what this meant, and she was even afraid to think about it too much, so she didn't, instead shoving her worries to the back of her mind.

Later. She'd work through the consequences later.

They breathed in tandem. It was provocative and hypnotic as they inhaled and exhaled in perfect harmony. How she wished they could stay locked like this forever!

"Why do you call me Tinker Bell?" she asked.

"Because you are small and compact and—"

"I'm not that small. I'm five foot four. You, sir, are just excessively tall. What seems small to you is normal-sized to most of us."

He stroked the side of her cheek with the pad of his thumb. "Truth. But there's much more to your Tinker-Bellness than your size."

"Oh?" Secretly, she was flattered that he called her Tinker Bell or Tink. She'd just never really delved into why.

"Tinker Bell is feisty and fearless, stubborn and determined." His voice softened with humor. "She's sassy, fiery, and hot-tempered."

"Some might not consider that a compliment."

"It's just her rough exterior." He added fingers to the thumb stroking her cheek, and it felt like a gentle spider crawling over her skin.

Good thing Jana liked spiders.

"Tinker Bell is empathetic, loyal, and deeply devoted to those she loves. She's concerned about helping others. She's really smart and has an amazing imagination," he said.

"How do you know so darn much about Tinker Bell?"

"Grace," he said. "*Peter Pan* is my niece's favorite movie, and when I babysit her, that's all she wants to watch. She sees herself as Wendy."

"Tinker Bell has a dark side too." Jana decided to give as good as she got and walked her fingers up his chest, tickling as she went. "She can be quite jealous, and she enjoys messing with people."

"Are you warning me?" He gave a low chuckle.

"Just saying."

"See what I mean? Honest and open, and she doesn't hold back. She reminds me of you so much."

"Maybe I should get a Tinker Bell tattoo," Jana mused. "What do you think?"

"Where would you put it?"

"Right here." She moved his hand to the inkless spot on her skin just under her left rib cage.

"Aw, I kind of like the blank space." He shifted around so he could kiss the spot.

"Does my ink bother you?" She knew her tats put off some people, and she supposed, on some level, that was why she'd gotten them. Armor. Something to hide behind and keep people at bay.

"It did when I first met you," he confessed. "Your skin has so much going on that I couldn't concentrate on *you*, but I don't even see them now. Unless I'm specifically looking at them."

"Are they a turnoff?" She heard the vulnerability in her voice and instantly hated that she had asked the question.

"No," he whispered. "Not at all. They're part and parcel of who you are. They are as much a part of you as Tinker Bell's fairy-dust sprinkles are a part of her."

"No one tells you when you're fourteen that covering your body in tattoos might not be the most employable move in the world."

"What do you mean? Everyone tells you that."

"Maybe in your world. Not out on the streets where most people have ink and encourage you to get more."

"How long were you homeless?"

Sudden sadness was a rock in her throat. "Months. It was an off-and-on situation. I couch surfed and spent time in homeless shelters. There's a whole world out there you know nothing about, MacGregor."

He stroked her hair. "Did you ever find your biological mother?"

"I did," she said.

She rarely talked about her past, especially this part of it, but she'd just been as intimate with Joel as two people could be, and she was feeling safe in the circle of his arms. He wouldn't judge her.

"How'd that go?" he prompted when she didn't answer immediately.

"About as badly as you'd expect."

"Really? I wouldn't expect bad at all."

"That's because you are a true son of Twilight, filled with

hope, and a rabid believer in happily ever after." Yes, okay, she sounded sarcastic. She'd own it. "You're projecting how you believe that you'd feel if you were in that situation."

He didn't say anything for the longest time, just held her against his strong, naked body.

She heard the pounding of his heart that matched her own intense beat. They were on scary ground here. At least it was scary for Jana, peeling back the layers of herself, letting him peek inside her psyche.

She had a sudden urge to jump up, put her clothes on, and run, but they were at her house. Where would she go? But, man, how she yearned to bolt! Fly away like Tinker Bell.

As if sensing her skittishness, Joel tightened his grip on her, anchoring her to his side.

"What happened with your mother?" he asked. "Why was it so bad?"

She didn't answer, because she couldn't. Salty tears filled her mouth, and her eyes burned. She was not going to cry. Not here. She was Tinker Bell. Tink didn't cry. She got mad. But getting mad at Joel seemed an easy trap to fall into, and she forced herself to resist the age-old anger that had burrowed deep beneath her skin so long ago.

"Wait. Don't answer that," he rushed to say. "It's none of my business."

Jana inhaled sharply and then let out her breath on a long, slow hiss. "My mom was a druggie. I won't go into the details. Let's just say she was not happy to see me, and when she regained her composure, the first thing she did was ask me for money."

"I'm so sorry."

"Why? It's got nothing to do with you."

"I shouldn't have brought it up. I didn't mean to kill the mood. Let's change the subject," he said.

"This is why I avoid pillow talk."

"Thank you for not avoiding it with me."

She couldn't see his face, but she could hear the smile in his voice. He was pleased with himself. Honestly, after that hot sex, she was pretty darn pleased with him too. Pleased enough to spill her guts, which was fairly concerning. She didn't want to turn into one of those wide-open women who revealed everything about themselves to their lovers and kept no secrets for themselves.

Lovers.

The word echoed in her mind. She and Joel had become lovers.

Oh snap!

The implications, which had kept her from going here before, fully hit her. What was this going to do to their friendship? Sticky wicket. She'd keep quiet about her concerns. Talking about the shift would just make it too real, and she wasn't ready for that. Not tonight. Not over Christmas weekend.

Joel must've sensed the tension running through her. He rose to kiss the top of her head. "It's going to be okay, Tink. I promise."

She trusted him more than she trusted most people, but she knew that promises were made to be broken.

"I won't ever hurt you," he said. "Not intentionally, anyway. All I want is to make you happy."

Oh, here it came. The expectations.

He assumed he possessed the power to affect her happiness. She didn't like that. It made her feel beholden. Like she *had* to be happy. Like being in a relationship with him required happiness.

She blamed Twilight for his irrational, romantic belief that love could conquer all.

"Should we talk—"

"No."

"But—"

"Shh." She reached up to press a finger against his warm lips. Lips that not so very long ago had been doing dazzling things to her body.

"Where do we go from here?" He mumbled around her finger.

"Now, see, that's not shushing."

"What—"

"Please don't ruin this."

"Is that what I'm doing?" He sounded disappointed.

"The sex was beautiful. We're together tonight. Live in the moment, Joel. Put away your labeler. We don't need it. All we need is now." It alarmed her to hear how desperate she sounded.

It must've concerned him too, because he said nothing else. Just propped his back against the couch, gathered her into his lap, and rocked her as if she were Gabriel.

Jana took her own advice and fully inhabited the moment. She savored the feel of his arms around her, not knowing how long they would be there or even if she would ever be in his arms again.

She'd learned a long time ago to treat each day as a treasured gift and be grateful for what she had. She often reminded herself, during moments of joy, that this time could be her very last and to savor it to the fullest.

That approach had given her a lot of flexibility and made her able to fully experience life in all its complicated splendor. She knew the skill was part of what drew people to her, even as her sharp edges sometimes pushed them away.

Joel seemed unconcerned by her dichotomy, and that gave her some hope that he could fully accept her unconditionally, ink, flaws, and all.

For the first time in years—hey, maybe for the first time ever—she felt the true meaning of Christmas.

Peace.

Joy.

Joel.

CHAPTER 19

THE KISMET COOKIES

Muted sunlight eased through the cracks in the shutters. Joel blinked, confused for a second about where he was. He'd been having the most amazing sex dream about Jana, and he was still floating in the fantasy.

Then he remembered.

It wasn't just a dream.

He'd made love to his good friend and part-time employee. His pulse quickened, and he rubbed his eyes. Glancing around, he realized he was on the rug in her living room, surrounded by gaily wrapped Christmas presents.

But he was alone.

His clothes were strewn around the room. Kismet cookies lay broken and crumbled beneath his body. How had that happened? Had they knocked the cookies off the coffee table at some point and crushed them beneath their bodies? Considering all their moves last night, it was highly likely.

Something else occurred to him. Last night had technically been the wee morning hours of Christmas Eve, and while there had been no pillow, he'd slept on a bed of kismet cookies and dreamed of Jana.

His one true love?

He gasped, literally. It was silly, pure Twilight whimsy, and yet he thought, Could Jana be his soul mate?

That idea sent his emotions into an upward spiral of hope, anticipation, and downright joy.

Hush up. You don't believe in that stuff. His rational mind didn't believe it, but his heart? There was no accounting for the sweet tightness pulling at his chest.

Speaking of Jana, where was she? They needed to get a move on. The float parade started at nine and it was . . . Joel searched the room for his phone, switched it on. Seven ten.

Feeling a slight stab of panic, Joel grabbed his clothes, pulled them on and was just zipping up his jeans when Jana appeared in the doorway holding a spatula and wearing a Christmas apron.

He let out a sigh of relief. She hadn't bolted and left him.

Ignoring his galloping pulse, he cocked his head and offered her a lopsided smile. The one he knew never failed to charm. "Hey."

"Hey," she answered in a softer voice than usual.

They looked at each other, the moment weighted and meaningful.

Oh Lord, there were so many things he needed to say to her, but he didn't know where to start, and he didn't know if she could tolerate it if he did. When he tried to talk to her last night, she'd shushed him. He didn't want to chase her off, so he turned up the heat on his smile to full-on boil.

"Looks like we crushed the cookies." He waved at the kismet-cookie crumbs sprinkled around the room.

"Yeah."

"Um . . . did you have any dreams?" He chuckled as if kismet-cookie legend was a huge joke, but his entire body tensed as he waited for her answer.

Of course, he didn't really *believe* in the legend, but hey, he'd slept on a bed of crumbs and dreamed of Jana. That's all he could attest to. Most likely, he'd dreamed of her because they'd had fantastic, mind-blowing sex, and his dreams had nothing at all to do with cookies.

"No." She held his gaze for such a long beat, he wondered if she was lying. A strange thrill went through him. Had she dreamed of him as he'd dreamed of her?

"No kismet-cookie dreams?" he asked hopefully.

"None. I guess there had to be a pillow involved for it to work."

"You think?"

"Maybe the cookies were defective," Jana said jokingly. "Either that or I'm immune to true-love mythology." She eyed him speculatively. "Did *you* have a dream?"

Okay, that line of questioning was going nowhere. If Jana had dreamed of him, she wasn't coming clean, so neither was he.

Joel snorted but couldn't hold her gaze while he lied. "*Pfft.* No."

"You sure?"

"Why would I?"

"You grew up in the lap of the legend. It would be logical if you did dream of your one true love." Her grin yanked his chain.

He shrugged, not knowing what to say to that, so he said, "We need to go get Gabriel. I'm guessing my twin and his bride have probably had their fill of a newborn."

"I already called them and told them we'd head that way as soon as we have breakfast."

"You're cooking?"

"Don't sound so surprised. I'm a woman of many talents. We're having vegan pancakes and facon."

"Fake bacon?"

"Yup." Her smile widened.

Joel's heart caught fire, and he gave himself a mission. Put a smile on that gorgeous face as often as possible.

"C'mon into the kitchen. Breakfast will be ready in a jiffy," she invited. "Then we'll load up the presents for later in the day and head on over to the Rockabye, pick up Gabriel, and be right on time for the float parade."

She had it all lined up. With efficient Jana on his side, they could conquer the world. They made one helluva team.

Was she thinking the same thing?

He studied her face, tried to read what was going on behind those inscrutable eyes. Argh! He was reading too much into everything. His earlier joy dribbled away. Despite his best efforts to keep a loose hold on his hopes, was he expecting too much?

Slow your roll, MacGregor.

"Good idea," he croaked, wondering why he sounded like a bullfrog with a bad cold. Maybe because he couldn't stop staring at her. Or maybe it was the memory of that sex dream and whether it had any rational significance or not.

There was nothing to the dream. Nothing at all.

But he sure as hell wasn't going to tell Flynn about the dream or what he'd done with Jana. His sister would imbue the cookie dream with weighted meaning that baked goods simply did not possess.

There was so much he wanted to say to Jana. To tell her how special last night had been for him, but he didn't want to jeopardize the delicate balance they'd achieved this morning. He was just going to enjoy the ride for as long as it lasted.

No expectations.

"Well," he said, rolling up his sleeves, "I'll help. Let's get to it."

"I'm thinking you need a shower first." Jana grinned at him.

He thought wildly, *That's the smile of a girlfriend.* And damn if his heart didn't flutter.

"I already had mine." She did look dewy fresh and smelled fantastic.

"Are you saying I stink?"

"I'm saying you're covered in cookie crumbs." A wide grin wreathed her face. "To the showers, tall man."

Then Jana did the darndest thing: she reached out and slapped his butt.

And Joel thought, *Yee-haw, she is my girlfriend.*

*   *   *

JANA WATCHED HIM go, her pulse beating as fast as humming-bird wings. She was scared. Scared of the shift in their relation-ship. Scared that this wouldn't work out. Scared that she would blow everything to high heaven. If she lost his friendship over sex, Jana had no idea what she would do.

Yet underneath the fear was a throbbing thrill. The kind of thrill she got whenever she drove a motorcycle fast or sat down in a tattoo artist's chair for new ink.

What if you got more than friendship? What if this bloomed into something spectacular?

Here was the truth: she'd lied like a rug to Joel. She *had* dreamed after sleeping on a carpet of kismet cookies.

It was a long and languid dream, and in her sleep, Joel had made love to her all over again. She didn't buy into that cocka-mamie cookie prophecy. She'd dreamed of him because she'd been with him, and that was all there was to it. Nothing mysti-cal or magical about it other than the stupendous sex. It was all a question of proximity and circumstances.

However, she wasn't about to let anyone in this myth-mad town know it. Most importantly of all, she wouldn't let Joel know. Joel, the one person she'd told more of her secrets to than anyone else in her life, ever.

Even if she had held back on her most momentous secret of all. Oh shit, this was getting deep, and she didn't know what to do with herself.

For now, she had breakfast to prepare, and that's where she'd spend her focus. Determined to tuck last night from her mind for now, she gathered ingredients. Arms full, she turned to set the supplies on the counter and caught sight of her reflection in the mirrored glass of the microwave.

Her hair was mussed, even though she'd brushed it, and her eyes were wide. Her lips were slightly swollen from so much kissing last night, and there was an inescapable smile on her face. With pancake ingredients in her arms and a jolly Christmas apron tied around her waist, she resembled a modern-day Betty Crocker.

She looked like, for want of a better word, a mom, and she *loved* it.

Excited by the prospect of a new life with Joel, Jana threw herself into breakfast prep.

He came into the kitchen with damp hair and eager eyes, and her heart tripped all over itself.

They ate and chatted, easy and comfortable with each other, then washed the dishes together, side by side at the kitchen sink. There was no dishwasher in the small rental, and the simple act felt cozy and companionable.

His elbow bumped gently into hers, and she thought, *This.*

This was solid. This was strong. This could work. They had a reliable place to grow from: mutual respect and admiration.

After they finished their tasks, they loaded up the presents they'd wrapped last night into the back of his truck. Joel closed the tailgate, pulled down the cover, and turned to her. "I'll meet you at the Rockabye."

"Wait," she said and put a hand to his forearm.

Gently, he smiled down at her. "What is it?"

"I'll go with you."

"And leave your Jeep here?"

She nodded.

"Really?" His smile stretched wider. "Whatever happened to never going anywhere without an exit plan?"

"I'm thinking maybe you *are* my exit plan," she whispered.

"Aww, Tink," he said, gathered her to his chest, and kissed her so thoroughly she was breathless by the time he let her go.

She climbed in on the passenger side, her heart throbbing from the high of his kiss. Things didn't get any better than this. Grateful, she hugged herself and grinned as he guided his truck around the town square.

Shoppers were hurrying home with packages from last-minute purchases. On a street corner, amid the hubbub, Jana spied the thin young woman in the faded jean jacket that she'd seen on the dock yesterday when they'd hung the banner on the Brazos Queen. The girl's dark hair was parted in two long braids, and she cast a sidelong glance at the pickup as they drove by. She appeared just as forlorn as she had on the Christmas Island pier, and Jana's heart went out to her. Not everyone got to have a merry Christmas.

No, but this year you do. Appreciate it. She could easily be that young woman on the street. Hell, she *had* been her more times than she wanted to admit.

"Is that the girl we saw yesterday?" Joel asked.

"I think so."

"The one you wondered if she could be Gabriel's mom?"

"I do believe it is her."

"She looks too young. Only thirteen or fourteen."

Jana placed a hand to her belly. "Biologically, totally possible."

"Do you think we should stop and ask her if she needs help?"

"Yes, let's do it."

Joel whipped over to the curb and put down the window, but the panic-stricken girl jumped back, turned on her heels, fled down the street, and ducked into an alley. "Well," he said, "that was suspicious. Should I go after her?"

Jana shook her head. "Leave her be. Most likely she's not Gabriel's mom and just a runaway."

"Still," Joel said. "I'm texting Hondo to keep an eye out. Just in case she is living on the street."

"We better get a move on," Jana said, her gaze on the alleyway where the young woman had disappeared. "The float parade starts in half an hour."

Nodding, Joel pulled back into the flow of traffic.

The radio was turned down low, and Jana could barely hear the song that was playing and smiled when she realized it was her favorite Christmas tune, George Strait's "Christmas Cookies," and she tried to get her happy mood back.

Fog, generated by the heavy humidity, rolled in off the lake, decreasing the visibility the closer they got to Christmas Island. Joel turned on the wipers to whisk away the gray damp from the windshield. They made a soft squeaking noise against the glass. He needed new blades.

As he left the town square and drove over the bridge to Christmas Island, where the Rockabye was permanently docked, he didn't speed up, even though the speed limit jumped by ten miles per hour.

"Anxiety got hold of you again, Tink?" Joel's tone was so gentle his words didn't sting.

Yes, yes it did. Then something occurred to her that she hadn't considered before. Something that tightened her muscles and sickened her stomach.

"Joel, what if Gabriel's mom is truly horrible, and he shouldn't go back to her? What if he really would be better off in foster care? I mean the woman did leave him in the manger for strangers to find. Who does that?"

"You were in the system. How awful would his mom have to be for foster care to be the better solution?"

"Pretty awful," Jana admitted as "Christmas Cookies" gave way to "Winter Wonderland." She sighed. "I mean most of my foster parents were decent people, but many of them put their own needs ahead of the children in their care. Some ignored me. Some turned me into the family scapegoat."

"I'm sorry you had such a crappy childhood," Joel murmured and reached over to hold her hand.

His touch comforted her, but it also threw her for a loop. Things were starting to get weird between them, boundaries blurring, feelings deepening.

Were these feelings she was having just because of the baby and the holidays? Would her emotions die down when things went back to normal? Would her euphoria be short-lived?

"Your childhood was crappy too. You lost your mom."

"Yes, but I had Flynn and Carrie and Noah and my mom's friends, and that made all the difference."

Slowly, so as not to seem abrupt and rude, she slipped her hand from his, pretending she needed it to smooth back her hair that had started to frizz in the humidity. Cautiously, she glanced over at him to gauge his reaction to her withdrawal.

He seemed unaffected, settling his hand back on the steering wheel and squinting hard at the wall of fog in his headlights and muttering, "Pea freaking soup."

All righty. He'd just been trying to comfort her as a friend. Nothing else. No harm, no foul. Don't read anything into it. Sleeping with him last night had spooked her, stirred her fears and insecurities. Nothing had changed between them. Her mind had fermented a shift that wasn't really happening.

"Not telling you what to do," Joel said, "but most of the things we worry about never come true. Usually everything works out in the end. Look at how far you've come since you arrived in Twilight."

While Jana liked Joel's down-to-earth practicality, his soft-pedaling of the situation ruffled her, although she couldn't say why. Anger made sense. So did tenderheartedness. But Joel's reasonable approach was confusing, and so was her own growing need to get back to the baby.

She'd bonded with Gabriel far quicker than she'd ever thought possible, and it opened her up on a whole new level.

In that opening, she saw a path to a whole new future. A future she'd never dreamed possible.

And it looked glorious.

But the only way to get there was to tell Joel her darkest secret of all, and she just didn't know if she was strong enough to do it.

Or if she ever would be.

Chapter 20

The Perfect Day

It was the best Christmas Eve of Joel's life.

No exceptions.

High on the sweet lovemaking of the night before, his heart overflowed with joy as he and Jana picked up Gabriel at the Rockabye.

Raylene Pringle was working the reception desk, while Kelsey and Noah, dressed as Santa and Mrs. Claus served brunch to the boatel guests in the dining area. Raylene kept an eye on Gabriel, who napped in a cradle beside the Christmas tree.

As Kelsey and Jana got Gabriel ready to go, Noah pulled Joel aside. "Dude, that baby is the sweetest thing. Kels and I are sold on having one of our own."

"Congrats. I'm glad you enjoyed keeping him. Thanks for looking after him for us. Jana and I appreciated the alone time."

"Ooh." Noah got a knowing look on his face and poked Joel in the rib cage with his elbow. "You two did it!"

"Shh."

"Hot damn! Congrats to you too, bro. Jana's the bomb, seriously."

"I'm not confirming or denying anything."

"You don't have to. The look on your face tells it all. I love it. You make a great couple. I've always thought so."

"Really?"

"Yeah, you just *get* each other. Haven't you noticed how you finish each other's sentences?"

"No."

"You do. Just like Kels and me."

"Do we?"

"Yep."

Hmm, maybe Noah was right.

"Joel and Jana sitting in a tree—"

"Stop it. What are you? Twelve years old?"

"Can't help it, bud. I'm excited for you."

"Could you keep a lid on it? I'm not sure Jana would appreciate word getting around that we're—"

"Shaking the sheets?" Noah chuckled.

"This is still new, and she's something special, Noah, so please, hush it."

"You're cute. Thinking that you're hiding something from everyone."

"We're just taking it slow. We don't know what this is ourselves. We're not throwing around labels."

"Sure, sure." Noah clamped a hand on Joel's shoulder. "But do I hear wedding bells in your future?"

Joel groaned and shook his head, felt his throat tighten. "Listen, Jana's had a tough life. She told me some things about her childhood. Things I don't know if she'll ever be able to get past, so—"

"But you're falling in love with her."

Joel wanted to deny it, but he couldn't. He was falling for her. Silently, he nodded.

"You know, Kelsey had a lot to overcome before she felt safe enough to trust me. If you need any advice or just want to talk, I'm here."

Joel cast a glance over at Jana, who was holding Gabriel while Kelsey was putting a little Santa suit on him.

He bit his bottom lip. He would like Noah's take on the situation. Quickly, he told his twin what Jana had confided in him the night before, about how she'd been abandoned in a honkytonk by her mother and then what had happened with the foster mom who wanted to adopt her and the sleazy older guy she'd gotten involved with.

"Life's kicked her in the teeth. Repeatedly."

"That does sound rough," Noah said. "Just give her time. Knowing you have her back, knowing that she can trust you will go a long way to making her feel safe."

"You're right. That's my plan."

"Good luck." Noah clapped him on the back. "Kels and I are rooting for you."

It felt good to tell his brother what was on his mind, but as Joel and Jana left the Rockabye with Gabriel, he couldn't help wondering if he should have kept his mouth shut. He started to tell her what he'd done, but Jana looked so darn happy with the baby in her arms, he just let it go.

Why ruin a perfectly great day?

The float parade was fun, the guests lively. Everyone on board the paddle-wheel wanted a chance to hold the manger baby in the little Santa suit and get their picture taken with him. Joel was surprised how much he missed the little guy and wished he didn't have to pilot the boat so he could hold him too.

Several times, he caught Jana giving him sidelong glances. He would smile at her, and she would smile back, and he had the best feeling that everything was going to be okay between them.

They were solid. They were good. They hadn't ruined their relationship, and sex had seemed to have enhanced it. He'd never seen her looking so happy, and his own heart had never felt so light.

The rest of the day was jam-packed with activities. After the float parade they met up with Joel's family at the busy holiday ice rink. Flynn and Jesse brought Ian and Grace, along with Carrie and her husband, Mark. Noah and Kelsey showed up too, and they were joined by Cousin Paige, Cash, and Zinnia. Joel's dad and stepmother drove up from the hill country for the weekend. They sat on the sidelines watching the skaters and tending Gabriel and Zinnia while everyone else skated.

While they were on the ice rink, to Joel's utter delight, Jana skated over and took his hand.

Right there in front of everyone.

"For stability," she said to clarify. "I'm not that accomplished on ice skates."

"Uh-huh." He grinned and let her have her little excuse. Ah, but he knew the truth. She *wanted* to hold his hand. His heart got a little crazy then, bumping and thumping. Joel squeezed her hand and held on tight.

From there, their group toured the life-sized gingerbread house constructed on the town square and attended the evening tree-lighting ceremony. Afterward, they convened to Paige and Cash's place on the lake for a charcuterie smorgasbord and a musical sing-along as Cash played his guitar.

They opened gifts and played games, and by eight o'clock the party started to break up. With lingering goodbyes and messages of hope and good luck for Gabriel, the guests slowly departed.

Paige insisted on sending everyone home with a bag of kismet cookies, including Jana and Joel. With a conspiratorial wink, she told Jana, "I expect a report on who you dream about tonight."

Joel rolled his eyes. "She's not sleeping with a cookie under her pillow. That's ridiculous."

"You're not the boss of her, Joel MacGregor."

"Neither are you, Paige Colton."

Jana ignored them both, in favor of blowing a soft raspberry against Gabriel's sweet little belly.

It was eight thirty by the time they got back to Joel's house. Jana changed and fed Gabriel and put him down to sleep in the

Pack 'n Play, while Joel tended the dogs. Jana prepared nondairy hot chocolate with minimarshmallows and peppermint sticks. Joel started a fire in the fireplace and got down on his hands and knees, putting together a train to run around the base of the tree.

"What are you doing?" she asked, coming into the room with two steaming mugs in her hands.

He grinned up at her. "It's the Polar Express. Part of my family tradition. On Christmas Eve, just before we went to bed, my mom would read *The Polar Express*, and my dad would put the same train together. Then we would set out kismet cookies and milk for Santa and head off to bed."

He got to his feet and took the mug she offered. They sat down together on the couch in front of the tree.

Joel stared at Jana, and his heart filled with wonder. Hell, his heart was filled with a whole lot more feelings than that. Serious feelings that had him squirming. Sometimes, he had trouble with the serious stuff, and he knew it was due to losing his mother at a young age. He and Noah had become the family jokesters, the class clowns, to lighten the dark atmosphere that descended after Mom had passed away.

The easygoing goofball had become part of his persona. He'd done a lot of wacky stuff in his life, often going the extra mile for a laugh, anything to blunt the harder emotions. Things like performing a public striptease. He wasn't irresponsible by any means. He just preferred to focus on the bright side, sometimes to his detriment.

He was pretty good at the good times, at parties and games, at being around people. It was one of the qualities that made him so accomplished at his job. He was friendly, open, and accepting. Until things turned solemn, and that's where he stumbled.

What he wasn't so good at was ambiguity. A long time ago, he'd learned to keep things on an even keel and squelch those moodier emotions. Ignoring the bad times and pretending they didn't exist was his MO.

And yet, all his carefully cultivated optimism wavered when he looked over at Jana and realized any quip or joke was an inadequate defense against the serious thoughts churning around in his head.

Her hair was mussed, her full lips pursed, her navy blue eyes wide and cautious. She was dressed simply, in jeans and a sweater again. The light makeup she'd put on earlier in the day had almost faded away.

In her simplicity, she looked absolutely stunning.

Her expression held a trove of things. Elation. Hope. An incendiary heat. But all that was quickly camouflaged by a look of feigned nonchalance.

"Today has been so beautiful," Jana said, echoing Joel's own thoughts. "I wish it could go on forever."

"Me too," he murmured, still afraid to say more. Things were so good. He didn't want to say or do anything to rattle her.

"I'd go as far as to say this might be my best Christmas," she said.

"Me too." He set down his mug, then took her mug from her hand and positioned it beside his on the side table.

"What are you doing?" she asked.

"This."

He swept her into his arms and kissed her. Kissed her long. Kissed her hard. Kissed her deep.

Then he pulled back and left her gasping.

"Wow," she panted, putting her fingertips to her lips. "What was that for?"

"Because it had been too long since I kissed you."

Her cheeks pinkened, and she ducked her head, smiling.

He moved to retrieve a package from underneath the Christmas tree and brought it back to her.

"For me?" She dropped her gaze to the package in her hand. "You really didn't have to get me anything. You've already given me the best gift of all by helping me take care of Gabriel and by being so understanding."

Throughout the day, he hadn't missed the look on her face whenever she held the baby. It was so sweet the way her eyes softened, but she was getting attached, and that hurt his soul, because she was going to have to give him up on New Year's Day.

Joel's chest tightened. He would miss the little guy too.

She slanted her head toward Joel and sent him a quick sideways glance before looking away, but he saw the tears brimming in her eyes.

"Well." Jana cleared her throat and put up a smile that seemed just a little bit forced. "Let's see what's in this box."

"It's no big thing." He shrugged.

She opened the box and unwrapped the Tinker Bell charm to add to her charm bracelet. "Oh, Joel!" She sighed happily and pressed the charm to her chest, "I love it."

"I'm glad."

Her face dissolved into a beautiful smile, and she leaned across the couch to hug him tight and whisper, "You're the best friend a woman could ever ask for."

Friend.

Yes, they were friends. And as of last night, lovers too. But he wanted so much more. Thing was he was too afraid of scaring her off to come right out and say it.

"Here," he said, "let me put the charm on the bracelet for you."

She held up her delicate wrist and he found a loop on her crowded charm bracelet and attached Tinker Bell.

Jana admired the charm, and then with a grin, clapped her hands. "Now open your present from me."

From her purse she pulled an envelope wrapped with a bright red ribbon. He opened it up to find two courtside tickets to an upcoming basketball game between the LA Lakers and the Dallas Mavericks.

"Sweet! I can't believe you sprung for these. It's been forever since I've been to a professional basketball game."

"I know," she said. "You can take Noah."

"No way. I'm taking you."

"Are you sure?" She sounded uncertain, as if she didn't believe she deserved to go with him.

Why was that? Or maybe he was just misreading her body language. "Don't you want to go?"

"Absolutely! I love the Lakers."

"Don't tell me you're going to root for them." He groaned.

"You better believe it, MacGregor." She gave him a gentle punch on his upper arm, in the same we're-just-friends way she usually did.

"You're the best, Gerard. C'mere." He held out his arms, and she went right to him. "I love the tickets, and I love that you're going with me. You can cheer at the top of your lungs for the Lakers if that's what you want to do."

"I like how you let me be me." She smiled and leaned in, and he kissed her again.

They kissed for a good long time, Joel savoring every second. Finally, she pulled back, suppressing a yawn.

"Are my kisses boring you? Because I can step up my game." He wriggled his eyebrows.

"No," she said. "Not at all. I'm just worn to a frazzle. It's been a big day, and Gabriel does like to eat every two and a half hours."

"I am pretty beat myself." He'd been looking forward to sex, but when she started yawning, he was yawning too.

"Would it be okay if Gabriel and I slept in your bed the way we did the first night? Just sleep?"

"Of course. Go get the little guy, and I'll meet you in my bedroom." Those were words he never expected to say to Jana. Two days ago, life had indeed thrown him an unexpected curveball. A curveball he was quickly coming to love.

A few minutes later they were curled up in the middle of his king-sized bed facing each other, the baby in between them. They gazed intently into each other's eyes over the infant's head.

Jana looked so adorable in the glow of the light with her hands stacked under her cheek and her honey brown hair spilling over her shoulders.

"This is nice," she said.

"Very nice."

"I never expected it to be so nice. You know, having a kid around."

Joel traced his knuckle over the baby's fuzzy little head. "We're going to miss the heck out of him."

Jana rolled over onto her back and stared up at the ceiling.

He studied her profile and wished he could see what was going on behind her eyes. "Are you going to be okay?"

"*Pfftt,* sure. I'll be fine." She said it just a little bit too loudly, a little bit too firmly for him to buy it. "You know me, easy come, easy go. We'll have achieved our goal. Taking care of him until his mother returns."

If she returns.

"We will." He paused. "Now it's time to get some shut-eye. We have another big day ahead of us tomorrow."

"You're right." She yawned again.

Joel blew her a kiss and turned off the light, and as he lay there in the darkness, found himself thinking, *I could spend the rest of my life doing this and die a very happy man.*

CHAPTER 21

THE FAMILY

Walking into Flynn's house—the same house Joel had grown up in—was always a pleasant experience. The old farmhouse near the Brazos River stirred nostalgic feelings of safety, warmth, and welcome.

But this Christmas morning felt extra special.

Flynn had gone all out with the decorating and cooking. It looked as if the North Pole had exploded inside her house, and hardly a bare patch of space existed without some tribute to the holiday, and it smelled like heaven on a plate. Fully decorated Christmas trees stood in every room. Christmas villages overtook dressers and tabletops. Homemade stockings embroidered with family members' names dangled from the mantel.

There was even a stocking for Jana. As if she was part of the family. That touched her in ways she hadn't expected.

Cinnamon, roasted turkey, vanilla, and pumpkin spice scented the air. Christmas music played, a different song from every device. It was cacophonous and joyous and submersed visitors in Flynn's version of the holiday like one of her warm, generous hugs. At Joel's sister's house you were treated to the full Christmas experience.

And yes, it could definitely be overwhelming for someone who wasn't accustomed to such high holiday spirits.

The minute they came through the door, Flynn went straight for the baby. "Oh, look at you! What a sweet boy!"

Without asking permission, Flynn scooped Gabriel from Jana's arms and waltzed him around the room, showing him off.

Joel's father and his second wife, Barbara, who'd once been the local librarian, were there already, as were Noah and Kelsey, Carrie and Mark, and Paige and Cash.

Mark and Carrie had been high-school sweethearts who'd broken up but reunited some years later. Mark was a successful TV game-show host, and they owned a ranch outside of Santa Barbara where they ran a pet rescue. They'd lived in Twilight for a time after their marriage, but then Mark had gotten a job offer he couldn't refuse, and they'd relocated. They didn't have children and seemed totally content without them.

Not everyone was destined to have children. In fact, Jana had believed she was one of those people who would skip both marriage and motherhood. She'd had no real maternal instincts. No strong role models in her early years, no urge to have a baby.

Until Gabriel.

Now, watching Flynn loving on the newborn, Jana felt a stark stab of both longing and jealousy.

Feeling unsettled and slightly claustrophobic, Jana escaped to the kitchen where the children were parked at the folding kids' table with crayons and coloring books.

"Hi, Jana!" Grace waved. "Wanna color with us?"

"I'm not very good at drawing," Jana said. "But please show me what you're coloring."

Proudly, Grace held up a nativity that she'd meticulously filled in with various shades of purple, her favorite color.

"Good job," Jana said and leaned over to peek at Ian's page. "What are you working on?"

"Dinosaurs!" Ian exclaimed and showed her his scribblings.

"Nicely done." Jana nodded.

"He colors outside the lines." Grace sniffed.

"Ian's still young. Give him time. You used to scribble."

Grace looked indignant. "I did not."

"Did too," Ian said.

"Not."

"Too."

"Not," Grace said, determined to get in the last word.

"Oops," Jana said, reaching across the table to take away the black crayon that little Zinnia was chewing on. "That's not candy."

Zinnia broke into tears.

Yikes! Before Jana could decide what to do, Flynn was there soothing the little girl, distracting her with a cookie while she expertly held Gabriel in the crook of her elbow. The woman was a mothering ninja.

"Grace, honey, could you please put away the crayons and coloring books?" Flynn asked her daughter. "We'll be eating soon."

"I'll help," Jana told Grace, feeling inadequate around Dynamo Flynn.

And you're not a dynamo? She heard Joel's voice in her head, plain as if he'd said it out loud.

Nah, she really wasn't a dynamo. Not a true go-getter. She just liked keeping herself busy. If left too long with her solitary thoughts, anxiety had a sneaky way of overtaking her mind, and that led to dark places she'd rather avoid.

"I was hoping you could help me." Flynn's bright smile was particularly blinding today.

Uneasiness tickled the back of Jana's neck. Was there a problem here? Was Flynn trying too hard, or was Jana's imagination in overdrive?

As a kid kicked from foster home to foster home, she'd learned to be hypervigilant. Relentlessly on the search for clues that helped her monitor her environment for threats—exaggerated smiles, forced cheerfulness, undertones and subtext in conversations, restless tics or twitches. Nervous habits. Any telltale signs of emotional outbursts forming on the horizon. It was a habit that no longer served her, but it was a tough one to break.

"Um, okay." Jana straightened. "What do you need help with?"

Flynn shifted the baby, bringing him to her shoulder and gently patting his back. "I've got some things in my bedroom that need sorting out."

Jana canted her head, watching Flynn through narrowed eyes. What was going on here?

"Oh, I thought you might need help putting lunch on the table." Jana shifted her gaze to Carrie, who'd come into the kitchen to open the oven and peek inside at the turkey.

"Care Bear," Flynn said to her sister, "could you hold Gabriel for a minute?"

"Sure." Carrie reached for the baby. "You want me to keep an eye on the turkey too?"

"That'd be great. Thanks." Flynn hooked her elbow through Jana's. "This way."

Flynn and Jesse's bedroom was just as decked out in Christmas bling as the rest of the house. Once inside, Flynn shut the door behind them, and Jana's sense of claustrophobia deepened.

Uh-oh. Jana hugged herself. What was up?

"Are you cold?" Flynn asked. "We kept the heat turned down because with so many people in the house it gets really toasty in the communal rooms. I can loan you a sweater."

"I'm fine," Jana said, fighting against her tendency to find trouble where there was none.

With a smile that Jana was afraid to trust, Flynn sat down on the edge of the bed and patted the mattress beside her. "Please, have a seat."

"Um, okay." Fighting her anxiety, Jana settled down next to Flynn.

Flynn put on a bright smile. "Just let me say, I've long admired you."

That worried Jana even more. "I admire you too."

"You inspired me."

"I did?"

Flynn reached over to take Jana's hand. It was all she could do not to flinch. People in Twilight were so touchy-feely. Nothing wrong with that. Jana just wasn't used to it, and she didn't know how to ask for her hand back.

"Jesse and I were thinking really hard about having another baby, but I'm getting close to forty, and there's so many children out there like little Gabriel who need parents. When I heard about what you went through in your life, how your mother left you in a bar under a pool table and how the one foster mother who truly loved you died and yet you've come out of it to be such an amazing person . . ." Flynn pressed her free hand to her chest.

Wait, what? Joel had told Flynn what she'd shared with him in an intimate moment? Stunned, Jana sat blinking as Flynn tightened her grip on Jana's hand.

"Well, when I told Jesse that I wanted to foster a child that we could eventually adopt, he was one hundred percent on board. I wish now we'd already gone through the process so we could put in to adopt Gabriel if his mother doesn't return for him."

Jana was still too gobsmacked by Joel's betrayal to speak. She would never have told him any of that if she'd known he was going to blab it to everyone.

Flynn was still just chatting away, oblivious to Jana's discomfort. "We shouldn't have any trouble getting approved, even though Jesse did spend ten years in prison. He was completely exonerated and pardoned when the real culprit who blew up the Brazos River bridge confessed."

"That's wonderful that you want to help a child," Jana said. "You are a really great mother, Flynn. Any kid would be lucky to have you as a mom."

"That's so sweet of you to say. I confess I was worried when I learned you and Joel were living together to take care of the baby."

"Why's that?"

"I was afraid Joel would fall for you and get his heart broken, but when I see the two of you together, I realize my fears were unfounded. You're a good person, Jana Gerard. I know you would never intentionally hurt him."

"No, I wouldn't."

"Oh my goodness, that sounded insensitive, didn't it? As if I didn't care about your feelings. I'm so sorry. Please forgive me."

"It's okay. I get it. I'm the interloper."

"That's not how I see you." Flynn's face was kind. "In fact, I have a gift for you."

Flynn got up and moved to the dresser and picked up a long skinny box wrapped in festive Christmas paper and brought it back to Jana.

Feeling self-conscious, she unwrapped the package. Inside was a beautiful gold necklace with a phoenix medallion.

"I saw it in the window of Linberg's Jewelry yesterday, and I thought, that's Jana. She's a golden phoenix rising out of the ashes of her past, and I just had to get it for you."

Jana stared at the fiery bird shooting heavenward, and she was so touched she couldn't speak.

"This thing with you and Joel, I don't know where it's going. I don't mean to put pressure on you, but my brother cares about you very much. I've never seen him look at any woman the way he looks at you, not even Tory."

Jana sucked in a deep breath. Was it true? Was Joel in love with her? Or were his feelings nothing more than a holiday-induced fantasy?

One way or another, she had to find out because she was falling in love with him.

"May I speak with you in private?"

Joel was standing beside the biggest Christmas tree in the center of the living room, surrounded by an impossible amount of gaily wrapped packages, drinking eggnog from a moose-eared cup inspired by *National Lampoon's Christmas Vacation* and conversing with Noah.

Jana seemed distressed but was trying hard not to let it show—pressing her lips together, shifting her weight from foot to foot, fingering a gold necklace at her throat.

"Sure, sure." He searched for a place to set the spiked eggnog far from the reach of any inquisitive little hands, but every inch of space was decorated.

"Now?" she urged.

"Here." He thrust the eggnog at Noah. "Hold this."

"Um, okay." His twin accepted the moose-eared mug that matched his own.

Joel took Jana's elbow to guide her from the room, wondering where they could go for a private conversation in this hubbub. There was the porch, but it was pretty nippy outside.

She wrenched away from his hand, and that's when he knew she was really upset with him.

Oh crap, what had he done?

He could take her to the bathroom, but with everyone watching, that seemed too intimate. He tried to take her hand again, but she shied away.

Not just upset, she was mad.

What *had* he done? Alarmed, Joel ran through a list of his possible sins but couldn't come up with anything.

"Tink?" he murmured.

She glared at him.

Okay, no nicknames. Got it.

"This way."

Jana's scowl deepened.

"The laundry room," he said.

She gave a curt nod and followed him, but that meant traversing the kitchen where the women were all gathered. He gave his relatives a jaunty wave and kept walking, Jana at his heels.

"Where you going?" Flynn called. "Food will be on the table in five minutes."

Joel raised his hand over his head. "We'll be right back."

Unless, he thought, *Jana skins me alive and eats me for Christmas brunch.* He was still at a loss for what he might have done.

He peeked over at her. From the way she was gnawing her bottom lip, he was about to find out.

Once they were in the laundry room, Joel closed the blue toile-pattern curtain that separated the laundry from the kitchen.

Jana was shaking her head. "They'll hear every word."

"No, they won't." Joel stepped to the clothes dryer and peered inside. It was filled with jeans that hadn't yet been unloaded. Those should make plenty of noise. He turned on the dryer and soon the clack of snaps and zippers acted as camouflage.

"What's up?" He turned to face her.

"You told your sister what I said to you in the strictest confidence."

Puzzled, Joel tried to take her hand, but she pulled back. He dropped his hand to his side. "I don't know what you're talking about."

"She *knows.*"

He canted his head, narrowed his eyes. Jana was upset, and it distressed him to think he'd caused it. "Knows what?"

"That my mother abandoned me under a pool table. That my foster mother Marjean died of cancer." She paused to take a deep breath.

"Oh," Joel said, guilt smashing into him. "I didn't tell her, but I did tell Noah. I asked him to keep it under his hat, and I know that he did. But I did tell him at the Rockabye, and Raylene was there. I should have been more circumspect. I didn't think about her eavesdropping, but knowing Raylene the way I do, I suspect that's the leak."

"But why did you tell Noah?" She said it in such a helpless voice it rocked him to his core. Jana was the opposite of helpless. Seeing her so hurt tore him up.

"He's my twin."

"So that makes it okay to betray me?"

"I get why you're annoyed," he said. "You have every right to be, but could you be overreacting?"

Her navy blue eyes flashed fire, and he felt the heat of her anger in the pit of his belly. "I trusted you, Joel. That's the big deal. I trusted you, and you let me down."

It dawned on Joel that Jana's upset had little to do with Flynn finding out about the past that she'd guarded so carefully. In Jana's mind, Joel had betrayed her trust, and that perceived betrayal had triggered her primal fears. She didn't trust easily, but she'd trusted him, and he'd let her down.

His heart ached, and he wanted so badly to take her into his arms and give her a big hug, but from the look on her face, that would be like hugging a cactus.

"I need you to know something. I know it's hard because you had no family structure growing up. No one you could depend on to have your back. I can't imagine what that's like. But I tell my family what's going on in my life. The good, the bad, the boring. We don't keep secrets. We help each other. Can you understand that?"

"I can try."

That little bit of agreement gave him hope. She was willing to try. For now, it was enough.

"I didn't mean to betray you. That wasn't my intention. I just needed some advice from my brother." Contrite, Joel pulled a palm down his face.

A mournful feeling came over him. They were twins, and twins shared everything. He couldn't expect Jana to understand that, but she made a good point.

"Advice about what?" she asked.

Joel held up both palms. This was it. The time to come clean. Time to tell her how he felt. If being honest caused her to bolt, then he had his answer—she wasn't ready for a real relationship—and he could decide from there whether to keep hanging on or not.

"About what, Joel?" She was trembling. It was slight, and someone else might not have noticed, but he saw the shakiness in her fingers, heard the quiver in her voice.

He gulped, cleared his throat, held her gaze. "Whether you and I have a fighting chance."

"A chance for what?"

"To be a couple."

"Oh," she said, then in a lower, softer voice repeated, "Oh."

"So do we?" Joel asked, searching her dear face.

"Do we what?"

"Stand a chance of making a go of it?"

She fingered the phoenix medallion at her neck and touched the tip of her tongue to her upper lip. "What are you suggesting?"

"I want to be with you, Jana. I've admired you from afar for a long time."

"You have?"

"Yes, and I think you know that."

She gave a quick smile. "I thought maybe . . . but then you were with Ursula, and I thought I was imagining it."

"You weren't. Living with you, taking care of Gabriel with you, it's deepened my feelings, and I can't keep quiet about it any longer. I can give you time. Lots of time. All the time you need, but first, I gotta know. Do you feel the same way about me?"

Silently, she nodded.

"C'mon on, then," he said, grinning big and taking her hand.

She balked, pulling back, but he did not release her. "Wh-where are we going?"

"To set things straight with my family."

CHAPTER 22

THE DECLARATION

"May I have your attention?" Joel announced to his family sitting in the living room. Everyone except Flynn and Carrie, who were in the kitchen clattering pots and pans.

Everyone quieted.

"Carrie, Flynn," Joel called to his sisters, "can you come in here too?"

The women appeared in the doorway, simultaneously drying their hands on dish towels as the interested eyes of the MacGregor clan fixed on Joel and Jana.

Jana straightened, feeling a little unnerved and crazy excited. It was real. She and Joel were an item. A couple. Boyfriend and girlfriend. Her mind filled with possibilities that she'd been too scared to entertain until now.

Joel wrapped his arm around her waist, anchoring her to his side. She looked over to Kelsey, who had Gabriel on her lap. Jana ached to hold the baby, but it felt nice knowing she had people eager to help out.

"Jana and I are officially dating."

"Hot dog!" Noah jumped to his feet and came across the room to pump his brother's hand.

"About time you realized it." Paige grinned.

"They're slow learners," her husband Cash chuckled. "Just like we were."

"Hon," Carrie said, holding out her hand to Mark, "you owe me a dollar." Mark stood, took the dollar bill from his wallet, and passed it to his wife.

"We were just waiting for you two to wake up to what was right in front of you." Kelsey sighed happily and passed Gabriel to Jana. "This little guy certainly worked his magic."

Yes, yes, he had, but as Jana cradled Gabriel in the crook of her arm, she couldn't help wondering if the magic would last once the baby was gone.

"I'm so happy for you both." Flynn held her arms wide. Hugged first Joel, then Jana. Then everyone was hugging them and congratulating them, and she felt herself swept away on a whirlwind of loving energy.

And just like that, Jana was accepted into the fold.

She cast a sideways glance up at her tall man, caught him looking down at her with such tenderness in his eyes that her breath hung up in her lungs. She wished she could tug his head down and kiss him right there in front of everyone. There was plenty of mistletoe around here to use as an excuse.

The impulse surprised her. She was a private person, not given to public displays of affection, but right now, she wanted to kiss him so badly, she almost did it anyway.

This was the dream Jana had dreamed for so long. A Christmas morning, and a closeness around the big family table after the tittering arrival of the guests, fresh scooting of chairs on the hand-scraped hardwood floors waxed shiny, the big platter of Belgian waffles deposited between the place settings with a declarative thump, the banter and laughter and echoing resonance of the family itself gathered, the last seats taken.

Jana sat reverent at her spot, breathing in the hubbub. She heard the sound of Joel's chuckle in the chair beside her, a rich vibration of good cheer and the crisp, bright clack of his fork against the china, then his rueful "Oops" as he started to pass the waffle to Jana and stopped midair.

"She can have them," Flynn said. "They're vegan. Christine Noble's recipe from the Twilight Bakery."

"You didn't have to go to special trouble for me," Jana said. "I could have just eaten the fruit salad."

"There's facon too," Carrie said and took the top off a serving dish.

Aww. They'd gone to all this trouble, and that was before Joel had told everyone they were dating. She was so touched that tears pressed against the back of her eyes, and Jana didn't do tears.

She'd always liked the MacGregors, but they were quickly becoming very important to her. Was it happening too fast?

There wasn't much time to dissect her feelings. The boisterous family ate and joked and enjoyed one another's company, and Jana was right there among them. After the meal, they made short work of cleanup, and everyone reconvened in the living room, where they opened gifts and took family photos.

While the children played and the adults put toys together, Jana sat on the couch beside Joel's stepmother, Barbara, and gave Gabriel a bottle.

"You're a natural," Barbara said. "A stranger seeing you with him would think you were Gabriel's mother."

Barbara meant nothing by it, but her words poked at old guilt inside Jana, kicked at the secret she had held so close to her heart for so many lonely years. The secret she'd never revealed to anyone in Twilight.

Not even to Joel.

She should tell him. Now they were officially dating. But she had no idea how to start that uncomfortable conversation, and the last thing she wanted was to wipe that grin off his face. He looked like a big kid, down on all fours playing with Ian.

Her heart melted in her chest. Ahh, she was in so much trouble here. What if things didn't work out between them? What if she told Joel her secret and he couldn't get past what she'd done? What then? What would happen to their friendship?

A fear sank its teeth into her.

Don't ever tell him, Jana. Take the secret to your grave. It's really none of his business. He never need know.

Keeping quiet had kept her safe for a long, long time. Why monkey with success?

Only problem? How could Joel ever completely trust her if she hid things from him? That wasn't an authentic relationship.

No, if she wanted an authentic relationship, she had to be fully honest about who she was—the good, the bad, and the ugly. She knew that. It was hard. She'd never revealed this much of herself to anyone, but Joel was worth the risk.

But what if it ruined everything? whispered fear. *What if, once he knows, he won't want you anymore?*

Wait. She'd wait. Until after New Year's. She wanted to enjoy the time she had left with Gabriel. No harm in waiting, really. Until their relationship was on solid footing. She'd waited this long. What was a week, after all?

Christmas night after they'd put Gabriel in the Pack 'n Play to sleep at the end of Joel's king-sized bed, they'd made love.

Twice.

Each time they had sex was better than the last. She'd never had a partner so attuned to her needs, so attentive and caring. At times, it was almost too much to have a man notice her so intently, and yet, it was what she'd always longed for. A deep emotional connection.

At one point, in the afterglow, as they lay side by side staring into each other's eyes, Joel had said, "Wow, your eyelashes grow all the way to the very corner of your eyes. I've never noticed that about you before."

His comment stirred her embarrassment as if there was something wrong with her for having eyelashes that grew differently from others. But honestly, it was more than that. His keen observation triggered her uneasiness. He saw her too clearly, and she ended up feeling as if he peered right through her, past her defenses and inside the very center of soul.

And that scared her.

A lot.

Sit with the discomfort. The words rose in her mind. That was the only way to get on the other side of this. To finally, fully let down her guard and allow him in.

Joel pulled her against his chest and kissed the top of her head. She could trust him. He'd never let her down. He was a man of his word. A man of integrity. He meant what he said and said what he meant.

She thought of Dr. Seuss's *Horton Hatches the Egg* and smiled big with her head tucked underneath Joel's chin. He was as loyal as Horton the Elephant, and he rounded out her rough edges in the most magnificent way.

And if she let herself dream, she saw an amazing future unfurling before them, the last tethers of her fears loosening.

If only . . .

"What are you worrying over?" Joel murmured.

"How do you know I'm worrying?" she asked, interlacing her fingers with his. "I might not be worrying."

He turned her in his arms so he could peer into her eyes again. "There's a part of you that's always worrying, Tink. It's part and parcel of who you are. That's perfectly okay. I just want you to know that you don't have to worry alone anymore. I'm here to help you carry the load."

She sucked in a sublime breath. How long she'd waited for someone to say those words to her.

"So let's worry together. Give me what you've got."

"What if Gabriel's mother doesn't come back the way she said she would?"

"What if she does?"

Jana cleared her throat. "That's not how my worrying works."

"Oh, you're a worst-case-scenario girl."

"Exactly."

"Okay, let's say his mother doesn't return. That means he goes to CPS."

She nodded.

"Granted, right now, that doesn't seem optimal, but it might be much better than being with his mom. We don't know her. We don't know what's in her heart."

"Okay, but what if his foster family is not a good one?"

"What if he gets someone like your Marjean?"

"What if he doesn't?"

"All right, let's go down that rabbit hole. What if he does get a sorry foster family? Will worrying about it now change that?"

"No," she mumbled and played with his chest hairs.

"You have some legitimate concerns. I'm not going to sugar-coat it and come up with some made-for-Twilight mythology. This situation isn't the way a child is supposed to enter the world. But we found him, and we're giving him the best possible start, and he has so many people rooting for him."

"True," she murmured. "But his life is going to be so hard. I know from experience."

"Playing devil's advocate here, but do you think you're projecting your past onto him? Could you be using him to work out your trauma?"

"Maybe."

No *maybe* to it. Joel was right. She *was* working through her own past traumas using Gabriel as a surrogate. She didn't know if that was a bad thing or a good thing. She only knew this one thing: despite all the worries, every minute she spent with Gabriel was precious, never mind that she was headed for a fall. Pain was an old friend. She could handle it.

"Try not to borrow trouble for him, if you can," Joel soothed.

"I don't know if I can do that."

"I trust you to take care of yourself," he said. "You've been doing an amazing job of it for twenty-six years."

His confidence in her calmed Jana's turbulent thoughts. He

didn't pooh-pooh her fears or offer false reassurances. He *got* her, and that was an amazing gift.

"Let's try to get some sleep." Joel stroked her hair.

It felt so good. So comforting. It reminded her of those early days with Marjean, and a bittersweet lump filled her throat. She closed her eyes and drifted in that fuzzy blissfulness between wakefulness and sleep, absorbing Joel's warmth and the easy sounds of his breathing.

What if every single night could be like this?

The dream was hers for the taking.

Smiling, Jana was almost asleep when Gabriel made a soft cooing noise. Joel was out like a light. She threw back the covers and slipped out of bed, reached into the playpen for the child, who looked at her with big, trusting eyes.

"For the next week I'm going to mother the heck out of you, baby boy," she whispered and kissed the top of his little head. "And I'll say the deepest prayer that your mama is a good person and she'll come back to you."

She carried him into the kitchen, balancing him in the crook of her arm while she one-handed the bottle prep. Once it was ready, she carried Gabriel to the living area and sat down in the rocking chair near the Christmas tree. Joel had left the lights on, and it created a magical glow throughout the room.

Feeding Gabriel, looking into his cherubic face, stirred impossible hopes and dreams of keeping him for her own. And on the heels of those dreams came memories of her past.

Blame the wee morning hours. She felt raw and exposed, vulnerable. A lump of hot regret clogged her throat. In the loneliness of the night, when it was only she and Gabriel awake, sorrow dug in and wouldn't let go.

Live in the moment, she told herself. *Be here now.*

The past was gone. The future forever out of grasp. All that mattered was now. She had lost so much, but she had so much to gain.

The entire world, actually.

Jana wouldn't tell Joel about how she was feeling. Not yet. Their deepening relationship was wonderful and growing stronger every day, but ultimately, she didn't know where it would lead. She didn't want to muddy the shiny happiness that had come over her with more secrets. She felt as if she'd given away too much already.

But that was the old fears that had no place in her new life. She didn't regret sharing anything with Joel; she just needed time to process and adjust to their newfound intimacy before sharing more.

One day soon, she would tell him everything about herself, and when that day came, Joel would own her heart one hundred percent.

AT DAWN, JOEL woke to find Gabriel in bed with them. Jana had her body curled around the baby, her arms encircling him protectively.

Smiling, he got out of bed and quietly put on his clothes to go walk the dogs. Yesterday had been one of the best days of his life, and he was still riding high on it.

Muffin, Puffin, and Filbert rushed to the mudroom door.

"Sit," Joel commanded to quell their unbridled enthusiasm.

Muffin and Puffin immediately plunked their butts on the tile, but lazy Filbert, an obedience-school dropout, refused to play along. Joel took the leashes off the hook on the wall by the door, gave Filbert a pointed look, and said, "Sit."

Reluctantly, Filbert sat.

Once their leashes were on, the dogs went nuts, barking happily and turning in circles.

Two minutes later, the three dogs were parading in front of him down the street as the sun peeked pinkly over the horizon, eager to melt the icy patches that had collected on the ground from a sprinkling of rain overnight. Their heads held high, the breeze off the lake ruffling their golden hair, mouths open and tongues lolling. Dogs were just so damn joyful. His pets never failed to lift his spirits.

But today, the lift was scarcely more than a blip, as his mind took out a shovel and started digging around in his emotions. He was feeling sad about Gabriel. Jana's worrying from last night had gotten to him.

He tried to stop the brewing analysis by noticing the leaves on the evergreen trees, inhaled the musky, fishy scent of water, heard the crunch of frozen gravel underneath his boots, felt the sleeves of his jacket ride up on his wrists. He probably should have worn sneakers or his rain boots instead.

The mindfulness didn't last long. As he turned his thoughts inward, trying to be fully in the moment by mentally listing sensory details, his emotions hijacked the proceedings. Across the way, the Brazos Queen was docked, and he thought about the fun they'd had during the Christmas Eve float parade. How maternal Jana had looked sitting in the pilot house with him as she fed Gabriel.

A sharp, pinging sensation in the center of his chest sent his thoughts skittering to all sorts of memories. Good memories of time spent with Jana. Memories he would cherish for the rest of his life.

The air was chilly but heavily humid here at the water's edge. Sadness, as gray as the winter sky, settled over him like a thick woolen blanket. An unexpected sensation of loss clung to him. He shook his head, determined to dispel the gloom, but it grabbed hold of him and wouldn't let go.

Sensing he wasn't in full control, the dogs took over the walk, pulling him down the street past neighboring houses and boat docks.

He let the dogs take charge, feeling like lake flotsam, floating and adrift. It occurred to him that this was how Jana went through life. Untethered, pushed around by wakes and ripples. While it kept her free to go where the current took her, she had nothing to ground her. No anchor to hold her safe and steady.

No family of her own.

He longed to be her rock. He wanted to be her family. Make his family hers as well.

Since making love to her, the feelings he'd kept buried for fear of scaring her off had moved to the forefront. Feelings of wanting to protect her, to keep her safe, to be her person. He'd loved her as a friend because it had been better than nothing. He'd held back. Kept his real feelings secret.

Waited for her to see what was right in front of her. A man who loved her and accepted her with all his heart.

Joel was in love with Jana. Had been for a long time, if he were honest. He'd just been scared to label it in case things didn't work out. Even though he and Ursula had been casual, she'd accused him of being in love with Jana. He'd denied it. She'd said, "Prove it. Fire her." Instead, he'd broken up with Ursula. He probably should have told Jana the real reason he'd broken up with Ursula, but he'd been afraid of scaring her off.

So here he was, unable to bury his feelings any longer. Terrified of telling her the truth, but knowing he couldn't go on like this anymore. Loving her as he did, he needed much more than friendship.

He needed a commitment from her.

And what if she can't give it to you?

Well, then, so be it. At least he would know where he stood.

Do it now! Today! It was the perfect time.

His mind started in on the excuses as to why he should wait, but he'd waited long enough, dammit. He couldn't wait to tell her that he was in love with her and had been for quite some time.

He turned the dogs, eager to get back to her, but Muffin and Puffin spied a squirrel, and in a surge, they bolted in the opposite direction. With the swift pivot, his boot heel struck a patch of ice.

The dogs yanked the leashes from his hands, and momentum sent him falling back, the loose leashes tangling around his feet.

The last thought, as his head hit the concrete, was of Jana.

Chapter 23

The Return

Jana fretted.

Worrying was part of her natural makeup, a habit created in childhood and a trait she would never entirely overcome, but this feeling was more than mere caution or sneaking suspicion. The hairs on her arms were raised, and her nape tingled, and the radar that had warned her of trouble in the past was going off like firehouse bells inside her head.

Something was wrong.

It was eight A.M., and Joel had been gone when she woke up. The dogs and their leashes were gone too, so she assumed he'd taken them for a walk.

She'd sent him happy emojis in her good-morning texts and waited . . .

He'd never responded.

She made excuses. He hadn't noticed the texts. He'd stopped to converse with a neighbor. His cell phone was out of juice.

Gabriel needed attention. She fed him, changed him, waited . . .

She sent a fresh round of texts. Opened the front door, peered out into the neighborhood, watched lazy snowflakes spin from the sky. Texted Noah to see if Joel had dropped by the Rockabye.

Noah texted back: Haven't seen him.

She put Gabriel down for a nap. Made coffee. Texted Joel again. Waited . . .

Fretted.

Heard the dogs bark. Opened the back door. Muffin, Puffin, and Filbert, with leashes dragging, bounded inside.

And that's when she called Sheriff Hondo.

JOEL REGAINED CONSCIOUSNESS in the emergency room.

The first thing he saw was Jana's dear face. She was sitting on the foot of his bed, yogi-style.

His head hurt like the dickens, and someone had placed an ice pack at his temple, but the person he loved most was in the room with him. All was well.

"You're awake!" Jana leaped off the end of the bed and rushed to his side.

"Hey," he said, surprised to find his voice shaky.

"Are you okay?" Jana took his hand. "How are you feeling?"

"Fi—" Speaking intensified the throbbing at his temple, and he winced. "Headache."

"You should see the goose egg on the side of your head."

Joel reached up to push away the ice pack and touched the tender, swollen spot and winced again. She wasn't kidding. It was a honker. Joel started to frown, but that made his head hurt worse.

"What happened?"

"You don't remember?"

He shook his head. Ouch, that hurt too. "The last thing I remember I was walking the dogs."

"When I woke up you weren't in the house, and the dogs were gone, so I knew you took them for a walk, but when you didn't answer my texts, I got worried and called Sheriff Hondo once the dogs showed up. He found you unconscious and called the ambulance."

It came rushing back to Joel then, how he'd turned to race

home to tell Jana he loved her and had slipped on the ice, fallen, and hit his head.

"Are the dogs okay?"

"Fine, fine. Belinda Murphey is looking after them."

"That's good. How are you?"

"Me? I'm fine. Don't worry about me."

"I must have scared you pretty good."

"Oh, we're not even going there. You know me. Worrywart Central."

"Does Noah know?"

"Your entire family is in the waiting room. That's what I love about them. A MacGregor in need rallies the whole clan."

"They should all go home. I'll be all right."

"You gave us quite a scare. They're not going to disperse that easily."

"Where's the baby?"

"Kelsey took Gabriel to the Rockabye. Everything's covered. Nothing for you to worry about."

"Leave all the worrying to you, huh?"

She grinned at him, and his heart soared. "You know it's my superpower."

A bouncy young nurse appeared in the doorway with a smile and a wink. "I see our Sleeping Beauty has awakened."

"I had trouble staying awake after I hit my head," Joel said. "Is that bad?"

"It's not cherry pie and whipped cream. You have a severe concussion. The doctor will be in later to give you the rundown."

"Will Joel be admitted to the hospital?" Jana asked, nervously fingering the necklace at her throat.

"Maybe for observation. We'll have to see what the doctor says." The nurse nodded at the monitor mounted on a bracket above Joel's head. "Your vital signs look good. I just need to take your temp and check your reflexes."

"You can get a fever from a concussion?"

"You might have an infection that caused you to pass out."

"I didn't pass out. I slipped on the ice."

"It's just protocol." The nurse took an electronic thermometer from the pocket of her lab jacket and ran it over his forehead. The device beeped. "A perfect 98.6."

Joel's eyes met Jana's. "Hear that? She said I was perfect."

"As if there was any doubt." Jana raised his hand to her lips and kissed his knuckles.

It was a tickly feeling that delighted him all the way to his toes.

The nurse snorted and rolled her eyes, pulled out a pocket flashlight, and checked his pupils.

"Perfect there too?" he asked.

"Pupils are equal and reactive," the nurse said.

"Just like us." Jana grinned at him.

"Good heavens." The nurse chuckled. "You two are way too mushy. If I stay here any longer, I'm risking diabetes."

"Hey," Joel said. "I almost died."

"Not by a long shot." The nurse shook her head good-naturedly. "The doctor will be by soon." Then she winked again and sauntered out the door.

"She's got your number." Jana giggled.

"And so do you. It's great to hear you laugh." Joel met her gaze, love pushing at the seams of his heart. She was magnificent.

Jana reached over to smooth the wrinkles from his covers with her free hand. "Seriously, how are you feeling?"

"I was about to ask you the same thing."

"I'm okay," she assured him. "Now that I know you're going to be okay."

He scooted over to the far side of the gurney and patted the space beside him. "Get up here, Tink."

Jana glanced over her shoulder. "I don't think the nurse would like that."

"I don't care. I'm here to heal, and the best healing for me is to hold you in my arms."

With a furtive grin, Jana kicked off her sneakers and climbed onto the stretcher beside him. Ignoring his pounding headache, Joel wrapped his arms around her and held her close, the scent of her hair filling his nose and lightening his heart. He wanted to smell her fragrance for the rest of his life.

"Here," Jana said, picking up the ice pack that had slid to one side of the bed. "Put this on your head."

"I'm so grateful for you," he whispered against her ear as he maneuvered the pack underneath his temple and rested his head against the cold.

"Ditto."

He tightened his arms around her, and they lay together in each other's embrace until footsteps drew their attention to the door.

Sheriff Hondo walked in, and with him was the scared-looking young teenager they'd seen around town.

THE SECOND JANA saw the girl with Hondo, she just *knew*.

"Jana, Joel," Hondo said. "I want you to meet Isabella Martin." He paused and added, "Gabriel's mother."

"Hello," Isabella said in a soft meek voice, her posture slumped, her eyes downcast. "Thank you for taking care of my baby."

Jana leaped off the gurney, and it was only when her stocking feet hit the floor that she recalled she'd kicked off her shoes. She didn't pause and, instead, grabbed the rolling stool in the corner and waved Isabella onto it.

"Please," Jana invited. "Sit down. You've had a trying week."

Isabella raised her head, her eyes misted with tears. Her long dark hair flowed down her shoulders, and her teenage skin was peppered with pimples. She was little more than a child herself with the hesitant manner of someone who'd yet to build a strong sense of self-worth.

Boy, did Jana ever know how that felt.

Tentatively, Isabella eased down on the stool. For a long moment, no one spoke.

Hondo cleared his throat, and everyone looked at the sheriff. "Isabella came into our offices just now and identified herself."

"I saw the ambulance come," she mumbled. "I worried."

"You've been watching us," Joel said.

Isabella nodded. "To make sure Gabriel was okay."

"Where were you?" Jana asked. "How did you know the ambulance came for Joel?"

"I've been hiding," Isabella confessed.

"I thought so." Jana met Hondo's gaze. "Joel and I saw her a couple of times, and I wondered if she could be Gabriel's mom."

"I was living on your big boat," Isabella said. "That's where I was when the ambulance came."

"I'd walked down to the dock on Christmas Island," Joel said to Jana. "I just now remembered what happened. I was headed back when Muffin and Puffin spied a squirrel, took off, and tripped me up on an icy patch of road."

"You were homeless?" Jana asked the girl as she backed up to Joel's gurney and sank down again.

"Uh-huh," Isabella said in a small voice. "I had nowhere to go."

Jana shot a quick glance over at Joel, who was sitting straight up in the bed, his gaze trained on her. The bump at his temple looked less swollen than it had when she'd first gotten to the ER. The ice was doing its job.

Their eyes met. His smile said, *I'm with you all the way, Tink.*

For a moment, everyone was silent.

Sheriff Hondo stood at the end of the bed, his hands on his hips, his observant eyes taking in the scene. Even for a man in his early seventies, he was sharp as a new razor.

Isabella fussed with a string bracelet on her wrist, avoiding eye contact.

Joel picked up the ice pack and held it to his head again. Jana got to her feet, hovered, unsure what to do.

Finally, Isabella said in a soft, hesitant voice, "I knew you would be good to him." She met Jana's gaze, tears misting her eyes, then sent a shaky smile to Joel. "I saw you two together at the nativity scene, and I instantly knew you would cherish him the way you cherish each other."

"We *did* cherish him." Jana pivoted to look at Joel.

His gaze latched on to hers, and she felt such a swell of love in her heart that it scared her. They'd hooked up because of Gabriel, but now that his mother had returned, what would happen to them? Would they go forward or, without the glue of the baby, would their closeness fade?

They hadn't had time to talk about the shift in their relationship, and now it was shifting again. They'd gone from friends to lovers. Where did they go from here? Back to just friends? To a commitment of some kind? Or—and this was the terrifying option—would everything they'd built start falling apart? There was so much love in his eyes that equaled the love in her heart, why would everything fall apart?

Why?

Because everything good that had ever come into her life eventually disintegrated. Even Marjean, who had loved her and cherished her the way she'd cherished Gabriel, had left her.

It could happen with Joel. His head injury could have been worse. He could have died and left her too.

But he hadn't.

"Gabriel and I were just so lucky it was you at the church that night when I needed you most." Isabella's voice quivered, and a single tear ran down her cheek. "It felt fated."

Jana reached for a tissue from the box on the nightstand and passed it to Isabella.

Smiling gratefully through her tears, the teenager blinked and dabbed her eyes. "Thank you."

"Why didn't you come forward and let us know who you were?" Joel asked. "We could have helped you."

"I was afraid *he* would find me."

"He?" Jana asked.

"My ex-boyfriend. His name is Felix. He beats me up."

A chill froze Jana's blood. She put a hand to her belly, briefly closed her eyes, remembered another baby, another abusive boyfriend.

"Felix Jenkins," Hondo said. "He's well known to the Parker County Sheriff's Department where Isabella is from. He's currently in jail over there on a DUI charge."

"Tell us what happened," Jana said. It might be nosy, but they'd cared for her son for five days. She needed an explanation.

"It's a long story." Isabella sighed.

From the hallway, the wheels of a cart that needed oiling squeaked, and a voice over the PA system paged Dr. Longoria to surgery.

Isabella fiddled with the bracelet, a self-soothing gesture. "I had just given birth, and Felix found out and showed up at the hospital. He wanted us to get back together. I said no. He threatened to take the baby away from me."

"That must have been terrifying," Jana said.

"Yes. I knew I had to get away from him, but I didn't know what to do. My grandmother had just died of cancer, and I couldn't pay rent on the house where we were living. The landlord locked me out while I was in the hospital."

Jana's legs were going numb from being crouched for so long, but she didn't want to move and interrupt Isabella's story. The teen deserved her full attention.

"What about your parents?" Joel asked. "Where are they?"

"I never knew my dad, and my mom died in a car crash when I was eleven. That's how I came to live with my grandmother."

"How old are you?" Jana asked, thinking the girl didn't look much older than eleven right now.

"I will be fifteen next month."

"How old is Felix?"

Sheriff Hondo supplied the answer through gritted teeth and a dark glower. "Twenty-two."

Jana was flooded with the weighted realization that there was no way Gabriel would be able to stay with his mother. She was homeless and a minor. Another chilling thought occurred. What if the courts gave Felix the baby?

"He was good to me at first. My grandmother liked him, and she said she would sign for me to get married so I would have someone to take care of me when she died, but that was before he started beating me. I couldn't tell her. She was dying, and I wanted her to believe I would be okay."

Jana's heart went out to her. As a teenager, she'd gotten trapped in an abusive relationship too. She knew what it was like to be gaslighted and trauma-bonded, trying to please an unpleasable monster.

She understood what it was like to be unable to break free from a tyrant's grip. People who'd never been in such situations and didn't understand the crippling dynamics between abuser and prey would often glibly suggest that victims just pack up and leave. As if it was that simple. As if the abuser would let them go without a fight. Abusers lived for conflict. The more you struggled, the more they came at you. Giving in to them was how you survived.

But somehow, Isabella had been able to flee.

What a brave girl!

Reaching over, Jana put a hand on Isabella's knee but stayed quiet, holding space for the teen's grief to unfold. Jana knew firsthand how much courage it took to walk away from an abuser that you knew could hunt you down and kill you for having the audacity to leave. Jana experienced Isabella's pain in the pit of her stomach. She'd been there. Knew exactly how it felt.

"I left the hospital in the middle of the night and hitchhiked to Twilight with Gabriel in my backpack. I had no idea where I was going to go, what I was going to do. I was terrified Felix would find me and take Gabriel away. I didn't know he was in jail until the sheriff told me just now." Isabella darted a glance at Hondo.

Jana sucked in her breath. She had such an urge to draw the girl into her arms and tell her everything was going to be okay, but that was a promise she couldn't make.

Hondo did it for her. "Felix will be prosecuted for his crimes. We'll get you and Gabriel into Child Protective Services. You will be taken care of."

Isabella hugged herself, her eyes wide. "Thank you, Sheriff. When can I see my baby?"

Hondo blew out his breath. "Jana?"

"I . . . I guess as soon as they let Joel go, I can pick him up from Kelsey and bring him to Isabella. Where will she be?"

"I'm taking her home to Patsy, and then I'll call CPS."

Isabella met Jana's gaze. Her eyes glistened with tears of gratitude. "I really can't thank you enough for looking out for my baby. Both of you."

"We bought some things for him. Other people gifted us with clothes and supplies," Jana said. "We'd like for him to have them."

"Thank you, thank you." Isabella bobbed her head.

Hondo put a hand to the teen's elbow to guide her from the room. He paused at the edge of the curtain separating Joel's gurney from the rest of the beds in the emergency department and looked at Jana. "We'll see you when the case worker and I come to get Gabriel."

With a wave, Isabella followed Hondo out the door.

CHAPTER 24

THE SURRENDER

After Hondo and Isabella left, Jana turned to find Joel staring at her with concerned eyes.

"You okay?"

She nodded.

"You sure?"

She shrugged.

"Don't want to talk about it?"

She shook her head. No, no she did not. Truth was, she didn't have the words to express what she was feeling. Sinking down onto the rolling stool that Isabella had vacated, she did her best to stanch the tears that threatened to flow.

When she took Gabriel in, she'd accepted that she'd get hurt as part of caring for the baby. What she hadn't expected was just how much it would hurt.

"Can you give me a hint of what's going on in that smart little head of yours?" Joel asked, looking concerned.

"I don't know what I'm thinking," she said, which was honest enough.

"Still too tender to talk about?"

She bobbed her head.

He mimed zipping his lips but then winced and clutched his head.

"Shh," she said. "You have a concussion. Stop trying to make me feel better. I'm tough. I'll get through this. You rest."

"It's okay. I'm here for you." He paused, added, "No matter what."

Relief and worry washed through her in equal measures. What would happen to them now that they no longer had the glue of Gabriel holding them together as temporary parents? Would they stay a couple? Did they really have something here? Where would it lead? What if things fell apart? What if she lost the one thing that mattered to her most?

Joel's friendship.

Yes. That was the truth. Somewhere along the line, she wasn't exactly sure when, Joel had become essential to her life, and she couldn't imagine a world without him in it.

Her pulse sped up. They had so much to discuss, but she didn't feel up to talking about any of it. At the moment, the ache in her heart was simply too big.

She'd expected to have more time with Gabriel.

Expectations.

She'd set herself up for the heartache. She'd gotten too attached. Overly identified with the abandoned baby.

"Tink?" Joel asked. "You okay?"

She nodded, tugged the cuff of her sweater sleeves down over her hands. Felt lost.

"Knock, knock." A lab-coated doctor with a black stethoscope around his neck pushed the curtain aside and stepped into the area. His ID badge identified him as Dr. Reddy.

He held out his hand to Jana. "Hello, Mrs. MacGregor?"

"No, no," Jana said. "I'm not—"

"She's my girlfriend," Joel said. "She can hear anything you have to tell me."

Girlfriend.

The word lit up her heart.

The doctor nodded and pulled the curtain around the gurney. "Your tests all look good. Let me do an exam, and if everything checks out, I'll send you on home."

Jana sat up taller on the stool and watched as the doctor examined Joel and asked him questions designed to test his level of awareness.

When Dr. Reddy finished, he straightened and offered an encouraging smile. "You did suffer a Grade 4 because you lost consciousness for longer than a minute, but your scans were clear. No intercranial bleeding. The main thing is to get lots of rest. Don't make any major decisions. Expect some fuzzy thinking. It's totally normal, so don't be alarmed if you have trouble concentrating. No strenuous physical activities for at least two weeks. No driving either."

"Um . . ." Joel said. "What about sex?"

Dr. Reddy shook his head. "Sorry, that falls into the category of strenuous physical activity."

"Darn it." Joel grinned, winced, touched the knot at his head.

"Take Tylenol or ibuprofen for pain, and avoid aspirin at all costs."

"You're discharging me?" Joel looked hopeful.

Dr. Reddy's gaze flicked to Jana. "If you have someone to stay with you around the clock for at least two days, I won't admit you for observation."

"I'll stay with him," Jana vowed. She'd cancel everything on her work schedule. She wasn't leaving Joel alone for a second.

"Great. The nurse will provide you with a list of symptoms to watch out for."

"What about snuggling?" Joel said. "Can we snuggle?"

"Snuggling is fine." Dr. Reddy chuckled.

"Kissing?" Joel wriggled his eyebrows.

"*Joel!*" Jana put her palm over her eyes.

"As long as kissing doesn't lead to other things, it's acceptable." Dr. Reddy shifted his gaze to Jana. "I can tell I need to put the burden of caution on you. Mr. MacGregor seems a little muddled on the concept of what constitutes physical activity."

"You've come to the right person," Jana said. "Caution is my middle name."

"In that case, I'm glad you're the one looking after him." Looking rueful, Dr. Reddy shook his head and left the room.

"You are naughty," Jana told Joel.

"You stopped thinking about Gabriel for a couple of minutes, didn't you?"

"Yes," she admitted.

"Mission accomplished." He winked.

"But now I'm thinking about him again," she said sadly. "I'm so happy his mom came back for him, but it's going to get really complicated for them both."

"I know you can't help worrying about them," he said. "I don't expect you not to, but really, Jana, it's not your problem to solve. We did the best we could. It's time to leave it in the hands of the professionals."

He was right. She knew it. But that didn't make the bitter pill any easier to swallow.

THIS WAS ONE time being laid-back was a blessing, Joel thought as he sat in the passenger seat while Jana drove him home. Dr. Reddy and the discharge nurse had both reiterated that he should take it easy. Taking things easy was Joel's forte.

He sprawled back in the seat as much as his long legs would allow and studied Jana's profile. "How you doing, Tink?"

"I should be asking you that question. How's the headache?"

"Headachy." He gave a rueful laugh that made it hurt more.

"You still have the ice pack?" She darted a quick glance at him.

He held it up for her to see. "What's going through your head?"

"Logistics of getting Gabriel ready to turn over to CPS. Kelsey is meeting us at the house."

"I am going to miss the little guy," Joel said, surprised by just how wistful he felt. What he really wanted to know, however, was how Jana was handling the loss. Tough as she appeared on the outside, she was so tender on the inside.

She gripped the steering wheel tightly in her hands and stared resolutely through the windshield, eyes on the road. She was a good driver. One of the best he knew.

"It's gonna be—"

"Joel—"

"You go first—"

"No, you."

"I just wanted to say it's going to be okay. We'll always remember Gabriel fondly. And who knows? Maybe we can still have some contact with him."

"Maybe," she said, a wan smile coming over her face, but he could tell she didn't really believe that. "I didn't know it was possible to love so hard so quickly."

"There will be other babies in our lives," he said.

She swiveled her head to look at him, her eyes growing wide. "What?"

He imagined them with a baby of their own, and his chest twisted so tight it was hard to get his breath. "It's possible."

She jerked her gaze back to the road. "Joel, there's something I really need to tell you."

He rubbed the knot at his head and squinted his eyes against the sun. "Sure, sure."

"Head hurting?"

"Nothing I can't handle."

"It's not worse, is it?" Anxiety lifted her voice. "I'll turn right around and take you back to the hospital."

"No, no. It's fine. I just . . . I'm having some trouble concentrating. The doctor said that was to be expected."

"Yes, okay. We'll wait on this conversation until you feel better."

"I'm eager to hear it," he said and reached across the seat to lightly squeeze her knee. "After CPS comes to get Gabriel."

"Look, Noah and Kelsey are already here," Jana said, turning into Joel's driveway.

His twin's vehicle was under the carport, and Noah was unloading the baby from the back seat. Kelsey stood beside him with Gabriel's diaper bag on her shoulder.

Joel's heart dropped to his stomach. "It's going to be okay."

"I know." Jana pressed a knuckle against her eyelid.

"We'll get through this," Joel reassured her. "This is what's best for Gabriel."

"I really wish I could believe you," Jana murmured.

"Jana?"

"Yes?" She killed the engine and turned in her seat to face him as Noah and Kelsey approached his truck.

"There is one thing you can absolutely believe."

"What's that?"

"I'm here for you. All the way. Never doubt."

She gave him a faint smile, and if his head hadn't been pounding to beat the band and CPS wasn't on the way to get Gabriel, he would have swept her into his arms and kissed her.

Concussion be damned.

IN JOEL'S BEDROOM, Jana changed the baby's diaper and put him in a cute little blue sailor's outfit that Flynn had given him for Christmas. Kelsey hovered by the bed, wanting to be helpful, but looking uncertain of how to do that.

Noah was helping Joel get settled in on the living-room couch and refreshing his ice pack.

And now she was giving the baby away. *Dammit, Jana, suck it up. He was never yours to begin with.*

Yes, yes. Her sense of loss was irrational. She understood that but felt bereft anyway.

How had she allowed herself to get so sucked in by a fantasy?

*Forget your feelings. Focus on Gabriel and his mother. They
need support.*

Jana had great friends in the MacGregors, and she had people
who cared about her all over town. Friends who had become
like family. She—like Isabella—had had no one when she'd first
come to Twilight, but now she had a strong support system.
Case in point, beautiful Kelsey was watching her intently.

If someone had told her seven years ago that she'd find such
acceptance and belonging in this wacky community, she would
have said something flippant or profane.

Back then, she'd had a wall up so high she could barely see
over the top of it. This town, and Joel, had knocked that wall
down to knee level, leaving her feeling exposed, vulnerable . . .
and far too open. But here was the kicker.

She liked it.

That was the scary part.

Opening herself up. Risking hurt and pain. Learning to trust.
It hadn't come easily. Getting there took hard work. She still
wasn't fully there. Didn't know if she would ever be the kind
of person who didn't hide behind the wall when emotions got
dicey.

Betrayal had been her lot in life. She'd learned people simply
couldn't be trusted, but that was defensive thinking, and it had
shut her down to love. Only through the kind patience of Joel
and the townsfolk had she started to dismantle the wall.

She wanted to offer that same gift of welcomeness and respect
to Isabella. But how did she go about it?

Buttoning up Gabriel's little outfit, she stepped back and
looked down at the baby in the middle of Joel's bed.

"Anchors away. Look at you, little fellow. You are so handsome," she murmured, not even realizing she was crying until
she saw teardrops wet the collar of his shirt. "Oh damn, damn,
damn."

The baby peered into her face.

"See, I'm too cussy to be a mom. It's better this way." She

swiped at her tears with the back of her hand and settled him into the carrier. "You're going to a place where you can be looked after properly, and people don't swear indiscriminately."

Kelsey grabbed a box of tissues from the bedside table and moved closer to silently pass the box to Jana.

"Thank you." She wiped away her tears.

The baby just kept staring at her.

"I'm not abandoning you. I'm making sure you're safe and cared for. You'll go live with a nice family who is more experienced with babies than I am."

Gabriel made a fussy little noise.

"Honestly, it really is better this way. What do I know about caring for babies? Zero. Zip. Zilch."

He raised a tiny fist as if he totally disagreed with her.

"Jana," Kelsey said, sounding shocked, "do you honestly believe that?"

She let her friend's words sink in. Did she?

"You're absolutely genius with Gabriel. Your love for him shines so clearly in your eyes. I've never seen you look at anyone the way you look at Gabriel . . ." Kelsey paused to take a deep breath. "Except maybe for Joel."

Jana couldn't meet her gaze. "I just feel like I was messing everything up."

"But why? From my point of view, you did a bang-up job mothering Gabriel."

"I guess it's because I didn't have a loving family like Joel and Noah. I never had a template for that. I don't know how to love."

"Oh, you most certainly do! And yes, you did lose the mother lottery, but so did I. A lot of people had crappy mothers but turned out to be wonderful moms anyway. You can overcome your past. Truly. But first, you have to face it and make peace with it."

Kelsey was right. She couldn't fully love and be loved until she admitted what she'd done. Until she told Joel her terrible secret.

Until she learned how to forgive herself. It felt like such a tall order. Especially when Joel wasn't feeling well. How could she spill her guts now?

Gabriel cooed at her.

"See?" Kelsey said. "He agrees with me."

Tears were flowing down her cheeks now. Why was she crying? Gabriel was a lot of trouble. For the past five days, her life hadn't been her own. It had consisted of ten feedings a day and almost as many diaper changes and carting around a bunch of extra stuff to the point where her shoulder ached from hoisting that damn diaper bag. Never mind the laundry piling up.

And she'd loved every second of it. Wished she had more time.

The doorbell rang.

Jana jumped.

Kelsey winced. "That'll be Hondo and the caseworker from CPS."

"I know." Jana scooped Gabriel off the bed in his little sailor suit and into her arms. She buried her face against his neck, breathing in his smell, fighting back fresh tears. She could do this. It would be all right.

Putting her arm around Jana, Kelsey guided her toward the front door just as Noah and Joel appeared in the hallway behind them.

Kelsey opened the door but stepped to one side. Hondo was there, along with a young caseworker named Willis Champion. Jana used to take his grandmother to her chemo appointments last year, and it was good to see a kind, familiar face.

"How is your grandmother, Willis?" she asked, keeping her palm braced against Gabriel's back.

"She's doing great. Just hit the one-year mark, and no evidence of disease," Willis said. "Thank you for asking."

"Tell her I said hi." Jana smiled softly.

"Will do. She forever sings your praises. You sure made her feel special when you had her favorite juice iced down and waiting for her when you picked her up."

"I knew she was going through a lot and just wanted her to know someone cared," Jana said.

Hondo cleared his throat and shifted his weight. Between Hondo and Willis stood Isabella, her gaze trained on Gabriel, her eyes filled with angst and longing. Jana had no idea what would happen to the teen and her infant, but she prayed hard that it was only good things.

"Would you like to come inside?" Jana invited them.

Hondo shook his head and readjusted his Stetson. "We've got a team meeting in ten minutes to discuss Isabella's and Gabriel's living arrangements."

"Yes, yes." Jana smiled, still clinging tightly to the baby. "I understand."

"Noah boxed up Gabriel's things for me," Joel said.

Jana cast a quick glance over at him. The knot at his head was red, and the dark circles under his eyes were tinged blue. This was as tough for him as it was for her.

"May I hold him?" Isabella looked from Hondo to Willis and back again.

Willis nodded, and Isabella reached for her baby.

Gently, Jana put Gabriel into his mother's arms. The minute she touched him, Isabella's entire body language changed—she went from quivering teen to protective mama bear, clutching her baby close to her chest, lifting her chin, and holding her head up. Proud and defiant.

Jana identified.

She'd been there. Understood the impulse to fight everyone tooth and nail, even people trying the hardest to help her.

Isabella darted a quick look down the street.

"Don't try to run," Jana warned, reading the teen's mind. "It'll only make things worse."

Isabella crashed her gaze into Jana's and then slowly nodded.

"They're going to help you." Jana locked her eyes on the teenager. "I promise it's going to be all right. I'll check in. I'll check up on you. I'll help any way I can."

"Why?" Isabella stared at her with suspicion and disbelief. "Why would you do that?"

"Because I was just like you once."

Isabella cocked her head, looked unconvinced.

"You can have a good life if you let people help you, but you've got to learn to trust."

"Ha!" Isabella snorted, clinging to Gabriel so tightly Jana grimaced.

"You've been hurt. Your distrust is understandable, but you can't do this alone."

Isabella wasn't convinced, and Jana understood that too. It would take time for her to let down her guard and start letting people in. Years, most likely.

How ironic she was telling Isabella she had to start trusting others when she'd never been able to fully do that herself.

She felt an arm go around her shoulders.

Joel. Standing behind her staunch as a soldier. Hondo picked up the box of baby things that Noah had set out as Willis took Isabella's elbow.

"Thank you," Isabella said. "For looking after Gabriel. I am grateful, and I do trust *you.*"

"Then, if you trust me, trust them." Jana nodded at the two men. "Things might be bumpy for a while, but give it time. Eventually, things will start looking up."

Isabella nodded. The look in her eyes said she'd already suffered hard times and knew how to weather it.

Then, with Gabriel in his little sailor suit, Isabella waved goodbye and let Willis and Hondo lead her into her future.

Permitting Jana to turn and take her own advice.

CHAPTER 25

THE PROPOSAL

Kelsey and Noah hung around for a while, and they discussed the upcoming New Year's Eve party on the Brazos Queen. They had dinner together, calling for takeout from Moe's diner. Halfway through the meal, Jana glanced over at Joel, saw he looked bone-deep exhausted, and suggested it was time for bed. He did have a concussion, after all.

He made a sexy joke.

She rolled her eyes and smiled.

Noah and Kelsey said their goodbyes and headed home.

"Time for bed, tall guy," she told him once their guests were gone.

"It's only seven thirty."

"And you can't keep your eyes open."

"I *am* pretty bushed."

She put her hand in his and, not feeling the least bit self-conscious, led him to his bed. It felt lonesome not having Gabriel in the room with them, but Jana pushed aside those sad thoughts to focus on Joel. She went over the discharge note from the hospital to make sure she wasn't forgetting anything.

Basically, it was her job to watch him for concerning symptoms that could send him back to the ER and make sure he stayed quiet.

Joel had a big jetted tub specially made for a tall man. She ran him a bath. He tried to get her to take one with him, but she reminded him the doctor had instructed him to stay calm and quiet.

He laughed and swatted her fanny as she walked away.

She pointed a finger at him. "Settle down."

He grinned and started stripping off his shirt.

Heating up, she gulped and ran. She had to keep him chill, and watching him get naked was not going to cut it.

In the bedroom, while he soaked, she turned on soft, soothing music, lit candles, and turned down the sheets.

Eeps! It was too romantic.

Just as she was about to blow out the candles, Joel appeared, slouching his bare shoulder against the doorjamb, a thin towel tucked around his waist, and giving her bedroom eyes. He canted his head and served her a lopsided grin.

She couldn't resist grinning back.

"Don't worry," he said, lowering his eyelids. "I'll be a good boy."

"Why do I not trust that?" She laughed.

"'Cause that's just you, Tink." He sauntered toward her. "I accept it."

Ouch. He was right. She was still holding back. Still keeping a part of her history hidden from him. Her one last secret, and she didn't want to let it go. "Wow, you sound so disappointed in me."

"Not in the least." He held out his arms to her, and she melted into his embrace.

He led her to bed, and they got under the covers, the scent of lavender filling the air, along with the gentle spa music. He murmured sweet nothings, and Jana allowed herself to drift on the moment, snuggled against him, happy to be here, and determined not to overanalyze things.

Joel was okay. She was okay. They were safe and with each other. Nothing else mattered.

When she was certain he was asleep, she got out of bed, went to the bathroom, blew out the candles, turned off the music, and crawled back in beside him.

She listened to his breathing, making sure it was slow and regular. All seemed well, but then, just as she was drifting off to sleep, Joel murmured something that took her breath away.

"I love you, and I want to marry you."

She froze.

Had she heard him correctly? Panic scrambled up her throat. She pretended he was talking in his sleep. Pretended she hadn't heard him.

"Tink?"

Purposely, she slowed her own breathing, which was difficult since her heart was shoving hot adrenaline throughout her veins, sending her nerve endings tingling in a wiry, electric way. Why had he said that *now* when she was completely defenseless? Her nerves shot from the day's roller-coaster activities.

She played possum. Not twitching a muscle.

"Tinker Bell?" His voice sounded strained, worried.

She didn't ease his mind. Overwhelmed by the fantastic idea of Joel being in love with her and wanting to marry her, she simply did not know how to respond. *It's the concussion. He's out of his head. He doesn't know what he's saying.*

"You asleep?"

Still as a statue.

He tightened his grip around her. "I'm glad you're asleep. That was a lousy way to vow my undying love and ask you to marry me. I'll do better tomorrow when you're wide awake and ready to hear it."

She imagined she was a huge granite rock—hard, immovable, lifeless—at the same time her body pulsed with life and energy.

Eventually, Joel's grip around her loosened and his breathing deepened, and when she knew for certain he was asleep, she crept from the bed, went to the bathroom, and sobbed her heart right out.

How could he love her when he didn't know her darkest secret? And yet how could she tell him, when that was the one thing that could send him walking away from her forever?

JOEL'S EYES FLEW open.

It was daybreak, and anxiety had hold of him as he tried to recall the details of last night. He and Jana had gotten into bed, snuggled, talked about Gabriel, and fallen asleep.

Wait.

Had he told Jana he loved her last night, or had he simply dreamed it?

Please, please, please, let it have been a dream.

Because it was absolutely the worst timing in the world. Not to mention unromantic as hell. Jana deserved a proper declaration of love—flowers, expensive dinner, a violinist. The whole nine yards.

The smell of coffee drifted in from the kitchen, and he could hear pots and pans clanging. She was cooking breakfast for him. What should he do? How should he react? Should he pretend that he'd never told her he loved her and wanted to marry her?

Since he wasn't sure he actually had, maybe pretending it hadn't happened was the right way to go.

Because if he had asked, he couldn't remember her answer.

Then another thought occurred to him. What if he *had* asked, and she'd said no? What then?

He'd have to play it by ear.

Moving slowly, he got out of bed and slipped into the bathroom for a wake-up shower. Briefly, he thought about coaxing Jana to join him, but the dull, constant ache in his head convinced him to cool his jets.

He turned on the cold water and stayed in as long as he could stand it and then got dressed. He found Jana making steel-cut oatmeal on the stove. There were pieces of cut-up fruit on a serving platter and homemade blueberry muffins as well. It was only seven. How long had she been up?

The floorboards creaked beneath his weight, and she turned at the stove, a bright smile on her face. Was that the smile of a woman who'd been told her man loved her and wanted to marry her? Or the smile of a woman who was simply happy to see her bed buddy was alive after his concussion?

"Mornin'," he mumbled.

"Good morning," she chirped.

He waited. Hoping she'd say something that would let him know for sure what he'd said last night.

"Have a muffin," she offered. "They're hot from the oven."

"Okay." He snagged a muffin. Took a bite. It was moist and warm, and although the texture was denser, he couldn't tell the difference between the vegan version and a regular muffin. "Um, how come you went to so much trouble for me?"

"Couldn't sleep."

"Why not?" he asked.

"Too much emotion over Gabriel and Isabella, I guess."

He studied her face, but Jana, the sphinx, gave nothing away.

"Oatmeal's ready." She gestured at the small dining table. "I've set out what I found in your cupboard—raisins, cranberries, bananas, chopped walnuts, dates, and brown sugar. Have at it."

"Thanks." He wasn't sure what to do. Should he mention last night and see how she reacted? Should he keep his mouth shut and act as if everything was normal? But what if he had asked, and she *had* told him she loved him back?

Dude, he heard his twin brother in his head, *if she'd told you she loved you, you'd remember.*

True enough. So either he hadn't told her that he loved her and it was a dream or he had told her and she hadn't said it in return.

He stepped to the stove, standing close enough so that they were almost touching, and reached for the serving ladle she'd stuck into the oatmeal. He caught a whiff of her fragrance and she smelled so damn good.

Joel leaned in, planning on kissing her cheek, but she zipped away from him and took her own bowl of oatmeal to the small bistro table into the alcove near the window. Outside, birds flocked to a feeder.

"All your feeders are empty except the big one," she said. "And I emptied the birdseed bag I found in the garage filling that one. Do you have more seed anywhere?"

"I'm out. I'll put it on my shopping list."

"I've let them down," she murmured.

"The birds?"

"I fed them on the first morning I was here. They expect food."

"There's still seeds in the feeder, Jana, and besides, it's not your responsibility to take care of all the world's birds."

"No," she said. "Not all the world's birds. Just the ones who've come to depend on a feeder."

"They'll figure it out," he said, only half listening. He was still wondering if he had told her he loved her. Should he say it again?

A male cardinal, with his proud red feathers, flew to the feeder and settled in beside the female cardinal already dining there.

"Cardinals are my favorite birds," she said. "They're so vibrant."

Joel studied her. "They brighten up any bird feeder."

"Did you know that red birds mate for life?"

His pulse jumped. "I did not know that."

"One of my foster mothers said red birds are too obvious. That they're just crying out for attention."

"Is that why you have a cardinal tattooed on your back? As a *nah-nah, nah-nah* to your foster mom?"

She grinned. "I was obviously crying out for attention."

"This foster mom, was she the woman whose husband tried to—"

"No, that was my last foster family. The cardinal-hating foster mom sent me away, saying I was too much to handle. A few years ago, she sent me a note of apology, so that was nice." Jana shrugged. "Although she did mention that I hadn't been an easy kid to love. Which, granted, was true." A strange expression came over her face, and she flicked her gaze back to the feeder. "I'm not easy to love."

That statement went all over Joel, and he felt anger rise to his throat. "The hell you're not!"

"I'm not. My foster mom wanted a kid she could dress in ribbons and bows and show off to her friends. What she got was a rebellious little shit who resisted everything she tried to do. I feel kind of sorry for her actually. She wanted a dream kid, and she got me."

Frustrated, Joel clenched his jaw. "Jana, why can't you see how amazing you are?"

"Because I have so many flaws."

"We all do! That's part of being human. If your foster mother couldn't see you for who you are, it's on her, not you. It's her loss."

"Mine too," Jana mumbled.

He reached across the table and rested his hand on top of hers. "Well, I see you for who you are, and I think you are the most incredible woman I've ever known, and I've known some pretty incredible women."

That brought a real smile to her face. "I think you're pretty incredible too."

He exhaled slowly and cleared his throat. Now was the time. This was it.

"Jana," he said. "We really need to talk."

WE REALLY NEED to talk.

Yikes! Was he going to bring up last night, his declaration of love and his quasi marriage proposal?

"Oh look, bluebirds!" She slipped her hand out from underneath his and pointed at the feeder. "I thought they'd migrated."

"Jana," he murmured, his tone insistent.

"It's Doonie," she said.

"Huh?"

"The bluebird. I noticed him the first day I was here. He's got a missing toe."

"You can tell me all about Doonie later. Right now, there's something I need to discuss with you."

Good grief, she couldn't just sit here and let him ask her to marry him again. Not until she told him about . . . Well, she didn't know how to start that conversation. She should have told him on the day before Christmas Eve, when they were spilling secrets, but she'd missed her window.

Last night, she'd been able to get away with feigning sleep, but that wasn't going to work in the stone-cold light of day.

"Jana." He reached out, took her by the shoulders, and turned her to face him. He would not be dissuaded.

She loved Joel with all her heart and soul, but she wasn't ready for marriage. Commitments had rarely gone well for her. Even her short-lived commitment to Gabriel. Opening her heart invariably left her battered and bruised.

"But first, there's something I need to tell you," Joel repeated.

Ah, crap.

"Oh," she said, tapping him in the center of his chest with her finger. "We've got to start decorating the Brazos Queen for New Year's Eve. And because we had Gabriel, we never cleaned up after the float parade. That'll take an entire day."

"I got Sean to do the cleanup. We can decorate tomorrow. There's something pressing we need to discuss."

"Can't it wait?"

"No." The earnestness in his eyes stalled her.

"Listen, Joel. I know what you're going to say."

"You can read my mind now?"

"Yes, and I really don't want to talk about it." She stepped back from him, raised both her arms, warding him off. "Things haven't been normal, and we've said and done and felt things that maybe we shouldn't have."

"Wait." He looked panic-stricken. "Are you breaking up with me?"

"No, no. I'm just saying there's no need for talky talky. Let's just go back to the way things were."

"So go back to being just friends."

"Well, maybe friends with benefits." She smiled, and her heart fluttered.

"You're worried about things changing."

She turned from him, shuffled over to the bistro table to pick up the carryall that held the fruits and nuts she'd set out.

He followed her. "Don't be worried. We're good."

She waltzed to the cupboard to stow the sugar, nuts, and dried fruit. "Uh-huh."

"Jana, what are you running from?"

"I'm not running."

"You're terrified of a deep conversation."

"If we're good, then why do we need to talk about it?"

"Tink." He hauled in a deep breath and swallowed so hard she could see his Adam's apple move. "I love you."

She nodded. "Sure, you do. We've become the very best friends."

"No, I love you as much more than friends, and I think you love me that way too."

Were they back to the proposal? "Joel, love and commitment are two different things. Last night, we were feeling vulnerable after losing Gabriel, and you'd had a knock to the head. A concussion. Your thinking is muddled. Now is not the time to—"

"So I *did* propose to you."

She crinkled her nose. "You don't remember?"

"I couldn't recall if I asked you, or if I dreamed that I asked you."

"You asked."

"What did you say?"

"I pretended to be asleep."

"Because you didn't know how to say no?"

"No," she said. "Because I didn't know how to say yes."

"Wait, what?" He shook his head. "Did you just accept my proposal?"

Had she?

Jana peered into the eyes of the person she loved most in the world. Why was she resisting him? He loved her; she loved him. They got along so well. Yes, it was scary, but hey, she'd been brave enough to take on Gabriel, knowing full well letting him go would break her heart.

And she trusted Joel, fully trusted him in a way she'd never trusted anyone, and that was huge for her. Monumental.

Was this really happening? Was Joel serious? Did he really want to marry her? Her heart overflowed with instant joy, and it felt so right she could draw a deep breath. She was scared as hell, but she wanted to be with him anyway. Maybe things would be okay after all.

"I can be bonkers sometimes," she whispered.

"That's what makes you so much darn fun to be around."

"I snore."

"I know that too."

"I can be passionate to the point of obstinance. I have a tendency to clam up when I'm hurt. I—"

"Shh." He took her into his arms and kissed her.

And then he kissed her again and again, and the next thing he'd coaxed her back to bed where he held her in his arms and listed one by one all the things that he loved about her, and she started to think that change could be a very good thing indeed.

CHAPTER 26

THE PLAN

Looking down into Jana's face as she lay in the bed peering up at him, Joel had so many things he wanted to tell her.

He wanted her to know just how much he appreciated and respected her. How much this Christmas season had meant to him. How taking care of Gabriel had bonded them in a way he hadn't dreamed possible.

How he wanted a future with her.

He kissed her again, and she kissed him back with a fierceness that left him breathless.

"We've got to stop," she gasped. "Your concussion."

"I know," he said reluctantly. "But I do feel fine."

"And we want to keep it that way."

He lay back against the pillow but kept his arms wrapped around her. It felt so good here, so right.

They started kissing again, but softer this time. Quieter. Not feeding a fire, just being together and drawing sustenance from each other.

They enjoyed themselves in a spectacular new way. More than just friends. More than mere lovers. They were forging an unbreakable bond.

At least to Joel's way of thinking, and he hoped her tender response signaled the same emotions on her side.

For over an hour, they played and teased, kissed and explored, delving into places they hadn't yet ventured. It felt freeing and fabulous, and he wondered why the hell he'd waited so long to tell her how he felt about her.

How he loved this complicated woman! She'd suffered so much in her short life, but the pain had honed her and sharpened her into a person filled with empathy and kindness. She'd learned and grown from her hardship, and his admiration for her courage and struggle knew no bounds.

In that bed, they quietly released their fears and anxieties and accepted each other for who they were, flaws and all. They found joy together and hugged it close. No orgasms needed to achieve it. No sex required.

Sighing, Jana rested her head on his shoulder, and he pulled her close, wrapping his arm around her. They turned to stare at each other, cross-eyed with their closeness, giggling together at the sheer fun of it all.

She trailed her fingers along his nipples, and he felt himself harden.

"Oh my," she whispered.

"Look what you do to me," he growled.

"I'll back off." She tried to roll away from him, but he held fast to her.

"Please don't go. It's okay. We don't have to pay any attention to *him*."

Giggling, she let him tug her close again.

They spooned, Joel cradling her against his belly, and he thought, *This is the very best moment of my life.*

And that's when the doorbell rang.

"CARMELA GARCIA, KXAS." The ambitious-looking young Latina woman on the doorstep thrust a microphone in Jana's face.

Startled, Jana jumped back, crashing into Joel's chest. They'd answered the door together, still rumpled and groggy from spending the morning in bed.

Behind Carmela hulked a camera crew. Jana didn't know if they were already recording or not.

"We're here for the story about the baby you two found in the manger," the newswoman said briskly.

"This isn't a good time," Joel said, moving to put his body between the reporter and Jana. Looks like local gossip about Gabriel had finally made it to the big-city news station.

Grateful for the barrier, Jana took the moment to draw in a deep breath and steady herself.

"Oh, please, talk to me," Carmela Garcia said in an I-will-get-my-story-one-way-or-another tone. "You think I'm the only one who is going to show up on your doorstep? I just got here first. This is a juicy story of holiday love. A manger baby! C'mon. Please, our readers are hungry for a sweet, heartwarming story. We've already spoken to Isabella Martin. She's the one who told us you were the angels who'd rescued Gabriel."

"Not now," Joel growled.

"It's okay, Joel." Jana turned to put a palm to his chest. "Ms. Garcia is right. This is an important story of hope that deserves to be told."

Joel turned to look at her. "Are you sure you're up to it now?"

Silently, she nodded and waved the reporter and her camera crew in out of the cold.

THE INTERVIEW TOOK over an hour. On the five o'clock news, the network reduced the story down to a few romantic sound bites designed to highlight how two friends had taken in the baby of a desperate teen mom, who was forced to abandon her newborn because she couldn't keep herself and him safe. The focus was on how Joel and Jana had adjusted to instant parenthood and how the whole community had rallied around to help them.

The story made it sound jovial and fun.

And Joel realized it had been. The only fly in the ointment was what would happen to Isabella and Gabriel. But Jana seemed convinced the story would bring forth someone willing to adopt Isabella and Gabriel together.

He prayed that was true.

"And so the enduring Twilight legend of Joel and Jana officially begins," Noah teased when the spot ended.

The family had gathered at Flynn and Jesse's house to watch the news story, and they were all piled up in the living area—including Carrie and Mark who were in town until after New Year's—while the delicious smell of vegan meat loaf wafted in from the kitchen.

"You're famous!" Grace clapped her hands and twirled ballerina-style in the middle of the rug.

"You're the next Jon Grant and Rebekka Nash," Flynn teased Joel, referring to the legend of the town founders, two lovers separated by the Civil War. Jon Grant became a Union solider, and Rebekka was a Southern belle, but fifteen years later, they were reunited on the banks of the Brazos River very near where the MacGregors' childhood home now stood. "The next thing you know, they'll be adding a statue of you, Jana, and Gabriel in Sweetheart Park alongside Jon and Rebekka."

"Okay, okay." Joel glanced at Jana. She looked uncomfortable with the conversation. She didn't like undue attention or the spotlight. "Enough ribbing. Is the meat loaf ready yet, sis?"

"Why not have a statue?" Carrie said. "This story is sure to bring more tourism to Twilight. I say go for it."

"My aunt Patsy's on the town council," Jesse said. "I could bring it up to her."

"No!" Joel and Jana said in unison.

"This might be beyond your control," Mark said. "The baby in the manger is a heartstring tugger."

Jana took a deep breath and briefly closed her eyes. Joel could tell she was drawing on inner strength. He reached over to squeeze her hand. She gave him a quick, tiny smile and moved her hand away.

He shouldn't get his feelings hurt. Jana wasn't big on public displays of affection either, but he wanted her to know he was here for her. That they were a team.

Always. From now on.

"Do you need any help in the kitchen?" Jana asked Flynn as the news program shifted to the weather report.

Flynn eyed her. "Sure. C'mon."

Jana wriggled her fingers at Joel and followed Flynn into the kitchen.

"I'll come too." Carrie hopped up from the couch. "Let's open that bottle of wine I brought."

"Don't leave me out," Kelsey said and trailed after them.

"How long before dinner is on the table, hon?" Jesse called.

"You got thirty minutes," Flynn hollered back. "Keep an eye on your kids."

Everyone scattered. Jesse and Mark took the kids to the game room to play video games, leaving Joel and Noah alone in the living room.

"Wanna take a walk on the dock?" Noah asked. "I've got a few things to discuss about the River Dreams Inc New Year's Eve party."

"Sure, sure." Joel shrugged into his jean jacket and followed his twin outside.

The air was nippy but not uncomfortable, although it was colder here at the water's edge.

They stood on the dock looking out at the river flowing in front of the home they'd grown up in, hands shoved into their pockets.

"Despite losing Mom, despite Dad hitting the sauce, we had a pretty darn good childhood," Noah said.

Joel nodded. "Thanks to Flynn, Mom's friends, and our community."

He thought about Jana and her rough upbringing. Basically,

she'd raised herself. It hurt him to think about her so alone in the world, forming that pugnacious persona to get by. Donning her tats and piercings like a warrior. Armoring herself with a don't-tread-on-me attitude. He wished he could have been there for her back then. Wished she could have lived in Twilight so at least she'd have had the community to fall back on as he and his siblings had.

Honestly, she hadn't needed it. Not only had she survived, she'd developed an iron will that he admired more than he could say.

Noah talked about business for a bit, and Joel tried to listen, but he couldn't get his mind off Jana. He thought of how brave she'd been giving up Gabriel. How understanding she'd been with Isabella.

He loved her. Had loved her for quite some time. But he'd settled for friendship. Anything really, just to be around her. Their main hurdle had been her caution and fear of opening up. She'd been betrayed so many times, but finally, he'd proven to her that he could be trusted. It meant the world to him that she'd held nothing back. Had told him all her secrets. He felt honored.

"Brother," Noah said sharply. "Where'd you go?"

"Huh?" Joel blinked.

"Your mind isn't with me."

"Sorry. What were you saying?"

"Wanna tell me what's going on? Is it the whole losing-Gabriel thing? Or should I be concerned about your concussion?"

"Neither."

"Wanna talk about it?"

"Not really."

"Does it have something to do with Jana?"

"Yeah."

"You're in love with her."

He nodded.

"Does she love you back?"

"I'm pretty sure she does."

"So what are you waiting for? Ask that woman to marry you. We all love her too. She's sassy and knows how to put you in your place. Bonus points."

"I already did."

"What! You're engaged!" A huge smile broke over Noah's face. "That's awesome, man."

"It's not. I blew it. I half-assed it." He told his brother then how he'd unintentionally asked Jana to marry him.

"Did she say yes?"

"Sort of. It was weird. We were talking about it, and then the doorbell rang, and there was the reporter, and we had stuff to do, and then Flynn invited us over for dinner and Jana jumped at the chance and—"

"You haven't had a chance to finish your discussion."

"That sums it up."

"So no biggie," Noah said. "Just do it up right."

"What do you mean?"

"Propose the correct way. She deserves that."

For sure she did. Joel exhaled. "I want to but—"

"No *buts*. New Year's Eve is the perfect time to ask her," Noah said. "We've already got a party planned. All you need is a ring."

"New Year's Eve is Friday. That gives me four whole days to find a ring, and I can't drive because of the concussion."

"Never fear." Noah grinned. "Your twin is here."

New Year's Eve. Ten P.M.

The scene was set. The real proposal planned. The ring was in his pocket. But Joel couldn't stop worrying. Why was he so worried?

Why?

What if Jana said no?

He convinced himself it wasn't a rational fear. The past few days had been magical as they hung out together. She stayed at his house, ostensibly to stay with him because of the concussion, but they never discussed her leaving. They'd stayed in the moment, just enjoying each other's company. They'd done quiet activities, based on doctor's orders. Board games and long walks holding hands. They'd cooked for each other and watched old movies and built fires in the fireplace. Roasted marshmallows and sipped hot chocolate.

It had been sweet. It had been bliss.

And he wanted more days like it.

Wanted to spend the rest of his life with her.

Tonight, because of his concussion, Jana was piloting the Brazos Queen while he and Noah played host to their guests. The festivities were in full swing. Music blared. The dance floor was hopping. The tempting smorgasbord Tasha had set out was a huge hit.

There was a small private room on the boat.

Earlier in the day, Noah and Kelsey had slipped over to decorate it for the proposal. Joel had gotten a quick peek at the room, and he was overwhelmed by the impressive job they'd done. They'd strung soft white twinkle lights from the ceiling and strewn rose petals on the floor. Iced champagne in a silver bucket. Cued up soft mood music on a tiny Bluetooth speaker.

At the appointed time, Noah would go up to the pilot house, tell Jana that Joel needed her help in the VIP room. Once Jana had said yes to the proposal, they'd go to the party and dance to "The Skater's Waltz."

It was a perfect plan.

Emboldened, Joel, dressed in his tux, gave Noah the signal, went into the private room and, with his heart in his throat, waited for the woman he loved.

CHAPTER 27

THE REJECTION

"Hey, Jana."

Jana turned from the captain's seat where she was piloting the Brazos Queen to see Joel's twin standing in the doorway.

"Hi, Noah. How's the party going?"

"Joel needs you in the VIP room." Noah pointed over his shoulder with his thumb.

"What's up?"

"Dunno."

"You can't handle it?"

"He said he needs your opinion on something, and I just won't do. I'm here to take over as captain."

Hmm. What was that about? "Okay."

Jana hopped up and let Noah have her seat. Out of concession to the party, and at Joel's urging because part of her duties included greeting the guests, she'd worn a little black cocktail dress and fancy black stilettos with red soles that she'd borrowed from Kelsey. She and Kelsey wore the same size shoes, and Kelsey, being rich, owned a crap ton of expensive designer footwear. Anyway, the shoes were sexy as all get-out and fit in nicely with Jana's plans for a special evening with Joel once the party ended after midnight.

She'd kicked off the shoes while piloting the boat and wriggled her feet back into them. Feeling like Cinderella at the ball, she went down the circular staircase, keeping a firm grip on the handrailing. Going to find Joel.

The ballroom was at the bottom of the stairs, and the band, led by Cash, was in a boot-scooting mood. Nattily attired guests line-danced to "Tush Push."

Jana wasn't much of a dancer. She'd never had the opportunity nor the inclination to learn, but she had a yearning to dance with Joel, who was a pretty decent dancer. Maybe he'd give her a twirl around the floor when the band played a waltz, although the stilettos would have to go. Then again, their height difference might create too much disparity on the dance floor without the extra four inches.

Plus, she'd have to make sure he didn't do anything too strenuous. Excessive physical activity was still off the table according to his doctor.

She skirted the dance floor and headed for the door leading into the hallway and the VIP dining room beyond. No one had rented out the room for the evening, so she didn't understand why Joel needed her in there, but she went without question. She was ready to help wherever she could.

The door to the VIP room was closed, and the closer she got the faster her pulse beat. She had no idea why, but suddenly she felt anxious.

She knocked gently, a light rap of her knuckles against the wood.

"Come in," Joel's rich, deep voice called from beyond the door.

Feeling cautious, she opened the door a crack. The room was dark except for the twinkle lights stretched across the ceiling. What was this all about?

"Joel?" Her pulse was in her throat, a hard, hot gallop. She pushed the door open wider, searching for him in the dimness.

She stepped over the threshold and onto a carpet of rose petals, as romantic violin music played from a speaker. She spied champagne in a silver bucket and a slideshow was being projected onto the wall.

Stunned, she watched the images play out. Photos of her and Joel over the past two years. It must have taken him hours to amass. There were shots of them in the summer, lounging on the beach at Christmas Island, and she'd been wearing a red string bikini, showing off her ink. Unbeknownst to Jana, Joel had been looking at her with such longing it now took her breath. She remembered that day, she and Joel just hanging out with Noah and Kelsey, playing like kids. They'd played volleyball, made sandcastles, and gone fishing. Later, they'd had a fish fry, cooking up their catch, with Joel frying up battered veggies for Jana in separate cooking oil. He'd gone to so much trouble for her.

When had he had the time to collect pictures from their family and friends to make the slideshow? Noah and Kelsey must have helped.

Her stomach squeezed, and she put a hand to her belly, overwhelmed.

There was a video of them at Noah and Kelsey's wedding on the Rockabye. Joel had been best man, Jana a bridesmaid. When Kelsey threw the bouquet directly at Jana, she'd sidestepped, and someone else snagged it.

Joel had caught the garter in the garter toss, and he looked disappointed that Jana hadn't gotten the bouquet. She barely remembered the incident, but it was clear from the video that Joel had wanted Jana's leg to be the one he slipped the garter onto.

She shifted her hand to her mouth. All this time, Joel had wanted her, and she hadn't seen it.

Next came a montage of the two of them around town together. Karaoke Night at Fruit of the Vine, singing Queen's "You're My Best Friend." Joel had picked the song. They'd put their heads together to sing in unison in a sweet moment that had drawn *aww*s from the crowd. Shots of the two of them helping

to decorate the Twilight Convention Center for the wedding of
the mayor's daughter last year. Images of Joel doing a striptease
for charity with the Christmas Bards, and Jana standing on a
chair throwing him whistles and catcalls. He'd come over to the
apron of the stage—to her—bumping and grinding like he was
the feature attraction in Magic Mike.

Holy Heart Chakra! He'd been in love with her for ages!

She had both hands on her cheeks now, and her heart was in
her throat. She spun around, tears streaming down her cheeks—
and dammit, she was not a crier—to see Joel standing behind
her wearing a tuxedo with a red rosebud in his lapel.

His dark hair swept sexily off his forehead, his gaze locked on
hers, in his hand he held a single rose, like in *The Bachelor*. She
smiled. It was a show they loved to make fun of together.

"Joel," she said. "I. Me. You. Us."

"Yes, Tink, it's been you all along." His voice quivered just
the tiniest bit, giving away his nervousness.

"What's going on?"

"I flubbed things the other night. I had to make it right." He
looked so adorable when he was vulnerable.

"This is beyond beyond. I never expected this."

"You deserve being treated like royalty. You're a princess in
my eyes."

"I *love* it."

He extended the flower. "Will you accept this rose?"

"Yes! Yes!" She took the rose, barely noticing the thorns had
been removed, and flung herself into his arms.

If she'd had any doubts before—not about Joel, but about her
being the right woman for such a magnificent man—they'd vanished completely. She might not understand why he loved her,
but he *did* love her. That much was clear.

He hugged her to him and kissed her passionately, his mouth
a determined punctuation to the sweet slideshow, this grandest
of gestures.

She absorbed his warmth, joy radiating from every pore in her body. How had she been blind for so long? She trusted this man as she'd never trusted anyone. In his arms, she found hope and the dreams she'd never dreamed.

It felt so good to let down her guard. Let go of her defenses. To open up and receive the love he offered her without any hesitation. In his arms, she was safe and secure, arriving at the place where she fit.

She had finally found home, and it was way more than she'd ever hoped for, and she couldn't wait to start her life with this man.

But reality sank its teeth into her, reminding her she'd foolishly let herself get carried away. She couldn't do this. Not until she'd told him everything about her past. She'd avoided it for too long, and the only excuse she had was her fear.

Tell him and risk losing him, the fear whispered.

Yes. It's what had kept her silent, but she couldn't accept his proposal without coming clean. There was no way around it.

He was taking a black jeweler's box from his pocket, getting down on bended knee.

Jana clutched the flower to her chest and stared into his eyes. No one had ever loved her the way this man did. He'd melted the ice block of her heart. She smiled at him, her body trembling with the impact of this moment. She knew him inside and out. He would never intentionally hurt her. She understood that with every fiber of her being.

But she was going to have to hurt him.

"No, no," she said in a rush. "Get up, get up."

"What is it?" He looked confused.

"I can't say yes. I can't agree to marry you."

He looked positively stricken. "Why not? What's wrong? How did I mess up?"

"It's not you, Joel. It's me." She hitched in a shuddering breath. "I'm not the woman you think I am."

HELL'S BELLS! WHAT did he have to do to convince Jana that she was a good and decent person?

"I should have told you all this before." She held out both hands to him.

He pocketed the ring, took her hands, allowed her to tug him off the floor, but the entire time his heart was beating so fast he feared he might pass out.

"Please sit." She waved at a chair and looked at him as if she was about to break his heart.

Not knowing what else to do, he sat.

Jana sank down in the chair next to him. She hauled in a shaky breath, held it, and then slowly exhaled. "I'm just like Isabella."

"I know that. You told me you got involved with an abusive older man."

She shook her head. "I left out a lot."

He raised both palms. "I've told you, Jana. I don't need to hear about all the details of your past. That's all gone. All I care about is the here and now—"

"I abandoned my baby," she blurted. "Just like Isabella did."

"Wait, what?" Stunned, Joel shook his head, trying to make sense of what she'd just said.

"Yes." Jana nodded stoically. "Not in a manger, but after I gave birth, I just walked out of the hospital and never looked back."

"You had a baby?" He rubbed the spot where he'd bumped his head. It was aching again.

"When I was Isabella's age."

"She's only fourteen!"

"Yes. Essentially, her story is my story. I had no father role model either, and my mother had mental health issues. Isabella was lucky she had a grandmother who cared, but then she lost her too."

Joel fisted his hands on the table, gritted his teeth, and tried to figure out what he was feeling.

She dropped her gaze. "I told you when I ran away from home I was out on the streets. I was looking for love in all the wrong places and wasn't knowledgeable about birth control. But honestly, getting pregnant woke me up and turned me around on the dark path I'd started down. The baby saved my life. I can't imagine what would have happened to me otherwise."

Still, he couldn't speak, hurt that when she'd had the opportunity to fully open up to him, she hadn't. How could he trust her to be honest with him in the future? What other secrets was she holding on to?

"I gave birth to a little girl on Christmas Eve. I didn't name her. I knew I couldn't keep her, and it killed me to let her go. But I was a wreck. I was living with that abusive older guy, doing what I had to do to get by."

"Was he the baby's father?" Joel asked, hearing his words come out hard and clipped. He was angry. Not at Jana but at himself for believing he'd gotten her to trust him. As if he had some sway with her that no one else had. Ego. It had all been his ego thinking they had something special.

"No." A long silence ensued. Finally, Jana said, "I don't know who the father was. I'd gone to a rave, and someone spiked my drink." She gave a half-hearted shrug but then angled him a sideways glance to see how he was taking her confession.

"That must've been so hard for you," he said by rote, his own feelings so numb he couldn't name them. "I can't imagine how difficult that was."

"The day I walked away was the absolute worst day of my life. But the guy I was living with told me if I didn't abandon her, I couldn't come back. I had nowhere else to go, no job, and no skills to raise a baby on my own." Tears glimmered in Jana's eyes, and the sight of them almost stopped Joel's heart.

"I don't know what to say, Jana."

"I'm just like my mother. I abandoned my child. I'm a horrible person. That's why I keep people at arm's length. To protect them, not me." She raised her hand to push back her hair, and he saw the tattoo of the angel with a baby's face.

"That's her picture, isn't it?"

"Y-yes. So I would never forget her."

"Do you know what happened to her?"

Jana shook her head. "No."

"You never tried to find out?"

"I didn't want to disrupt her life."

"Do you want to find her?"

"Maybe. Some day. I figure I'd leave it up to her."

"She'd be a teenager now?" he asked.

"Almost, she'd be twelve."

"So she could come knocking anytime. She's old enough to ask about you." Joel pulled his palm down his face. He had to get off by himself and think. "Look, I'm going to need some time."

"I get it. I get why you wouldn't want to marry a woman who could walk off and leave her own baby, even if it was for the baby's highest good. I mean, what if we got married and we had a baby? Would I just walk away?"

That had never occurred to him. Joel had no doubt her mistakes in her past had been due to her circumstances and young age. The Jana he knew would never, ever leave her baby. Of that he was as certain as the sun would rise in the east.

But this new revelation was a lot to absorb.

He got to his feet.

She jumped up beside him, anxiety pulling at her face. "Joel, I—"

"Jana, I don't mean to hurt you, but I've got to get out of here. Could you please just leave me alone?"

"I—"

"Please."

With that, Joel turned and left his own party, uncertain how he could ever heal the broken places inside of Jana's heart.

CHAPTER 28

THE DESPAIR

Midnight.

A brand-new year.

Happy freaking New Year.

Jana should have been spending the moment with her fiancé. Would have been in Joel's arms right now if she'd only been honest with him from the beginning.

Knees to her chest, arms wrapped around her knees, Jana rocked in front of the fireplace in her living room, mourning what might have been.

Tears burned her eyes as she tried her best not to cry. Look what Joel had reduced her to. He'd gotten her to trust him and let him in. She'd shucked her defenses for him and fallen in love with him. Discovered he was no different than anyone else from her past. He'd walked away from her when she needed him most.

That's not fair. He couldn't handle the fact you abandoned your own baby. You should have told him sooner. You should have fully trusted him when you had the chance.

This was her fault, and she knew it. She'd wrecked her own life. Stretching out prone on the area rug, Jana rested her forehead on the floor and closed her eyes.

Misery grabbed hold of her, heavy and sour. The acidic taste of despair filled her mouth, astringent as vinegar. She dug her fingernails into the rug, heard the sharp *pop* of wood burning in the fireplace.

Stop feeling sorry for yourself.

Softly, she pounded her forehead against the floor. Dammit! She had no idea how they'd work through this. She loved Joel and wanted to be with him, but could he forgive her for holding back?

She'd been by herself for so long and hadn't had anyone she could rely on to be there when the going got tough. That's why she'd held back. Fear, plain and simple. But that's why he was so upset. She couldn't let herself fully trust him.

Long ago, she'd learned how to rely on herself and had come to cherish her independence. How could she be expected to suddenly embrace coupledom? How could she put herself out there, knowing that she might get hurt again?

It's called being vulnerable, numbskull, and it's a good thing.

Yeah, well, she wasn't so sure about that.

So how long are you going to lie here and whine?

She closed her eyes. Where was he when she needed him most?

It's late. Give him space. He asked you to give him space.

She thought of the trouble he'd gone to with the elaborate proposal. He was a kind, good man. It wasn't him. He wasn't the problem.

It was her.

She was the problem. She was the broken one. Sure, she'd worked hard on herself and had found balance in her life. But when the going got tough, she'd held back, desperate to protect herself at all costs.

That's who she was at her core. A woman who hid behind walls.

You could change that.

Yeah? How?

Start with going to bed. Then get up tomorrow, and go about her day. After that, she had no idea what to do.

One step at a time.

With that, she got up, banked the fire, and crawled into bed, still wearing the cocktail dress she'd had on when Joel proposed.

WHILE JANA WAS lying on the rug in front of the fire castigating herself, Joel sat outside in his truck parked at her curb, engine idling to run the heater. It was edging toward one A.M., but there was still a light on in her living room.

His mind warred with his desire to see her, hold her, and apologize profusely for walking out. He'd texted Noah and told him what had happened. Noah advised him to take his time and let Jana come to him.

It went against his every instinct. Right this minute, he had to grip the steering wheel with both hands to keep from jumping out of the truck, running up the sidewalk, and pounding on her front door to tell her he was a fool for putting up walls of his own.

He'd told her to give him space. How could he expect her to come to him?

It killed his soul that she was inside the house suffering, when he was right here and could be sorting things out with her.

He killed the engine, pocketed his keys, and put his hand on the door handle. *Maybe she needs to be alone too.*

He hesitated.

Go to her, or head home?

He stared at her window, his heart urging him forward but his twin's wise advice holding him back.

More than anything in the world he wanted to be with Jana. Not just for tonight, but for the rest of his life. If he pushed too soon, came on too strong, he could blow it. They both had a lot to process. As much as it hurt him to turn away, it was for the best right now.

The light in the living room went out.

It was a sign.

Stuffing down his feelings, Joel started his truck and drove home.

TWO DAYS LATER, Jana sat in Naomi Luther's bedroom working on piecing squares for her unborn daughter Heather's baby quilt. The doctor had put Naomi on bed rest until her due date, and she'd called begging Jana to come keep her company. Naomi was propped in bed, while Jana sat on the settee in the bay window.

She pulled a sewing needle through the soft cotton fabric, a pink print featuring frolicking lambs and bunny rabbits, and felt her throat clog with unshed tears. She'd told Naomi everything. About the baby she'd abandoned at the hospital when she was fourteen years old, about her sketchy past, about Joel walking out on her after she'd finally confessed everything.

Naomi had taken the revelation in nonjudgmental stride and had avoided any mention of Joel after that, which Jana greatly appreciated, and they quilted in silence for several minutes, but now she wanted to talk.

"I'm thinking of leaving Twilight," Jana said.

"What?" Naomi looked shocked. "Why would you do that?"

"This breakup with Joel, I don't know if I can ever get over him. Even if I quit working for him, I'll still see him around town all the time."

"B-but where would you go?"

Jana raised a shoulder, feeling listless. "I dunno. Back to Austin, maybe."

"But you've got so many friends here. Your business. Look how hard you worked to get that going. Why would you throw all that away just because you and Joel didn't work out? And, by the way, I think you're overreacting about that too."

"I haven't heard a word from him in two days."

"Have you contacted him?"

"No," Jana admitted. "He said he needed to be alone, and I'm honoring that."

"Do you plan on ever talking to him, or are you leaving the ball fully in his court? Because that's not the Jana I know. The Jana I know has agency."

"I don't know what to do." Jana dropped her gaze, pulling her sewing needle through the cotton fabric.

"You have to talk to him, Jana. I've never seen you this down. I'll text him right now and get him over here." She searched through the bedcovers, looking for her cell phone.

Jana could see the edge of Naomi's phone underneath a stack of material. She didn't tell her where it was.

Joel *had* let her down when he'd walked away. She'd feared it, and it had happened. But she couldn't blame him. She hadn't fully trusted him, and he'd gotten his feelings hurt. The major question: Was her past a deal-breaker?

Jana pulled a palm down her face. She was regressing. Turning back into that terrified nineteen-year-old who'd rolled into Twilight seven years ago, searching for refuge and a place to lie low. She'd found so much more in this town: kindness, compassion, acceptance, and love. Yes, many people in Twilight loved her. If she left, she'd be surrendering a lot.

"You're scared," Naomi said. "Things got really real with Joel, and you're terrified that it won't work out, so you're sabotaging things between you two before they ever got started."

Jana sucked in a gasp of air, startled by her friend's perceptiveness.

"It's understandable, considering your childhood, but you can't hide forever, Jana. Unless you want to stay isolated and lonely for the rest of your life, you've got to stop hiding behind those emotional walls."

Presented that way, Jana's actions sounded immature and irrational. And yet she couldn't simply dismiss her feelings with a wave of her hand. She couldn't, because she'd developed a pattern of accepting other people's dismissal of her.

Jana blew out her breath. "I know."

Her friend's tone chided. "You're running scared."

"Well, obviously."

"So own it," Naomi added. "Joel's gotten under your skin, and you're terrified that all the defenses you've spent a lifetime assembling are cracking and falling away."

Too true.

"But that's a good thing. The best thing. I'm guessing here, but I suspect no one has ever gotten this close to your heart before, and you don't know what to expect. You're afraid he'll morph into someone who'll eventually hurt you."

Bingo. Yes, she was. No denying it, no matter how much she might wish she could. Jana placed a palm to her chest, felt her heartbeat beneath her fingers.

"You have to admit that Joel's not just some random guy," Naomi continued. "He's your friend. How can you possibly think he would do something to harm you? He'd never once intentionally hurt you. But I know a rational argument has little sway over strong emotions. You feel what you feel, and if you feel like you can't trust Joel to be there for you, then you can't. I'm just so deeply sorry you feel that way."

Jana dropped her face into her upturned palms. When she raised her head, she saw Naomi's husband Shep standing in the doorway studying her intently. Had he overheard their conversation?

"Where are the boys?" Naomi asked.

"Upstairs playing with their new video games." Shep strolled into the room, eyeing Jana. "You probably don't want me butting into the conversation, but can I say something?"

Jana met Naomi's gaze. Naomi shrugged and gave her a look that said, *A male opinion might be helpful.*

At this point, Jana wasn't so sure about that, but Shep was a nice guy, and it did seem like he wanted to help.

"Whatcha got?"

"Guys can be really thick sometimes. You gotta know, at our core, we really don't understand women, no matter how hard we try. You are a fascinating mystery to us."

Jana shifted her gaze to Naomi, who was grinning at her husband. Shep, however, seemed absolutely serious.

"Please cut Joel some slack," Shep went on. "He's a really good guy. Please don't judge him based on your previous experiences with men."

"I'm—"

"I had a pretty rough start as a kid too, and Naomi will tell you I've had some serious trust issues myself. I get where you're coming from, Jana. I understand why Joel putting a little distance between you feels monumental."

Why did *this* feel like a lecture?

"But at some point . . ." He beaded her with a dead-eye gaze. "You have to decide whether you're going to come in from the cold or not."

"I did. I moved to Twilight. I embraced the town—"

"And yet, you never risked giving away your heart," Naomi said. "Shep was the same way."

Shep turned his gaze to his wife, his entire face softening as his eyes filled with love and he murmured, "Until you."

Aww, Shep and Naomi were so cute together. Could she and Joel have a love story like that? The center of her chest tightened as if someone had inserted a screwdriver into her and twisted.

"Did Joel act like a butthead?" Shep continued. "Maybe, probably, but here's the truth. I've never seen a man so much in love since I fell for Naomi."

"You were besotted with me." Naomi laughed. "But no more than I was with you."

Shep crossed the room and sank down at the end of the mattress. Leaning over, he hugged his wife and gave her a soft, quick kiss. He straightened, took Naomi's hand, and glanced back at Jana.

"You deserve the same kind of love we've found," Shep said to Jana. "But until you can beat your fear of abandonment, you won't be able to find what you so desperately want. Your prickly armor will grow thicker and thicker until you push everyone away. I know. Been there. Done that."

Shep was one hundred percent right. Jana fingered her bottom lip, realized it was trembling. That *she* was trembling. "How do I fix this? How do I fix *me*?"

"You're not broken," Shep said. "That's your first mistake. You think you're broken because of your childhood, and while it's understandable that you believe that, it's simply not true."

"That sounds nice, but it doesn't give me the tools I need to get over my fears. How do I do that?"

"Lean into it," he murmured kindly and patted his wife's rounded belly. "That's how Naomi showed me to deal with my PTSD."

Jana canted her head and studied Shep. "Meaning?"

"Instead of running from the fear, let it teach you. Understand that there is nothing wrong with you. That you're not broken. That you don't have to constantly have your guard up to protect yourself."

"What do I do when these feelings of abandonment crop up?"

"Evaluate them logically."

"Spoken like a guy." Naomi laughed with a roll of her eyes.

"What's wrong with logic?" Shep asked.

"Feelings are important to women."

"Feelings are mercurial, butterfly. Logic is not." Shep leveled a smile at his wife. Returning his attention to Jana, he said, "Ask yourself if your standards for what you consider betrayal are way too high. Ask if you've set people up to disappoint you. Ask if you're expecting other people to live by some standard that they don't even know you hold."

Was that what she'd done with Joel? The pang in her heart was so sharp, she knew the answer was yes.

Naomi tightened her grip on her handsome husband's hand. "You're something else, Mr. Shepherd."

"I love you, sweetheart." All Shep's attention shifted to his wife.

Naomi patted the left side of her chest. "I'm more in love with you today than I was yesterday. Thank you for taking the time to help my friend."

Shep turned his head back to Jana, a shiny smile on his face. "See what you can have when you stop running from your fears?"

"You love Joel," Naomi said. "Whether you say it aloud or not. And he loves you. When you're in a room together, it's electric."

"But what if I commit to him, and it doesn't last?" Jana asked, expressing her greatest fear. "What if I fully surrender, let down my guard, open myself up to him completely, and it blows up in my face?"

"But what if it *doesn't*? What if you've found true and lasting love?" Naomi asked. "You're so focused on the risks you've forgotten about the rewards."

Her friends were right. She'd been laser-locked on the downside of commitment. Terrified of being hurt yet again.

Jana smacked her forehead with the heel of her palm. "You're absolutely right. My stars, I *know* it."

Naomi and Shep smiled the same indulgent smile.

"And I *do* love Joel. So much. That's the biggest hurdle of all."

"How is your love a hurdle, Jana?" Naomi asked.

"Because I love him so *very* much. I love that he cared for Gabriel as if he were his own child. I love his steadiness and his reliability. I love how close he is with his family. I love his holiday spirit. I love the way he looks after other people. But most of all, I love how he looks at me, as if I'm a special treasure he can't believe he unearthed. I love the taste of his kisses and the feel of his calloused palms against my bare skin and the way his outdoorsy scent teases my sense of smell and . . ."

A delighted little laugh escaped Jana as she thought of all the ways she loved Joel. "Just all of him. Strength, flaws, all of it. I love him in a way that I have never loved anyone or anything. That's the problem. I'm terrified of losing him. Of screwing up.

Of him waking up one day and realizing who I really am and that he doesn't want to be with me anymore. Both of you are totally right. And I know how utterly foolish that is."

Shep's phone dinged, signaling that he'd gotten a text. Letting go of Naomi's hand, he fished in his hip pocket, pulled out his phone, and peered at the screen. Shaking his head, he said, "Speak of the devil."

"Joel?" Naomi asked.

"Yep." Nodding, Shep looked at Jana. "And he wants to know if we've seen you."

CHAPTER 29

THE LOVE

"Tell Joel I'm not here!" Jana jumped up, scattering sewing supplies around her. She wasn't ready for this. "Tell him—"

"You're scared?" Naomi chuckled. "That you're desperate to hide from your feelings?"

Oh no, she was swamped with feelings. What she was desperate to hide from was the man himself.

"Running away won't work," Shepherd said as his phone dinged again.

"Why not?"

Shep held up his phone with the screen turned toward her so Jana could see the second message from Joel.

Walking up your front steps.

Ack! Joel was here. Right now. No doubt he'd seen her vehicle parked at the curb. No place to go. No quick getaway.

The doorbell chimed.

Jana started to dart one way and then the other and ended up spinning in a circle, knowing she was trapped. Like it or not, she would have to talk to Joel. Eep!

Shep got up.

"Don't answer it!" Jana's pulse thundered in her ears.

The doorbell chimed again.

"I'm not hiding out from your boyfriend." Shep shook his head and went to the front door.

Dang it.

Okay, fine. She'd face him.

"It'll be all right," Naomi said. "He loves you."

Yeah, that wasn't the issue. The problem was her. Jana didn't know how to accept someone's unconditional love. Conditional love was all she'd ever known.

Shep came back into the room, Joel trailing behind him.

Jana's radical heart skipped two beats and left her feeling breathless and naked in the intensity of Joel's dark-eyed stare.

He wore Wranglers and cowboy boots, with the collar of his shearling jacket turned up against the cold, damp weather. Raindrops clung to his hair, and she recalled the inclement night they'd found Gabriel in the manger. His face was expressionless, matching what she hoped was her own blank face.

Her heart was pounding so hard and fast she couldn't hear anything else but the wild *bump, bump, bumpity-bump.*

"Hey, Joel," Naomi said. "Were your ears burning? We were just gabbing about you."

Grinning at Naomi, Joel covered his ears with both palms. "Freezing my ears off is more like it."

Jana stood there with her hands curled into her fists, her lungs hardly expanding, her brain leaping from one fractured thought to another. *My friend. My lover. My man.*

"How's bed rest treating you?" Joel asked Naomi, as if there were nothing else going on in the room.

"I'm not used to taking it easy." Naomi wrapped an arm around her belly. "But I'll do anything to keep this little one in place until she makes her grand entrance."

"Keep up the good work, Mama." Joel ran a hand through his rain-dampened hair.

"Do you want coffee or hot chocolate?" Naomi asked him. "Jana brought lemon squares from the Twilight Bakery."

"Lemon squares are my favorite," he said. "But not right now. I need a word with Jana. Could we use your living room?"

"Be our guests." Shep motioned toward their living area. "We'll just hole up in here."

"Thanks." Joel turned his attention to Jana and held out his elbow for her to take.

Not knowing what else to do, she slipped her arm through his, and he led her from the bedroom. Shep closed the door behind them.

In the living room, a fire crackled, and the Christmas tree was still up. Jana let go of his arm and made a beeline for the fireplace. She wasn't cold, but she needed an excuse to catch her breath. His touch, his scent, the sound of his voice was simply too distracting. Whenever she was around him, she couldn't think straight.

He plunked down in the plush armchair in front of the fireplace and motioned for her to sit in the twin chair across from him.

"I'm good right here." She backed up to the fire, felt the heat warm her hands as she clasped them behind her.

Joel popped back to his feet. "Okay, if that's the way you want it. We'll stand."

Jana felt the pulse at her neck flutter hard as she looked up at him.

"We need to talk." His tone was soft, but his gaze was solid. "And I want you to really listen to what I have to say. Will you do that?"

Silently, she nodded, mainly because the lump in her throat was so big that she didn't know if she could force enough air around it to form words. She folded her arms over her chest, a thin barrier against the firm set of his chiseled jaw.

He stepped closer.

She would have backed away but, hey, fireplace.

He took another step and then another until the toes of their boots were touching. He slipped his palm around her chin, his fingers fanning to her cheek as he tilted her face up. His gaze held her in place, his eyes filled with worry and concern.

Beard stubble ringed his jaw, and there were dark circles beneath his eyes as if he hadn't slept much. His masculine fingers were rough from the cold weather, and she could smell the scent of soap on his skin. Everything about him was so achingly familiar, and it triggered so many memories and an intense desperate yearning.

She was trembling all over again, her knees weak and her pulse thready.

Without taking his eyes off her, he lowered his head and murmured, "Promise me that you'll hear me out."

Listen, buddy, she was tempted to say, *you were the one who walked away.*

"Please?" he whispered, begging. It wasn't something this big man did.

Stalwart Joel. Salt of the freaking earth. The guy who thought for some insane reason that she'd hung the moon and dusted the stars. She didn't know why he loved her. She only knew that he did. Of that she had no doubt.

Silently she nodded, and he visibly relaxed, his breath leaving his lungs on a shaky sigh. Had he really thought she wouldn't listen to him?

He jumped right in. "I had to get off by myself because I had a few things to sort out."

"Things like what?"

He pulled a piece of paper from his pocket. "I went to see a friend of mine who just happens to be a private detective in Austin."

"Joel, what did you do?" She splayed both hands on her chest scarcely daring to hope.

"I found your daughter."

She gasped, and a tingling chill washed over her entire body. "You didn't."

"I didn't go see her. I just got a name. I wouldn't presume to do that without you."

"Tell me about her!" All those feelings she'd had for her daughter, that she'd shut down so solidly twelve years earlier, came rushing back.

"Her name is Charlotte, and she was adopted by a couple called the Klepperholts. She has a nice life in an upper-middle-class home. Her father is a CPA, and her mother is a stay-at-home mom." Joel passed her the piece of paper. "Their phone numbers and emails are there."

Jana's hand was shaking as she took the paper and stared down at the information. "This is why you left? To locate my daughter for me?"

"Yes."

"You weren't turning away from me because I kept my secret. You were trying to help," she murmured, distressed by the depth of her lack of trust in him.

"I hope you don't mind."

"Are you kidding? This is the nicest thing anyone has ever done for me." She clutched the paper to her chest. "I thought you didn't want me because I was the kind of woman who'd give up her child."

"Sweetheart." He cupped her cheek. "Why would I judge you like that? You were a child having a child. Just like Isabella and Gabriel. You were caught in something beyond your control, and yet you cared enough about your child's well-being to give her up. I admire your bravery more than you can ever know."

"Really?" Her voice quivered.

"I'm just sorry you didn't feel like you could trust me sooner, but hey, you finally told me. We're getting there."

"I'll never again keep anything from you, Joel."

"Even if you did, Tink, I'd never leave you over it. Don't you know me better than that by now?"

She nodded, tears springing to her eyes. She did know that. "I'm sorry I didn't trust you. I'm sorry I didn't call you for the last two days. I overreacted. I reverted back to old Jana. I felt hurt, and I momentarily forgot that you are my best friend and that you've *always* had my back."

"And I always will," he said. "If you'll let me. I do apologize for not letting you know where I was going and what I was up to. I didn't mean to cause you distress."

"Joel, there's nothing to be sorry for. I kept my secret from you out of my own insecurity. Naomi and Shep helped me see that."

"You mean it?" His voice cracked, and his eyes softened with hope.

"Here's the dealio. I've grown up a lot since I came to Twilight, but in this one area, in being able to fully trust, I got stuck. I reverted back to that scared kid."

He put his hand to her cheek again, reaching up with his thumb to wipe away the tear she hadn't even known she'd shed. "My behavior triggered your reaction, and I wonder, if on some level, you were just waiting for me to disappoint you so you could have a reason not to trust me."

"That's not—"

"Be honest with me, Jana . . . and yourself." His eyes were sad. "Please."

She sucked in a shuddering breath. "Okay, maybe. You might be right. Subconsciously, I felt you were too good to be true, and I braced myself for the other shoe to drop. It happened with my biological mom, it happened with Marjean, and in every romantic relationship I've been involved in. Because until I came to Twilight and began my healing journey, I repeated bad patterns by getting involved with people destined to abandon me."

His jaw clenched, and she saw frustration in his eyes. "But now, we've learned an important lesson."

"Yes," she whispered. "We've discovered that when we're feeling vulnerable, rather than run away or hide our feelings, we should talk it out."

"Lean into the scary places and shine a light on those pesky fears."

"Exactly." She caught her breath, hope blooming fresh inside her. "It's time for me to stop hiding behind walls."

"Do you mean that? I hope you mean that because I'm not hiding from you. Not now. Not ever." A troubled look darkened his eyes. "If you want that too."

Overwhelmed, she couldn't find the words to express her gratitude.

He leaned forward, looming over her, forcing Jana to look up at her big, tall man. "I let you take the lead on deepening our relationship because I knew you felt more comfortable when you have control over things. I knew you were less likely to run. And I was okay with it. Want to know why?"

"Because the sex was hot?" She dared a small smile.

His face stayed serious. "Well, yeah, obviously, but I need more than hot sex now. The reason I let you set the parameters on our relationship was because I wanted to be with you, no matter what it took. I'd go at your pace, even if it didn't match my own. I told myself it was enough."

She felt her smile fade.

He cleared his throat. "I love you, Jana, with all my heart and soul. I want to marry you and build a life with you. Are you in, or are you out? 'Cause I just gotta know."

Jana stared into his eyes, not answering his question.

She is gonna say no. Panic filled Joel, and he wondered where he'd gone wrong and how he'd managed to screw this up so badly. He'd spoken what was in his heart. He loved her, and he could swear she loved him.

A door opened somewhere in the house, and then came the pitter-patter of little feet. He glanced toward the stairs, saw Naomi and Shep's kids Hunter and Henry peering at them through the rungs of the railing. He hadn't meant to propose to her at the Shepherds' house and wished he could take it back and start all over.

"Before I answer, there's something I have to know first," Jana said.

He froze. Finally, his jaw unhinged and he croaked, "What's that?"

"I plan on having as active a role in Charlotte's life as she and the Klepperholts will allow. I might drive to Austin twice a month or have her come visit me just as often. Are you good with that?"

"Why wouldn't I be?"

"She'll be a teenager soon. That's a difficult age."

"We can handle it . . ." He locked eyes with her. "Together."

"Are you sure? Even a part-time child is a big responsibility."

"Jana, don't you know by now that I live for responsibility?" He wrapped his arms around her and pulled her close. He dipped his head down and hooked his thumb underneath her chin to tilt her face up.

"You think I'm worth all the extra complications? Sometimes I need to withdraw a little in order to figure out what's going on in my head."

"That's great! I can give you all the space you need."

"And while I'm working on the trust issues, it is a process, and I'll have days where I'm frustrating to be around."

"Ditto, babe. That's called a relationship. I want to be the one you can always count on. I want to be your person."

"Are you sure?" She looked at him with awestruck eyes, as if she couldn't believe her good fortune to have found love at last.

He made a tsking noise. "I love you, Jana Gerard. I've loved you for ages. You're my best friend in the entire world, and that includes my twin brother. I love everything about you. I love your determined walk and independent spirit. I love your ink and how you're not afraid to put yourself out there. You're honest and genuine, and you do what you say you'll do. I know fear is your driver, and I want to be your copilot. I want to be your soft place to land."

Joel removed a ring box from his pocket, cleared his throat, went down on one knee, and cracked open the ring box.

"Holy Snickers, Joel! That's a two-carat diamond!"

"I'm a traditionalist," he said. "What can I say? But don't worry about the ethics. It's a made diamond. Kelsey said many vegans prefer them."

"Oh, Joel." She sighed. "You get me. You really get me."

"Jana, did you really doubt me?"

"No." She shook her head. "Um, we have an audience."

"I know. Do you mind?"

"Not at all." She laughed.

"Jana Gerard, will you marry me?"

"Yes, yes!" She tugged him to his feet and flung herself into his arms. Tears spilling down her cheeks, laughter shaking her sides.

He tightened his arms around her, lifted her off her feet, and spun her around. When he set her back on her feet, he kissed her with every ounce of love he had inside him, and she kissed him back, Jana-fierce.

She had come through so much, and even though she could be a bit guarded, it was clear she loved people as much as they loved her. That's why she was so guarded. She'd loved big and gotten hurt so many times. But now here she was opening up, ready to take a chance on love again.

Ready to love *him*.

"Mommy," Hunter called from the stairs, "Joel's kissing Jana in our living room."

"Stop spying on them," Naomi called back to her son.

Shep peeped around the corner of the room. "Naomi wants to know if Jana said yes."

"Yes!" Joel and Jana said in unison, then went back to kissing.

"You know," Shep said, "Pastor Luther is right next door if

you want to start planning your wedding. I mean, you two have been dancing around this thing for two long years. No sense wasting any more time."

"Do you want a big church wedding?" Joel asked. "I'm up for anything."

"Heavens, no! I don't like all the fuss. The courthouse will be just fine. Unless you want to elope."

"Don't you dare elope!" Naomi hollered from her bedroom.

"We could go next door and get Naomi's dad to marry us right now," Joel said. "How is that for spontaneity?"

"What's happening?" Naomi yelled. "Are they getting married right now?"

Grinning, Jana hollered back to her friend. "No, Naomi. We won't have a wedding without you. Don't worry."

"Oh, thank heavens."

"We can get married on our boat," Jana said picking up Joel's hand and interlacing their fingers. "Just like Noah and Kelsey got married on theirs."

"Poetic," Joel said. "I like it. If you're sure that's what you want."

"I just want to be with you."

"Well, you've got that. For now and forever, Tinker Bell."

"Why are we still here?" Jana whispered. "Shouldn't you be taking me home?"

"Your house?" he asked. "Or mine?"

"Mine. It's closer."

With a laugh bursting from him, Joel bent, scooped up his petite bride-to-be, and carried her the full three blocks to her house.

SOMETIME LATER, SATED and spent, they snuggled together in Jana's small bed.

Jana kept holding up her ring finger, admiring the man-made diamond. This was one of the things she loved most about him.

His kindness and consideration. The diamond caught the light and glimmered bright.

"It's real," he said. "We're engaged."

His long legs were hanging off the end of her small mattress, and she was tucked securely against his side. He kissed her cheek, toyed with one of her curls. "Thank you for giving me a second chance. I intend on spending the rest of my life proving you trusted the right guy."

From the cottonwood tree in the side yard, red birds called from the branches. Grinning, Joel traced the cardinal inked onto her skin. "I looked up the meaning to every single one of your tats."

Stunned, she sat up and looked at his handsome face. "You didn't."

"I did." With an index finger, he reached out and started cataloging her ink. "This wolf in blue ink obviously stands for true-blue loyalty. The dolphin represents trust. This guy?" He traced the elephant in the center of her chest. "Family."

"Yes."

"And this angel not only represents Charlotte but unconditional motherly love."

She nodded, the lump in her throat strangling her speech. Her eyes welled with tears as her heart swelled with love for this man.

"You've been inking your values all over your body. I'm sorry it took me so long to wake up to that." He reached up his hand to cup her cheek.

"You're the only one who ever saw it," she whispered. "The only one who cared enough to look past the surface."

"That's because I love you, Jana. With all my heart and soul. And I got a tat to prove it."

"You did? Where?" She yanked back the covers and scanned his body. They'd just made love, and she hadn't seen any ink. "I thought you were scared of needles."

"I am." He laughed. "But for you? I'd walk through hell and back."

"Where is it?"

"Check out my foot." He rearranged himself on the bed, sitting up to rest his left ankle on his right knee, exposing the sole of his foot.

There was a small tat of two red birds, heads together, inside the frame of a heart. "They mate for life."

"It looks brand-new. When did you get it?"

"Yesterday."

"Before you even knew I'd say yes to your proposal."

"I had faith in you, Tinker Bell. You might have had more struggles than the average person, but you've overcome them. You're the strongest woman I've ever known. With all these symbols of love, trust, loyalty, and devotion inked onto your body, I knew, once you let yourself stop hiding and opened your heart to what was right in front of you, you'd accept your fate."

"Oh?" she said, feeling giddy and effervescent with love. "And you think that's you?"

"I know it, my love, and so do you. I love you, Jana Gerard, with all my heart and soul."

That was all she needed to hear. Tears brimmed in her eyes, and she gave him a watery smile. "I love you too, Joel Mac-Gregor."

He kissed her then and pulled her back into the circle of his arms, and for the first time in her life, Jana knew she'd finally found home.

EPILOGUE

Christmas, one year later

The MacGregor clan assembled for the holiday. Not at Flynn and Jesse's house as had been the tradition for the past ten years but at Joel and Jana's new home on Christmas Island, not far from the Rockabye Boatel.

But far more than just immediate family had gathered in the living room with the wide picture window looking out onto Lake Twilight. The Shepherds were there with their three children, along with the Klepperholts and Charlotte, and Isabella and Gabriel. It was a joyous time of community and celebration for the wonderful year just past.

So many lovely things had happened for their friends and family that Jana could hardly believe all the good fortune. How grateful they were for such blessings!

After spending time in Twilight, Isabella, who'd been declared an emancipated minor by the courts, was so taken with the town, she'd moved there with Gabriel. Once she got out from under her controlling boyfriend, she'd blossomed. Joel and Jana got to babysit for Gabriel while Isabella took night classes to get her GED. He was growing into a bright, gregarious child with an avid interest in taking things apart and putting them back together. For Christmas, they'd gotten him a set of building blocks. He'd bonded with Naomi and Shep's daughter, Heather, since they were close in age, and at the moment, they were sleeping side by side on a pallet beneath the Christmas tree.

Charlotte had just turned thirteen, and she was riding high on the adrenaline of winning her first regional gymnastic competition. Once a month, Joel and Jana alternated between driving to Austin or having Charlotte come visit them. During the summer, Joel had taught her how to water-ski. The more Jana learned about her daughter and the Klepperholts, the more she appreciated the important sacrifice she'd made to give her child a good life. With the help of a good therapist, all five of them were learning how to navigate the intricacies of an open adoption. They'd had a few challenges along the way, but communication was key, and since Jana had learned to stop running and face challenges, she'd not only grown as a person, she'd invited more love into her life.

Kelsey had recently given birth to a baby girl she and Noah had conceived the previous Christmas. Currently, they sat on the couch, ogling their little angel, Willow.

On Christmas Eve, Flynn had announced that she and Jesse were expecting their third and final child. It was quite the baby boom in Twilight.

Jana curled her arm around her own extended belly and glanced over at Joel, who was dressed as Santa and was preparing to start handing out packages from the huge pile of gifts underneath the tree. Just as they were about to start the festivities, the doorbell rang.

"I'll get it," Joel said, stepping around packages and children.

Satisfied to let her husband handle things, Jana sat on the couch beside Naomi. If she craned her neck, she could see the front door. She'd been expecting a special delivery that no one else knew about.

"We're going to have to wait to open the gifts for just a little bit longer," she announced as Joel opened the front door.

"Aww," said Hunter and rolled his eyes. "We've already waited for*ever*."

"Aww," his younger brother, Henry, echoed.

"Sons," Shep said, "mind your manners."

"There's cake," Jana told the boys.

"Yay!" The boys and Charlotte did a happy dance around the room.

Joel came back into the room carrying a white cake box. "It's from the Twilight Bakery," he said. "I can't believe they delivered on Christmas Day."

"Christine sent it as a favor," Jana told him.

Joel gave her a sexy look. "But why? We have plenty of sweets."

"It's the gender-reveal cake," Jana confessed.

That got everyone's attention, and they all abandoned the living room for the big farmhouse-style kitchen.

Joel took the cake from the box and settled it on the kitchen island while their guests gathered in the room. He rummaged in the drawer for a knife and serving fork, while Jana went for the plates.

"You ready to find out what we're having?" Joel asked the collective and settled his arm around Jana's shoulders.

She leaned against her tall, handsome husband. She was the luckiest woman in the entire world. Thirteen years ago she'd never have dreamed such a wonderful life could be hers.

"Yes!" everyone hollered.

"Charlotte?" Joel looked to his stepdaughter. "Would you like to do the honors?"

"Me?" Charlotte's face flushed prettily as she pressed a hand to her chest. "You want me to cut the cake?"

"Please?" Jana smiled at her.

"Sure!" Charlotte took the knife and cut into the Christmas-themed layer cake.

Jana held her breath, the anticipation killing her. She really didn't care about the sex of the baby. Joel said he didn't either, but he spoke often of playing catch and shooting hoops with his son, while Charlotte often talked about having a baby sister.

Everyone leaned in to get a peek of the color of the cake.

Charlotte met Jana's gaze and looked confused as she dished up the first slice. "I don't get it. The bottom layer is blue, and the top layer is pink." Her eyes widened along with Jana's, and they said in unison with everyone else in the room, "Twins!"

Joel tightened his grip around Jana. "Tinker Bell, we're having twins! Can you believe it?"

No, no she could not.

Stunned, Jana's mind filled with possibilities. Twins. They were having twins!

Everyone congratulated them and went in for cake, chattering about the joy of having two babies to love at once.

Joel reached down and took her hand, slowly eased her from the kitchen and into their bedroom. He shut the door behind them and turned to her.

"You okay, Tinker Bell?"

"I've never been happier."

"You sure?" Tears of joy misted his eyes. "You're not afraid?"

"With you by my side? Not in the least. You were made for fatherhood, Joel MacGregor, and I think this might just be the second-happiest moment of my life."

"What was the first?" he whispered.

"The day we found Gabriel in the manger. It was when everything changed, and I saw clearly what I had been denying for two long years. I was in love with my best friend."

"You know," he said, "if we didn't have a houseful of guests, I'd take you to bed and show you exactly how much I love you."

"Kissing will have to do for now," she said. "There's a passel of kids waiting to tear into their Christmas presents."

"This is how it's going to be from now on," he said. "A life filled with love and children."

"I wouldn't have it any other way," she said.

Then there was a knock on the door, and Noah poked his head in, urging them to rejoin the fold.

Joel shooed his brother away and took Jana's hand, and together they walked into their very happy future. Love was all around them as they celebrated a Christmas filled with second chances.

Keep reading for a look at

THE CHRISTMAS BACKUP PLAN

by Lori Wilde!

Chapter 1

Cupid: In skydiving parlance, slang for altitude expressed in hundreds of feet above ground level.

Wednesday, December 16
The Silver Feather Ranch, Cupid, Texas

"You gotta be shi—"

"Remington Dewayne Lockhart! Watch your language!" At thirty-five, his stepmother, Vivi, was just three years older than Remington, but she lectured him as if he were the same age as her twin toddlers.

Vivi clapped her palms over the ears of Remington's half brother, Rory, who was sitting in her lap. "Reed," she called to Rory's twin halfway across the den stacking blocks. "Cover your ears, son."

Reed looked up, wide-eyed.

"Ears." Vivi nodded and gave him a pointed look. "Now."

Like a well-trained puppy, the boy plastered his palms over his ears.

"I swear I think you Lockhart men just enjoy testing the limit of my patience," Vivi muttered.

"Do you think making a big deal over curse words might draw more attention to them?" Remington drawled, leaning one shoulder against the doorjamb that led from the foyer to the den.

"Swear jar." Vivi snapped her fingers at the bookcase where a glass mason jar sat. Dollar sign stickers and the symbols %$#@^ decorated the jar.

"Hey." Remington raised both palms. "I didn't say it. You cut me off at the knees."

"The intent was there." Vivi got to her feet, rested her fisted hands on her hips.

"Wicked stepmother," he said affectionately. "To my way of thinking, my foul mouth is all your fault for springing Aria Alzate on me."

"Your father and the US Army are to blame for your foul mouth, not me." Vivi retrieved the swear jar and shoved it under his nose. "Five dollars."

"Five dollars? Highway robbery," Remington grumbled, but he got out his wallet and opened it up. "I only have twenties."

"I'll take one." Vivi leaned over to pluck the twenty from his wallet. "You'll cuss around my boys again. Consider your next three curse words prepaid."

"No doubt I will, especially since you blindsided me with Aria. Low blow, Vivi, low blow."

Vivi fluffed her shoulder-length blond hair and grinned. "I do try my best."

His stepmother ran a cowboy wedding venue on the Silver Feather Ranch, and Aria worked for her as a wedding planner. Because of Aria's connection to Austin, where she'd lived for a time, she'd managed to get a write-up in *Texas Monthly*. Vivi's business had exploded as people sought them out for authentic cowboy weddings, and Aria, rising to the occasion, dazzled. They had so much work they'd upped their prices and started turning away business.

Much as he disliked Aria, the woman was pretty good at her job. Remington valued hard work, and he admired that about her, if nothing else.

"Would you have agreed to drive cargo to a wedding in North Central Texas if you'd known Aria was part of that cargo?" Vivi asked.

"Hells to the no."

"Exactly." Vivi held up two fingers. "You only have two curse words' credit now."

"Hell isn't a curse word, it's a place, and you just put me in a vehicle with it for the next eight hours."

Vivi waggled her index finger. "You have one prepaid swear word left."

Tempted to give her all the money he had in his wallet so he could swear up a blue streak, Remington reached for the cash, but his toddler half brothers watched him with mesmerized eyes.

"I'm no more thrilled to get stuck in that paramilitary black SUV with you than you are to have me there," said a tart female voice from the other entryway into the den, this one from the dining room.

He stared across the room, his gaze clashing with the woman standing there. Their eyes narrowed at each other like gunslingers squaring off on the dusty streets of Tombstone.

Looking at Aria Alzate, knowing what was ahead of him for the next several days, Remington made a brash forecast. Thrown together for several days in forced proximity, they would either learn to get along or tear each other from limb to limb.

Remington's money was on the latter. He groaned and briefly closed his eyes. "You could have warned me that she was in the next room, Vivi."

"Look," Vivi said, "I know you two get along like cats and dogs, but I need you both to play nice and get this done. Got it?"

Remington opened his eyes and studied the stunning woman standing in the doorway.

Aria Alzate was a major pain in the ass, but she was sure pretty to look at. Slim and trim, but curvy in all the right places, she studied him through lowered eyelids thick with long dark lashes. Her father, Armand, was Mescalero Apache, and she'd inherited his straight black hair and high cheekbones, while also inheriting a pale creamy complexion from her Irish mother, Bridget.

She was an interesting contrast of dark and light.

Remington had known her his entire life, although he hadn't seen her much in the twelve years he'd been in the Army, most of those spent as a paratrooper. On the few occasions she'd been home when he'd returned on leave, they'd made a point never to be in the same room alone together. They'd always rubbed each other the wrong way, and they literally had nothing in common.

Aria was impulsive, rebellious, quirky, and something of a busybody. Everything Remington was not. They'd grown up together on the Silver Feather in an arid, isolated stretch of Trans-Pecos nestled in the shadow of the Davis Mountains. Her family had worked for the Lockharts. Her father had been the ranch foreman until he'd retired, and his son Archer took over. Her mother had been their housekeeper.

In those terrible times, after his mother, Lucy, died when Remington was ten, Bridget acted as a surrogate mother to him and his three brothers, Ridge, Ranger, and Rhett.

At the moment, Remington was living on the Silver Feather because his paternal grandfather, Cyril, had left the four oldest Lockhart grandsons—this was before Dad had Rory and Reed with Vivi—two-acre parcels of land on each quadrant of the hundred-thousand-acre spread.

Nice of him, but as with everything involving his father's family, there was a catch. None of the four brothers could sell their places without approval from the entire family. And Remington's father would never grant his permission.

So, knowing he had few options with the land, he had a house built on his property while living in a fifth-wheel trailer. His contractors had just finished building the house, giving him something to occupy his mind while he recovered from his injuries and adjusted to civilian life. But things still felt alien. He'd been away for twelve years. Living in a third-world country had shown him a whole other way of being. And he wasn't really sure who he was anymore, now that he was no longer an Army Ranger.

Besides, Aria reminded him too much of who he used to be. The wild kid he'd worked so hard to shed.

Yes, he and Aria found themselves forever tied, and not just because of their pasts, but also since his three brothers had all married her three sisters. He might as well get used to having her around. It was a weird family dynamic, especially when everyone seemed to expect him and Aria to get together too, just because the others had all gotten together.

Yeah, over his dead body. The woman was sexy, but she was a bona fide flake. She acted first and thought . . . Well, Aria didn't think, did she? Neither before, during, or after jumping in with both feet.

"Why can't she drive herself?" Remington asked, feeling a bit petulant. He wasn't proud of it, but neither was he ashamed.

Aria drilled down on her glare.

"One," Vivi said, "it's a long drive in the winter with a potential ice storm brewing. Two, she's got a lot of stuff to haul, and three, she needs help to set things up once she gets there—"

"It's okay, Vivi, you don't have to make excuses for me," Aria interrupted.

"Excuses?" Remington lifted an eyebrow. What had the harum-scarum woman done now?

"My doctor says I can't drive, okay?" Aria folded her arms over her chest and jutted out her cute little chin. "If it wasn't for that, you can bet your sweet booty I'd drive myself."

"You think my booty is sweet?" he drawled, intentionally provoking her.

Aria made vomiting noises.

"Stop it, you two." Vivi sounded exasperated. "This wedding is important." She turned to Remington. "Besides being one of

Aria's best friends, the bride, Olivia Schebly, is the daughter of Twilight's mayor. If we do a good job, we'll have an 'in' with Texas politicians."

"A lot's on the line then," Remington said.

Vivi nodded and turned back to Aria. "So, follow the checklist. Got it?"

"I've got it right here." Aria tapped her temple with an index finger. "Olivia is my bestie. I won't disappoint either of you."

"Write it down, please." Vivi's expression brooked no argument.

"I don't need—"

Vivi interrupted her. "Write it down. I know you have a good memory, but considering recent events, write it down."

"Yes, ma'am." Aria rolled her eyes.

Without missing a beat, Vivi reached down and took a piece of carpet fuzz out of her son's mouth. "Let Remington rub off on you. He's a great planner."

"*Eww*, I don't want Mr. By-the-Book rubbing off on me." Aria pantomimed dusting herself off.

"Don't worry," Remington said. "I have no intention of getting close enough to you to rub off."

"Good." Aria tossed her head, and her long straight hair swished like a curtain. "I hate being boxed in. I follow my muse."

"You can plan and still find inspiration," Remington said.

"Maybe I can." She put a palm across her heart. "But can you?"

"You're ironic, you know that?"

She narrowed her eyes and widened her stance. "How so?"

"A wedding planner who doesn't plan." He snorted. "How does that even work?"

"I plan. Just not in the dead boring, extreme minutiae way that you do."

"Why can't you drive yourself?" Remington changed the subject. He didn't want to get into what his first and last serious girlfriend had called his "intractable" ways.

"Not that it's any of your business," Aria sassed, "but I suffered a concussion two days ago—"

Alarm shot through him. Concussion? That wasn't good.

Remington had suffered one helluva concussion two years ago in Afghanistan, and he'd had lingering health issues for months. He knew firsthand just how serious a concussion could be. While he disapproved of the scatterbrained woman, he didn't want bad things happening to her.

"Are you okay?" he asked.

"It's a mild concussion, I'm fine. I have a slight headache." Aria kneaded her temple. "But no biggie. Still, to be on the safe side, my doctor forbade me from driving for ten days."

Remington shifted his gaze to Vivi. "Should she even be doing this?"

"Dr. Kemper says she's fine to work, just not to drive and especially not to overdo it. As long as she gets plenty of sleep and keeps hydrated, she'll be fine," Vivi said. "That's why she's adding an extra day to her schedule."

Remington eyed Aria. "How did you get a concussion?"

Aria looked embarrassed. "I . . . um . . ." She dropped her gaze and fiddled with the hem of her sweater. "I fell out of the hayloft."

"What were you doing in the hay—" It hit him then that she might not have been alone in the hayloft. Aria dated a lot. "Oh," he said. "Oh."

She fluttered her eyelashes at him and offered up a knowing smirk. "Sometimes I get a little too adventuresome."

"A little?" He arched his eyebrows. It sounded irresponsible to him. Falling out of a hayloft.

She shrugged and stabbed him with a piercing stare as if daring him to judge her. "What can I say? I like to have fun. Unlike some people in this room."

"There's fun and there's just plain foolishness. What's wrong with having sex in a bed like anyone else?"

Aria hooted. "You thought I was having sex in the hayloft?"

"That's what you implied." He scowled. She loved to poke fun at him.

"No, that's what you inferred."

"What were you doing in the hayloft?"

"Hanging Christmas decorations."

"In a hayloft?"

"It was for ambience."

"In the horse barn?"

"Don't be dopey. It was in the wedding reception barn."

That didn't make it any better. People needed to consider the consequences of their actions and plan ahead. If she climbed up in the hayloft to string lights, she should have had help, and a backup plan in case she fell out and concussed herself.

"No one else can drive her?" Remington shifted his gaze back to Vivi.

"Hello!" Aria waved a hand. "In case you haven't noticed, I'm standing right here."

Oh, he'd noticed plenty. That was part of the problem. Annoying she might be, but he found her hot as a firecracker, and that vexed him to no end.

"Duke's out of town," Vivi said. "Ridge and Kaia's third baby is on the way any day, Rhett is running the Christmas toy drive—"

"How about your brother?" Remington asked. Archer seemed the prime candidate to drive her to Twilight, at least in his book.

"Archer has his hands full with the ranch, and Casey doesn't want him traipsing off for five days just before Christmas."

"Maybe a ranch hand then?"

"We give the ranch hands two weeks off at Christmas in case you've forgotten," Vivi said. "That's why Archer is so busy."

"There's absolutely no one else?"

"Everyone's eyeball deep in work. While you, Mr. Dark and Broody, have been moping around your new house feeling sorry for yourself ever since you got discharged from the Army."

Things were a lot more complicated than that, but Remington wouldn't get into the lingering effects of PTSD with Vivi.

"Don't think you're alone in hating this," Aria said. "I've already gone through all the other possible chauffeurs. I even thought about calling an Uber from El Paso to take me, but the cost is beyond astronomical."

"Dammit," Remington muttered.

"Curse again and you'll need to cough up more money." Vivi rubbed her thumb and forefinger together. "You've maxed your twenty."

Okay, he was dragging his feet and grasping at straws. A knot of dismay settled in his gut. He didn't want to do this, but he was a former Army Ranger. He knew how to suck it up and get the job done whenever he got a rotten assignment.

And Vivi was right about one thing. He'd been in a dark cloud mood ever since he'd received the medical discharge for losing the ring finger and pinky of his left hand in a parachuting mishap.

His hand had healed, but in his head, he was still struggling. For the past twelve years the Army had ruled his world. Now he was clueless about his future.

"Well?" Vivi's tone irritated him, and if he didn't like his stepmother as much as he did, Remington would have walked off. But Vivi had corralled his old man, who could be a humdinger, tamed Duke as much as was humanly possible, and brought a softness to the family that hadn't been there since his mother died.

"Fine." He sighed. "I'll drive her."

"You can hang out in Twilight until after the wedding." Vivi nodded. "Then drive her back?"

"Yes, yes." He grunted and rolled his eyes. He would do it. He would drive her, but first, he needed to formulate some kind of plan to keep his sanity around the harum-scarum Miss Alzate.

"Don't worry," Aria said. "I'll make it fun."

"That's what I'm afraid of," he muttered.

"Are you always such a sourpuss?" Aria clicked her tongue.

"Pretty much."

"I know how to cure that."

"I have no desire for a cure," he said. "And I have ground rules."

Aria groaned and dropped dramatically onto the couch, clutching her chest as if he'd just stabbed her through the heart. "I'm not a fan of rules."

He caught a flash of her thigh in thin black leggings as the hem of her red-and-green plaid wool skirt rode up, and he felt an odd heat bolt through his body.

Stop that, Lockhart.

"Do you want me to drive you or not?" He stuffed his hands into his pockets and intensified his glower.

"As if I have a choice."

"Good, I'm glad we agree." He nodded but kept his scowl in place just in case she didn't get how serious he was about this.

Vivi was watching them, a bemused smile on her face. Haha. At least someone found entertainment in this farce.

"I'm going to let you two sort out the details," Vivi said, gathering a twin in each arm and balancing them on her hips. The boys peered at Remington and Aria over their mother's shoulder as she waltzed out the door.

"We need a plan," Remington said after Vivi disappeared.

Aria blew out her breath through pursed lips. "Here's the plan. We get in your SUV and drive northeast."

"Not so fast. First, I've got to check the weather." He pulled his phone from his back pocket. "I want to get ahead of this ice storm."

"Then get on it." Aria snapped her fingers. "Chop-chop, time's a-wastin'. It's almost nine."

"Second rule," he said. "No side trips. We're driving straight to Twilight, no delays, no detours, no jacking around."

"Okay, okay." She held up both palms, the many bracelets at her wrist jangling merrily. "But Vivi built an extra day into the schedule just in case something comes up."

He ignored that. "Third rule, no Christmas music."

"No Christmas music! Who are you, the Marquis de Sade?"

"Who's that?" Remington asked. "If the guy hates Christmas music, then yes, I'm the Marquis de Sade."

"He was a famous sexual sadist."

"Then no! I am not the Marquis de Sade."

"Figures," she mumbled. "So, does that mean I *can* listen to Christmas music?"

"On your own device where I don't have to hear it. That's why they make earbuds."

"You are such a grinch."

"Thank you. I consider that a compliment." He nodded. He'd never been a fan of Christmas. At least not since his mom had died.

"His heart is two sizes too small," Aria muttered.

"What?"

"Forget it. How many rules are there?" Aria scrambled to her feet, landing gracefully on the spiky heels of her ankle boots. "Because I've got a really short attention span—"

"Rule four. No putting your feet on my dashboard. I hate it when people put their feet on my dash," he said.

"Good grief, you're such a fussy old man."

"Five," he went on, laying out his plan. "Keep conversations to a minimum."

"No Christmas music, no talking—what? Am I just supposed to sit there like a silent lump?"

"That would be nice."

"You're impossible."

"Look, I've been through some stuff, okay? I don't like idle chitchat. Or cheerful music—"

"Or cheerful anything, apparently."

"Right. The less cheer, the better."

"I get that you're a war hero and all that . . ." Her gaze went to his missing fingers.

Self-consciously, he tucked his left hand into his right armpit. No one talked about his injury to his face and that's just the way he wanted it.

"But I don't like when people try to micromanage me," she said.

"I don't think this will work." He shook his head. "At all."

"Me either."

"Vivi!" they called in unison, simultaneously rushing for the door.

They made contact at the threshold, Remington's big shoulder plowing into hers. He was so much bigger than her that the impact of their bodies knocked her off her cute little boots. Her arms windmilled in the air, and she teetered.

Adrenaline shot through Remington, and he grabbed her just before she fell, holding her securely in the crook of his elbow. The last thing she needed was concussion number two. What the hell was wrong with him?

"I'm sorry, I'm sorry," he apologized, alarm tightening his chest. "I didn't mean to do that."

Her long dark silky hair trailed down the back of his arm, and she peered up into his face. Her eyes widened and her lips pursed, and that adrenaline in his veins turned to pure testosterone.

Creamed cow chips, what in the hell was this? He was not having a sexual reaction to Aria Alzate. No way, no how, no, no, no.

NO.

"It's okay," she said, her voice softening. "Not your fault. I charged for the door like a galloping rhino."

"There is nothing rhino-like about you," he murmured, shocked to hear how raspy his voice sounded.

"I think you're right," she said, still in his arms and breathing as hard as he was. It was not his imagination.

"I am?" Remington blinked. "About what?"

"A plan. We do need one."

He gulped, nodded, righted her, and stepped away. "And what's your plan?"

"We stay away from each other as much as possible."

"Agreed," he said, his mouth suddenly dry as the Chihuahuan Desert. "I like that plan very much."

"Once we hit Twilight, you go your way and I'll go mine. We meet back up on Monday after the wedding, drive home together, and we never speak of this experience again."

"I'm on the same page. Absolutely."

"Deal?" She stuck out her palm and the charm bracelet at her wrist jangled. The charm bracelet was as disorganized as she was. It held too many charms, and they were an eclectic mix of metals—copper, gold, silver, bronze, even some glass and plastic. But oddly, the charms were cohesive in their messiness.

A lot like Aria herself.

"Deal." Remington sank his hand into hers.

The instant their skin touched, static electricity snapped through them with a charge so strong the air literally crackled. Simultaneously, they both dropped their hands and jumped back.

"Wow," she said, her eyes growing wider. "Static electricity is a humdinger this time of year."

"For sure."

"Well." She brushed her palms together, as if by doing so she could discharge the feeling and sent her charm bracelets jangling again. "We better get your SUV loaded and get on the road."

He nodded. "The sooner the better."

"Yes." She sounded breathless. "The sooner we get this party started, the sooner we get it over."

"I couldn't agree with you more."

"I'll round up the supplies," she said.

"I'll gas up the SUV."

With a curt nod, she turned in one direction and he turned in the other, his pulse thumping the way it did every time he jumped from an airplane.

His reaction to her was weird.

Too weird.

And unwanted. Remington knew one thing with unshakable certainty. It was going to be a very long trip.